Decorated to Death

Debby Grahl

Decorated to Death

by

Debby Grahl

Debby Grahl

Published on IngramSpark by Debby Grahl 2017

Paperback   ISBN-10: 0-9994630-5-5
ISBN-13: 978-0-9994630-5-5

E-book   ISBN-10: 0-9994630-6-2
ISBN- 13: 978-0-9994630-6-2

Cover Design: Niina Kokko / Image credit: @ivelly/DepositPhotos and @Wavebreakmedia/DepositPhotos"

Dedication

To my friends and neighbors of the Oregon Historic District, Dayton, Ohio, especially those who opened their homes to the public for the annual Christmas tour, the tour guides, and those who served on the Christmas tour committee. You inspired me to imagine murder.

Debby Grahl

Cast of Characters

Alex Mackenzie:	police chief
Abigail Mackenzie:	Alex's wife, owner of Abigail's Tea Room
Henry Butterfield III:	bank chairman, a Founding Father
Victoria Butterfield:	wife of Henry
Charles Butterfield:	son of Henry
Agatha Butterfield:	wife of Charles
Pauline Silverspoon:	widow of Ethan Silverspoon, a Founder
Henrietta Silverspoon:	librarian, daughter of Pauline & Ethan
Samantha Edwards:	realtor, granddaughter of Ethan and Pauline Silverspoon
Carl Edwards:	bank president, Samantha's husband
Dr. Jack Monroe:	the village doctor
Claire Monroe:	Jack's wife
Ben Schenker, Sam Cooke:	owners of the Cork & Bottle Inn
Molly Bright:	postmistress
Sally Bright:	Molly's teenage daughter
G. H. Greeley:	publisher of the Newcomsville News
Kathleen Cooper:	owner of Kathleen's Corner Shop
Nan Katz:	best friend of Kathleen Cooper
Tom and Judy Scraper:	owners of Two Bits Barber Shop and Yesteryears Antiques
Carolyn St. John:	owner of Indulgence Spa
Bob O'Neal:	owner of O'Neal's Service Station
Peggy O'Neal:	Bob's wife, works at the Tea Room
Margaret Mary O'Neal:	daughter of Bob and Peggy, works at the Cork and Bottle
Patty O'Neal:	daughter of Bob and Peggy
Beatrice Studebaker:	widow, Abigail's cook at the tea room
Josephine Grill:	owner of Flapjacks Diner
Stewart Wallberger:	widower, owns Stewart's Books
Grant Cummings:	friend of Alex, his college roommate
Sylvia Schmuckler:	decorator, from the city
Bonnie Schreiber:	Alex's secretary

Debby Grahl

Often in winter the end of the day is like the final metaphor in a poem celebrating death: there is no way out.
- Agustin Gomez-Arcos

Prologue

Nov 20
Dear Diary,

I think $20,000 would be a nice Christmas present for little old me. Don't you agree, Diary? I think I'll visit my little fish in person. Hee, hee, hee.

*A lovely thing about Christmas is that it's compulsory, like a
thunderstorm, and we all go through it together.*
- Garrison Keillor

1

Newcomsville, Population: 2454

**Newcomsville Annual Candlelight Christmas Tour
Saturday, December 4th, and Sunday, December 5th
from 5:00 PM to 9:00 PM**

Please join the residents of Newcomsville as we open our houses
and businesses for our annual Candlelight Christmas Tour. You will
be guided through four wonderfully decorated homes and two of our
unique specialty shops.

Desserts and beverages will be served at the historic Cork &
Bottle Inn.

Tickets are $20, available at all Newcomsville businesses.

"You wait right there, Abigail Mackenzie," shrieked a familiar
female voice.

Knowing it was too late to bolt, Abigail plastered a smile on her
face and turned to see Kathleen Cooper storming out of her shop's
front door.

Good grief, she still has her hair that awful orange color was Abigail's first thought as the short, stocky woman stomped toward her, face suffused with anger.

"Hello, Kathleen. I was just admiring the tour posters. Don't you think they look great?"

"I don't give a damn about the posters," Kathleen shouted, pointing a stubby finger at Abigail. "I want to know how that snooty Samantha Edwards gets away with hiring an interior decorator to do her house for the Christmas tour contest while the rest of us are expected to do our own work. I want that woman disqualified."

"Kathleen, I don't know what you're talking about," Abigail replied taking an involuntary step back.

"You're on the Christmas Tour committee, aren't you?"

"Yes, but I haven't heard anything about Samantha and a decorator."

"Then perhaps you and your committee should pay more attention to what's going on. For your information, Nan Katz and I were in Flapjacks this morning having breakfast when Samantha sashayed in with her *decorator,*" emphasizing the word with total disgust, again poking her finger at Abigail. "She introduced her to Granny Jo telling her all about how *Syl-vi-a* is here from the city and how *Syl-vi-a* is going to help decorate her house."

Abigail took a couple more steps back. "Kathleen, I…," but before she could continue, Kathleen persisted.

"Now you can just tell Claire Monroe that I'm not going to stand for it. Your committee can inform Samantha Edwards that for once she has to do something on her own and not expect someone else to do it for her. Throughout her entire pampered life, she's had everything handed to her. I was under the impression the tour contest was to be judged on originality, not on what some fancy decorator can do." She began to gesticulate wildly, her face an alarming red. "I'll tell you something, Abigail, I can decorate better than she can, and I'm going to prove it to this entire town."

Abigail glanced at her watch. "I'm really sorry, Kathleen, but I can't stay. As it happens I'm on my way to a tour committee meeting, and I'm already late. I'll be sure to tell everyone what you've said. I'll be seeing you." Then, before Kathleen could utter another word, Abigail turned and hurried toward the Cork & Bottle Inn.

"Hello, here I finally am," Abigail called a few minutes later when she spotted Claire standing in front of the inn. Claire, a retired legal secretary, was an attractive middle-aged woman. Tall and willowy, she had short light-brown hair and shrewd brown eyes.

"Sorry I'm late," Abigail said gasping for breath. "You wouldn't believe the incredible conversation I just had with Kathleen."

"For heaven's sake, Abigail, slow down," Claire said. "Your face is about as red as your hair."

"I know Christmas tour meetings can be exciting, but not worth having a stroke over," Ben Schenker said looking down from the top rung of his stepladder, brush in hand, green paint speckling his dark wavy hair. He flashed his infectious grin. "But do tell, what has crazy Kathleen done now?"

"Does this have something to do with the tour?" Claire asked.

Abigail nodded.

"Then we should wait until Nan and Molly get here."

"That's fine. I only want to have to tell it once." Abigail smiled up at Ben. "The door looks great."

"Thanks," Ben said as he stepped from the ladder. "I'm so glad we're going to have the pleasure of the tour committee meeting at the inn. You know, Sam and I were just saying the other night that the day wouldn't be complete without at least one visit from an alert Christmas tour lady on the lookout for tacky decorations such as dancing snowmen or vulgar blinking Christmas lights, and now you're all going to be here together. What a treat!"

"Benjamin."

"Yes, Claire?"

"Didn't anyone ever tell you nobody likes a smart ass?"

"I'm afraid that's one lesson Ben has trouble remembering," Sam Cooke said, his husky frame blocking the doorway, a white chef's hat perched precariously on his shiny bald head.

"Hello, Sam," Claire and Abigail said as one.

"Hello, ladies."

"I was just about to tell Ben how pleased we are you've opened the inn to serve the desserts for the tour," Claire said. "You've both done a marvelous job restoring this old place."

"Thank you. It's been quite an undertaking, but worth it," Ben said.

"It's taken almost three years for us to get to this point, and we're still not through working on our living quarters in the carriage house out back," Sam said with a frown.

"Sam refuses to call our home anything but 'the carriage house'," Ben said. "He thinks the word 'stable' makes people think of horse shit."

Abigail laughed. "Seriously though, with Sam's culinary talents and your carpentry skills, this place was bound to be a success."

Ben grinned. "With his last name being Cooke, what else could he become but Newcomsville's premier chef?"

"During the renovations were you able to discover how old the inn is?" Claire asked.

"We think it was one of the town's earliest buildings, dating from around 1855," Sam answered. "The bar, or tap room, as we call it, was the original log structure. You can tell the main dining room was added later, around the 1870's."

"How many guest rooms are upstairs?" Abigail asked.

"There's one large suite and two smaller rooms." Sam said.

"We call the decor 'yuppie rustic'," Ben added.

"Here's the last of your committee," Sam said.

Abigail turned to see Nan Katz and Molly Bright coming toward them. Nan, a retired telephone operator, was a tall gaunt woman with a perpetually sour expression. She had tightly permed iron-gray hair, small beady eyes, and a thin pointy nose.

Molly, a widow in her thirties, is Newcomsville's post mistress. She only stands five-foot-two and is 'pleasingly plump' with wavy chestnut hair and big brown eyes. Molly and her daughter, Sally, had come to Newcomsville when the former postmaster retired. She and Sally live in what was once a small schoolhouse.

Ben leaned down to whisper in Abigail's ear. "Nan looks her usual cheery self. Lucky you."

Abigail rolled her eyes.

"Let's go in and sit down," Claire said when Nan and Molly had joined them. "We have a lot to go over this afternoon."

"Watch out for the wet paint," Ben said ushering them through the front door.

The group entered the low-ceilinged taproom with its centuries-old smoke-darkened beams and painstakingly restored hardwood floors. On the exposed log walls gas-lit sconces gave off a welcoming glow. A crackling fire burned in the large stone fireplace, and the ornately carved oak bar was a lovely example of nineteenth-century craftsmanship. They sat themselves down at a round maple table in front of the glowing fire.

"Sam, I'll bet these ladies would like something to drink. How about getting us a round? Then we can hear about Abigail's little encounter with Kathleen."

"What's this about Kathleen?" Nan asked.

"In a minute," Claire said.

"Unfortunately, ladies, I won't be able to stay and hear the story," Sam said. "I have things to do in the kitchen. At least one of us has to do some work around here."

"Hey, I deserve a break," Ben said. "I've been painting all morning."

"I'll have iced tea, Sam, if you don't mind," Nan said glowering at Ben. "I personally don't drink alcohol in the middle of the afternoon."

"That's just fine, Nan. Iced tea it is," Sam replied, ignoring the stunned faces around him. "And you're absolutely right. Hard telling what drinking in the afternoon might lead to. Also, I have some nice bruschetta left from lunch. Would you ladies care for some?"

"That sounds great, Sam. Thanks," Claire said. "Okay, Abigail, let's hear what happened with Kathleen."

"Oh, *please*," Ben interjected. "The suspense is killing me."

"It was while I was passing her shop," Abigail began. "She came running out hollering for me to stop. Oh, by the way, did you know her hair is still that unusual orange color?"

"She sure made a great-looking pumpkin at the Halloween party," Ben said.

Nan sniffed. "I think her hair looks rather festive."

"Festive isn't quite the word I was thinking of," Ben replied.

Clair cleared her throat. "Go on, Abigail."

"As I was saying, Kathleen came running out demanding to know what we were going to do about Samantha Edwards and the Christmas house contest. She was carrying on about a decorator and how it wasn't fair to all the other entries. She said Samantha's house should be disqualified. I told her I didn't know what she was talking about. I have to tell you, she was getting so worked up at this point I was afraid she would have a stroke. Then she went on about how the contest was supposed to be judged on originality, not on an idea designed by a decorator. I just told her I was late for the meeting, and I would be sure to let the committee know about her complaint."

"Doesn't Samantha usually hire someone to help her with all her decorating?" Molly asked. "This shouldn't really be a surprise to anyone, should it?"

"It's certainly not a surprise to me," Nan replied. "I can't help but agree with Kathleen on this. For god's sake, can't Samantha at least put up Christmas decorations without help? She has to be the most incompetent person I've ever met."

"Except when it comes to selling real estate," Claire added. "I believe she's rather successful at that."

Nan snorted. "It's not like she needs the commission money from the houses she sells. Everyone knows she inherited millions when her grandfather Silverspoon died. And I ask you, just how do you think Carl Edwards managed to become president of the Newcomsville Bank and Trust? Kathleen has had to work hard for everything she has, just like I have and…"

"Nan, I honestly don't see what relevance Samantha's finances or her husband's job have to this discussion," Claire said interrupting Nan's tirade. "Besides, I believe the inheritance was more like hundreds of thousands, not millions."

Before Nan could respond, Sam arrived with the bruschetta placing the oval plate in the middle of the table.

"That looks great," Abigail said.

"It certainly does," Claire replied. "Thanks, Sam."

"No problem. You folks enjoy your meeting. If you need anything else, Ben will be happy to oblige."

Ben smiled. "Sure thing. I'm at your beck and call."

"No thank you," Nan said as Abigail offered her a small plate. "I personally prefer to eat in an establishment which doesn't reek of foul cigarette smoke."

The thunderous expression on Ben's face had Abigail scrambling for something to say when Molly spoke up.

"I've been thinking about Samantha, and I can't help but feel sorry for her. It seems no matter what type of domestic project she undertakes it never turns out quite right." Molly pushed her oversized glasses back up on her nose. "Correct me if I'm wrong, but didn't we start the Christmas house contest a few years ago because some of the houses on the tour weren't decorated very well, and some of the ticket-buying tourists complained? In other words, it's a way to make sure everyone on the tour goes all out."

"You're absolutely right," Claire agreed. "I don't understand why Kathleen is so concerned about how Samantha decorates her house. I'm sure Kathleen will do a wonderful job with her shop and her apartment upstairs."

Abigail nodded. "Whenever I've been in her shop, it looks great. She truly has a flair for artfully arranging her displays."

"She's the queen of the glue gun. That's for sure," Ben said.

Nan's nostrils flared. "Kathleen happens to be extremely talented. Her silk flower wreaths and Christmas centerpieces are beautiful."

"I have to say, if Samantha thinks she needs help, and the result is a beautifully decorated home, who cares how it got that way," Abigail stated.

"I absolutely agree," Claire said. "We have enough to do organizing this tour without worrying about Samantha using a decorator. I don't need to tell you how difficult it is to get new houses each year to be on tour. When Kathleen and Samantha both volunteered at the last town meeting, I was happy to accept. The Christmas tour is this town's largest fundraiser, and we certainly need the extra income."

"That's true," Molly said. "As the town treasurer, I can honestly say we need to sell as many tickets as we can. We've been getting complaints about the condition of the old lumber mill's water wheel. We're going to have to eventually restore it or tear it down."

"Are you guys still at it?" Sam asked, coming out of the kitchen. "Ben, did you know it's after four o'clock? We need to start setting up for happy hour."

Ben got to his feet. "Sorry, ladies, as much as I'm enjoying this fascinating conversation, my services are needed elsewhere, so if you wouldn't mind, I'll leave you. Please don't hurry off. You're welcome to stay as long as you like."

"I have to get back to the tea room so we need to finish up," Abigail said. "Peggy is going to be wondering what happened to me."

"I have other things to do as well," Nan said. "I can't sit around here all day."

Molly grinned. "Look at it this way. With Kathleen and Samantha in competition, this should be one of our more memorable Christmas tours."

"Or one of the worst," Abigail murmured.

Nan glanced around the room and lowered her voice. "There's one other issue I'd like to address. I didn't want to say anything while Ben was here, but Kathleen and I have been wondering whether this inn is, well, the appropriate type of place for serving the desserts."

Molly looked puzzled. "What do you mean, Nan? The decor in the dining room is wonderful. I imagine by the time Ben and Sam get done with the Christmas decorations it will look fantastic."

"Oh, I don't doubt the dining room will look superb. That type are known for their decorating. No, what I'm talking about is, well, we're afraid some of our tour guests may find Ben and Sam's living arrangement offensive. Remember these people are paying to go on our tour. We wouldn't want to discourage them from returning next year."

Fury in her eyes, Claire replied, "You know what, Nan? Somehow I really don't think the people who buy our tour tickets are especially concerned with the personal lives of the owners. I truly think they're more interested in seeing historic architecture with unique holiday decorating, eating outrageously fattening desserts, and drinking fine champagne. Your brand of narrow-mindedness isn't as widespread as you might think."

With her face flaming and eyes bulging, Nan opened her mouth to respond. Claire, cutting off whatever Nan was about to say, stood and began to gather her papers. "I think it would be advantageous at this point for me to adjourn this meeting. Jack will be joining me here soon for dinner. How about if we meet next Tuesday? We can go over any last minute problems and hopefully have a more productive meeting. Abigail, would you mind staying for a minute? Molly, I hope you and Sally have a happy Thanksgiving." Without another word, Claire turned smartly on her heel and headed for the bar, ignoring Nan's indignant sputtering.

"I'm going to owe Molly a huge apology," Claire said when she and Abigail had taken seats at the bar. "She didn't deserve being left with Nan, but I couldn't take that woman one minute longer."

Abigail gave her a reassuring smile. "I know, and I'm sure Molly understood."

Ben came over to where they sat. "Is the meeting over? Did things improve after I left?"

Claire shook her head. "Hardly. We'll both have a glass of wine."

Ben laughed. "That bad." He glanced up at the clock over the bar. "I guess it's okay. It's almost five and no longer the middle of the afternoon."

"I shouldn't let Nan Katz get under my skin the way she does, but she has to be one of the most rude, opinionated people I've ever met," Claire said.

"She and Kathleen have made it clear they don't approve of our relationship," Ben said. "Don't get me wrong, they've never said anything to us directly, but as the old saying goes, actions speak louder than words."

"What do you mean?" Abigail asked.

Ben sighed. "The other day we received what one could consider a menacing anonymous letter in the mail suggesting Sam and I and our inn aren't the appropriate image the town wishes to project to the public. So for the welfare of the town and the Christmas tour, we should withdraw from serving the desserts."

"What?" Claire exclaimed.

"It really isn't a big deal. Sam and I have received homophobic letters like it in the past. We just consider the source."

A mixture of outrage and concern filled Claire's eyes. "Ben, this is terrible. I suppose we can guess who the anonymous senders were."

"Well, there isn't any proof, but Kathleen and Nan would be my first choices. Then again, who knows?"

"I have no doubt it's those two." Claire slapped her hand on the bar. "I knew they could be spiteful, but this is going too far. People should learn to mind their own business and live and let live. Ben, I hope you and Sam know that their narrow-minded opinions are not those of the majority of your neighbors."

"We know that. Trust me, we don't feel privileged when it comes to their poisonous pens nor their viperous tongues."

"I think they deserve each other," Abigail said. "Two bitter women who blame everyone else for their problems. And this thing about Samantha is typical."

"Why does Kathleen dislike Samantha so much?" Ben asked. "It can't just be this decorator business."

"There's been animosity between those two for quite a while," Abigail said. "How it all began, or what it's about, I really don't know. I have a feeling the problem goes way back."

"I have to say I've always liked Samantha," Claire said. "When Jack decided to close his practice in the City and open an office here, Samantha was the realtor who sold us our house. She told us her grandfather had passed and she'd inherited his Maple Street house. She also said that one day Carl shocked her with the news he had quit his job. The stress at his brokerage firm in the city was getting to be too much to handle, and he needed a change."

"Really?" Ben said with surprise. "I was under the impression that this was the last place on earth Carl wanted to live."

A few more people sat down at the bar and Ben excused himself. Abigail paid for her wine and stood. "I'm sorry, Claire, but I have to go. I've left poor Peggy long enough." She gave Claire a hug. "If I don't see you, have a happy Thanksgiving."

Claire hugged her back. "Same to you. I'll call you in a day or two."

***

"You're getting a little swamped," Claire said as Ben placed a bowl of pretzels in front of her. "Where's Meg?"

Ben frowned. "Miss Margaret Mary O'Neal is a half hour late for work. I think the little minx has a new boyfriend."

"Ah, don't get your knickers in a twist, boss. I'm here," Margaret Mary said, coquettishly tossing her long black braid over her shoulder as she came up behind Ben.

12

"Hi, Claire."

"Good evening, Meg."

"Now that you're finally here, pretty Meg, why don't you earn the outrageous amount of money I pay you and wiggle your cute little self over to that table and take their order?"

"Sure thing, boss," Meg said smiling to show her dimples.

Ben turned to Claire. "Where's the Doc this evening?"

"He had to go into the city for a conference. We're to meet for dinner. I'm not sure what time he'll get here, so if the dining room fills up, don't worry about us. We'll just eat right here at the bar."

"The bar is fine with me," Jack Monroe said sitting down on the stool next to her. Jack's tall and well-built with receding salt and pepper hair, matching mustache, and kind green eyes.

"Hey, Jack, how's it going?" Ben asked.

Jack smiled. "Much better now that I'm here, and I'll feel even better once I have an ice cold martini."

Ben reached for the martini shaker. "Coming right up."

"So how was your day?" Jack asked kissing Claire's cheek.

"Rather infuriating. How was yours?"

"Extremely boring. So tell me about yours."

Ben placed Jack's drink in front of him. "If you'd like to move into the dining room, we have an open table."

"Actually we're fine right here," Jack replied.

Claire agreed. "How about a couple of steak sandwiches with lots of grilled onions?"

"And a basket of fries," Jack added.

Ben nodded. "Sure thing."

Jack popped bar nuts into his mouth. "So, let's hear about your infuriating day."

"It was going along rather well until the Christmas tour meeting this afternoon. Nan Katz was even more obnoxious than usual."

"Hard to believe."

"Well, believe it. And that's not all. Ben told me they received a nasty anonymous letter telling them to withdraw from the tour because their lifestyle isn't what this town wishes to project to the public."

"That's incredible. Do they have an idea who sent it?"

"Our first thought was Nan and Kathleen, but we can't prove it."

Jack shook his head. "For god's sake, what's wrong with those women?"

"I think they have nothing else in their lives but to see how much trouble they can cause. Kathleen stopped Abigail on her way here to the meeting ranting about Samantha hiring a decorator from the city to help her get her house ready for the tour."

Jack smiled. "Okay, I'll bite. What's wrong with hiring a decorator?"

"Nothing as far as I'm concerned, but I guess Kathleen doesn't think it's fair to the others. Naturally Nan agreed with Kathleen, but the rest of the committee was fine with it. I just hope they can behave like mature adults and there isn't any trouble during the tour. That reminds me, Jack. Do you remember when Samantha was showing us our house? Didn't she give you the impression Carl was the one who wanted to move here?"

Jack nodded. "That sounds right. I can't help wondering if that's the true story."

"What makes you say that? Ben kind of indicated the same thing."

"I'd say Ben was thinking about the night Carl was in here totally drunk and being an obnoxious pain in the ass. He was emphatically telling all of us he couldn't believe he let Samantha bully him into leaving the city and moving to this boring, piss-ass, hick town. According to Carl, the main interest of the citizens of Newcomsville is sticking their noses into other people's business. I tell you, Claire, he was starting to piss off Bob O'Neal to the point I thought Bob might punch him."

"My goodness, Jack, that's awful."

"Two steak sandwiches with grilled onions and a basket of fries," Ben said as he set the food on the bar. Can I get you anything else?"

"It looks great," Jack replied.

"Jack was just telling me about the time Carl Edwards was in here drunk and mouthing off."

Ben nodded. "That was just a few months ago."

"I'm a little confused," Claire said. "I was under the impression it was Carl who instigated their move, but now, according to you and

Jack, Carl isn't at all happy here. Do you know what might have changed his mind?"

Ben shook his head. "I have no idea what's going on with those two, but I tell you, after Jack and the rest left that night, Carl kept drinking. When I threatened to cut him off, he became extremely obnoxious. He said that unfortunately the only place he was going was home to that controlling bitch, and he was walking anyway so what did it matter how drunk he got. I was tired of arguing with him, and I was busy getting ready to close. I didn't notice when he left. If you want to know the truth, the last time he was in here, he pretty much told Sam and me just exactly what he thought of us. Sam took it until Carl started getting really nasty, then Sam, ah, decided to help him out the door."

"That's terrible," Claire said. "What is going on in this town? First Nan and Kathleen and now Carl."

"I don't think your regular customers will miss Carl not taking up space at your bar," Jack stated.

Ben smiled. "After the other night, I don't think we have to worry about him coming back. Meg told me that not only is he a drunken asshole, he's put the moves on her more than once, and she's also seen him coming on to some of the female tourists. Meg likes to flirt and have a good time, but she's a good kid. I'll tell you what, if Bob O'Neal hears that Carl has been messing with his girls, I feel sorry for the guy."

"Are you going to stand there jabbering all night, boss, or are you going to fill these drink orders?" Meg hollered from the other end of the bar.

Jack smiled. "It sounds like you're needed."

"That little minx needs a kick in the pants," Ben mumbled as he walked off.

"Jack, I hadn't heard anything about Carl drinking too much or harassing women," Claire said. "Have you? I mean other than the time you saw him in here."

"No, not really, but I'm usually not here in the evenings when Carl would be. Although..."

"Although what?"

"Just the other day, Pauline Silverspoon was in the office. You know she had a bad case of the flu. Anyway, when I asked her how she was, she said she was feeling better, but I could tell by the look on her face that she wanted to talk to me about something."

Claire leaned closer. "Jack, what did she say?"

"You know I can't discuss what my patients tell me, not even with my extremely discreet wife."

Claire gave him an exasperated look. "Jack, you know I won't tell anyone."

Jack sighed. "I know. And I also know you won't stop pestering me until I do. Actually, she really didn't say much, just that she was concerned about Samantha. She said Carl had been acting strange lately, and Samantha had been looking a little pale. I said maybe she had a touch of the same flu Pauline just had. She didn't think that was the problem. She ended by saying she really didn't know how to explain what she meant. I told her to let me know if Samantha started acting or looking worse. She said she would, and then she left. I don't know if any of this has anything to do with Carl, but I'll tell you one thing. I hope if Bob O'Neal, or anyone else in this town, has a reason to show Carl their displeasure, I'm not the one who has to bandage up what's left."

"My god, Jack, do you think Carl's behavior could lead to something like that?"

"I sincerely hope not, but nothing would surprise me."

They had just finished their meal when Ben placed two slices of yummy looking cake in front of them.

"Here's dessert. Sam made a wonderful pumpkin cake."

"I shouldn't, but that looks delicious," Claire said. "Speaking of pumpkins, what are you and Sam doing for Thanksgiving?"

"Abigail and Alex have taken pity on a few of us lost souls and invited us over. There will be Sam and me, Molly and Sally, Carolyn, and I think Judy and Tom."

"Sounds like a fun group," Claire said as they were preparing to leave. "Don't forget you and Sam volunteered to help decorate Main Street Saturday morning."

"Sam doesn't know yet that he volunteered, but we'll be there with bells on."

Mortals are easily tempted to pinch the life
out of their neighbor's buzzing glory,
And think that such killing is no murder.
- George Eliot, Middlemarch

2

When Abigail left the taproom, the winter sun was dipping down behind Main Street's brightly-painted shops with their beautifully restored facades. A cold wind blowing through the bare branches of the trees lining the street caused her to turn up the collar on her cashmere jacket. She hurried around the small traffic circle. In the spring, the ladies of the garden club would fill the stone planters with an array of colorful flowers. Now a tall, freshly cut pine tree stood in the middle of the circle waiting to be strung with red and green Christmas lights.

Abigail took time to hurry into Stewart's, a wonderful bookstore, its tall shelves packed to overflowing with both the used and the new. In the back, welcoming worn chairs were clustered around a small brick fireplace where you could curl up with a book.

"Stewart, are you here?" Abigail called.

"Back here," came a muffled reply. Stewart Wallberger, retired history professor, a dapper little man with sparse gray hair and gold-rimmed pince-nez perched precariously on his slightly pointed nose, lives in a small but fastidious apartment above the bookstore.

Abigail worked her way through the stacks of books waiting to be shelved. She found him sitting on the floor in front of the fireplace. His face, hands, and usually pristine white shirt with its jaunty red bow tie were black with soot. Webster, the bookstore's resident tuxedo cat, was perched on the carved mantle looking amused.

"Stewart, are you alright?" Abigail asked.

"Oh yes, my dear, I'm fine. The chimney wasn't drawing well. I thought I'd take a look."

Abigail couldn't help but laugh. "Stewart, you're a sight. I wish you'd called Alex. He would have walked over and looked at the chimney for you." She gave Stewart her hand to help him up.

"I know, dear, but I dislike bothering folks if I don't have to. Anyway, I think it's fine now."

"I stopped by to invite you for Thanksgiving dinner tomorrow. We're just having a small group."

"That's awfully kind of you, but Henrietta has invited me to go with her and her mother to the Butterfield's."

Abigail opened her eyes wide. "Wow, dinner at the Manor. You'll have to tell me all about it."

'The Manor' is how the residents affectionately referred to the Butterfield's spacious ancestral home. Located on a ridge, it has a wonderful panoramic view of the town and surrounding countryside.

"I have to say I'm quite pleased with the invitation. I do enjoy visiting with Henry and Victoria, you know. Oh, my goodness, there's the front bell," he exclaimed. "And just look at me."

"Don't worry. I'll see who it is. Go on and clean up."

"Oh, thank you, dear," he said with a grateful smile. "I'll just be a minute." He turned and hurried toward the back stairs.

When Abigail reached the front door, Henrietta Silverspoon, the town librarian, was just coming in.

"Oh, hello, Abigail. My, that wind certainly is getting brisk." Henrietta's softly-rounded cheeks were pink, and her bright blue-framed glasses had steamed up. "You know, I just heard on my radio that they're predicting snow tomorrow."

Abigail grinned. "Good, I love snow. I hear you're going to the Manor tomorrow. You and Stewart be careful driving up the ridge. The roads may get icy."

"We'll be just fine. Charles is going to drive down and pick us all up, but thank you for being concerned."

"How is Pauline? I heard she hadn't been feeling well."

"Mother is doing much better now, thank you. I'm so glad she decided to move in with me after Daddy died. She's getting up there in years, and with her heart condition, well, I didn't like the idea of her living alone."

"I'm sure having her close has to be a comfort for both of you." Abigail gave the older woman a hug. "I'm sorry, but I have to run. Peggy is holding down the fort, and she must be wondering where I am. Stewart had a slight accident with the chimney. He went upstairs to clean up. Will you watch the store until he comes back? Tell everyone at the Manor I said 'Happy Thanksgiving'."

"Happy Thanksgiving to all of you as well," Henrietta called as Abigail hurried out the door.

Abigail's tea room is located in a three-story Victorian home she inherited from her Grandmother Bohn four years ago. She darted across the street, through the back door, and into the kitchen, a sunny room with bright yellow walls, a blue and white tile floor, and glass-front cupboards.

Beatrice Studebaker, Abigail's sturdy seventy-year-old cook, exudes a no-nonsense air. She was pulling a new batch of delicious-smelling apple scones from the oven. She turned and gave Abigail a disapproving look over her glasses.

"I'm sorry I'm so late, Bea," Abigail said. "The meeting went on longer than it should have. Has Peg had any trouble?"

Before Beatrice could answer, Peggy O'Neal walked through the swinging kitchen door, her dark hair in a neat bun and her green eyes dancing.

Peggy and Bob, and their five children, live in a rambling house behind O'Neals', a nineteen-thirty style service station where one of the O'Neal children will pump your gas from Bennett pumps with their illuminated glass globes.

Peg smiled. "Well, Abigail, here you are. I was beginning to think you ladies decided to stay at the Cork & Bottle and party."

"I'm sorry, Peg. The meeting went on and on about nothing except Kathleen Cooper and her latest beef with Samantha."

"No problem. Everything is under control," Peg replied. "It's been a light afternoon. Although it's funny you mentioned Samantha. She was in earlier with an attractive blond woman I didn't recognize."

Abigail rolled her eyes. "That was probably the infamous decorator."

"Who?" Peg asked.

"I'll tell you later. It's quite a story. Has anything else happened?"

"The only other interesting thing is that 'the Queen is in your parlor eating bread and honey' and has been asking for you."

"Peggy, you really shouldn't talk about Miss Victoria like that," Beatrice said reproachfully. "Newcomsville wouldn't be what it is today if it weren't for the Butterfields and the Silverspoons investing in this town. You two girls weren't here when most of the good folks were out of work, and the town began filling up with no-account trash. Let me tell you it wasn't a pretty sight."

Peg lightly touched Beatrice's arm. "I'm sorry. I didn't mean to upset you. I truly like Victoria, but I can't help it. With her high and mighty demeanor she reminds me of a queen."

"Do you know what she wants?" Abigail asked.

"She just said it was in regard to Kathleen and Samantha."

Abigail groaned. "Oh, great. I've had about enough of Kathleen for one day."

"Okay, what's going on?" Peg asked. "The suspense is killing me."

Beatrice placed her hands on her hips. "I know what's going on in here. My pastries are getting cold while you two stand around gossiping."

"Sorry, Bea," Abigail said. "I'll go see what Victoria wants and be right back. Peg, has she been here long?"

Peg reached for another tray of pastries. "About thirty minutes. Don't worry about keeping Victoria waiting. Agatha is in the front parlor trying on hats."

"Who would have ever thought Victoria would have a daughter-in-law like Agatha?" Beatrice shook her head in wonder. "I don't know which of those two girls goes around this town acting crazier, Kathleen or Agatha. Last time I saw Kathleen, her hair was dyed orange, and Agatha always looks like someone from a nineteen-thirties movie."

Abigail slid a tray of scones into the oven. "Her hair is that color because she came to the Halloween party dressed as a pumpkin. Maybe she's decided to keep it orange through Thanksgiving."

Beatrice again shook her head. "If you ask me, I think it looks dang silly, but who am I to judge?"

"Did you know Samantha and Kathleen while they were growing up?"

Beatrice placed chocolate éclairs on a pretty crystal tray. "I surely did. Kathleen has always been shy and insecure. Although she seems to have outgrown the shyness, the insecurity is still there. That's why she tries so hard to make everything perfect. When that no-account husband of hers left, it truly affected her mind. She could always be temperamental, but these last couple of years, she's been a lot worse."

"I know what you mean. Kathleen stopped me on the street hysterical because Samantha hired a decorator to help her for the tour. Kathleen doesn't think that's fair to the other contest entries. I personally think she's way overreacting."

"I'm sure she is. Kathleen has always been envious, and no matter what Samantha does, she's bound to find fault. Kathleen grew up here. Her family was hard working but still poor. Then you have pretty little blond Samantha, a granddaughter of the Silverspoons. Kathleen would see her wearing her new clothes and, when she was old enough, driving around in fancy little cars."

"With Kathleen's shop doing so well, you wouldn't think she'd still feel such animosity toward Samantha." Abigail frowned. "As hard as I try to like Kathleen, I just can't."

"You're not the only one. She rubs a lot of people the wrong way. She can be nice as pie one minute and mean and spiteful the next. Even with their age difference, I can see how Kathleen and Nan Katz became close friends. They're two peas in a pod who like nothing better than saying as many hateful things about other folks as they can think of."

Peg popped her head around the kitchen door. "Abigail! Vic-to-ria."

"Oh, damn. Please tell her I'm coming. Beatrice, I'll be right back. I want to talk to you about Thanksgiving."

Abigail found Victoria Butterfield seated at a glass-topped wicker table next to a charming little fountain in the small conservatory that overlooked the side yard. It adjoined what her grandmother used to call her "comfortable sitting room." These two spaces had been converted into the tea room. Abigail had kept the same color scheme of rose and cream, just adding some wicker tables and cushioned chairs to go along with the padded settees.

The walls are tastefully hung with watercolor garden scenes. Displayed about the room are flowered straw hats, lace gloves, fans and colorful parasols. Abigail likes to say, "It's always spring in my tea room."

A large Victorian china cabinet holds a collection of mismatched teacups, saucers and dessert plates Abigail found in boxes in the attic. There are teapots of every size and shape and a lovely assortment of embroidered napkins and place mats.

"There you are, Abigail," Victoria said with her upper-crust Boston accent. Petite, with an elegant appearance and a regal bearing, she has china blue eyes, and her thick snowy white hair is always worn in a fashionable twist. "Please tell Beatrice that her pastries were delicious as always."

"I'll certainly do that. Sorry to have kept you waiting. The Christmas tour meeting ran a little longer than expected."

Victoria smiled. "Meetings have a tendency to do that. And the Christmas tour is exactly what I need to discuss with you. First, tell me, how are the ticket sales going?"

"As far as I know, we're doing well. I haven't had a chance to call all of the businesses and check on their totals, but last I heard they thought sales might be up from last year."

"Wonderful. That's what we like to hear. I'm concerned that some of our new people do not understand that the entire town benefits from increased ticket sales. Henry was just saying at breakfast that a decision needs to be made soon in regards to the old mill. If we decide to restore it, the repairs are going to be extremely expensive."

"Well, perhaps in the spring we can consider doing another type of fundraiser. I'd be happy to chair the committee. A friend of mine was telling me about going to a Monte Carlo Night at her husband's country club. She said they really had a great time. Who knows, something like that might be worth considering."

Victoria nodded. "I'm open to any suggestions. I'll leave it up to you to get the wheels in motion. Just let me know if I can be of any help. Now, Abigail, we need to discuss a rather incoherent call I received from Kathleen Cooper before luncheon today. You know, I find her a rather peculiar young woman." She waved a well-manicured hand. "But that's really neither here nor there. From what I could comprehend, it seems Kathleen is in distress over something to do with Samantha and the Christmas tour. Why she chose to call me, instead of one of the tour committee members, is beyond me. Would you happen to know what this is all about?"

"As a matter a fact I do," Abigail replied with a sigh, then proceeded to tell the story one more time ending with, "She probably called you thinking that because you're president of the Historic Society you could do something about Samantha and her decorator."

"Do you think it will be a problem with the others on the tour?

"No, not really. I think everyone else knows the house contest is basically for fun. The objective is to have all the homes nicely decorated. Naturally at the meeting I told Claire about Kathleen, and she didn't seem to think it would be an issue with anyone else."

"I certainly haven't a problem with Samantha hiring a decorator. And Claire Monroe is a competent woman. I feel comfortable leaving all of this in her capable hands. I'm sure she can deal with any problems that may arise."

At that moment, Agatha Butterfield's boisterous baritone voice could be heard from out in the hall. To Abigail's amusement, she saw Victoria wince as if in pain.

"Here I finally am, Mamaw-in-Law," Agatha boomed as her tall buxom form approached like a looming thunderstorm.

Abigail always thought Agatha was a dead ringer for Mae West. Today Agatha was wearing a black gabardine suit with four round silver-toned buttons. The jacket had wave-like seams down each side and a peak style lapel.

"I didn't think I'd ever be able to make up my mind what wonderful treasure to choose from Abigail's lovely shop. Don't you just adore my new hat?" Her big brown eyes were bright with excitement. "Won't it just look marvelous for Thanksgiving?"

Abigail had to bite her tongue to keep from laughing out loud at the horrified look that crossed Victoria's face upon seeing the tutti-frutti style hat perched on Agatha's large bleached blond head.

"Abigail," Agatha exclaimed with her friendly broad smile. "You're such a clever little girl. Using all those marvelous old clothes and accessories of your grandparents' to open a vintage clothing shop is nothing short of pure genius."

"Thank you, Agatha. I'm glad you're enjoying yourself. I honestly didn't know what to do with all the things in Granny's trunks. She saved everything and kept them in perfect condition. It actually was Alex who came up with the idea of using the parlor as a shop." Abigail smiled. "Although I have to admit that collecting vintage clothing has become kind of an obsession. If I don't quit, I'm going to have to find a larger space."

"Agatha," Peggy called from the tea room door. "Charles is here."

Charles Butterfield strolled through the door. Victoria's youngest son, he'd just celebrated his fortieth birthday.

"Chucky," Agatha again boomed hurrying across the room. "How do you like my new hat?"

"It's swell, Aggie," Charles said in his high reedy voice.

Agatha, beaming with pleasure, gave her husband a loud smacking kiss.

Charles, a man of slight stature, has a receding hairline, slightly protruding blue eyes and a Charlie Chaplin mustache. A bit of a fop, he was wearing a dark green and tan checkered suit, a dark brown bowler, and a tan trench coat with matching spats. He shares Agatha's delight in vintage clothing and murder mysteries, and a passion for classic movies. They absolutely adore each other.

"Did you have a nice tea, Mamaw?" Charles asked, as he helped Victoria on with her coat.

"Yes, thank you. It was very pleasant. Where did you have to park the car?"

"I found a spot right out front. It's turning rather cold out, but we'll have you nice and cozy in a jiffy."

"Tell everyone on the ridge we said 'Happy Thanksgiving'," Abigail said walking with the little group down the paneled hall to the front door.

"Happy Thanksgiving, happy Thanksgiving to all of you," Agatha and Charles sang, as they walked arm in arm following Victoria's regal back.

Abigail, chuckling, closed the front door and headed into the little parlor which was just to her right.

"That Agatha cracks me up," Sally Bright said from behind the sales counter, "But Mrs. Butterfield scares me half to death."

Sally, who works for Abigail after school and on weekends, is a pretty sixteen-year-old with a happy freckled face and a bubbly personality. She likes over-sized pink-framed glasses and wears her dark hair in a long ponytail.

"Victoria can be a little intimidating," Abigail said as she came into the room, "but I think her bark is worse than her bite. So, Sally, how did we do today?"

"Pretty good. Besides Agatha's hat, I sold a couple pairs of gloves, a beaded handbag, and Samantha bought a scarf. Oh, and I sold a few pieces of jewelry."

Abigail nodded. "Not a bad day at all. You can go on home. I'll close up later. Molly probably has your dinner ready. I'll see both of you tomorrow. Remember to be here by three o'clock. We're going to have dinner around four-thirty or so."

"We'll be here. You know Mom's bringing her famous pumpkin pies."

"Yes, I know. They're always delicious."

As Abigail made her way to the kitchen, she glanced into the large front parlor to make sure everything was in order. The large and small parlors are on either side of the front door. Each has a bay window overlooking the porch. The smaller room had become the Victorian shop. The large parlor on the left had pocket doors which led into the formal dining room. Abigail had removed most of the Victorian furniture out of these two rooms and replaced it with small tables and chairs using the combined space to serve her customers Beatrice's savory lunches.

When she reentered the kitchen, Beatrice and Peggy were sitting at the table having a cup of coffee and finishing up a plate of cherry tarts.

"Are you all closed up?" Peg asked filling Abigail's cup.

"Yes, the Butterfield's were the last to leave. I'll go through and get the lights later. She gratefully sat down and slipped off her shoes. "Thanks a lot, you two, for leaving me a tart. She gazed longingly at the empty plate.

Peg laughed. "Don't look so sad. There's some pumpkin pound cake left. Would you like a slice?"

Abigail brightened. "Sure, that would be great. You know I get so tickled watching Victoria around Agatha. I would have given anything to have seen the look on Victoria's face when Charles first brought his bride home."

"I can tell you it about killed Miss Victoria," Beatrice said. "I was their cook at the time. Charles called and said he had met a great girl from Atlantic City, and they had eloped."

"So they met in Atlantic City?" Peg asked.

"No. Agatha's from Atlantic City, but they met on some kind of mystery train weekend. It was the one where all of the suspects stab the body. Agatha played one of the characters from the book."

"Murder on the Orient Express," Peggy and Abigail answered together.

Beatrice nodded. "That's the one."

"I've heard of those trips," Abigail said. "They're supposed to be a lot of fun."

"Had Agatha been an actress?" Peg asked.

"From what I understand, she used to have some small parts in an Atlantic City theater group," Beatrice replied.

"I didn't know that," Abigail said. "As expressive as Agatha is, I can see her being an actress. Wouldn't it be fun if we could get Agatha to put together a local theater group? I've always thought acting would be exciting."

"Oh, wouldn't that be great," Peg exclaimed.

Beatrice frowned. "Well, I don't know about theater groups, but I can tell you that when Miss Victoria heard about Charles and Agatha's marriage, she was so upset she took to her bed, and that was before she had even laid eyes on Agatha."

Abigail and Peggy were laughing so hard they didn't hear Abigail's husband Alex come through the back door.

"Are we starting the Thanksgiving party a day early?" he asked, smiling at the women.

Alex Mackenzie, a tall handsome man with wavy chestnut hair, a thick mustache, and smoky gray eyes had been Newcomsville's police chief since leaving the county sheriff's office.

"Hi, Hon. Beatrice was telling us a story about Victoria and Agatha," Abigail said still chuckling. "Where's the turkey?"

Alex frowned. "Turkey? What turkey?"

"The turkey you were supposed to bring home."

Alex's eyes opened wide. "I was supposed to get the turkey?"

"Alex, this isn't funny. You were going to stop at Buyers' Market and pick up the turkey on your way home." Abigail jumped to her feet and glanced at the clock. "Oh no, they're probably closed by now."

Alex couldn't keep from smiling. "I'm sorry. I couldn't resist teasing you. The bird is in a bag out on the porch."

Abigail's face flooded with relief. "Real funny, Alex. Only a man would think forgetting the turkey is funny."

Peg laughed. "I agree. Now I'd better head on home and see what my brood is up to. Abigail, are you planning on opening for lunch at the usual time Saturday?"

"Yes. If everything goes according to plan, we should have all the Christmas decorating done on Friday."

"What time would you like me to send the girls over?" Peg asked, as she slipped on her coat.

"Any time after nine. Sally Bright is coming as well. Tell the girls I really appreciate their help."

"It's not a problem. They're all excited. Those girls love decorating for Christmas. I'll see everyone on Saturday. Have a happy Thanksgiving," Peg called as a blast of cold air blew through the open back door.

Beatrice reached for her coat. "I'm going home too. I need to call Josephine and see what time her daughter is picking me up tomorrow."

"Beatrice, are you sure you want to go to Josephine's?" Abigail asked. "I thought her grandchildren gave you a headache. You know you're more than welcome to have dinner here with us."

"Actually the children aren't as bad as they used to be. Jo bought one of those things they play video games on, and it keeps them busy for hours. Besides, I promised Jo I'd be there. Her daughter can get on her nerves after a while. She's always onto Jo to sell the diner and move into a retirement community. You know how much Jo loves Flapjacks. She enjoys visiting with folks when they stop in, and she doesn't want to leave Newcomsville. So I think she feels that if I'm there her daughter won't bring up the subject of retirement communities."

Abigail kissed Beatrice's cheek. "You and Josephine have a nice Thanksgiving. Don't forget we'll be closed Friday, so I'll see you Saturday. Hopefully we'll have a nice lunch crowd."

"I plan on being here at noon on Friday to make lunch for all of you," Beatrice stated heading for the back door.

Abigail opened her mouth in protest but abruptly closed it when she saw Beatrice's stubborn expression.

"Now don't you argue with me, Abigail. I've seen this place while Christmas decorating is going on. And if I'm not here, I know doggone well that none of you will stop and eat. I'll just make something simple out of the turkey leftovers, and I'll feel better knowing you've all eaten. Now that's settled." She gave a satisfied nod. "You have a happy Thanksgiving." And with that she was gone.

Alex grinned. "She's quite a character."

"She certainly is. I'm so glad she agreed to live in our carriage house. I feel better knowing she's close by in case she needs us. You know she and my granny were like sisters."

He gave her a big hug. "I'm glad she's close by as well. I know how much she means to you. I'd better get the turkey off the porch before Thomasina carries it away. Speaking of turkey, what's for dinner tonight?"

"I thought we'd order a pizza. I'm almost through down here. I just need to check a few things."

"That's sounds good. How about getting an extra-large with the works?"

She laughed. "You must be really hungry. Why don't you order it, and I'll be up soon."

As Abigail walked through the first floor rooms, straightening chairs and turning off lights, she thought back four years ago to her grandparents' sudden death in a car accident and how it had changed her life a week before her twenty-fifth birthday. She had sat in stunned silence at the reading of the will as the family attorney told her she'd inherited her grandparents' house and all its contents.

Her parents were retired and living in Florida. Her sister and her family were settled on the East Coast. They were all happy that Abigail had inherited the house, but they weren't exactly full of suggestions as to what she was supposed to do with it. Abigail loved the old place and knew she wouldn't sell. The thought of renting it out and having strangers living there didn't appeal to her either. It seemed the only option left was to live there herself.

And do what for a living? she had wondered. *I don't think there's a large demand for marketing consultants in Newcomsville.*

Sitting alone in the empty kitchen, overwhelmed with grief and thinking of the daunting task ahead of sorting through the entire contents of the large house, Abigail had heard a scratching sound on the back door. She'd turned and seen Thomasina, her grandmother's fat tabby cat, looking in through the glass panel. Abigail had let her in and scooped her up and buried her face in the thick fur. "Oh, Thomasina, what are we to do?" With tears running down her cheeks, she'd jumped when she'd heard a male voice from behind her.

She'd turned to see Alex Mackenzie leaning against the open back door. Having forgotten he'd been taking care of Thomasina, she'd wiped the tears from her face and invited him in.

If it weren't for Thomasina, Abigail thought, *Alex and I wouldn't have sat at that scarred kitchen table drinking coffee and talking for hours.*

Over the next few weeks it was Alex who helped her sort through the numerous trunks, closets, dressers, sideboards and the capacious attic. They had given a number of boxes to charity, but there had still been an overwhelming amount left. She'd had no idea what to do with the house and all the wonderful things she couldn't bear to part with.

They'd been sitting in Alex's cozy kitchen in the carriage house eating a delicious pasta with cream sauce he had made. Alex had asked if she'd decided whether to stay in Newcomsville. She'd told him she'd like to but needed to make a living. He'd smiled and said, "You're a marketing consultant. All you need to do is incorporate the house and its contents and figure out a way to do what you do best, market them to your best financial advantage."

Abigail, still smiling at these memories, climbed the stairs to their living quarters on the upper floors of the house.

"Just in time," Alex said. "The pizza just got here. Would you like a glass of wine or a beer?"

"I'll have a beer thanks. I've just been reminiscing about how you and I first met and how I came up with the brilliant idea to open the house as a restaurant for lunch and high tea."

Alex lifted a questioning brow. "Whose brilliant idea was it?"

She smiled. "Well, you may have had the idea, but I'm the one who made it work."

"Yes, love, you did. Granny would be proud."

She reached for a slice of pizza. "Speaking of Granny, Agatha and Victoria were in today. Agatha bought another of Granny's hats. It was the one with all the fruit. I wish you could have seen the look on Victoria's face. I truly believe Agatha and Charles are oblivious to Victoria's chagrin over their total disregard for convention, and I love it."

"I know. You can't help but like them both. I get a kick out of watching them drive through town in that classic Packard. You know Charles is really rather handy when it comes to restoration work. I think he can rebuild just about anything from antique furniture to old cars. That reminds me. I had a rather odd phone call from Henry Butterfield. He wants to meet with me in my office on Friday. It sounded important, but he wouldn't say what it's about."

Abigail cocked her head. "He didn't give you any idea at all?"

"No, he just said he needed to see me, and he didn't want to discuss it over the phone. Since I'm the police chief, there could easily be any number of issues he wants to talk about. I'll have to wait and see. It's just not like Henry to be so vague."

"That's for sure. Henry's usually not one to beat around the bush."

Just then the phone rang and Abigail reached to answer it. "Hello."

"Hello, is this Abigail?" an unfamiliar voice asked.

"Yes, this is Abigail. Who's this please?"

"Abigail, this is Grant Cummings. We've met a few times, but it's been a while. I was Alex's college roommate."

"Of course I remember you, Grant. How are you?"

"Well, to tell you the truth, that's why I'm calling. I seem to be at loose ends."

"I'm sorry to hear that. Is there something we can do?"

"It's just, well, you see, my divorce was final a couple of weeks ago, and as I was telling Alex on the phone, even though it was an amicable divorce, I've still been a little disconcerted over it all. So when Alex invited me for Thanksgiving, I was at a loss as to what to do, so here I am."

"Here you are? Grant, I'm a little confused."

"Sorry, I'm here at the Cork & Bottle. I decided to get away for a while so I just threw some clothes in a suitcase and started driving and, as I said, here I am. I hope you don't mind another guest for dinner tomorrow?"

"Of course I don't mind. I'm glad you decided to spend Thanksgiving with us. There's always more than enough food, and we have plenty of room for a guest. I'm looking forward to seeing you. Alex is right here. I'll let you speak to him."

Abigail handed Alex the phone giving him one of those wide-eyed wifely looks that said, "Dear, just when were you planning on telling me we're having an out-of-town guest for Thanksgiving, which happens to be tomorrow?"

***

"Hey, Grant, how's it going?" Alex asked, while mouthing to Abigail, "I forgot."

"Alex, I hope it's okay I took you up on your invitation?" I needed to get away from Pittsburgh. I'm staying here at the Cork & Bottle."

"Sure, no problem. I'm glad you decided to come. But why did you go to the inn? As Abigail said, you're welcome to stay here with us."

"Thanks, but I'm fine right here. I explained to Ben and Sam who I was, and they said I could just ride over with them tomorrow."

"Okay, that's great. You're in good hands. We'll see all of you around three o'clock."

"I'm sorry, Abigail," Alex said as he put down the phone. "I honestly forgot to tell you about Grant last week. He's taking the divorce a lot harder than he thought he would."

"You know I don't mind you inviting Grant. It just took me by surprise. Do you know why he got divorced?"

"From what Grant says, he and his wife began having other interests and kind of drifted apart. Grant enjoys the outdoors and loves to travel and meet new people. His wife was more married to her job than she ever was to him and doesn't like to leave Pittsburgh. Grant told me that when they would go on a trip, she would insist on taking office work along and spent more time working than enjoying herself."

Abigail rolled her eyes. "She sounds a lot like Carolyn's ex." She grinned. "Wouldn't it be ironic if Grant and Carolyn hit it off tomorrow?"

"For heaven's sake, Abigail, the man has only been divorced for two weeks. Don't you think you should at least give the poor guy a break before you start match making?"

"You don't need to be such a killjoy. You never can tell when romance will blossom."

Murder is always a mistake. One should never do anything that one cannot talk about after dinner.   -Oscar Wilde

3

On Thanksgiving morning, the residents of Newcomsville awoke to a vista of gently falling snow. Abigail clapped her hands in delight as she looked through her second floor bedroom window.

"Alex, wake up. It's snowing!"

"Hmmm."

"I just love Newcomsville in the snow. Don't you?"

"Hmmm."

"It looks like one of those Dickens Christmas villages."

"Hmmm."

"Alex, I have a great idea," she said watching the snow fall. "Let's get all bundled up and go for a walk."

"Abigail, Hon, I have a much better idea," came his husky sleepy voice from their bed.

Abigail turned from the window to see Alex propped up on one elbow, his smoldering gray eyes making her body tingle all over. "Oh, really, what's that?"

"If you come back to bed, I'll show you exactly what I have in mind."

Abigail pursed her lips, pretending to consider her husband's offer by glancing from the enchanting view out her window to the tantalizing man in her bed.

She gave him a coquettish smile and drawled, "Well, I guess the snow can wait." She shook out her hair and let her silky nightgown fall to the floor.

***

Quite a few hours later...

"I know I'm a half hour early, Abigail, but I didn't know how long it would take to clear the snow from my car," Carolyn St. John said as she breezed through the front door past her. "But I did remember to bring the wine, a superb pinot grigio from Oregon. Where would you like me to put them?"

Carolyn is the owner of Indulgence, an opulent salon and day spa. Abigail and she met while working for a marketing agency in New York City. Two years ago Carolyn showed up on Abigail's doorstep, bags in hand.

"I've left that social-climbing, cheating, son-of-a-bitch husband of mine," she'd cried, tears running down her cheeks. "I need a place to stay until I take that bastard for everything he has." She opened Indulgence one year later.

Abigail took the wine from Carolyn. "You drove in all this snow? Why didn't you walk? It's only a couple of blocks."

Carolyn gave her a horrified expression. "Don't be absurd, Abigail. Snow, especially this much snow, is for looking at through one's window while curled up on a comfortable sofa by a nice fire, not for walking around in freezing one's butt off. Besides, do I look like I'm dressed for tromping around in the snow?"

Abigail laughed. "No, you certainly do not. Let me take that wonderful coat, and I'll hang it up."

Carolyn's coat was a rich chocolate sable with a fur-lined hood that covered her honey blond hair and framed her beautiful heart-shaped face. Under this she was wearing a hunter-green cashmere sweater with a pleated calf-length black wool skirt. Black Italian leather high-heeled boots completed her ensemble. Draped around her slender neck she wore Mikimoto pearls with matching earrings.

"Carolyn, you are every woman's walking nightmare. If you weren't one of my best friends, I'd hate you. Come into the kitchen. You can help finish the hors d'oeuvres."

"Thank you. I guess I'll take that as a compliment." She followed Abigail down the hall. "It smells wonderful in here. Did you do all the cooking yourself?"

"Goodness no. Alex is great about helping me out. Besides, everyone is bringing something."

"Speaking of which, where *is* that handsome husband of yours?"

"He's in the solarium setting up the bar. We'll have drinks and hors d'oeuvres in the tea room and dinner in the dining room."

Abigail placed baked stuffed mushrooms on a crystal serving dish.

"Who all did you end up inviting?" Carolyn asked.

"It's going to be a nice size group. Ben and Sam, Molly and Sally, Judy and Tom. Oh, and there's Alex's friend Grant."

"Abigail, I don't like the way you're smiling at me. Just who is 'Alex's friend Grant'?"

"He's a friend from college, recently divorced, and feeling a little lost. So Alex invited him for Thanksgiving. He stayed at the Cork & Bottle last night."

Carolyn cocked her head. "So what's he like?"

"From what I remember, he's very nice. There's the doorbell. Would you please go answer it and take this tray to Alex. I'll be done in a few minutes."

***

"Just what I love to see, a beautiful woman greeting me with food," Ben said as Carolyn opened the front door.

She kissed his cheek with affection. "Hello, horse's ass, where's your better half?"

"He's getting his sweet potato something-or-other out of the trunk. What's that you have there, stuffed mushrooms?" He promptly popped one into his mouth. While still chewing, he asked, "Where's Alex, and where's the bar?"

But Carolyn's attention was no longer on Ben. Her eyes were glued to the drop-dead gorgeous man walking through the door in front of Sam.

"Close your mouth, love, you're drooling," Ben whispered in her ear.

"Take this to Alex," she hissed through gritted teeth, shoving the tray of mushrooms at Ben.

"Hello, I'm Carolyn St. John, a friend of Abigail's," she said giving Grant her most dazzling smile and holding out her hand.

Grant returned her smile. "Hello, I'm Grant Cummings, and it is certainly nice to meet you. I'm a friend of Alex's."

"Hi, Carolyn," Sam said coming in behind Grant.

Ben rolled his eyes. "She won't hear you, Sam. Her hormones are raging."

Carolyn glared. "Ben, I thought you were going to take that tray to Alex."

"I'd be happy to love, if I knew where he was."

An unusually flustered Carolyn laughed. "I'm sorry. Alex is in the solarium with the drinks. You can all hang your coats here in the hall closet. Oh, hi, Sam. What's that you have there, a casserole? It smells great. Let me take that to the kitchen." She reached for the dish. "As I said, the bar is set up in the solarium. We'll join you in a minute."

Seeing Ben's amused face as she turned to go, she gave him a sugar-sweet smile and managed to accidentally step on his foot with her two-inch heel as she hurried toward the kitchen.

***

"What on earth is going on out there?" Abigail asked. "Is that Sam's casserole? Let me put it in the oven to stay warm. Doesn't that look yummy?"

Carolyn narrowed her eyes. "Why didn't you tell me he was an absolute hunk?"

"Who? Sam?"

"Abigail! You know damn well who I'm talking about, Alex's friend Grant."

"Yes, well, now that you mention it, I guess he is an absolute hunk, isn't he?"

"Real cute, Abigail. You wouldn't believe what a babbling ass I just sounded like out there."

Abigail shook her head. "I can't imagine that. Let's go join the others, and we'll see if you can knock Grant off his feet."

When the two women walked into the tea room, they found that along with Molly and Sally Brite, Judy and Tom Scraper, the owners of Yesteryears Antiques and Two Bits Barber Shop had arrived.

Judy was of medium height with straight light brown hair, brown eyes, and a wide friendly smile. Her husband, Tom, was tall and thin with serious hazel eyes set in a long narrow face.

"Hello, everyone," Abigail said. "Happy Thanksgiving."

"Happy Thanksgiving!" they replied in unison.

"Abigail, I brought the pies," Molly said. "Alex told me to put them in the dining room. Is that okay?"

"That's fine. Thanks for making them."

"Sally, did you bring the bowl of whipped cream in?" Molly asked.

"Oh, I'm sorry, Mom. I left it in the car."

"No problem," Tom Scraper said. "I just remembered I left Judy's salad in our car as well. Give me your keys, and I'll retrieve both dishes."

"Abigail, this room looks so festive with all of your Christmas decorations," Judy said. "And with the fire in the fireplace and the snow falling outside, it's absolutely charming."

"It's a real winter wonderland," Ben added around a mouth full of cracker and crab.

Abigail smiled. "Thanks. The rest of the decorations are going up tomorrow, but I wanted to finish the rooms we'll be using today."

"Abigail, these hors d'oeuvres are delicious," said Sam. "I'll have to get your recipes."

"Thanks, Sam. Coming from you that's quite a compliment. There's plenty more in the kitchen if we run low."

Abigail went to where Grant stood talking to Alex. "Hello, Grant, it's so nice to see you again. Has Alex introduced you to everyone?"

"Yes, and it's nice seeing you as well. They've all made me feel right at home. I was just telling Alex what a terrific job you've done with the house."

"Thanks. If you'd like, I'd be happy to take you on a tour after dinner."

"That would be great. I'm sort of an old house buff. I've always dreamed of buying an older home and fixing it up, but my ex-wife wouldn't hear of it."

"If you want a fixer upper, you've come to the right town," Ben said. "Although you're lucky there aren't too many left that are in really poor condition."

"Grant, are you pretty good with your hands?" Tom asked. "What I mean is if you're able to do your own carpentry work, it really helps cut down on the cost of repairs."

"Well, not really. My carpentry skills are pretty limited. I would need quite a lot of help and advice."

Tom laughed. "I'm sure you could get endless amounts of both. What is it you do in Pittsburgh?"

"I'm the chief financial officer for the ZX Corporation."

"There are still a few wonderful homes for sale. Would you seriously consider relocating to Newcomsville?" Carolyn asked.

"It's a possibility. You see my ex-wife is from Pittsburgh. I'm originally from New York City, but I'm getting a little tired of big city headaches if you know what I mean."

Carolyn's smile widened. "Oh, yes, I know exactly what you mean. I'm also originally from New York. I've been here two years now."

"Do you have a business here in town?" Grant asked.

"Yes, I run a day spa and salon called Indulgence."

"Really. I like the name."

"Thanks. I've always believed a little indulgence is good for the soul."

"I agree. I must confess I do enjoy a good massage."

Carolyn raised one perfectly arched brow. "As it just so happens, massages are one of our specialties."

Grant sipped his drink. "Is that right? I don't suppose you personally give massages?"

She gave him a slow sexy smile. "As a matter of fact I do. But only for special customers."

"Carolyn, isn't your masseuse's name Burt?" Ben asked. "When did you start giving massages?"

Carolyn smiled at Ben, her sapphire eyes shooting daggers. *"Benjamin."*

"Yes, love?"

"Why don't you…"

"Why don't I do what love?" He asked, giving her a wide-eyed innocent look.

"Stuff another mushroom in your mouth."

His lips twitched as he tried to suppress his laughter. "Sure thing."

Molly cleared her throat. "Grant, if you decide you'd like to look for a house here, Samantha Edwards, who is a friend of mine, is our local realtor. I'm sure she would be happy to help you find something that would suit your needs."

"That would be great. My problem is ZX doesn't have any offices near here, and unfortunately I'd still need a job."

"You know, Grant, it's only a thirty-minute drive into the city. A number of Newcomsville's residents commute," Carolyn said. "Perhaps you could find work there."

"It's definitely a possibility. I'll keep it in mind."

"Speaking of Samantha," Judy said. "She was in the antique shop yesterday with her new decorator. She introduced her as Sylvia Schmuckler from the city. I also heard a rumor that Kathleen is all upset about Sylvia helping Samantha decorate for the tour."

Abigail frowned. "Unfortunately, it's not just a rumor. If we can get through this Christmas tour without Kathleen causing any more problems, I'll be shocked."

"When Kathleen was in Yesteryears the other day," Judy continued, "she was looking at a pair of ruby and diamond earrings. I usually don't carry jewelry at that price, but they were from an estate sale, and I had bought a few pieces I couldn't resist. Anyway, Kathleen really liked them. I mentioned how expensive they were and, well, she got really defensive. She said something like, 'Don't you think I can afford to buy them?' I said I didn't mean that. I don't know why, but I just felt I needed to apologize for the price. Well, she gave me that cut-you-dead look of hers. Then she slapped her credit card down on the counter and told me to wrap them up. They were really pretty. I shouldn't say this, but I wish a nicer person than Kathleen had bought them."

Ben grinned. "You mean like Dracula's mother?"

"Good one, Ben," Carolyn said. "I also had an encounter with 'Classless Kathleen' last week. I was in the bank when she came sashaying out of Carl Edward's office and did she ever look smug. I said hello to her, and she stuck that pug nose of hers in the air and walked right past without saying a word. Which really shouldn't be surprising considering I've heard she thinks I'm nothing but a rich conceited slut."

Ben shook his head. "Come on, Carolyn, giving me an opening like that."

Carolyn laughed. "Thanks for restraining yourself."

"Okay, I'll bite. Who's this lovely-sounding Kathleen?" Grant asked.

"She's a mean, spiteful, crazy bitch that runs a craft shop here in town," Ben replied, "and has the nauseating habit of sticking her nose in other peoples' business."

Judy snorted. "Gee, Ben, don't hold back. Tell us exactly how you feel."

"I'm sorry. I know I sound like a real jerk, but I'm tired of the way she's constantly ridiculing Sam and me over a situation she knows nothing about."

"It's not just Sam and you," Molly said. "I've heard her say some really hateful things about a number of our neighbors. When she starts that around me, I just tell her I don't care to hear it."

"She was saying some really ugly things about Ben, Sam, and Meg O'Neal in Flapjacks the other day," Sally said in a hesitant voice.

Her quiet remark got everyone's attention, and Sally turned as bright pink as her glasses.

"You didn't tell me about this, honey. What did you hear?" Molly asked.

Sally stared down at her hands and mumbled. "I'm sorry. Maybe I shouldn't have said anything."

Ben spoke up. "It's okay, Sally. Go ahead. I'm sure it's not any worse than we've already heard."

She gave him a grateful smile. "Patty O'Neal and I were having a coke and fries. Kathleen and Nan came in and sat down in the booth behind Patty. They hadn't been there for very long when Kathleen said, 'Nan, I understand Meg O'Neal is working for those two unnatural heathens at that so called inn of theirs, which probably is the perfect place for someone like her. I mean with her questionable reputation, she should feel right at home with those two.

God only knows what kind of perversion goes on at that place. In fact, I heard a little hanky panky has been going on between Meg and our town princess' husband. You would think Bob O'Neal would have more concern about where his children are and what they're up to. But after having five of them, what can you expect? Except to have them running wild all over town, getting into who knows what kind of trouble. Besides, everyone knows Peggy O'Neal never was any better than she should be, and her daughters are just like her. In fact, I wouldn't be surprised if Bob and Peggy *had* to get married. We'll just see which one of her girls gets herself pregnant first.' Patty was so upset she was starting to cry, so we paid our check and left."

Judy looked horrified. "What horrible things to say right in front of you girls. Peggy O'Neal is one of the nicest people I've ever met. As far as the children, I think both Bob and Peg have done a great job raising all of them. It doesn't seem as if Tom and I can escape Kathleen's poison tongue either."

Tom squeezed Judy's hand. "Don't get yourself all worked up over this again. That woman isn't worth a second thought. I'm ready to tell Kathleen she's not welcome in the shop." He continued, addressing the rest of the group. "Every time she comes in, she says something to upset Judy, and I'm tired of it. I just wish she'd learn to mind her own damn business."

"Kathleen has a problem with the age difference between Tom and me," Judy said. "Most of you already know Tom is fifteen years older than me. She says I'm nothing but a gold digger who found herself a sugar daddy. If two people are happy, what difference does age make?"

"It shouldn't make any difference at all," Abigail replied. "And honestly it's nobody's business."

"I agree," Molly said. "I hate to say this, but I think Kathleen is truly a cruel person."

"One of these days, she's going to go too far and say the wrong thing to the wrong person and discover she's finally pissed off someone who isn't going to take any more of her shit." Sam stated.

Although Ben had remained quiet during this last exchange, when his and Abigail's eyes met, she silently shuddered at the utter fury and hatred she saw in their blue depths. She plastered a smile on her face. "Okay, well, let's talk about something more pleasant. What is Grant going to think of us?"

Ben, his usual good-natured expression back in place, laughed. "You're right. After hearing what a congenial, happy little town we have here, I'll bet he can't wait to go home and pack his bags."

Grant shook his head. "Unfortunately, I don't know of anywhere that's perfect."

Abigail rose to her feet. "Newcomsville really is a nice town to live in. Alex, would you build up the fire? I'll check on dinner. It should be about ready. I'll be right back."

"Can we help?" the girls asked.

Abigail nodded. "Sure, that would be great. The table is all set. I just need to put the dishes on the sideboard in the dining room. We're going to serve buffet style if that's okay."

"The table looks beautiful set with your grandmother's china and silver," Molly said. "Are those wine glasses antique crystal?"

"I believe they are, but Judy would be the expert on that."

"Waterford by the marking and very old," Judy said. "They're wonderful."

"Abigail, this room feels so Victorian. Every time I walk in here, I feel as if I've stepped back a hundred years," Molly said.

Alex pulled the cork on a bottle of wine. "Who would like some of this fine wine Carolyn brought?"

"None for me thanks. I can't drink alcohol for about seven more months," Judy said.

"Judy," Abigail exclaimed, are you expecting?"

Judy's brown eyes sparkled. "Yes. It's finally happened. We just found out from Doc Jack yesterday that my test was positive."

Everyone hugged and congratulated the couple. They'd been trying to have children for several years, had just about given up hope, and were beginning to think about adoption. Though they'd always seemed extremely happy together, now the two of them were absolutely glowing.

"How in the world could you keep quiet about this until now?" Molly asked.

Judy laughed. "It wasn't easy. I wanted to wait for the right moment."

"She swore me to secrecy, but I honestly can't believe she kept quiet for this long," Tom said. "I'm surprised she wasn't calling all of you as soon as we heard."

"Okay, everyone please have a seat," Abigail said. "Here's Sam with the turkey."

"Abigail, is there any certain place you would like us to sit?" Grant asked.

"No, not really. Sit wherever you'd like."

"Why don't you sit next to Carolyn, Grant?" Ben suggested. "She is known for her witty dinner conversation."

Abigail had to put her hand over her mouth to hide her smile at the murderous glare Carolyn gave Ben.

Alex rose from his chair. "I'd like to propose a toast. First, congratulations to Tom and Judy. We're all delighted with your news."

Lots of cheers and "hear, hears" went around the table.

"Abigail and I also would like to toast our dear friends and great neighbors. We're both happy all of you could join us today. Now everyone eat and enjoy."

***

The congenially festive mood at the Mackenzie Thanksgiving dinner table was not at all in evidence at the Butterfield home up on the ridge.

Actually, if looks could kill, one of Victoria's guests would have slid silently from his chair onto the thick Aubusson carpet and for evermore been silent.

Victoria inwardly sighed. *The only thing I'll be thankful for is that this dreadful day should end.* She momentarily closed her eyes, willing away the headache which had begun at breakfast with the arrival of Agatha looking like a poor imitation of Carmen Miranda. She gazed around her elegant dinner table at her guests. *It's incomprehensible to me how Samantha can tolerate that drunken, disagreeable, vulgar Carl Edwards.* She watched as he emptied another bottle of wine into his glass. I certainly can understand why Pauline looks as if she just discovered something rather offensive on her shoe every time she looks at him.

A loving smile touched Victoria's face as she gazed at her son Charles. The smile vanished when she realized Agatha was still wearing that dreadful hat. With her headache increasing by the minute, Victoria silently reminded herself that for some inexplicable reason Charles was besotted with the woman.

Victoria was seated at the foot of the massive cherrywood dining room table which was covered with Irish linen and laid with Royal Doulton china and heavy antique silver. The crystal glasses sparkled softly beneath the exquisite Baccarat chandelier.

Henry was seated at the table's head. To his right sat their daughter-in-law Agatha and her husband Charles. Next came Henrietta and her friend Stewart seated to Victoria's left.

I'm so glad they're enjoying each other's company. They make such a delightful pair. At least we can count on both of them for some intelligent dinner conversation, Victoria thought.

On Henry's left sat Pauline Silverspoon, a tall slim attractive woman in her late seventies with a rather formidable disposition. Pauline's short auburn hair was streaked with gray, and at the moment her clear green eyes were shooting daggers at her grand-son-in law Carl seated next to her, his wife Samantha on his left.

"Shall we remove the salad plates and serve the main dishes, Miss Victoria?" Annie Stokes, the Butterfield cook, asked.

"Yes, Annie, that would be fine. Mr. Henry will carve the turkey if you would please bring in the other dishes."

"Hey, Annie, tell Brooks to bring more wine," Carl slurred, "This bottle's empty."

The strain showed in Samantha's taught face. "Carl, don't you think you've had enough for now?" she asked in a quiet voice.

"Hell, no, I haven't had enough," Carl replied in a biting tone which would have been hard for anyone at the table to miss. "It's Thanksgiving, and I'm celebrating ev-er-y-thing I have to be thankful for. Would you like to hear what all I'm thankful for, my dear wife?"

"Here's Annie with the turkey," Agatha interjected. "Doesn't old Tom Turkey look yummy? I'd like a drumstick please, Papa-in-law."

Victoria didn't miss the grateful smile Samantha gave Agatha or the mortification in her eyes.

"Finally, here's Brooks with the wine," Carl said. "Put it down right here, my good man."

The glare Victoria gave Carl should have turned him to stone on the spot, but being oblivious to everyone around him he happily filled his glass.

Victoria knew her husband well enough to see his patience was about at an end. He scowled at Carl and began carving the turkey filling everyone's plates which were soon heaped with turkey, dressing, and wonderful-smelling side dishes. To Victoria's relief, the meal progressed in merciful quiet for a time.

Henry finally broke the silence. "Stewart, I understand you've received a shipment of new books. Are there any I'd be interested in for my rare book collection?"

Before Stewart had a chance to answer, Carl scoffed, "Henry, you've got to be kidding. How could you think you'd find a rare book in that dusty old store? Maybe a tattered old paperback or two."

Henrietta visibly bristled in outrage. "I'll have you know, Stewart not only carries the latest releases, but his selection of the classics, including a number of rare books, is quite impressive."

"In order to know that, Henrietta, one would have to occasionally emerge from a bottle and enter establishments other than taverns," Pauline said.

Samantha, her eyes blazing, turned to Carl, but before she could speak, Agatha said, "Henrietta, don't you just love my new hat? I bought it at that delightful shop of Abigail's."

Henrietta smiled. "It's really quite something. I also enjoy Abigail's shop, especially the antique jewelry. In fact, I decided to treat myself to an early Christmas present, a beautiful broach that belonged to her grandmother."

Carl sneered. "Agatha, that has to be one of the ugliest hats I've ever seen you wear, and believe me you wear some ugly hats. Besides, isn't it in poor taste to wear a hat at the dinner table? But I doubt you were taught proper etiquette in backstreet Atlantic City hotel rooms."

An audible gasp was heard around the table as Agatha's large happy face suddenly crumpled. For the first time since she'd met her, Victoria's heart went out to Agatha for she seemed on the brink of tears.

Victoria watched in horrified fascination as Charles slowly rose to his feet. With a murderous look on his normally placid face, his hands clenched into tight fists, visibly trying to control his anger, he said, "Carl! I demand you apologize to my wife for that despicable and vulgar remark. I also demand you apologize to Mamaw for your crude behavior at her dinner table. Then I want you to leave this house immediately. If your inebriated state will inhibit you from removing yourself on your own, I'll be happy to assist you. Samantha, I'm sorry but I think we've all had quite enough of Carl and his drunken rudeness for one day. On the other hand, just because Carl is leaving, I don't want you to feel that it is necessary for you to leave as well. We would all truly prefer it if you would stay."

After a stunned silence, with everyone looking at Charles, mouths agape, Carl got unsteadily to his feet and with an obvious effort to keep himself from weaving back and forth, nastily slurred, "Who the hell do you think you are telling me to leave? I'm not apologizing to anyone, you little…"

"EE-NOUGH!"

A tense silence came over the group as all eyes turned to the head of the table. Carefully laying down his knife and fork, the formidable Henry Butterfield stood and called, "Brooks."

"Yes, Mr. Henry, I'm right here."

"Mr. Edwards is leaving. Please bring him his coat. Carl, your behavior today has been indefensible. Your manner has been offensive and you've undeservedly insulted Agatha, not to mention your despicable behavior towards your own wife. Therefore, the way I see it, you have exactly two choices. You can either walk home or you can let Brooks drive you. The choice is yours, but you will leave my house immediately. I will be in your office at the bank at nine AM Monday morning. Make sure you're there. Now here's Brooks with your coat. He will escort you to the door."

His face burning, Carl opened his mouth, closed it and with a thunderous scowl at Henry, turned and unsteadily left the room.

When Samantha began to rise, Pauline gently placed a hand on her arm. "I think you should stay for a while. He's drunk and looking for a fight. We don't want him to take his anger out on you."

Samantha's eyes filled with tears. "I'm so sorry everyone. I don't know what's wrong with Carl. He hasn't been acting like himself for months, and he refuses to tell me anything. Please excuse me," she said her tears flowing freely now. She hurried from the room.

Henry let out a long breath and resumed his seat. "I'm sorry, Pauline. I guess I didn't handle that situation very well."

Pauline smiled. "Oh, I think you handled it much better than Ethan would have. If he were here, he wouldn't have bothered saying anything. He would have just punched Carl in the nose. I'm glad Ethan isn't here to see what's become of Carl. Something is definitely wrong. And I'm terribly concerned about Samantha. She looks as if she hasn't slept in days."

"Carl used to be such a nice young man," Henrietta said. "It breaks my heart to hear the cruel way he speaks to Samantha."

Henry let out a sigh. "Unfortunately, Pauline, I'm afraid I may know at least one reason for Carl's erratic behavior."

"What's that?"

"I'd like to wait and tell you after dinner. We've already had this delicious meal interrupted long enough."

Pauline nodded. "That will be fine. I'll be happy if you can shed some light on all of this." She turned to Victoria. "It seems my family has managed to ruin your lovely Thanksgiving dinner, and I apologize."

Victoria gave a dismissive wave. "Don't be ridiculous, Pauline. You're hardly responsible for Carl's behavior. As far as Samantha goes, I can see why you're concerned. She doesn't look well at all. I honestly can't imagine how she tolerates that odious man."

"I'd also like to extend my apologies for my outburst, Mamaw," Charles said. "I shouldn't have lost my temper at the dinner table, but when he insulted my Aggie, I couldn't restrain myself."

"Oh, Chucky, you were my gallant knight," an adoring Agatha said with a wide watery smile.

Victoria shook her head. "That's quite alright, Charles. To be honest, I was at the end of my patience with Carl as well."

"I must say I'm also concerned about Samantha," Henrietta added. "I've tried my best not to interfere, but something has to be done about the way Carl treats her."

"I agree," Charles said emphatically. "Carl Edwards is an out and out rotter who needs to be brought down a peg or two."

Victoria rose. "I believe we've all had quite enough of discussing Carl for one day. Shall we try to enjoy our pie and coffee in the living room? I believe Brooks has added more wood to the fire. I'll inform Annie that's where we wish to be served."

Henrietta also got to her feet. "If you don't mind, Victoria, I'd like to check on Samantha before joining you for dessert."

"I'll come with you," Agatha said. "I think the poor dear could use some girl talk."

"Pauline, if you'd please step into the den, I'll explain to you what I know," Henry said. "Victoria, dear, this shouldn't take very long. Then we'll join the rest of you."

Victoria smiled at Stewart. "Well, it appears that leaves just you and me. Shall we retire to the living room?"

He offered her his arm. "Dear lady, I'd be delighted."

For the poison of hatred seated near the heart
Doubles the burden for the one who suffers the disease;
He is burdened with his own sorrow,
and groans on seeing another's happiness.

-Aeschylus

4

Friday morning dawned clear but cold. The snowfall from Thanksgiving Day had stopped leaving three fresh inches on the ground. Kathleen, up by six, was pleased to see they were plowing the roads. She was in a hurry to be on her way to the mall in the city. This was the big after-Thanksgiving sale day, and she wanted to get as much of her Christmas shopping done as possible.

She drove her new cherry-red van while tapping her fingers to her favorite country music. *Life is finally treating me fairly. I'm no longer going to be one of the poor have-nots.* She gave herself a smug grin in the rear view mirror. *I'm going to buy Nan something really special this year for Christmas, so she can wear it on our surprise cruise. I can't wait to see the look on her face when I tell her what I have planned for us.*

She pulled into the mall parking lot. A resentful expression filled her face when she thought of her friend going out of town for Thanksgiving, leaving her home alone. *Oh, well, Nan will be back Sunday night, and we can have a nice visit on Monday.* She entered the already crowded mall.

A few hours later, she'd finished her shopping and was ready to leave when she spotted someone familiar going into The Wine Cellar, a trendy Italian cafe popular for its gourmet carry out.

Oh-ho, what are you doing here? She slowly headed for the café's entrance. Giving her eyes time to adjust to the dim light, she searched for the person she had seen enter. She spotted her quarry in a corner booth. *Well, well, what do we have here?* She sat down where she could watch the two, but thanks to the placement of large potted plants, she couldn't easily be seen across the crowded room.

Giddy with excitement, Kathleen left the café as unobtrusively as possible and drove home as quickly as she could. *This is too good to be true! If only a certain person knew what all I know.* She laughed aloud with malicious glee. *Oh, what a fool you are, my little fish.*

When Kathleen arrived home, she put away her purchases and began packing her handmade Christmas wreaths in several large boxes. She'd been asked to make wreaths for the town hall, and she was to deliver them today.

When she arrived at the hall, she stacked her boxes on the lobby's marble floor. Not seeing anyone to assist her, she resentfully picked up one large box and headed for the elevator in the back.

A thick burgundy carpet covers the grand staircase which rises gracefully up three floors with a landing at each floor. The lobby is Italian marble, and a breath-taking thousand-prism chandelier hangs from the frescoed ceiling.

Kathleen angrily jabbed the elevator button. *Where in the world is everyone? Hopefully I'll find someone on the second floor who can come and help me with all these boxes. You would think that since I took the time to make their wreaths, they would at least have the courtesy to have someone here waiting for me.*

Alighting onto the second floor, she still didn't see anyone. "Hello," she called. Getting no reply, she headed toward Alex Mackenzie's office in the front of the building. Alex's secretary, Bonnie Schreiber, wasn't at her desk, but the door leading into Alex's inner office was ajar, and Kathleen could hear voices coming from within.

She sat the box of wreaths on the floor and crept toward the slightly open door. With her ear to the crack, her eyes opened wide as she listened to the conversation on the other side.

"Are you sure you have the right person?" Alex asked.

"Unfortunately, yes," his visitor replied. "When this was first brought to my attention, I didn't want to believe it, but now, after listening to Barb Winters, I feel her suspicions may be sound."

"How would you like to handle this?"

"I plan on addressing the problem Monday morning, and I'd like you to be present."

"Are you sure it's wise to wait until Monday?" Alex asked.

"Considering the presumptuous behavior shown so far, I think we're pretty safe in waiting. I have to tell you, Alex, this situation has made me feel a murderous rage I've never felt toward anyone. If my suspicions are correct, not only is this going to devastate a few people I care deeply about, but think about the reaction of the town. I'd like to prolong it as long as possible. There's only one other person besides you and me who knows what I'm planning to do."

"Can I help you, Kathleen?" came the icy tone from behind her.

Kathleen turned to see Bonnie standing behind her, bristling with indignation.

"I was, ah..." Kathleen franticly tried to clear her mind. The conversation she had just overheard had left her thunderstruck. "I was looking for someone to help me with the Christmas wreath boxes," she finally managed to sputter. "I couldn't find anyone around, and I heard voices from Alex's office. See, here's one of the boxes."

"Is this all you have?" Bonnie asked with irritation.

Kathleen's eyes flashed. "No, this isn't all I have. There are more boxes in the lobby. I wasn't about to carry them to all three floors by myself. Where is everyone today anyway?"

"Today does happen to be the Friday after Thanksgiving," Bonnie replied. "Most of the employees aren't expected back until Monday. Don't worry about the other boxes, I'll find someone to take care of them."

Her mind still reeling, Kathleen hurried from the town hall. *I should have told that snooty secretary to shove it.* Kathleen got into her van. *The stuck up woman not only treated me like a nobody, she didn't even bother to thank me for delivering the wreaths.* She took a deep breath. *I need to calm down and keep a cool head. When I get home, I'll make a pot of tea, then think things through and decide what to do.*

"Oh, Nan, Why aren't you here when I need you?" she cried aloud, thumping her fist on the steering wheel. Not paying attention, she had to slam on her brakes to keep from hitting Sam Cook as he was crossing the street in front of Buyers' Market.

"You stupid crazy bitch, watch where you're going." he yelled jumping out of her way.

When she realized who it was, she flashed him a rude gesture as she sped past.

***

The Mackenzie household had been bustling with activity since early Friday morning. Thomasina, thoroughly enjoying herself, thought it already had to be Christmas what with all the brightly colored ribbon scattered around and the silver and gold Christmas bulbs she kept finding on the floor to play with.

Alex and Abigail had gone out early and cut down three large Fraser firs, one for the tea room, another for the dining room, and the last for their living room upstairs.

Now Meg O'Neal was busily decorating the tree in the tea room, and Abigail and Claire were working on the one in the dining room. Sally and Patty O'Neal were stringing fresh garland and hanging wreaths in the little parlor. There were garland swags hanging in all the doorways, and Christmas candles surrounded by more garland decorated the mantles. The house was full of the unmistakable and wonderful smell of fresh cut pine. After making everyone stop for lunch, Beatrice insisted on ironing all of the Christmas tablecloths, napkins, and place mats for the tea room and dining room tables.

Leaving his office a little early, Alex stopped in at the Cork & Bottle and coerced Grant into coming home with him to help string the outside garland and hang wreaths.

"Abigail, I have a number of tablecloths ironed, and I'm going to put them on the tables," Beatrice said as she came into the dining room. "Where do you keep those pretty Christmas candle centerpieces?"

"All I have left should be in a box in the tea room," she replied. "I had to order new silk holly rings for the candles from Kathleen. I hope to pick them up tomorrow. How do you like the gold and maroon decorations I chose for this tree? I had Meg put silver and blue on the one in the tea room."

"That looks real pretty," she replied. "But I think the angel on top may be crooked. Have you heard about what happened at the Butterfield's yesterday?"

"No, what?" Claire asked moving the stepstool closer to the tree.

"Well, from what Josephine says, and mind you she heard this from Annie Stokes who you know is Miss Victoria's cook," Beatrice stated with the assurance of one who knows her source has firsthand knowledge, "it seems Carl had been drinking heavily all day, and by the time they were ready for dinner he was in pretty bad shape. Annie says he kept asking for more wine during dinner, and she could tell Miss Victoria was getting real upset with his behavior. I guess it all came to a head when Carl said something mean about Agatha. Charles was so mad he was ready to punch Carl when Mr. Henry stopped him and threw Carl out of the house. Samantha spent the rest of the evening in Agatha's room crying until Charles drove Pauline and her home."

Abigail stared, incredulous. "Beatrice, are you telling us the amiable Charles Butterfield almost struck Carl at the dinner table, then easy-going old Henry threw him out of his house?"

Beatrice nodded. "That's exactly what happened. And that's not all. While Jo's daughter was bringing me home last night, we saw Carl driving like a crazy man out of town. I'll tell you, if the police didn't stop him for drunk driving, he probably landed himself in a ditch."

Abigail shook her head. "This is unbelievable. I feel so bad for Samantha."

Claire nodded. "I know."

Beatrice headed for the hallway. "I'll tell you one thing. I've never trusted Carl from the first day I saw him, drunk or sober. He's no good, and the best thing for Samantha would be to get rid of the bum."

Before Claire and Abigail could resume their conversation, the girls came hurrying into the dining room, faces glowing with excitement.

"We're all through, Abigail," Meg said. "If you don't need us for anything else, we just heard there's a group going sledding on the ridge. We'd like to go home and change our clothes."

Abigail smiled. "No, there's nothing else I can think of. Go on. Have a good time. Thank you for your help."

On the heels of the girls' departure, Alex and Grant could be heard at the front door stomping the snow from their boots.

"We're through with the garland and wreaths, Hon," Alex said heading toward the welcoming fire. "All that's needed is your stamp of approval on our creativity."

"I'll go out and look, but I'm sure it's terrific. Grant, I really appreciate you helping Alex. Hanging Christmas decorations isn't one of his favorite things to do. Would you like to join us for dinner?"

"Thanks, but Carolyn has already invited me over. I can't tell you both how glad I am I decided to come here for Thanksgiving. This is exactly what I needed."

"We're happy you came, but next time please stay here with us," Abigail said.

"Did you say Carolyn is cooking dinner?" Alex asked with chagrin. "Buddy, I hate to have to tell you this, but she's a terrible cook."

"Alex," Abigail cried, "that's not a very nice thing to say."

Alex shrugged. "I'm sorry but it's the truth. It wouldn't be right not to warn him."

Grant smiled. "Don't worry, Carolyn has already told me cooking isn't one of her specialties. She said there's a gourmet café in the city where she gets carryout. I need to get back to the inn to change. Where can I pick up a nice bottle of wine on my way?"

"Panatellas," Claire said slipping on her coat. "I'm heading home. I'll show you where it is."

Abigail gave Claire a hug. "Thanks for all your help. I'll see you tomorrow morning. Alex and I will be there to help with the Main Street decorations."

"Remember we start at nine o'clock sharp," Claire called as she and Grant headed for the door.

***

Samantha Edwards stopped her pacing and, for what must have been the hundredth time, stared out her front window. *Where are you, you son-of-a-bitch?* She'd arrived home after the disastrous Thanksgiving at the Butterfield's to find Carl's car gone. She had been wakeful most of the night listening for his return. Now here it was Friday afternoon, and he still wasn't home. She'd been fluctuating between hating the bastard and worrying he might be lying in a ditch dead somewhere. If she found out he'd been with his latest whore, she was going to kill him herself.

At three o'clock in the afternoon, the phone rang. Heart pounding, she slowly went to answer. She just knew it was bad news. "Hello?"

"Hello, Samantha, this is Sylvia Schmuckler."

Heart still pounding, it took her a minute to recognize the caller.

"Oh, hello, Sylvia, what can I do for you?"

"I just wanted to let you know I've checked into the Cork & Bottle."

Samantha frowned in puzzlement. "I don't understand. You live in the city. Why are you at the inn?"

"I know it sounds crazy, but to tell you the truth I'm really beginning to like this little town. I've thoroughly enjoyed myself these last few days while you've been showing me around. So I've decided to spend the weekend here. Tomorrow I thought you and I could get an early start on your decorating. I have some ideas I think you'll like."

Distracted by a sound outside, Samantha barely registered what Sylvia was saying. "That's fine. What time did you say?" *Was that his car door? Yes, there's his key in the lock.* "Sylvia, I have to run. I'll see you in the morning." Not waiting for a reply, she hung up the phone. Now that she knew the drunken son-of-a-bitch was alive and hadn't killed himself in his car, she was ready for one hell of a battle.

***

Late that evening, an absolutely seething Kathleen was staring through her bedroom window not really seeing the snow that was falling heavily on Main Street. The more she thought about what she'd overheard that afternoon, the angrier she became.

"Damn, Damn, Damn," she said through gritted teeth. *Just when everything is going so well, it all has to fall apart. Why can't anything ever go right for me? All my plans are ruined.* Frustration and self-pity brought on more tears. *Get a grip, Kathleen, you need a clear head.* She reached for another pink tissue. *This isn't getting you anywhere. You have to think this through. You have two days. Nothing can happen before Monday.*

Oh, how I wish Nan would stop being so stubborn and buy a cell phone. I'm going to burst if I don't talk to her soon, she thought as she turned from the window. *At least I can leave her a message on her land line.*

"Nan, I know you're not home," she said into the answering machine. "But I have to tell you something very important. I was going to explain everything on Christmas, but something distressing has happened which may ruin all my plans. Now I don't think I can wait. Please call me as soon as you hear this. I need your advice. I…"

Damn there's the downstairs doorbell. Who in god's name could that be at this hour? "Nan someone is at the shop door. Please call me as soon as you can. This is really really important.

The most effectual way to be deceived is to believe oneself more cunning than one's neighbors.
                    -François, Duc De La Rochefoucauld

5

When Abigail awoke Saturday morning, she was excited to see there was fresh snow on the ground. *I'll go for a quick run and be back before Alex wakes up.* She fed Thomasina her breakfast and put the coffee on to brew. Wearing her down jacket and snow boots, she headed out into the pristine whiteness. There was a pale light in the eastern sky, and the Victorian lampposts with their triple glass globes gave off a comforting glow. *This town could be a Currier & Ives print.* She ran past the closed shops on Main Street. The only sound was the snow crunching beneath her boots, and there wasn't another soul to be seen. As she passed Kathleen's Corner Shop, from across the street something bright orange in the window caught her eye.

Oh good, Kathleen's already up. I'll stop on my way back by to see if she has my candle rings ready. She went as far as the inn before turning back. When she approached Kathleen's shop, she slowed her pace. A horrified scream lodged in her throat as she stared into the store's bow-front window. Stumbling backwards she fell heavily into a mound of snow.

"Oh my god, oh my god, oh my god," she cried trying to get to her feet. Shaking uncontrollably, she slipped, fell again, then finally managed to stand. She franticly looked for help, but the street was still deserted.

Her teeth chattering, she tried to think clearly. *Alex.* She patted her pockets. *Damn.* She'd forgotten her phone. *Home is too far away, so where should I go? Claire.* Without another thought, she started running toward the Monroe's home.

When Jack opened the front door, Abigail, sobbing, threw herself into his arms.

"My god, Abigail, what is it? Claire, come here," Jack yelled as he helped Abigail into the house.

"What in the world?" Claire asked, as she hurried down the stairs. "Jack, what's going on?"

"I don't know. She was like this when I opened the door." Jack gave Abigail a little shake. "You have to settle down and tell me what's wrong. Claire, get me some brandy, and then call Alex. Maybe he knows what's going on."

Abigail shook her head and stuttered, "A-Alex d-doesn't kn-know anything. He's s-sleeping."

Jack led Abigail to an over-stuffed chair. "Come sit down and drink this brandy. Take a deep breath. Then very slowly tell me what's happened. Claire, would you please bring me a blanket."

"Jack, it's Kathleen Cooper," Abigail stuttered through trembling lips.

Jack helped Abigail out of her coat. "Okay, tell me about Kathleen."

Abigail buried her face in her hands. "Oh my god, she's in the window, Jack. She's in the window."

"Abigail, please, I don't understand."

She raised her tear-streaked face. "Jack, she's in the window."

"I'm sorry, you're not making any sense. Who's in a window?"

With a trembling hand, Abigail took a large swallow of brandy, and with a deep breath she began. "I was running past Kathleen's shop and saw something orange in the window. I thought it was her working on a display so I stopped to pick up my candle rings. Jack, Kathleen is sitting dead in her display window. It's horrible. Oh god, her face."

"Claire, call Alex. Tell him Abigail is here, and tell him I'll meet him at Kathleen's," Jack said, putting his overcoat on over his pajamas and slipping his bare feet into boots. "Make some coffee, and get Abigail out of those wet clothes," he said as he went out the front door.

Jack thought he'd make better time through the snow on foot, so he ran toward Main Street. It wasn't quite eight, and the town was still quiet.

"Good god," he murmured as he looked at Kathleen's lifeless body sitting in the shop's window. *What kind of sick bastard would do something like that? No wonder Abigail was hysterical.* With relief, he turned to see Alex's Bronco approaching.

***

"What have we got, Doc?" Alex asked, as he stepped from his vehicle.

Jack motioned to the window. "This is unreal. I can't believe what I'm seeing. I think Kathleen's been strangled."

"Christ," Alex exclaimed, as he stared at Kathleen's slack gray face and lifeless body. She was propped up in a chair in the window, her hands demurely folded in her lap. Around her neck, the murderer had placed a large Christmas wreath complete with a big red bow. This wasn't enough degradation; it also appeared her mouth was glued shut.

"Jack, is Abigail alright? When Claire called me she said something was wrong with Kathleen, and I was to meet you here, and Abigail was there with her."

Jack nodded. "She'll be fine once she gets over the shock. She was starting to settle down when I left."

"I didn't know she was gone. Had she been running?"

"Yes." Jack explained what Abigail had told him.

"I need to get in touch with the coroner, but I need to secure the scene. Jack, can you contact him for me?"

"Sure, I know Louis. I can make the call."

"I don't see any reason to worry about footprints. The new-fallen snow has taken care of any old ones. Those we're seeing have to be Abigail's, and it also looks like she fell."

"Yeah. Her clothes were pretty wet when she got to our house. Alex, I'm going to have to use your phone."

"It's in the Bronco. I'm going to see if I can get into the building. It looks like there are blinds in this front window. I'd like to close them before anyone else sees her. If someone comes by, try to keep them away. I know it's going to be hard. Just say it's police business."

Before going to the back of the building, Alex retrieved the camera he kept in the Bronco and took photographs of the front of the shop. Then he tried the street door entrance. Not having any success, he trotted around back. He found the shop's rear door closed, but not locked. He took more photographs, and then with his gloved hand he carefully opened the door.

After his eyes adjusted to the dark interior, he saw that the shop was long and slightly narrow. Along the right-hand side, he could see high shelves holding a large quantity of Christmas craft items. In front of these shelves, tables were also laden with what looked like handmade decorations. Along the left-hand side, a curving staircase led to Kathleen's second floor living quarters. Further down the left wall stood a long counter with a cash register at one end and boxes piled high with more decorations.

Alex moved quickly, but with great caution, down the center aisle. On reaching the front window, he gingerly stepped around Kathleen's body to let down the blinds. Then switching on the overhead lights, Alex unlocked the front door and let Jack in.

"I got hold of the coroner," Jack said. "He's going to come as soon as the roads allow." Jack turned to Kathleen. "My god, Alex, she looks grotesque. Who in the hell would do something like this?"

"I can tell you, Jack, during my years with the county sheriff's office before I became Newcomsville's police chief, I never came across anything this vile. Kathleen wasn't a pleasant person, but she didn't deserve to die like this. What scares the hell out of me is that the person who did this probably lives right here in Newcomsville. I say that because there wasn't any sign of a forced entry or any type of struggle. Kathleen may have innocently let her murderer in."

Jack ran his fingers through his hair. "I know. I had the same thought. Throughout the years, she's managed to offend a number of people."

"Without touching her, Jack, can you tell what was used to strangle her?"

He hunkered down in front of the body. "I can try. It's hard to tell without moving the wreath out of the way, but it looks as if it may have been the ribbon from the bow."

"I need to take some more photographs before the coroner arrives," Alex said. "I hear voices outside. Would you look and see what's going on?"

"Damn! It's the group gathering to start decorating Main Street. They're going to wonder where Claire is."

"Do you still have my phone on you?" Alex asked.

"Yes, it's right here."

"Then call Claire and tell her to come as quickly as she can. Ask her to gather the group and take them to the other end of town and waste as much time decorating as she can. If Abigail is still shook up, tell Claire to leave her at your house." Alex then began to take photographs of the body and the surrounding area while Jack stepped to the back of the shop to make his call.

"Okay, she's on her way," Jack said. "She was already one step ahead of us. She had thought about the Main Street decorators and was going to drive Abigail home, then gather up the group. I guess the garland and wreaths have been stored at the O'Neal's garage which helps since that's at the other end of town."

"Hopefully Claire can keep everyone occupied for quite a while," Alex said. "The last thing I need is a bunch of people hanging around asking questions. There's a car door. Maybe it's the coroner."

Jack peered through the front door window. "No, it's Claire. She's talking to the group. She's beginning to move them off."

Practically on the heels of the departing decorating team, Louis Tate, the coroner, pulled up in his van out front.

"Hello, Jack," Louis said as he came through the door. "This sounds like a pretty nasty business you have here."

"I can tell you it's not what I expected to wake up to this morning," Jack said. "Louis, do you know Alex Mackenzie?"

"Yes, Alex and I have met on occasion."

Alex shook the older man's hand. "Thanks for getting here so quickly. The body is right over here." He pointed to where Kathleen sat.

Louis went to examine Kathleen. "Well, son, you seem to have a rather ugly murder on your hands. It also looks as if someone has a depraved sense of humor. Did you take photos of the body?"

"Yes I've taken a number of photographs and we haven't disturbed anything."

Gingerly Louis tried to remove the wreath from Kathleen's neck. "Gentlemen, here's your murder weapon, and what a cunning weapon it was."

The long ends of the Christmas ribbon had been tightly wrapped around Kathleen's neck causing asphyxiation. Then the ends were brought forward and tied into a festive looking bow beneath her chin. Afterward, to make the scene even more absurd, the murderer had placed the wreath around her face.

"I'll know more once I do a full examination," Louis said. "But I'm ninety-nine percent sure strangulation by this Christmas ribbon is what killed her."

"Can you give me an approximate time of death?" Alex asked.

"Based on rigor and lividity, I'd say between eleven and two last night, but as you said that's just an approximation. I must say, this is one of the last little towns I would have expected to be called to for something like this."

Jack shook his head. "Tell me about it. I'm still having a hard time believing what I'm seeing. This is going to be a horrific shock to Newcomsville's residents.

"It will be a shock for everyone, except for the last person to visit Kathleen," Alex said. "And I'm damn sure going to find out just who hated her enough to do this to her."

After Louis took Kathleen's body away, Alex began a scan of the shop's interior. "Jack, let me have my phone. I'm going to call the county sheriff's office and have them dust for fingerprints, but I'm not expecting anything useful to come from it. Look at this place. Not only are there Christmas decorations piled on every surface, between the tourists and residents coming through there could easily be thousands of different prints."

Jack gazed around the room. "This place really is a mess. She must have been getting ready to decorate for the tour."

"Probably, but there seems to be a number of identical items. There's a pile of wreaths and another of what looks like centerpieces with candles. I'll bet over there in those boxes are the holly candle rings Abigail mentioned to me last night. It's as if she was organizing items into groups."

A few minutes later, Alex pocketed his phone. "Okay, Jack, the sheriff's office said the forensics team will be here within the hour. Would you like me to drive you home? You may want to change before people wonder what you're doing out in your pajamas," he said with his first smile that day.

Jack looked down with surprise at his red-striped pajama bottoms visible beneath his long coat. He laughed. "I forgot I didn't dress before I left the house. Are you sure you should leave to drive me home?"

"That's not a problem. I want to check on Abigail anyway. I'll make sure the county boys have everything they need, then we'll leave. I'm not planning on being gone for very long. Do you know anything about Kathleen's relations? I need to notify her next of kin."

"Even though she was a patient of mine, I can't say I saw her that often. But I'm sure there must be family emergency information in her file. If I find what we need, would you like me to call her family?"

"I'd appreciate that. Tell whoever you talk to I'll call them as soon as I can." As the two men walked toward the back door, Alex turned to view the narrow room one more time. He spotted something shiny on the floor near one of the front display tables. He bent down for a closer look and saw it was a lady's brooch.

Jack knelt down next to Alex. "What did you find?"

"I think it's an old-fashioned lady's pin. It's a lot like the ones Abigail has from her grandmother."

"Kathleen's?" Jack asked.

"Most likely. It could have fallen off if she struggled with her assailant. We'll see if the boys can get a print. Then I'll have Abigail take a look at it. She should be able to tell if it's an antique."

Just then they heard cars pulling in behind the shop.

"Hopefully that's Pete and CSI," Alex said opening the back door.

"Hey, Alex, it's been quite a long time," Pete Vanderwood said as he entered. "What's this you've gotten yourself mixed up in?"

Alex gave his old partner a hardy handshake. "How've you been, Pete? You're right. It has been a long time, and we certainly do have a mess on our hands. Pete, this is Jack Monroe, our town physician."

Jack smiled and shook Pete's hand. "You'll have to excuse my appearance. Alex was just going to give me a ride home so I can put on some proper clothing. This all began rather early."

"Don't worry about it." Pete returned Jack's smile. "You wouldn't believe some of the clothes I've had on at early morning crime scenes."

"You're going to have your work cut out for you, Pete," Alex said. "Miss Cooper's shop is a crafts store, and there are Christmas decorations piled everywhere. There was a glue gun used on the body, which I haven't been able to locate, although I did find a lady's pin lying under one of the front tables. Also I'm going to need you to go over her apartment upstairs. This back door wasn't locked when I arrived, so please dust the knob as well."

"No problem, but it's going to take us at least a couple of hours."

"Take your time. Here's my card. Call me if I'm not back when you've finished."

After leaving the sheriff's forensic team to do their job, Alex dropped Jack off at home and went to check on Abigail. On his way he saw Claire with her group of decorators coming toward him. He pulled to the curb and motioned for her to come over.

She stopped next to the Bronco. "I'm sorry, Alex. We finished this end of town, and I hadn't any reason to keep everyone here."

"That's okay. The coroner has taken Kathleen's body away. I just dropped Jack off at home, and I'm heading over to check on Abigail."

"What the hell is going on? Abigail told me Kathleen was dead and that it was horrible, but she was so upset I didn't want to press her for details."

"How was she when you dropped her off?"

"She was still a little shook up, but she'll be fine. You're going to have to tell everyone what's happening. They're already asking questions, and I don't know how to answer them."

"I know. You're right. I'll go talk to them now. I wanted to wait until I had decided what to do next, but I guess this is as good a place as any to begin."

Alex parked the Bronco and walked up to the little group standing on the corner: Ben and Sam, Peggy O'Neal, Tom Scraper and Charles Butterfield, along with Claire.

"Good morning," he said, trying to sound as natural as possible. "From what I've seen of the town so far, the decorations look great."

"What's up with Kathleen?" Ben asked, with unusual abruptness. "Sam said he saw the county coroner's van parked in front of her shop."

"Alex hesitated before answering, scanning each familiar face. The last thing he wanted was a town full of panic-stricken people. But keeping the truth from them was nigh on impossible. Besides, chances were that eventually he'd be questioning a number of these folks anyway. So he took a deep breath and told them. "It seems Kathleen has been murdered."

As he said the word murder, Alex studied the reactions of the little group looking for any sign that one of them wasn't surprised by his news. One by one he saw shock, disbelief, then fear cloud their familiar faces. *My god, how can I be thinking someone in this group could be capable of committing such a horrible act against another human being? I've known these people for years, and they're my friends.* Then he thought of Kathleen's dead defiled corpse. Not only was it a vicious act of murder, the utter cruelty of bedecking the body like a holiday display stiffened his resolve.

Peggy's usual rosy complexion began to turn a chalky white, and her voice shook. "Alex, did you say murdered? How?"

"It seems she was strangled sometime last night."

Upon hearing this, Peg's face turned even paler, and she began to sway. Alex gently guided her toward a brightly painted yellow bench.

Claire hurried to sit down next to Peggy and put her arm around her trembling shoulders.

"Put your head down. That's it. Now take slow deep breaths."

"You say Abigail found her?" Sam asked. "Is she alright?"

"I understand she's pretty shaken, but Jack tells me she'll be fine."

"How in the hell did it happen?" Ben asked. "I mean how was she strangled?"

Alex again hesitated over what exactly he should tell them, deciding to say as little as possible. "Last night in her shop she was strangled with some Christmas ribbon." At the sight of Peggy's stricken face, he was glad he hadn't mentioned what else had been done to the body.

"Oh dear god." Peggy could be heard softly crying as her entire body shook uncontrollably.

"Claire, why don't you take Peggy home," Alex said. "I'm sure the men can finish up the decorating."

Claire nodded. "That's an excellent idea. After I get Peg settled, I'll check on Abigail. Come with me, Peg. We'll get you a nice hot cup of tea."

"Alex, do you know what time this happened?" Tom asked after the two ladies had left.

"The coroner thinks Kathleen must have been killed last night sometime between eleven and two. Do any of you remember seeing or hearing anything out of the ordinary?"

"I didn't see anything last night," Sam answered. "But yesterday afternoon, Kathleen about ran me down in front of Buyer's Market. She had to slam on her brakes to keep from hitting me. It was as if she didn't see me at all, and you have to admit I'm pretty hard to miss."

"What time was this?" Alex asked.

"Let me think. It would have been after the lunch crowd, so I would say sometime after two o'clock."

"It was around three, Alex, when you stopped at the inn to pick up Grant," Ben interjected. "Sam came back right after you two left."

Alex frowned wondering if Kathleen was on her way back from dropping off the wreaths at the town hall. He'd have to ask Bonnie what time she was there.

"I was in the antique shop rather late last night," Tom added. "I was decorating the display window. I remember stepping away to get more tacks. When I got back, I saw someone hurrying past in the direction of Kathleen's shop."

"Did you see who it was?" Alex asked.

"No. It was snowing pretty hard, and I just caught a glimpse as they went by. I remember thinking I was glad it wasn't me out there in the cold and snow."

"Could you tell if it was a man or woman?"

"I'm sorry, Alex. No, I really couldn't."

"Do you remember what they were wearing, or how tall they were?" Alex's increasing frustration must have been obvious for Tom began to flush with embarrassment.

"Again, I'm sorry, Alex. I didn't know at the time it would be of any importance. All I can tell you is that it was before midnight. I think they were wearing a dark coat with a hood."

"How about Judy? Is there a chance she could recall more about this person?"

Tom shook his head. "Judy was tired, so I sent her to bed before I began working on the window."

Alex gave Tom a reassuring pat on the shoulder. "Okay, thanks. If you remember anything else, let me know."

As he'd been questioning Tom, Alex had noticed Charles shifting nervously from one spat-covered shoe to the other.

"Charles, is there something you wish to tell me?"

Wiggling his eyebrows up and down like Groucho Marx, and shifting his slightly protruding eyes back and forth, Charles' silent message was clear — *get rid of the others.*

"Okay, that's all for now. I won't keep you any longer," Alex said. "I know you want to finish this decorating so you can get about your day. I'll be in and out of my office, so if you need to get ahold of me, call my cell. I'll give you the number before you leave. If you hear or remember anything, please call me. Don't discuss it with anyone else if you think it may be of importance. This is difficult to say, but someone we all know and think of as a friend may be involved in this. So I want everyone to be very careful about what you say and who you say it to."

"You think the murderer could be one of Newcomsville's residents?" Sam asked in disbelief.

"I don't care for that idea any more then you, Sam, but until I find out who did this, everyone is under suspicion. Remember, if any of you need me, here's my number." He gave them his card, then watched as the somber little group walked away carrying the rest of the decorations.

He turned to Charles. "Let's sit in the Bronco and talk. It's getting colder out here."

"Alex, you see, something rather peculiar occurred last night," Charles began, his excited thin voice sounding reedier than usual. "And I feel you should be apprised of this. You know how Aggie loves to go for sleigh rides. Well, we have that old one of father's. So last night, considering all the snow, we decided it would be jolly fun to take it for a spin. By the time Aggie got herself all bundled up and had made a large thermos of hot chocolate, I had the horses hitched up, and we started out. By this time it was getting pretty late." At this point in his narrative Charles stopped and sat staring bug-eyed at Alex with an expectant look on his face.

"Charles, are you trying to tell me you saw someone around Kathleen's while you and Agatha were out in the sleigh?"

Charles frowned. "Oh, no, this doesn't have anything to do with Kathleen's murder. At least I don't think it does. You see we weren't anywhere near Kathleen's shop."

Alex tried his best not to lose patience. "Charles, did you see something last night I should know about?"

"Well, you see, it was really Aggie who saw him. I, ah, had drunk a little too much hot chocolate, and I had to, ah, well, find a tree, if you know what I mean."

Reminding himself he truly liked Charles, Alex went doggedly on, "Who did Aggie see?"

"Why, it was Carl Edwards."

Alex wasn't sure whose name he'd expected to hear, but it sure wasn't Carl's. "Where were you two when Agatha saw Carl?"

"We thought the snow would be relatively deeper for the sleigh on the side streets, so that's why we were back there."

With total exasperation, Alex demanded, "Just where in the hell was that, Charles?"

Oblivious to Alex's annoyance, he replied. "Oh, sorry, didn't I say? We were in that little street that runs behind the bank."

Alex's pulse quickened. "Did Carl see you?"

"I don't think so. It was snowing pretty hard when I got back in the sleigh. Aggie told me she thought she'd seen Carl's car pull into the parking lot behind the bank. It must have been after midnight, and we were wondering what he was doing there at that hour. We decided to check the situation out. When we arrived, we saw Carl's car, but he wasn't anywhere in sight. Alex, don't you think that's a little odd? I mean where could he have gone except into the bank? But why would he do that?"

"Son-of-a-bitch," Alex exclaimed through clenched teeth. "Charles, do you know where Henry is?"

"This morning at breakfast he said he was going to get a haircut, then play checkers with Stewart. Why, what's wrong? I must say your agitated reaction to my narrative leads me to conclude with all confidence that Aggie and I were spot on in thinking something was definitely amiss."

"Charles, I can't go into details now, but it's very important that I talk to Henry. Do you want to get out here, or go with me to Two Bits?"

"I knew that blackguard was up to no good. I should have mentioned our encounter to Father this morning at breakfast." Then, with eager anticipation on his thin face, he reached for his seat belt. He settled his fedora more securely upon his head. "Alex, let's show a clean pair of heels."

When they arrived at Two Bits, an old-timey barbershop complete with a striped barber pole and an impressive display of late nineteenth and early twentieth century barbers' paraphernalia, Tom Scraper, the owner, hadn't returned from decorating Main Street. His assistant was just finishing Henry's cut while Stewart Wallberger set up the checkerboard.

"There you are, Alex," Henry said, as Charles and Alex hurried through the door. "What in the hell is all this about Kathleen Cooper being murdered?"

"It's true, Father," Charles exclaimed before Alex could reply. "It seems someone strangled her with Christmas ribbon last night. And it may have happened while Aggie and I were out in the sleigh. And all we saw was that louse Carl." At the mention of Carl's name, his excitement vanished, and there was such utter disappointment on his face that Alex almost wished Aggie and he had stumbled across Kathleen's murderer instead.

Henry stared at his son in total bewilderment. "Alex, what in hell is Charles talking about?"

"What Charles says is true. Kathleen Cooper was murdered last night, but, Henry, I need to talk to you in private. It's important. Can we step outside?"

"Alright, Alex, what's going on?" Henry asked as soon as they were standing on the snowy sidewalk.

When Alex glanced back through the shop's window, he saw Charles looking as if someone had just stolen his prized 1948 Packard. He then motioned for him to come out and join them.

"Henry, I think you need to listen to what Charles and Agatha saw last night. I have a feeling you won't need me to go with you to the bank on Monday. I think we're already too late. I have to get back to Kathleen's shop. I'll meet you at the bank as soon as I can. Charles, tell your father exactly what you told me you saw last night."

As Alex stepped into the Bronco, his cell phone rang. The screen showed the caller was Abigail.

"Hon, I'm so sorry I haven't called you. Are you alright?"

"I'm okay now, but this is unbelievable. Alex, I feel like we're living in a nightmare. Where are you now?"

"I'm in the Bronco on my way back to Kathleen's shop. The forensic boys should be finishing up."

"Oh, god, I keep seeing her horrible face. Who could have done such an awful thing?"

"I don't know, Hon, but I intend to find out. Are you sure you're alright? Do you need me to come home?"

"No, really, I'm fine. Beatrice and Claire are here. I wasn't up to opening for lunch, but I'm planning on opening for tea. Although Claire said there didn't seem to be a lot of tourists in town today. Maybe it's because of the snow."

"Did you say something about lunch? What time is it?"

"Alex, it's after one o'clock."

"No wonder I'm hungry. I've lost all track of time. When Claire called me this morning, I just threw on some clothes and left."

"Would you like me to bring you something?"

"No, that's okay. I'll grab a bite. I'll call you later. I have to go to the bank and meet Henry after I secure Kathleen's. I haven't a clue what time I'll get home tonight, so don't wait up. Maybe you should see if Jack can give you something to help you sleep."

"Don't worry about me. I'll be fine. Why are you meeting Henry at the bank? It's closed on Saturday."

"I'm at Kathleen's, Hon. I've got to go. I'll call you as soon as I can."

The men were just finishing up with their fingerprinting when Alex walked through the back door.

"I was getting ready to phone you," Pete Vanderwood said. "We're done here."

"I'm sorry it took me so long to get back," Alex said. "How did it go?"

"As you expected, there are a number of prints. I'll let you know if anything comes up when we run them. I didn't get much of a print off that broach. The texture was too rough. And the glue gun had been wiped clean. I bagged everything I thought you'd want to look at. It's all over there on the counter."

"You found the glue gun? I looked around but didn't see it."

Pete pointed. "It was shoved under that stack of little wreaths over there on that front table."

"Did you find anything else I should know about?"

"No, not really, just what you would expect to find in a shop like this. There were a few odds and ends lying on the floor. I bagged them and put them with the others."

"Thanks again for getting here so quickly," Alex said. "How are the wife and kids?"

"They're just fine, thanks. In fact, they're waiting for me to get back so we can all go cut down a Christmas tree. I'd rather buy an artificial one and be done with it, but my family won't hear of it. They call me Scrooge."

Alex laughed. "At least you only have to cut down one. Abigail had me out at the crack of dawn yesterday cutting three trees down."

Pete shook his head. "I guess I shouldn't complain. I wish you luck with this case," he said getting into his car. "This is a nasty one. Oh, and by the way, Merry Christmas."

"Yeah, thanks. Same to you."

Alex made sure the front and back shop doors were locked then placed yellow police tape across both. He planned on coming back later and having a good look around. But first he wanted to see what Henry turned up at the bank.

"The scoundrel has bolted," Charles exclaimed as Alex walked into Carl's office. "If I had known about Father's suspicions, Aggie and I could have nabbed the little swindler last night."

Henry sat behind Carl's desk looking apoplectic.

"I take it your suspicions were right," Alex said.

"It certainly seems that way," Henry answered with disgust. "I just got off the phone with Samantha. It took me awhile to get her to tell me the truth. Alex, I can't understand why, but that girl is constantly covering up for Carl or making excuses for his behavior. I had to tell her what I suspect happened before she'd tell me that he's been missing since early last night. Now the poor girl is practically hysterical. I called Pauline and she's on her way over there. Hopefully she can calm her down. I told you there was one other person who knew about my suspicions. Well, that was Pauline. I knew when this all came out Samantha would need the support of her grandmother. Her parents are constantly traveling. This time they're in Europe."

"Father, you know you could have taken me into your confidence," Charles said, crestfallen. "If I had been aware of the situation, I might have been able to prevent the miscreant from committing this outrage."

Henry let out a long sigh. "Charles, it was only a short time ago that Barbara brought this to my attention. She didn't have proof that Carl was helping himself to funds that didn't belong to him, but she thought I should look into the situation. I did and I found she was right. So on Friday I went to see Alex and explained all of this. We were planning on confronting Carl Monday morning. I wanted to keep this as quiet as possible. I not only didn't want Carl to learn of my suspicions, I didn't want Samantha upset if it wasn't necessary. I thought the fewer people involved the better. Evidently my decision to wait until Monday was a colossal mistake."

"Henry, do you know how much is missing?" Alex asked.

"I'm not sure, but he must have been in a mighty big hurry."

"Why do you say that?"

"Look at his desk. It's usually extremely neat. Not only are there papers scattered all over, the drawers were left open, and I found this safety deposit box key lying on the floor."

"Do you know what was in the safety deposit box?" Alex asked.

"No. To tell you the truth, I haven't looked any further then his desk. Even though the proof is right in my face, I still can't believe Ethan and I were so easily convinced Carl was an honest man who would make a good president for our little bank."

Charles' face lit with eager anticipation. "Father, let me try that key. I may be able to find a clue."

"I seriously doubt there's anything in there now, but it's worth checking. You'll need the other key to get into the box. You know where they're kept." Henry turned to Alex. "Until I can get the security system code and all the bank's locks changed, I'd like to hire a security guard. Can you recommend someone? I can't imagine Carl will come back, but if he's gone off the deep end, hard telling what he might do next."

"Sure, I can give you a couple of names to call. As far as Carl, I really can't do anything until you can show me proof of embezzlement. Then I can get in touch with the county sheriff. Until that time, he's an adult. I can't declare him missing for at least seventy-two hours."

Henry nodded. "I understand. I'm going to call Barb Winters and see if she'll come in this afternoon to help me go through Carl's office, although I don't know how we'll get into his safe. I can't find a combination anywhere in this mess. You don't happen to know any safe crackers, do you?"

Alex smiled. "Unfortunately no. If you're in luck, either Carl was absent-minded enough to have the combination written down, or maybe he has an office or study at home. Samantha may be helpful in that regard."

"Father, Alex, I believe I've discovered a clue," Charles cried, as he hurried into Carl's office, waving a strip of white paper.

Henry reached out his hand. "What is it?"

"Carl's nefarious ways may prove to be his undoing." Charles handed the paper to Henry. "I found it taped to the back end of the safety deposit box, but I'm not sure what it means."

"What does it say?" Alex asked.

"It could be some kind of bank account number."

"Let me see," Alex said. "Charles, is this all you found?"

"Yes, the box was empty, but I didn't need to use the keys. The box wasn't pushed back in all the way."

"These numbers don't look at all like the ones on my bank account. Henry, do you think perhaps they're some kind of international number?"

"It certainly could be, but Barbara would know more about that. Ethan and I were on the board, but we didn't actually run the bank. That's what I thought I hired Carl to do," he said with a sour expression.

"I'm sorry, Henry, but I'm going to have to get back to Kathleen's shop. Call me if you turn up anything. Also here're the names and phone numbers of two men who might take the security job."

"My god, Alex, what's happening here in our congenial little town?" Henry said with dismay. "Not only do we have an embezzler, we also may have a murderer living among us."

Alex gave a wan smile. "Look on the bright side; at least we have an idea who the embezzler is. I haven't a clue who killed Kathleen."

Charles knitted his brows. "What we need to do, in order to solve this murder, is put our heads together and think like Lord Peter, Roderick Allen, and Sam Spade."

Incredulity could be the only word to describe the expression on Henry's face as he stared at his son.

"As soon as you learn something, Henry, call me," Alex said as he headed for the door.

Out on the sidewalk, Alex's rumbling stomach reminded him he still hadn't had anything to eat. Glancing at his watch he was surprised to see it was almost two o'clock. The Cork & Bottle wasn't far, so he decided to grab a bite before he went back to give Kathleen's a thorough search.

For how can you compete, being honor bred,
with one who, were it proved he lies, were neither shamed
in his own nor in his neighbors' eyes.
- William Butler Yeats

6

"Hi, Chief," Meg O'Neal said as Alex sat down at the bar in the unusually quiet taproom. "What can I get you today?"

"Hi there, Meg. I would like the biggest cheeseburger Sam has with the works and some onion rings. I haven't eaten all day and I'm starving. Where is everyone? I don't think I've ever seen it this slow on a Saturday."

"It's been like this all afternoon." Lowering her voice until Alex could barely hear her, she whispered, "I hope it's the weather, not the murder, that's keeping people away."

Again speaking in her normal tone, she continued, "Let me give Sam your order, and I'll be right back." With just a hint of her usual sunny smile, she asked, "What would you like to drink?"

"A tall iced tea with lemon please."

Alex watched as Meg stopped to speak to a young couple loaded down with colorful Historic Newcomsville shopping bags. Her manner was friendly and courteous, but the unique Meg O'Neal sparkle definitely wasn't there.

"Aren't you in a little earlier than usual?" Alex asked as Meg set down his tea.

"Yes, my normal hours are five to eleven, but Ben asked me to come in early. He wasn't sure when they'd finish decorating Main Street."

Assuming Meg's subdued behavior was due to natural upset over Kathleen's murder, Alex decided to ask. "Meg, you don't seem to be yourself today. Does it have to do with Kathleen's death?"

Giving him a questioning look, she began to wipe the already spotless bar with a clean white cloth.

"I guess what I mean is, how are you and your friends handling this. I know violent death can not only be confusing, but downright scary."

"Meg!" Sam yelled from the kitchen. "Burgers up!"

"Here you are, Chief. Can I get you anything else?"

"No thanks. This is fine, but please answer my question. I'm truly concerned what effect Kathleen's death is going to have on our young people."

She folded her arms and leaned on the bar in front of him. "To be perfectly honest, I don't think Kathleen was liked by very many people, including the younger crowd. I'm sorry she was murdered; nobody should have to die like that. I can't speak for anyone else, but I'm not real sad she's dead. She was a mean, spiteful, horrible woman who constantly went around town saying nasty things about people that weren't true. It seems to me someone finally got tired of it."

The utter contempt on her normally cheery face, mixed with the bitterness in her voice, made Alex's stomach clench. *Could this vivacious twenty-year-old girl be capable of murder?* As he watched her serve the young couple their food, he recalled all too clearly Sally Bright on Thanksgiving telling the story of the malicious things Kathleen had said about the O'Neal's that had sent Patty running out of Flapjacks in tears. He took a big bite of his burger. Meg may have intensely disliked Kathleen, but he couldn't seriously consider her not only as a murderer, but wicked enough to deface Kathleen's body after death. Nevertheless, he needed to know where she was last night.

"Chief, that couple over there was just asking me about the murder," Meg said as she refilled his glass of tea. "I'm not sure what

I should say when I'm asked. Was she really strangled with a Christmas bow?"

"Meg, when anyone asks you about Kathleen, just tell the truth, that you don't know any more than anyone else."

Alex felt that the less gossip there was about how Kathleen died the better. Besides, Meg looked troubled enough as it was. "How's your mother? She seemed terribly upset this morning when I told the decorating team about Kathleen's death."

"She's fine. Why?"

Alex was surprised at the sharpness in her reply and noticed that what little laughter there had been in her blue eyes had disappeared as she again busied herself wiping the bar. "I don't mean to press, but are you sure you're alright?"

"Yes, Chief, I'm fine. I just need to get back to work. You know what a slave driver the boss is." She smiled, attempting to put some humor back in her voice. "Why, take last night; he kept me here until after midnight while he left and…"

That answers my unasked question about where she was last night, but what the hell is wrong, he thought, seeing her face pale.

Alex pushed his empty plate aside. "Okay, Meg, what's going on?"

Alex sighed when he saw shiny tears begin to pool in her eyes. "Meg, I'm sorry if I've upset you. I don't like the fact that I have to ask what may seem like intrusive questions of people I consider my friends, but I have a murder on my hands. I need to know where people were last night so I can eliminate them from suspicion. It's obvious you're upset about something. If it has anything to do with last night, the best thing for you to do is tell me. Now you started to say Ben left the inn last night. I need to know what time he left and when he came back."

She visibly tried to swallow back her tears. "Chief, Ben often has to leave for one reason or another. It doesn't mean anything." Now her pretty young face not only radiated fear, but hostility as well.

"It's alright, Meg. I'll take care of this," a familiar voice said from behind Alex. "The bar is beginning to fill up. Go on back to work."

Alex turned in his seat to see Ben with a troubled expression on his normally congenial face.

Meg gave Ben a grateful look and Alex a rather sour one before she hurried off to wait on new customers.

"Let's go into my office," Ben said. "We can have some privacy there." As they entered the hallway leading to the back office, an attractive blond who looked to be in her thirties came through the front door and headed for the stairs to the guest rooms. The scowl on the woman's face as she glanced at them made Alex raise a questioning brow at Ben.

With an 'I-don't-know' shrug, Ben continued toward his office.

Once Alex was seated in a comfortable armchair with a cup of coffee, Ben sat down behind his antique oak desk.

"So who's the unhappy blond?" Alex asked. "She doesn't seem to be having a very pleasant day."

"Sylvia Schmuckler, Samantha's decorator from the city. She checked in yesterday afternoon for the weekend. She was supposed to meet with Samantha this morning. Maybe her decorating ideas didn't thrill Samantha," Ben said, his impish grin back in place.

Alex couldn't imagine Samantha concerning herself with Christmas decorations this morning, but nothing would surprise him. He sipped his coffee.

"So how is the investigation going?" Ben asked. "I still can't believe someone finally murdered that witch."

"Considering that the only things I know for sure are that Kathleen was murdered and that you seem to have been away from the inn about the time it happened, I'd say things aren't going real well. As I told Meg, I don't like this any more then you do, but Kathleen was murdered, and I mean to find out who did it. I'm going to ask questions which might seem offensive, but they have to be asked. From Meg's behavior, it's obvious something happened here last night. Your feelings toward Kathleen are well known. Now I hear you left the bar. I need to know what time you left and where you went."

"Alex, I didn't kill Kathleen," Ben replied with a steady gaze. "I might have wanted to, and I'm not overly sorry she's dead, but I'm not the one who did it. As to where I went last night, a customer needed help getting home, and I gave him a lift."

"I need to know who the customer was."

Ben rose and walked over to the window which looked out toward the carriage house. He stood silent for a time before turning back to Alex.

"Bob O'Neal."

"Bob O'Neal?" Alex said with disbelief. "I've never known Bob to drink to the point he couldn't get himself home. Besides, why didn't Meg just drive him when she got off work?"

"Unfortunately there's a little more to the story."

Alex ran his hand through his hair. "You'd better tell me all of it. I already have a feeling I'm not going to like what I hear."

Ben went to a small drinks cabinet and poured himself a glass of scotch. "I guess I should start at the beginning." He leaned against the edge of his desk and lit a cigarette. "It all started yesterday morning. Kathleen stopped at O'Neal's service station on her way out of town. It was young Patty's day to help out on the pumps. Well, I guess she let some gas trickle down the side of Kathleen's new van which caused her to have a royal fit. Patty said it was an accident, but Kathleen didn't believe her. She made her go and get Bob. Naturally he apologized and told Patty to get a hose and wash it off. To Bob's disbelief, Patty refused. She said she hoped the gas ate the paint off the witch's car and ran into the house. You can imagine Bob's reaction. He runs a pretty tight ship and isn't used to one of his kids disobeying him, especially in front of a customer. After Kathleen's non-stop stream of remarks about negligent parents, daughters with loose morals, and totally uncontrollable children, Bob, furious, told one of the boys to wash off Kathleen's van and went looking for Patty. I guess he found her at the kitchen table with Peg and Meg. Peg told Bob to calm down and listen to what their daughter had to say. Patty started crying and told them what Kathleen had said when she and Sally were in Flapjacks."

Ben then rose and began to pace restlessly back and forth in front of his desk. "The rest is pretty easy to figure out. Bob, needless to say, was extremely pissed off. He told Patty not to worry; he'd take care of Kathleen. When he came in last night, he'd already had a few and began making unflattering remarks about Kathleen. He kept going on about how tired he was of hearing Kathleen bad-mouth his kids' behavior and his and Peg's parenting."

Alex nodded. "I can imagine what he said. But I still don't understand why you had to drive him home instead of letting him go with Meg."

"Are you sure you wouldn't like a little scotch?"

"Why? Am I going to need it?"

"You might."

Alex shook his head. "Just tell me."

"Okay. I drove Bob home because he kept threatening to go tell Kathleen what he thought of her. Now you and I both know when Bob's Irish temper is up, he can be quite intimidating. Meg was afraid that if he decided to get out of the car as they passed Kathleen's, she wouldn't be able to stop him. So I told her to help Sam close up, and I'd take him home. At first he wasn't going to let me. He said he'd walk. But I finally convinced him to get in the car and we left. Bob normally isn't mean when he drinks, but he can get stubborn. The last time I saw him he was standing on his front porch."

"Why don't I like the way you say 'the last time I saw him'?"

Ben sighed and sat back down behind his desk. "Well, probably because that's not the end of the story. And you're really really not going to like this part. You see, Meg called when she got home and told me Bob wasn't there. I guess Peg had been reading in the den waiting for the two of them to get home. I can imagine Meg's surprise when Peg asked where her father was."

"I thought you said you left him at his front door."

"I did."

"Let me get this straight. You left Bob on his porch, but when Meg got home, he wasn't there."

"That's about it."

Alex rubbed his temples. There was an unwelcome throbbing beginning behind his eyes. "Do you know where he went?"

"Ah, actually, no, I don't. When I asked Meg this morning, she said he came in about one-thirty. He said he'd just been out walking, trying to calm down and clear his head."

"That's just great. What time did you say you dropped him off?"

"It was between eleven-thirty and quarter-to-twelve."

"And Meg arrived home at...?"

"Well, we close at midnight. She said it was around quarter to one by the time she'd finished helping Sam and driven home. It took her longer than usual because of the snow.

"So Bob's whereabouts are unknown from around midnight until one-thirty," Alex concluded. "That's terrific. No wonder Peg reacted the way she did when I told all of you about the murder."

"I would imagine the O'Neal's are a little freaked thinking you'll suspect Bob."

"So now I guess I'll go and have a talk with the O'Neals." He got to his feet. "Thanks for filling me in on all of this. By the way, what time did you get back from dropping Bob off?"

"It must have been around quarter-after-twelve or so. In fact, I went out with Meg and helped her clear the snow off her car."

"I don't suppose I'd be lucky enough for you to suddenly remember seeing something out of the ordinary last night while you and Bob were driving down Main Street?"

"You don't know how much I wish I could," Ben replied while walking him to the office door. "Alex, I didn't like Kathleen, but I didn't kill her, and I can't honestly believe Bob purposely went back to her shop and murdered her. Besides, if he was going to strangle her, I think he'd use his bare hands, not fool with a Christmas ribbon."

Alex gave him a half-hearted smile. "You're probably right. By the way, I need to know who all is staying here at the inn."

"That's easy. Just the decorator and your friend Grant. That's if he hasn't already found more interesting accommodations elsewhere," Ben said with a grin.

"I know Grant checked in Wednesday night. How about the decorator?"

"Friday afternoon. I'd say around three o'clock. I can check the exact time if you'd like."

"I'd appreciate that. Do you know how long she's staying?"

"I think only until tomorrow night."

"Okay, Ben, thanks again. I'll be in touch."

As the two men entered the hall, GH Greeley, editor of the Newcomsville News, was standing just inside the taproom doorway. Spotting Alex, GH's expression resembled that of a hunter who has at last cornered his prey.

GH is a likeable, short, stocky man in his late forties. He has beetled brows, a thick mustache, and an ever-increasing bald spot which shows above the green visor he's rarely seen without. GH swears he's a direct descendent of the New York Tribune's editor, Horace Greeley. GH can be seen typing away on his vintage Remington typewriter and printing his weekly paper on his early-twentieth-century press. He's an avid collector of printing memorabilia and loves to show off his treasures. The building where the Newcomsville News is published today once held the town's first telegraph office expanding to house the paper in 1861.

"There you are, Chief," GH exclaimed quivering with excitement. "I knew eventually I'd track you down. What can you tell me about this murder?"

Alex quickly headed for the front door. "Hey there, GH. I can't tell you any more right now than you already know."

"Details. I need details," GH called following on Alex's heels. "Any leads? Any suspects? Was it really done with a Christmas bow? What time did she die? Why did you have to talk to Henry Butterfield in private outside the barbershop, and where are you going now?"

Alex lifted his hand to halt the reporter's verbal onslaught. "Slow down, GH. This is all I can tell you. No, I don't have any leads or suspects. Yes, a ribbon was used. She died late last night, and what I was talking to Henry about has nothing to do with the murder. If I learn anything I think you should know, I'll be sure to let you in on it."

Alex got into his Bronco. As he pulled onto Main Street, he glanced into his rear view mirror and saw GH hurrying toward his own car, his white trench coat flapping around his knees. *No, you don't. You're not going to follow me.* Alex made a quick right onto Poplar and a left onto Elm, eventually bringing him to the O'Neal's back door.

"Hello, Alex," Peggy said with a tremulous smile. "Come on in." A frisky puppy named Tramp ran in circles around Peg's feet while Lady, a pretty cocker spaniel, slept in her basket. "You caught us about to sit down for dinner."

"I'm sorry, Peg. I won't be long. I'd like to have a word with Bob."

“Come on back, Alex,” Bob called from somewhere beyond the kitchen. “I’m in the den. Peg, would you bring us some coffee?”

When she turned to Alex, her green eyes were huge with fear and her face taut with strain.

Alex placed a reassuring hand on her shoulder. “I’m just going to talk to him. I’ll try not to be too long, and a cup of coffee sounds great. In fact, I have the beginnings of one hell of a headache. You wouldn’t happen to have a couple of extra-strength aspirins handy, would you?”

She gave him a slight smile. “Go on into the den. I’ll bring you coffee and aspirin. Are you hungry? You’re more than welcome to stay for dinner.”

“Thanks for the offer. It smells great, but I just came from the inn. I stuffed myself with one of Sam’s deluxe cheeseburgers.”

Alex found Bob relaxing in a worn, over-stuffed chair by the fire. His stocking feet were propped on the matching footstool, and he looked as if he hadn’t a care in the world.

“Man, you look like hell. Have a seat.” Bob gestured to the easy chair on the opposite side of the fireplace. “Maybe you need something stronger than coffee.”

“Coffee will be fine.” Alex fingered the beard stubble on his chin. “Do I really look that bad? I didn’t exactly have time to clean myself up this morning. I left the house in kind of a hurry. But I must say you don’t look any the worse for wear, considering your activities last night.”

“Ah, so you’ve heard about that.” Bob’s ruddy face, with his bright blue eyes, took on the appearance of one who’d just been caught with his hand in the cookie jar.

“Yeah, Bob, I did happen to hear. Purely by chance I might add. I stopped at the inn for a bite and found Meg and Ben not exactly happy to see me. I finally got Ben’s version, and now, if you don’t mind, I’d like to hear yours.”

“I can understand you being a little miffed. I admit I may have had a few too many and may have said things about Kathleen I shouldn’t have, but there’s really no more to it than that.”

Annoyed at Bob’s nonchalant attitude, Alex struggled to control his temper. “A little miffed? Bob, Kathleen was murdered last night, and your whereabouts around the time of her death aren't known. When exactly were you going to tell me this?"

Alex looked up to see Peggy standing in the doorway with the coffee tray in her trembling hands.

Alex rose. "Let me help you with that. How about if you get the kids settled with their dinner, then come back, and we'll talk this all out." He set the tray down on the table between the two chairs, gratefully helping himself to the aspirins.

"I've already taken care of that," Peg said. "I made a pot of vegetable soup, so it won't matter if Bob and I eat later."

"That's fine. Why don't you sit where I was sitting, and I'll use this desk chair." Alex pulled the chair over. "Now I'd like you two to relax. I think the easiest way to do this is for me to tell you what I know, and then you can fill in the blanks. Will that be alright?"

They took a minute to look at each other then somberly nodded their agreement.

"Okay, first, I know about Kathleen's malicious comments in front of the girls in Flapjacks. I also know about the incident with the gas on Friday morning. Then there are Bob's rather vocal feelings he expressed toward Kathleen in the inn last night. That leads us up to when Ben dropped Bob off and the time Meg got home to find her father wasn't here. Now, Bob, I need to know where you were between midnight and one thirty."

Bob removed his feet from the stool and sat up straight in his chair. He ran his hand through his thick dark hair and began. "As you know, Alex, when Ben dropped me off, I was pretty drunk and pissed. I knew I wouldn't be able to sleep. I needed to walk it off. I do that a lot when I'm upset."

"That's true," Peggy interrupted earnestly. "Depending on what's bothering him, he's been known to wander for hours."

"Thanks, Peg," Alex replied. "Bob, in what direction did you walk?"

"I headed up Ridge Road."

Alex stared at him in disbelief. "Wasn't that a pretty hard walk considering all the snow?"

"Not really, I keep an old pair of tall boots and a heavy coat in the garage. Besides, I could see a light on in the Butterfield's barn on the ridge. I thought maybe Charles was up fiddling with one of his cars. He's been known to work out there at all hours. They keep the barn heated because of the horses."

"So did you see Charles?"

"Not in the barn. But as I was coming back down the ridge, I could hear loud singing voices. It turned out to be Charles and Agatha in the sleigh. As they got closer, I was able to tell they were singing a rather off key version of Rudolf." Try as he might, Bob couldn't hold back a grin.

"Did they see you?" asked Alex.

"No, unfortunately they didn't. The snow had let up a little when I started up the ridge, but it was coming down harder on my way back. I was standing near a group of trees when they went by. They were quite enthusiastic with their singing and drove right past me. If I had to guess, I'd say they'd been drinking a little Christmas cheer." At this point he no longer tried to hold back his laughter. "Alex, I swear they were wearing reindeer hats."

Alex smiled. "Do you know about what time this was?"

"I'm really not sure. I leaned against a tree and had a smoke while I watched the sleigh go up the ridge. When I finished my smoke, I walked on home."

"It was twenty-after-one, when he came in," Peggy interjected. "I'm sure about the time because I kept looking at the clock wondering where he was. I was worried the damn fool had fallen and was out there freezing to death."

She turned toward her husband and gave him what Alex thought of as 'the female look'. This seems to be a universal language unique to women. Bob clearly understood Peg's green-eyed message for the laughter left his face, and he appeared rather contrite.

"Peg, when Bob got home, where did he tell you he'd been?" Alex asked.

"He said he'd been walking on the ridge. He told me he saw Charles and Agatha in the sleigh having a great time."

"Did he mention what happened at the inn?"

"He didn't need to. I'd already heard all about it from Meg." She nervously twisted her hands in her lap. "I asked Bob about it this morning. He said he was tired of Kathleen's nasty remarks and was just blowing off steam. Ever since we moved here, Kathleen has been saying awful things about Bob, me, and our kids. Bob and I can stand up for ourselves, but it was a different story when she attacked our children. Alex, you've known Bob and me for years. I hope by now you realize Bob's big mouth is much worse than his bite, and he would never hurt another human being."

Alex's cell began to ring. "Sorry, I have to get this." He reached into his pocket for his phone. "This is Alex."

"Alex, Ben here. I'm sorry to bother you, but after you left I was thinking about last night and you asking if I saw anything odd after I dropped Bob off. Well, I don't know if this will mean anything or not, but I remember seeing Carl Edward's car coming out of that street behind the bank."

"About what time was this?"

"It was after I helped Meg clear off her car. So I'd say around twelve-thirty or so."

"Could you tell if it was Carl driving?"

"No, I really wasn't paying close attention. I just saw the car turn onto Main Street and head out of town. I didn't think any more about it. I guess I thought it was just Carl out and about as usual."

"Thanks for letting me know."

Alex clicked off the phone. Rising, he studied the two O'Neal's anxious faces. "Well, I guess that's all for now." He turned to leave. "I'll let you get on with your dinner. Thanks for talking with me. I'll be in touch."

Reacting to the relief on their faces, Alex paused in the doorway. "Remember that until the killer is found, I'm not ruling out anyone whose actions last night are in question. I'll talk to Charles and Agatha. With any luck, they'll remember seeing Bob. I'm not trying to frighten you, but I want you to understand that even though we're friends, I have a job to do, and I intend to do that job fairly and to the best of my ability. I am going to nail this guy, whoever it is and whatever it takes."

Peg got to her feet. "I'm so sorry, Alex. We've been unforgivably selfish. We've done nothing all day but worry about ourselves when this has to be terribly difficult for you."

"Questioning my friends and neighbors about a murder isn't exactly what I thought I'd be doing when I took this job. But we'll all make it through this."

"How's Abigail doing?" Bob asked, as they walked to the back door.

"I was planning on calling her," Peg said. "She sounded a little shook up when she called to tell me we wouldn't be opening for lunch. I felt better when I heard that Claire and Beatrice were with her. I can't begin to imagine her horror when she found Kathleen."

"Abigail's a tough cookie. In fact, it wouldn't surprise me to find her trying to do some detective work on her own." As soon as the words left Alex's mouth, a feeling of trepidation came over him imagining what his inquisitive little wife might be up to. Thinking he'd better give her a call, he hurried back to the Bronco.

"Alex, thank goodness it's you," Abigail said excitedly. "The phone has been ringing off the hook. But don't worry. We've been writing down the information from any call that sounds possibly useful."

"Abigail, slow down." Who's the 'we' you're talking about?"

"Claire's here with me."

"I'm on my way back to Kathleen's. Give me the short version of the messages. If there's anything of real importance, I'll call them back now. Otherwise they can wait 'til I get home."

"Well, Jack said he got hold of Kathleen's brother. He'll be here sometime tomorrow. Henry wants you to call. He said to tell you they're still looking through the books. Alex, what books does he mean? Does Henry know something about Kathleen's death?"

"No, Hon, that's a totally different matter. I'll explain when I can. Is there anything else?"

"Let me see." Alex could hear shuffling paper. "Oh, you'll love this. Agatha called and said she and Charles have read a great number of detective novels and would be happy to assist you in the investigation."

"That's terrific. Just what I need, Agatha and Charles running all over town thinking they're Jerry and Pamela North."

Abigail chuckled. "Can't you just picture them?"

"Hon, I'm at Kathleen's. Is that all?"

"There's one more from Carolyn. I could hear Grant in the background. I think he may have stayed with her last night."

"Good for him, but what did she want?"

"Oh, sorry. Carolyn wanted you to know she saw Kathleen at the mall yesterday in the Wine Cellar. She said Kathleen was acting, as Carolyn put it, 'more peculiar than usual.'

"What does she mean by that? No, wait. Tell me when I get home. I want to go through Kathleen's as quickly as possible. I'll see you as soon as I can."

"Fine. I made a pot of spaghetti sauce in case you're hungry when you get here. I'll be waiting. I love you. Be careful."

Anyone can put paint on a canvas,
but only a true master can bring the painting to life.
Anyone can kill, but only a genius can make murder an art.
- Shaun Jeffrey, The Kult

7

A menacing chill went up Alex's spine as he entered Kathleen's darkened shop. *Get a grip. You just need some light.* He felt along the wall until he found the switch. Fluorescent lights illuminated the tables with their stacks of Christmas decorations and the evidence bags Pete had left on the checkout counter.

As Alex placed the clear evidence bags in a paper sack, his eye was caught by a black book of matches with gold lettering. His stomach clenched as the words 'The Cork & Bottle' leaped out at him. "Damn," he murmured.

Pete had made a list of where the few items in the evidence bags had been found. Alex quickly read, 'Book of matches-on the floor, to the right of back door, between large box of candles and the table.'

Alex went to the spot Pete had indicated and looked around. It was just off of the center aisle, and anyone could have dropped the matchbook there. But how many people with Cork & Bottle matches would come in here?

Sighing, he carefully searched through the drawers behind the counter finding only what one would expect: tape, scissors, wrapping paper, decorative bags, string, etc. The cash register held around seventy-five dollars in small bills. He'd checked the register earlier and had ruled out robbery.

He made sure the shop's back door was securely locked before he climbed the narrow curving stairs to Kathleen's apartment. Again a feeling of cold unease surrounded him. He gritted his teeth. *I do not believe in ghosts.* When he reached the top, he found the door ajar. His nerves taut, he slowly eased the door open. When he saw a dim light burning over the kitchen sink, he eased his tight muscles.

As he entered the compact kitchen, he had an unrestricted view through the rest of the apartment. It was long and slightly narrow like the shop below. A combination living room/dining room led off the kitchen, with Kathleen's bedroom and bath along the front facing Main Street.

There were boxes labeled 'Christmas Decorations' stacked along the left-hand wall of the living room next to an entertainment center that held a television, stereo, DVDs and an assortment of arts and craft books. Tucked among these, Alex found a number of well-thumbed self-improvement and how-to-make-the-most-of-your-dollars paperbacks.

On an angle facing the entertainment center sat a small sofa with a matching recliner. Between the two sat an end table with a Tiffany-style lamp. Alex opened the drawer in the table to find an array of Caribbean cruise brochures, an ad for a Lexus SUV, and a Saks Fifth Avenue Christmas catalog. Frowning, Alex looked through a cruise brochure in which Kathleen had made the following notations on the margin, 'Check first class availability for two. Check departure dates. How long on island? How long at sea?'

Alex let out a slow whistle as he turned to the back of the brochure where the cruise rates were listed. Kathleen's shop must have been doing extremely well. He slipped the brochures into a large manila envelope he found in the drawer.

He turned his attention to a reproduction Queen Anne style desk sitting beneath a window on the opposite wall from the entertainment center. Alex sat down and turned on the PC. It was password protected so he began to go through the desk's two drawers. In the second of these Alex found what might explain Kathleen's interest in expensive trips and fancy cars.

There was an account book labeled 'Kathleen's Corner'. Apparently she preferred old-fashioned pen and paper. At a glance, Alex thought it looked to be in order. It was the other book marked 'Personal Accounts' which made the hair on Alex's neck prickle.

Up until five months ago, all financial entries such as household expenses were what one would expect to see. It was in August that the entries drastically changed. On the fifteenth, Kathleen had made a deposit of $5000. Looking ahead he saw $10,000 listed for September, but in October the amount went up to $15,000. 'Still not enough' was written next to this entry.

Damn Kathleen, what have you been up to? He placed the account books in the envelope with the travel brochures.

When Alex stepped into the bedroom, the phone on the desk behind him began to ring. As it switched to voice mail, Alex could hear Nan Katz's screechy voice.

"Kathleen, where are you? What in god's name is going on? I came home a day early and got your phone message. I couldn't stand my uppity sister and her pompous ass of a husband another day. What do you have to tell me that's so important? Call me as soon as you can."

Alex hesitated for only a second before picking up the phone.

"Hello, Nan, this is Alex Mackenzie."

"Alex, what are you doing there? Why are you answering Kathleen's phone? Where's Kathleen?"

Alex didn't want to break the news of Kathleen's death over the phone.

"Nan, I need to talk to you. Are you at home?"

"Yes, I'm at home. Didn't I say I just got back? Alex, I have a bad feeling about this. What's going on?"

Hearing the growing hysteria in Nan's voice, Alex silently cursed. "Nan, there's been an accident." Before she could interrupt, he continued. "I need to see you. I'll be there in a few minutes. Is there someone you can call to come and be with you until I get there?"

Her voice broke on a sob. "Alex, what's happened? I knew by the way Kathleen sounded on my voice mail there was something terribly wrong."

"Nan, please try to calm down. I'll be there as soon as I can. Who should I call to come be with you?"

"I can call Josephine, and you hurry up!" and with that she slammed down the phone.

He hoped by the time he got to Nan's, Josephine would have already told her about Kathleen's death. He probably should have told her himself, but he thought Granny Jo would know how to gently break the news. Apparently Kathleen had left Nan a message. That call may have been the last one Kathleen made. He hoped Nan had enough sense not to delete it.

Back in the bedroom, he opened the small drawer on the nightstand. Under a couple of romance novels with unrealistic-looking men on the covers, Alex found what seemed to be a diary. He felt like a voyeur as he thumbed through the pages. Reading what Kathleen had written on August tenth chilled him to the bone.

Aug 10
Oh, Dear Diary,
I can't believe what I just saw! How the high and mighty can fall. I have to think what to do. Should I tell Nan what I found out tonight? No, not yet. I need to make a plan. I'll write more when I'm thinking clearly.

Alex read further,
Aug 11
Dear Diary,
I've decided what I'm going to do with my secret. Why should some have it all! I admit I'm a little afraid of this backfiring on me, but I'm willing to take the chance. This is my lucky break and I'm going to use it. Besides there's more than enough to go around.

Aug 12
Oh Dear Diary,
I did it! I can't believe I had the nerve to do it in person, but I did it! I said I wanted $5000 by the 15th or I'd tell their dirty little secret. I've heard people say they've seen the color drain from someone's face, but today was the first time I've seen it. It was

wonderful! I've decided not to tell Nan right now. I'm going to let this play out.

Alex began paging through to her final entries.
Aug 15
Oh Dear Diary,
I have it! $5000! I can't believe how easy this was. I'm thinking if I could get five, why not ten? Why not take as much as I can? It's my turn now!

Sept 2
Dear Diary,
I've decided to ask for $10,000 this month. I was having second thoughts until the town meeting. No matter what, there are some people who think their shit don't stink. Well, I'll show them who's in control now. Let them try and treat me like I'm a nobody.

Sept 3
Dear Diary,
I just mailed a nice little note explaining how my silence is worth more than a piddly $5000. In addition, how ten would be more appropriate for my continued silence. What fun! I'm just sorry I won't be there when my note is opened.

Sept 4
Dear Diary,
I love watching the rich grovel. Just imagine little old nobody Kathleen Cooper now has the power to bring the hoity-toity to their knees. I had a phone call asking me not to increase the payment. What a thrill listening to my little fish-on-a-hook beg. It's not my fault if they got themselves caught. I said I thought I was being rather reasonable only asking for ten. I'm sure they will see my point of view and come through on the 15th. I feel so good I think I'll invite Nan out to dinner, my treat. We'll go somewhere nice, but not that seedy "Cock and Bottom" Inn.

Sept 15
Dear Diary,
This is too good to be true! I now have $15,000. Just think. If I hadn't been in the right place at the right time, none of this would be happening. The possibilities are endless. Maybe I'll look into buying a new van, or maybe taking a trip. Wouldn't Nan be surprised if I told her we were going on a fancy trip. OH, LIFE IS GOOD!

Oct 16
Dear Diary,
What a great day! I bought a candy apple red luxury van right off the lot! I can't wait for Nan to see it. She'll wonder where I got the money. I won't tell her what I've been up to until we're on the cruise after Christmas. She doesn't know about the trip yet. I want it to be a surprise. I hope I didn't ask for too much. I think my little fish is beginning to panic. I'll just drink from the well until it goes dry.

Nov 6
Dear Diary,
I'm so mad I could spit! The only reason Samantha volunteered to have her house on the Christmas tour was to show me up. Well, I'm more creative than her. I'm going to make my little apartment a Christmas showplace, and the hell with her.

Nov 20
Dear Diary,
I think $20,000 would be a nice Christmas present for little old me. Don't you agree, Diary? I think I'll visit my little fish in person. Hee, hee, hee!

Nov 24
Dear Diary,
What a bitch! I'm so mad I could rip her hair out. I'll make her pay! Oh, will I ever make her pay. She thinks she can outdo me. I'll show her. Oh, will I ever show her.

Feeling bile rise in his throat, Alex closed the book on the last words Kathleen would ever write. *Well, Kathleen, I believe I know why you were killed. Now I just have the delightful task of finding which of Newcomsville's residents was your blackmail victim.*

With disgust, Alex put the diary in the envelope with the other items. As he switched off the bedroom lights, he caught a movement from the corner of his eye. He turned to see a fluffy white tail disappear around the corner into the living room. On entering the tiny kitchen, Alex found a small black and white cat cowering in the corner next to a couple of empty dishes.

"Hello there, little one. I didn't know you were here. It looks like you're in need of food and water. Let's see what we can do about that."

He searched the cupboards and found dry food and some kitty treats. After filling the dishes, Alex watched as the tiny kitty overcame its fear and began gobbling up the food. "I imagine you also have a litter box somewhere." He located the box in a small utility room off the kitchen. He began to scoop fresh litter from a covered plastic bin.

"Little one, what do we have here?" Ignoring him, the satisfied cat was contentedly washing its face.

Alex reached in and removed a plastic ziplock bag hidden in the bottom of the bin. He extracted a sealed brown envelope. "Well, I'll be damned," he murmured as he pulled out a large stack of hundred-dollar bills. Wrapped around the money was a thin band of paper which read, 'Newcomsville Bank and Trust'.

He smiled ruefully. *This will certainly help narrow my search for the blackmail victim — to only those hundreds of people who have an account at the Newcomsville bank.* He slipped the money back into the envelope.

Making sure the cat had all it would need until he found it a home, Alex locked the kitchen door and went back down into the shop. As he gazed around at the Christmas decorations Kathleen had crafted, an overwhelming feeling of sadness came over him.

Why can't we all just be happy with what we have? He replaced the police tape on the back door and slowly walked away.

Nan Katz lived in a small wood frame house on Elm Street. When Alex arrived, she and Granny Jo were drinking large mugs of coffee which, judging by the aroma, must have been liberally laced with bourbon.

"It's about damn time you got here," Nan screeched as he stepped into the tiny living room. Her pinched face was blotchy from crying, and her hands shook as she held her mug.

"It took longer at Kathleen's than I thought," Alex replied. "Nan, I'm truly sorry. I know how close you and Kathleen were."

"Alex, can I get you a mug of coffee?" Granny Jo asked.

"Yes, please. That would be great. Thanks."

"Nan, I'm sorry, but I'm going to need to listen to the message Kathleen left you."

Nan dabbed her eyes with a tissue. "As soon as I heard her voice, I knew something was wrong. Oh, why did I go to my sister's? I should have stayed here with Kathleen."

"Now you just calm down, Nan Katz," Granny Jo said, handing Alex his coffee. "All this carrying on isn't doing you any good. You have no idea if you being here would have made a difference, and fretting is going to make you sick."

"Alex, the phone recorder is in the kitchen which is down the hall," Granny Jo directed.

"Thanks, I'll be as quick as I can."

Alex found the recorder sitting on a small table under a window facing the back yard. He hit Play Messages but all he heard was silence. "Damn, it has to still be here," he whispered as he went back to the menu and tried again. "You have three new messages," a robotic voice announced to his relief.

Again pushing Play he heard Kathleen's gruff voice. "Nan, I know you're not home, but I have to tell you something very important. I was going to explain everything on Christmas, but something distressing has happened which may ruin all of my plans. Now I don't think I can wait. Please call me as soon as you hear this. I need your advice. I... Oh, damn, there's the downstairs doorbell. Who in god's name could that be at this hour? Look, Nan, someone is at the shop door. Please just call me as soon as you can. This is really very important."

Alex checked to see if the machine had recorded the time the message had come through, but this was an old model and didn't have that feature. He removed the cassette from the machine and placed it in his jacket pocket.

When he returned to the living room, he was pleased to see Nan in a much calmer state. It seems they had dispensed with the coffee and were now drinking the bourbon neat.

"Nan, I'm going to have to take the cassette with me. I'll return it as soon as possible. Now I'd like to ask you a few questions if you feel up to it."

"Alex, do you want me to leave?" Granny Jo asked.

"No, please stay. Who knows, you may think of something that will be helpful. Nan, I'd like you to take your time and think. Do you have any idea what Kathleen may have been talking about on her phone message?"

"I don't have the slightest idea. Don't you think that if I did I'd tell you? Don't you think I want you to find the sick person who did this to Kathleen?" Nan continued, not giving Alex a chance to reply. "The one thing I know that she was really upset about was the Christmas tour contest and that dreadful spoiled Samantha Edwards hiring a decorator. I told the committee it was unfair, but they didn't listen."

"I believe Kathleen's feelings about Samantha are common knowledge," Alex said, interrupting Nan. "On her message, she said something important had happened, and she needed to talk to you right away. Do you know what she meant?"

"That's what I don't understand. She didn't let on there was anything wrong, and she tells me everything. For the last few months she's been real happy. I mean happier than I've ever seen her." Nan's voice broke and her eyes again filled with tears.

"I'm sorry, Nan. I know this is difficult for you. But anything you can tell me may help. Now please think hard. Has she said or done anything lately which you would consider peculiar?"

"I can tell you one way Kathleen has been acting unlike herself," spoke up Granny Jo.

"How is that?" Alex asked.

"I've known that girl since she was little, and if there's one thing she was always complaining about, it's the fact she didn't have enough money to do what she wanted. It was always woe-is-me poor Kathleen. That is until a few months ago."

"Now, Josephine, that's not fair. Kathleen's always had to work hard for what she wanted, and it finally paid off. She told me her shop did real well this past summer," Nan said, her composure, and her usual sour disposition, back in place. "So if she's managed to have a little extra, good for her."

"Are you saying she had money problems?" Alex asked.

"I'm saying that poor girl was pretty much on her own," Nan stated. "Her parents are both dead, and that snob brother of hers left Newcomsville right after high school and only comes back if he has to. Her husband left her for some floozy and didn't leave Kathleen a dime. Then there were all those medical bills left after her mother's death. She's always had to scrimp and save."

Granny Jo snorted. "You wouldn't think so considering the way she's been acting lately."

Alex could see where this was headed, but he thought he'd let it play itself out. "How is that, Jo?"

"Like I said, Kathleen was always going on about money. Then a few months ago, everything changed. It began with small things, like a new bracelet, some new clothes, and an expensive handbag. She and Nan used to come into Flapjacks for dinner on Friday or Saturday nights for my meatloaf or pot roast specials. But here lately my cooking isn't good enough. They have to go to fancy restaurants in the city. Then to top it off, she shows up in a brand new van. So one day I asked her, 'Did you win the lottery or something?'"

"What was her response?" Alex asked.

Jo shook her head. "It was all crazy talk. At first she got that sly look on her face like children sometimes will get when they're up to no good. But then she laughed and said, 'Oh, no, Granny Jo, it's not the lottery. The Newcomsville Bank gives me thousands of dollars every month just for being one of their most likeable customers,' or some such nonsense as that."

"Did she say anything else?"

"No. She was picking up a carry-out order. She just kept up her crazy laughing all the way out the door."

"Okay, thanks, Jo. You never know what might be helpful."

He turned his attention back to Nan. "I need to ask if you can think of anyone who hated Kathleen enough to do this to her."

Nan sat staring at her hands folded in her lap for a few minutes before she replied. When she looked up there were rivulets of tears running down her thin bony face. "Kathleen could have her good days and bad just like all of us. She knew she wasn't well liked. People just didn't understand how hard and unfair life had been for her. No, Alex, I don't know who could have done this to her, but there's a number of vindictive people in this town. I suggest you begin with those two no-good heathens that run that inn."

"Nan, I'd like you to look at something and tell me if you recognize it." Alex took the plastic bag holding the brooch from his pocket.

She settled steel-framed glasses on her nose, took the bag from Alex, and stared intensely at it. "Where did you get this?"

Alex didn't answer, just asked, "Do you recognize it?"

"It looks like something Abigail would sell in her shop. Why are you showing it to me?"

"Could it be Kathleen's?"

"Kathleen's? Why, no. I've never seen her wear anything like this. She likes modern pieces."

"You're sure?"

"Yes, Alex. Of course I'm sure. Once again, why are you showing this to me?"

"It was found on the floor of Kathleen's store. I wanted to know if it could have been hers."

Nan narrowed her eyes. "It certainly wasn't hers. I don't see what importance some brooch is. Instead of wasting time showing me old jewelry, you should be out trying to find Kathleen's murderer."

Alex rose. "Ladies, I won't keep you any longer. If either of you thinks of anything that might be important, please call me at any time." As he turned to leave, a small cat figurine sitting on the mantle caught his eye. "By the way, do either of you have any idea who would take Kathleen's cat?"

"Oh, my lord, I forgot about Precious," Nan cried.

"Don't worry," Alex said reassuringly. "I gave her food and water. She'll be just fine for a couple of days."

Nan was becoming more agitated by the second. "I can't leave Precious all alone. We'll have to go over there and get her." She began to rise from the sofa.

Alex held up his hand to stop her. "Wait just a minute. I can't let anyone into Kathleen's apartment at this time. Precious will be fine tonight. How about if I get her tomorrow and bring her here to you?"

"That will be fine, but don't you forget," she said, settling back on the sofa. "Josephine will see you out."

"Well, Alex, you can probably tell that as far as Nan is concerned, Kathleen does no wrong," Granny Jo said as they stood in the small front hall. "It's always someone else's fault."

"Do you know how they became such close friends?"

Jo nodded. "Let me see, that would be about five or six years ago, right after Nan moved here. Kathleen was having dinner at my place when Nan came in. She sat at the counter next to Kathleen, and they hit it off from the start. Since Nan didn't know Kathleen growing up, she believed all the hardship stories she told her. Don't get me wrong. Kathleen's family was poor, but Kathleen makes it sound a lot worse than it was. Not to speak ill of the dead, but Kathleen could be a really nasty person, and I'm not surprised she came to this kind of end."

Alex sighed. "From what I'm hearing, it sounds as if Nan may have been the only friend Kathleen had in this town."

"You're probably right, but Kathleen brought it all on herself. Alex, how's Abigail? I understand she's the one who found Kathleen."

"She's doing okay. I'm heading home now. It's been a long day."

"My word, you do have your hands full, but I know you'll figure this all out."

"I sure hope so."

Alex decided to stop by his office and put the evidence from Kathleen's shop in his safe, then finally go home. When Alex walked in, he found Abigail curled up in the corner of the sofa with a legal pad on her lap. Thomasina had taken over a scattering of paper on the coffee table for her evening toilette. Before Alex could say a word, Abigail was up and throwing herself into his arms.

"Oh, Alex, I'm so glad you're home," she said her voice muffled by his shirtfront.

"I know, Hon, so am I." Holding her trim body close, he breathed in her fresh sweet smell. "I'm so sorry you had to be the one to find her."

"I've never seen anything so horrible in my life. Who would do something like that?"

"I don't know, love."

"Claire and I were trying to remember if we'd heard anyone criticizing Kathleen lately. She took her arms from around him and stepped back. "I mean, more than usual. I've been going over the ideas we wrote down and, Alex, it's awful. Except for Nan, we couldn't think of another person who might have actually liked Kathleen."

"I'm finding that out myself. I'd like to take a shower and put on clean clothes. Then we can talk. The spaghetti sauce smells great. Is it ready to eat?"

"I just have to make the pasta. Go take your shower, and it will be on the table when you get out."

Afterward, with his hunger appeased, Alex sat in his favorite wingback chair looking through his phone messages. "Abigail, did Carolyn explain to you what she meant by Kathleen acting peculiar in the Wine Cellar?"

Abigail, seated on the sofa, sipped her cup of tea. "She just said she was standing in the carry-out line when she spotted Kathleen's orange hair. You know they have that low wall with latticework separating the dining area from the carry-out. I guess Kathleen was sitting in the dining room peeking around a large potted plant. The place was packed so Carolyn couldn't see who Kathleen was looking at. By the time she got her food, Kathleen was gone. It's obvious Kathleen didn't want whoever she was watching to see her, but who could she have been spying on?"

Alex sighed. "Who knows why she did what she did. I found something in Kathleen's apartment which explains why she was murdered. Whether it has anything to do with the way she was acting in The Wine Cellar is beyond me."

He proceeded to tell about finding the cruise brochure, the van ad, her account book, and Kathleen's diary.

"Blackmail. Alex that's truly vile. I know Kathleen could be callous, but blackmail. I wouldn't have thought she could stoop that low."

"You never know at what point a person will step over the line from common decency to utter malevolence. I brought Kathleen's diary home. I'd like you to look through it. There may be a clue to the identity of her blackmail victim I've missed."

"So you think her blackmail victim is also her murderer?"

"Not necessarily. The blackmail may have had nothing to do with her death. As we both know, Kathleen's malicious tongue has managed to piss off a number of Newcomsville's residents, including a few of our friends, who, I happened to find out today, were out and about in the snow last night. So I'm not ruling out other possibilities."

Abigail leaned forward. "Really, who were they?"

Alex smiled. "You know I can't tell you that. It's privileged police information."

She narrowed her eyes. "Don't you dare tease me like that. You know I'll keep anything you tell me to myself."

He snorted with laughter. "Is that right?"

"Alex."

"Okay, Hon. Let's see, Charles and Agatha were out in their sleigh. Ben, Sam, Bob and Meg, and who knows who, all were at the inn. Judy and Tom had been decorating Yesteryears' window when Tom said he saw someone hurry by. Oh, and I can't forget Carl Edwards. It seems he helped himself to some of the bank's money on his way out of town last night. And that's only the ones I know about."

"Wait a minute, Alex. What did you say Carl was doing?"

"Oh, yes, we not only have a murderer in town, it looks as if we have an embezzler as well."

"Carl's been embezzling money from the bank? How did you find this out?"

"Remember when I told you Henry wanted to talk to me, and he wouldn't discuss it over the phone? Well, that's what it was about. Barb Winters told Henry she thought Carl was up to something and thought he should look into it. Henry and I were supposed to confront Carl on Monday morning, but we were too late. Carl's been missing since yesterday, and Charles and Agatha saw his car behind the bank last night around midnight.”

“What’s Henry going to do now?”

“He and Barb Winters spent this afternoon at the bank trying to figure out how much damage Carl has caused. That’s what today’s call from Henry was about.”

“This doesn’t make any sense. Why would Carl steal money from the bank? Samantha has oodles of the stuff.”

“I think that’s what Henry’s also wondering. If Barb is right, it looks as if this has been going on for a few months now.”

“You know, Claire told me she heard Carl’s been acting rather odd lately. I guess he’s drinking a lot. In fact, Beatrice told Claire and me yesterday that Carl got so drunk at the Butterfield’s on Thanksgiving Henry ended up ordering him to leave.”

Alex yawned. “Now that you mention it, I remember Jack telling me about Carl getting really drunk at the inn and angering Bob to the point Jack thought he was going to punch him. Maybe the drinking is guilt from stealing his neighbors’ money.”

Abigail set down her teacup and stood. “I think we should call it a night. It’s definitely been a long, emotional day. I just hope I can sleep without seeing Kathleen’s horrible face in my dreams.” She shuddered. “That reminds me of something Claire and I were talking about. We can’t understand how Kathleen could sit in her window all night without anyone seeing her. Especially now that you tell me there were people out late.”

“I thought of that as well and came up with two possibilities. Either someone did see her and is afraid to come forward, or it could be as simple as being too dark for anyone to see in the window. There weren’t any lights on when I went into the shop this morning.”

Abigail shook her head. “Talk about nerves of steel. I mean don’t you think the murderer took a big chance of someone seeing them?”

“There’s a pull down blind that covers the entire window. The murderer probably used it, then raised it before they left. It’s obvious they wanted Kathleen to be seen, or why bother decorating her like that? Actually it’s hard to tell where the murder took place. What I mean is, there aren’t any signs of a struggle. Kathleen could have been standing anywhere when the murderer came up from behind.

That's why I think Kathleen knew this person. She must not have felt any fear because at one point she had to have felt secure enough to turn her back."

"Were any lights left on?"

"No."

"Kathleen always kept her display window lit," Abigail said. "Especially during Christmas. I guess the murderer didn't want the body to be seen until morning." Abigail covered her face with her hands. "Oh, Alex, I still can't believe this has happened."

He stood and took her into his arms. "I know, Hon." He looked into her troubled blue eyes, then bent to nuzzle her neck. "Mmm, you smell good. Let's get a couple of small brandies and take them to the bedroom. Perhaps I can help make sure you have pleasant dreams."

Sunday: A day given over by Americans to wishing that they themselves were dead and in Heaven, and that their neighbors were dead and in Hell.   — H. L. Mencken

8

On Sunday morning, Alex found Abigail seated at the table in their cozy kitchen. When they'd opened the dining and tea rooms downstairs, they'd made the second and third floors into living quarters with a combination great room, kitchen, and office, and the master bedroom and bath all on the second floor. Guestrooms, guest bath, and Abigail's sitting room, which overlooks Main Street, are on the third.

"You look busy. What have you been up to?" Alex asked, coming up behind her chair and kissing the top of her head. She had Kathleen's diary open on the table and had been writing on a legal pad.

"I hope you don't mind. I found the diary in your coat pocket and thought I'd start reading through it."

Alex poured himself a cup of coffee. "That's fine. What do you think?"

"Before we get into this, do you want me to make us some eggs or something?"

"That's okay. I'll just have cereal. So what are you writing?"

"I've been working on a couple of lists."

"Lists of what?"

"After reading the diary, I have no doubt Kathleen was blackmailing someone, but who? There're only a few people I can think of that live in Newcomsville who could afford to pay that kind of money. They'd also have to be involved in something they could be blackmailed over. So I've made a list of people who might fit."

"Let me see what you have."

Possible Blackmail Victim	Possible Reason
1. Henry Butterfield	?
2. Charles and Agatha	Agatha's past
3. Pauline Silverspoon	?
4. Samantha Edwards	Carl...
5. Carl Edwards	bank business, mistress
6. Jack Monroe	malpractice
7. Carolyn St. John	?

"It's not very helpful, is it?" said a disheartened Abigail. "But I can't think of anyone else who could afford to pay out thirty thousand dollars. And, Alex, what on earth could these people have ever done that Kathleen could hold over their heads? The other question I have is whether there's anyone on this list you can picture being crazy enough to strangle Kathleen. I sure can't."

Alex poured cereal into a bowl. "Can I picture it? No. Could it have happened? Yes."

"You know we could be looking at this totally the wrong way. Maybe the murderer isn't a Newcomsville resident at all. It could be a total stranger."

Alex shook is head. "I really feel it has to be someone she knew. Remember there wasn't any sign of forced entry or signs of a struggle."

"That doesn't necessarily mean the person lives here. It still could have been anyone she knew."

"That's true, but how many people would drive here from out of town to call on her after eleven o'clock on a bad snowy night?"

"Maybe they came to pick up something for Christmas that Kathleen had made for them."

"What, they didn't like the way it came out so they strangled her? Abigail, I know you don't want to think of someone you know doing this. Neither do I. But I'm afraid it may turn out that way. Look at it like this. If you were the murderer and, say, lived in the city, why would you pick a snowy night to drive out here and confront her? Why not just wait?"

"Maybe Kathleen didn't give them any choice. She could have insisted that they come right then, and if they were planning on killing her, well, they had the perfect opportunity."

Alex sighed wearily. "I just don't believe that's what happened. On her phone message to Nan she sounded surprised that someone was at her door. I don't think she was expecting anyone."

"What phone message to Nan?"

"Didn't I tell you about that?"

"No, Alex, you didn't."

"Sorry. While I was in Kathleen's apartment, her phone began to ring so I answered. It was Nan Katz. Kathleen had left an urgent message asking her to call as soon as she got home. After I finished going through Kathleen's apartment, I went over to Nan's and listened to the recording. At the end, Kathleen tells Nan there's someone at the door. She sounded annoyed. That's why I don't think she was expecting anyone. Then there's the money I found."

"What money?"

"The cash in the cat litter."

"Alex, what in god's name are you talking about?"

"I take it I didn't tell you about that either."

She rolled her eyes. "No."

"I'm sorry. I must have been more tired last night than I thought." He told her about finding the cat, giving her food and water, then discovering the money in the litter bin.

"How much did you find?"

"I didn't count it, but I'd say about $10,000."

"Do you think it was her blackmail money?"

Alex nodded. "I would imagine so. The only reason I can think of for someone keeping $10,000 in a bin of cat litter is so neither the bank nor the IRS knows about it."

"What does the money have to do with your belief the murderer could not have been a stranger?"

"Because the paper band around the money said "Newcomsville Bank & Trust."

"That still doesn't mean the person was someone we know. We don't know everyone who lives in town."

Alex let out a long breath. "You're right. I'm only saying I don't think someone drove here last night in all that snow purposely to kill Kathleen. Whoever it was had to have already been here." He glanced at the clock. "I need to get to work. Are you opening the restaurant today?"

"Yes, why? What time is it?"

"It's almost nine o'clock."

"Damn, I'm late and I need to take a shower. Beatrice will be here any minute to start prepping for lunch. What are your plans for the day?"

"I'm going to start by returning a couple of phone calls. Then I'd like to get my notes in order. After that I have to go and get Kathleen's cat and take it to Nan. While I'm out I may walk through town talking to people." He hesitated. "Hon, don't mention Kathleen's blackmail to anyone. If the blackmailer is the murderer, I don't want them to know about the diary."

She smiled. "You don't have to worry about me saying anything. My lips are sealed."

Alex poured another cup of coffee and made his way to his home office to call Henry. "Hello, Henry, this is Alex."

"Good morning, Alex. Well, it's not a good morning at all, is it?" Henry replied sounding tired.

"I'm sure we've all had better. I was wondering if you and Barb discovered anything at the bank."

"We certainly did. To begin with, the numbers Charles found were for a bank account in the Caribbean. We're still not sure how much money is missing. We were able to get into his office safe, and it's empty. The only good news, if you can call it that, is it looks like he's only been at this for a few months. I think the financial loss will be substantial, but not detrimental to the bank's existence. Alex, I can't express how angry and disheartened I am over all of this."

"It's all pretty unbelievable. I take it Samantha hasn't heard from Carl."

"No, and she's absolutely inconsolable over this. Pauline ended up calling Jack last night, and he went over there and gave Samantha something to help her sleep. Pauline said she'd stay with her for as long as she needed to."

"Okay, what do you want to do now?"

"I'd like to beat the little bastard within an inch of his life."

"I can understand that, but we need to find him first. Does Samantha have any idea where he might have gone?"

"Hell, I can tell you where the son-of-a-bitch probably is. He's sitting on some beach somewhere drinking a god-damned pina colada. I tell you, Alex, when I think of all the hard work the citizens of Newcomsville have put into reviving this town and the trust they put in Ethan and myself when we told them this town could really prosper; when I think of how that bastard abused that trust, throwing it back in our faces, I swear if he were in front of me right now I'd kill him with my bare hands."

"If, or should I say when, word of this gets out, I don't think you'll be the only one feeling that way. Let's start by seeing if we can track him down. Then we can see how he likes our jail. When I call the sheriff, it would be helpful to have the make and license number of his car."

"I'm sure we can get that information from Samantha. I know Kathleen's murder has to be your first priority, but I'd appreciate any assistance you can give in finding Carl. I'm not going to give up until he's found."

"Henry, I want to find him as much as you do. I think I'll go over and talk to Samantha. She may know of someone Carl might get in touch with. Before you go, is Charles there? I'd like to ask him a couple of questions."

"Yes, he is. Hang on a minute. I'll go get him."

"Good morning, Alex. How's the murder investigation going?" Charles asked excitedly.

"Actually, that's why I wanted to speak with you."

Before Alex could continue, Charles rushed on, "Aggie and I have been ardently reading about the case in GH's special edition this morning."

Alex gritted his teeth. "GH put out a special edition?" *He sure didn't waste any time.* "I haven't seen the paper, Charles. What does it say?"

"Wait just a minute. Aggie, do you have the Newcomsville News in there with you?"

Alex could hear Agatha's boisterous voice in the background followed by the sound of crinkling paper.

"Okay, Alex, I have it here. Would you like me to read the article to you?"

"That would be great."

"It says, 'Newcomsville News Special Edition'!

Murder on Main Street   by GH Greeley

Our little town's tranquility was shattered yesterday. While out for a morning run, Abigail MacKenzie, the wife of our police chief, Alex MacKenzie, stumbled upon the dead body of Kathleen Cooper, owner and proprietor of Kathleen's Corner, sitting in her craft shop's front window. Miss Cooper had been brutally strangled by the use of a large Christmas ribbon.

But was strangling Miss Cooper enough for the murderer? Oh, no! Not satisfied with just murdering Miss Cooper, the "Yuletide Strangler" sadistically desecrated her body, decorating it like a Satanic Christmas display.

A large holiday wreath was placed around Miss Cooper's neck complete with a big red bow. Then this devil incarnate ornamented her hair, dyed orange for the fall holidays, with sprigs of holly. Still not happy with his work, the murderer, by the use of Miss Cooper's own tool of the trade, hot-glued her mouth shut!

According to our Chief of Police, there are no suspects at this time. If you have any information that will assist in apprehending Miss Cooper's murderer, please contact Police Chief Alex Mackenzie's office immediately.

"Then it goes on to tell about Kathleen growing up in Newcomsville, how she began her shop, and a little on the Christmas tour. Would you like me to continue?"

Alex could hardly control his anger. *How the hell did GH get the information on Kathleen's body?* He would definitely be paying the star reporter a visit.

"Alex, are you there?" Charles asked.

"Yes, Charles, sorry. Thanks. I think I've heard enough. I wanted ask if while you and Agatha were out in the sleigh Friday night, did you see anyone besides Carl?"

"Actually, Aggie and I have been mulling over that very thing. After we saw Carl's car behind the bank, we waited for a few minutes. When Carl didn't appear, we thought perhaps he'd had just parked his car there and gone somewhere else on foot. Now we know the sneaky little crook was in there the entire time. Anyway, Aggie was beginning to get cold so we drove for a little ways on that gravel road that winds around and eventually brings you out on Main Street next to the Cork & Bottle."

"About what time was this?"

"Hang on. Aggie, could you come here please. Alex wants to know what time it was that we saw that shadowy figure in front of the inn."

Alex frowned. *Shadowy figure?*

"Aggie says it must have been just before one o'clock because we were back on the ridge by one-thirty."

Alex rubbed his temples where another headache was beginning to pound. "Charles, let me see if I understand all of this. You're saying, after you and Agatha left the bank, you drove for a while. Then you ended up coming out on the road next to the inn that runs into Main Street."

"That's right. That's when we saw the shifty-looking character."

"Please, Charles, I need to know exactly what you saw."

"Well, you see, that's our dilemma. We're not exactly sure what we did see."

Alex ground his teeth. "That's fine. Just tell me what happened."

"While we were turning onto Main Street, we saw a man. Excuse me, Alex. What's that, Aggie? Aggie says she thinks it was a woman. You see, we're just not sure if it was a man or a woman. What we know for certain is that the figure was wearing dark clothing and was standing on the corner by that large oak tree near the inn."

"Were they heading toward the inn or walking away?"

"That's another problem. We're really not sure about that either. About the time we were passing the inn, the horses began moving at a pretty good clip, and it was snowing rather hard. We weren't really paying that much attention to our surroundings. It wasn't until Aggie and I were reading GH's paper this morning, and it jarred our memories about seeing someone on the corner. But unfortunately, Aggie and I still disagree on the sex of this person."

"Could you tell if this person was tall or short?"

"No, although I do recall the figure looked to me as if they were hunching over. Just a moment and I'll ask Aggie what she thinks. She also thinks this person was hunched over."

"Thanks, Charles. If either of you remembers anything more, please call me. Now, other than this person, did either of you see anyone else on your way up the ridge?"

"No, I don't recall seeing anyone else. Aggie, did you see anyone as we came up the ridge? Aggie says she didn't see anyone either. But Alex, Aggie and I have been studying the case, and we have a working hypothesis on why this crime happened, and we'd like to run it by you."

"Go ahead, Charles." Alex tried to hide the impatience in his voice.

"Aggie and I were thinking that perhaps Kathleen unwittingly came upon or overheard something she shouldn't have, and whoever discovered this indiscretion knew she had a big mouth. So they needed to permanently silence her. Gluing her mouth shut was their way of letting others know they'd better stay clammed up. So, Alex, what do you think?"

"That's quite an interesting theory. I'll definitely keep that in mind. Let me ask you this. Who do you and Agatha think the warning to keep clammed up is for?"

"Why, it would be for whoever else is in on the scheme Kathleen must have stumbled upon."

"So you and Aggie think there's more than one person involved in this?"

"Oh, yes, certainly. Although we believe there's only one person who actually perpetrated the crime. We feel somehow there's another person involved in this. Like Richard Jury and Melrose Plant, Aggie and I plan on keeping our eyes and ears open for anything or anyone that may look suspicious."

"Charles, I appreciate you and Agatha wanting to help, but if you hear something you think is important, please call me. Don't approach anyone with your suspicions on your own. Remember this person is a killer, and if they feel threatened, they may strike again."

"We'll be sure and let you know immediately," Charles replied with great enthusiasm. "Aggie and I are confident we'll be of great assistance to you."

Alex silently groaned. "Just remember what I said. Don't do anything on your own."

"Righto," Charles replied. "Alex, father has that information for you. Hang on."

"Carl's car is a dark green Cadillac," Henry said. "Plate number JRK4279."

"Thanks, Henry. I'll call Will Boone at the county sheriff's office and fill him in. Who knows, we may have Carl by nightfall."

After speaking in depth with Will Boone, Alex began typing his notes into his computer. When he finished, he sat back in his desk chair and thoughtfully reviewed the file. He was pretty confident who the blackmail victim was. *Blackmail victim, yes. Murderer, I can't see it.*

He made his way downstairs to tell Abigail he was leaving. As he entered the kitchen, the aromas of fresh baked bread and simmering homemade soup made his mouth water. Beatrice, standing at the stove, was busily ladling what looked like thick potato soup into two large bowls.

Alex sniffed appreciatively. "That smells wonderful. Is there enough for a neglected starving husband?"

"Abigail told me you two didn't have a proper breakfast this morning," Beatrice replied with disapproval. "Set yourself down and I'll get you some soup and a slice of my chicken pot pie."

As Alex sat down at the scarred wooden table, Abigail came rushing through the swinging kitchen door.

"Three more specials, Beatrice," Abigail said breathlessly. "Oh, hi, Alex. My goodness, you wouldn't believe how busy we are. We hardly have time to get a table cleared before Peg is seating someone else. Yesterday Claire and I were wondering if the murder would keep the tourists away and hurt ticket sales for the tour. Well, we needn't have worried. The murder is all everyone is talking about."

Beatrice glared reproachfully. "You shouldn't sound so pleased, Missy. Kathleen wasn't the most liked person in town, but her death is still a tragedy."

Abigail's cheeks turned pink. "You're right. I'm sorry. But it's true. The town is packed."

"That doesn't surprise me," Alex said. "Situations like this always bring the curiosity seekers out in droves. Abigail, after I've finished eating, I'm going to be out and about most of the day."

"Okay, I'll let you know if I hear anything that could be important."

"You do that, Hon. Beatrice, thanks for a delicious lunch. I'll see you two later."

As Alex was reaching for his coat, the kitchen wall phone rang. "I've got it. Hello, Abigail's Tea Room."

"Hello, Chief, is that you?" Bonnie Schreiber, Alex's secretary, asked.

"Yes, Bonnie, it's me. You just caught me on my way out. What's up?"

"Chief, I was calling about GH's special edition. The office phone is going to be ringing off the hook. Would you like me to go into the office and take care of it?"

"If you don't mind, I'd appreciate it. I'm sure we're going to have a number of calls from residents with quite vivid imaginations. Please just keep the tips that sound plausible. I'll stop in later."

Before Alex had a chance to replace the phone, Abigail was asking, "What's happened? What did Bonnie want?"

When he turned, he was confronted with Abigail and Beatrice. They'd stopped what they were doing and stared at him with expectant faces brimming with curiosity.

"Sorry, ladies, no new gossip. Have a good day." With an amused smile he went out the back door.

***

"ALEX, you infuriating man," Abigail exclaimed.

"I'm glad you two have time to hang around laughing," Peggy said, her arms laden with dirty dishes.

"I'm sorry, Peg. Let me help you with those."

114

Peg handed Abigail the stack of dishes. "What's so funny?"

"It was just Alex being an incredible ass," Abigail stated. "Peg, are we still busy?"

"We're beginning to slow down, but Carolyn and a really good looking guy just came into the dining room, and they were asking for you."

Abigail smiled. "That good looking guy is Grant Cummings. You know, I don't think he and Carolyn have been apart since Thanksgiving. Wouldn't it be something if they ended up together?"

"Really, that's fantastic," Peggy said with a true matchmaker's heart.

"While you two are standing in here grinning at each other like a couple of cats who got the cream, there's folks out there wanting something to eat."

"Yes, Beatrice," the two said in unison. "We'll be good and go back to work." Still chuckling, Abigail and Peggy went through the swinging kitchen door.

"There you are, Abigail." Carolyn said. "I told Grant what a wonderful cook Beatrice is, so we decided to come and have lunch. Henrietta will be joining us."

"I'm glad to see you two, but I haven't seen Henrietta. When were you supposed to meet?"

"About ten minutes ago," Carolyn replied. "Pauline is considering selling her house, and Henrietta is going to show it to Grant."

"Really, that's wonderful. So, Grant, you're thinking of moving to Newcomsville?"

Grant nodded. "If I can find a house, and, more importantly, a job. Carolyn has been showing me around, and I'm really beginning to like it here."

"That would be great if you could work things out. I know Alex would be pleased to have you as a neighbor. I can't imagine Pauline's house will need much repair."

"No, not really," Carolyn said. "Even though she's living with Henrietta, Pauline has made sure the house is kept in good shape. If anything, the interior could be updated, and I could help Grant with that."

Abigail studied the two and smiled. *They absolutely glow when they look at each other. I can't wait until I tell Alex how well this is working out.*

"There's Henrietta," Carolyn said waving to the older woman.

"Hello, everyone. I'm so sorry I'm late. Stewart and I stopped after church to see Samantha, and the time got away from me. Oh, thank you, Grant," she said as he held out the chair for her. "I hope I haven't kept you waiting."

"No, you're fine. We haven't been here that long, but what's wrong with Samantha?" Carolyn asked.

Henrietta looked flustered. "Oh, dear. You haven't heard."

"Heard what?" Carolyn asked.

Realizing Henrietta didn't know quite what to say, Abigail spoke up. "It seems Carl has left town. He hasn't been seen since sometime on Friday, and Samantha doesn't know where he is."

Henrietta gave Abigail a grateful smile. "Yes, and she's beside herself with worry. I know I shouldn't say this, but Samantha has always been my favorite niece. I can't help worrying about her. There's something about Carl that's always made me uneasy."

"Good riddance to bad news is all I have to say," Carolyn replied. "I've always said Samantha deserves better than that useless sleaze ball."

"Carolyn!"

"Abigail, don't say 'Carolyn!' The man's a toad, and she's better off without him. She doesn't feel that way now, but she'll come around. I'll call her and tell her to come into the spa for an all day pampering. Afterward she'll feel great. You'll see."

Abigail laughed. "Only you, Carolyn, would think a manicure, a pedicure, and a facial will make everything alright."

Carolyn opened her eyes wide. "Well, doesn't it?"

"I guess it can't hurt," Abigail agreed. "Now I imagine all of you are hungry. Would you like to order?"

"Yes. What delightful dish does Beatrice have for us today?" Henrietta asked.

Abigail handed them the menu, then took their orders. "I'll be right back with your beverages. When she returned to the table, the trio was lively, discussing the topic on everyone's tongue — Kathleen's death.

Carolyn was saying, "Well, I personally hope Alex never finds out who did it, and hats off to whoever it is."

"Carolyn, what an awful thing to say," Abigail said.

"I know I sound unfeeling, but I don't care. I'm not going to sit here and be a hypocrite and say I'm sorry she's dead when I'm not. She was a horrible person, and most of this town feels the same way."

"I understand dear," Henrietta said. "Why, the awful way she would criticize Samantha was disgraceful."

"Oh, I know," replied Carolyn. "One day while Samantha was showing her decorator around town, Kathleen stormed into Indulgence right after them and started screaming at Samantha like some crazy insane woman. It was all over the Christmas tour contest. I can tell you I think Samantha could have strangled her right there on the spot." A look of horror swept over Carolyn's face as she realized what she had just said.

"Oh, here's Peggy with your lunch," Abigail said with relief. "I'll let you eat then I'd like to hear about Pauline selling her house."

***

Alex decided that since the town was full of tourists, it would be easier to walk to Kathleen's instead of trying to find a parking spot. When he arrived, the little cat eagerly greeted him at the apartment door.

"Hello, Precious. I've come to take you to live with a nice lady. Now I want you to be a good kitty and be nice and quiet. We're going to leave through the back and hopefully avoid all the curious people out front."

As he passed by Kathleen's bookcase, a title he hadn't noticed before caught his eye. Thumbing through the small paperback, he was even more convinced he was on the right track. He placed the book in his pocket, and then, with the little cat tucked under one arm and her supplies under the other, they slipped unseen out of the back door.

It was a short walk to the kitty's new home where Alex was pleased to find Nan much calmer than on the previous night.

"Oh, you poor baby," was Nan's greeting, as she grabbed for the cat. "Alex, thank you for bringing her to me."

"No problem. Here are the rest of her things. There are extra food and litter at the apartment I can bring to you another time."

At the mention of Kathleen's apartment, Nan's entire demeanor changed. Her appreciative tone disappeared, and her words became scornful.

"I don't suppose you're any closer to figuring out who killed Kathleen, are you?"

"Nan, I've just begun the investigation. And it's going to take time."

"If you want my advice, you should ask Samantha Edwards what she was doing Friday night."

"Why Samantha?"

"Because she's always hated Kathleen." Her voice had increased in volume, and there were two bright pink spots on her thin cheeks.

"I need specifics," Alex said with irritation. "Did you ever see or hear Samantha threaten Kathleen?"

"No, not to her face, but she said some awful things behind her back."

Alex had a hard time refraining from telling her that was a little like the pot and the kettle.

"You go and ask Josephine what she saw Friday night."

"Okay, relax. I'll talk to Granny Jo."

"You do that." And with that she slammed the door in his face.

Alex decided he needed a hot cup of coffee. He could stop off at Flapjacks on his way to the Edwards' home. When Alex walked into the diner, Granny Jo was wiping down her red '50s style counter. The old jukebox was playing Elvis, and there were only a few customers sitting in the red vinyl booths.

Alex took a seat on a stool at the counter. "How about a cup of coffee for a weary cop?"

Jo smiled. "Just coffee? No doughnut?"

"Real funny, Jo, but sure. Why not? What do you have?"

"Today I have glazed and chocolate."

"I'll have glazed, please. Jo, I need to talk to you. Do you have a minute?"

"I always have time for you. What's up?"

"I just came from dropping Kathleen's cat off at Nan's. She's still pretty upset, and she said something I'd like to ask you about."

Jo poured fragrant black coffee into a thick white mug. "What's that?"

"She told me to ask you who you saw Friday night."

Her round jovial face reddened with anger before she replied. "I told Beatrice on our way home from church that I thought Nan was eavesdropping on us while we were setting up the coffee and cookies this morning after services. Evidently I was right."

"Jo, I'm sorry, but I'm going to need to know what Nan overheard."

She gave him a long solemn look before quietly saying, "Alex, I didn't say anything to you because I'm not really sure if the person I saw that night was really who I think it was."

"But you did see someone out on Friday night?"

"Yes."

"Who do you think it was?"

"Alex, I can't be sure," she said in earnest. "What if I'm wrong, and I end up getting her in trouble for no reason?

"I understand your reluctance, but if they're innocent of any wrongdoing, you telling me their name won't matter. Please just tell me who you thought it was, and I'll handle it from there."

Her mouth formed a thin line. "If it wasn't for my daughter getting me so upset that night, none of this would have happened. You see, I couldn't settle myself down. My daughter called and we got into it again over selling this place and moving into a retirement community. Anyway, I decided to make myself some hot chocolate, and I didn't have any in my apartment upstairs so I came down here to get some. I happened to glance out the front door, and I saw her hurrying past."

"Granny Jo, who did you see?" Alex asked, nobly holding onto his patience.

She hesitated then reluctantly said, "It looked like Samantha. But Alex, I know she couldn't have killed anyone."

Alex silently cursed. *Was the entire town running around in the snow that night?* He saw the fear in Jo's eyes and gently laid his hand over hers. "Don't worry. You did the right thing. Do you remember what time it was?"

She nodded. "Right after the eleven o'clock news. I remember because I wanted to have my hot chocolate before I went to bed."

"What exactly did you see?"

"I saw a woman hurrying past the door."

"And this woman looked like Samantha?"

"I couldn't say for sure. She kind of reminded me of her."

Alex sighed. "Granny Jo, I understand you don't want to involve Samantha, but you must have had a strong impression it was her, or you wouldn't be so evasive. Can you tell me what she was wearing?"

"It looked like a black parka with a hood. Alex, if it turns out to be Samantha, I have to believe there was a good reason for her being out."

He took the last sip of his coffee. "I'm on my way over there now. Hopefully Samantha will be able to sort this all out. Jo, I appreciate you being honest with me. I truly don't like having people I know as suspects in a murder investigation, but I do have a job to do."

"I know, Alex, and you're a good man. I'm sure you'll do your best getting to the bottom of this."

As Alex was leaving Flapjacks, an attractive blond was on her way in. It took him a minute to recall her as Samantha's decorator, Sylvia Something, who had been staying at the inn. He'd wanted to talk to her before she left town.

"Excuse me," Alex said. "Are you Sylvia?"

She hesitated. "Yes, I'm Sylvia Schmuckler."

"Miss Schmuckler, my name is Alex Mackenzie. I'm Newcomsville's police chief. May I speak to you for a moment?"

"I suppose, but why? Have I done something wrong?"

Alex held open the door. "Let's go in and sit down. Then I'll explain."

Granny Jo glanced up as they entered the diner. "Back so soon?"

"I'll have another cup of coffee, please, Jo. Sylvia, let's sit in a booth. It will give us more privacy."

Alex studied Sylvia as she removed her black fur-trimmed hat and matching coat. She had a slim figure and looked to be in her thirties with big brown eyes set in an oval face framed by short blond hair.

"So, Chief Mackenzie, what can I do for you?" She leaned back into the red vinyl cushion, reached into her purse, and pulled out a pack of cigarettes. Alex shook his head.

"Sorry, there's no smoking in any business in town."

She sighed and replaced the pack in her purse.

"I'd like to ask you a couple of questions if you don't mind," Alex continued.

She gave him a provocative smile and in a slightly husky voice asked, "What if I do mind? Am I allowed to refuse?"

Alex smiled. "You can refuse, Miss Schmuckler, but I don't think that would be a very good idea."

She laughed and said, "I apologize, Chief Mackenzie. Obviously this is about something important. Please ask me anything you'd like."

"Let's begin with why you're staying at the inn?"

"I'm staying there because I'm working for Samantha Edwards."

"Will you be checking out today?"

"No, I've decided to stay on for a few more days. I'm helping Samantha decorate her home for the Christmas tour, and we've had a slight delay."

"Here's your coffee, Alex. Miss, do you know what you'd like?" Granny Jo asked.

"I'll also just have coffee for now, thanks."

"Do you live nearby?" Alex asked after Granny Jo had walked away.

"I live in the city. What's this all about?"

"I'm sure by now you've heard about the woman who was murdered on Friday night."

"Yes, but what does that have to do with me?"

"Well, Miss Schmuckler, hopefully it has nothing to do with you at all. But you're a stranger in town, and I don't know anything about you."

"Okay, what would you like to know?"

"For starters, why are you staying at the inn when you don't live that far away?"

"Besides the fact that I like this town, I thought it would be easier for Samantha and me if I was close at hand. Chief Mackenzie, are you saying I'm a suspect? For heaven's sake, I didn't even know the woman."

"Well, Miss Schmuckler, until I discover who murdered Miss Cooper, everyone is a suspect. So I'd like to know what you were doing on Friday night."

"I don't have a problem answering your questions. I just feel you're wasting your time with me. I don't see how I can be of any help."

"I've never felt talking to people is a waste of time, so please tell me how you spent Friday night."

"Okay, well, I checked in around three in the afternoon. Then I called Samantha to let her know I was here. I decided to walk around town for a while then had dinner at the inn. After dinner I went to my room and got my plans in order to show Samantha the next morning. And there you have it, dull as it may sound."

"Once you went to your room, you didn't go back out?"

"No. I was supposed to meet Samantha at nine the next morning. I wanted to get up in plenty of time to have breakfast, so I made it an early night."

"Do you know anyone else in town besides Samantha?"

"She's been showing me around, and I've met some of the shop owners. But before that I didn't know anyone."

"How do you know Samantha?"

"A couple of years ago I did some decorating for her home in the city. Why?"

Alex stood. "No reason. Just my curiosity. Miss Schmuckler, thank you for your time. I hope you enjoy the rest of your stay in Newcomsville."

***

"Good afternoon, Alex," Pauline said, answering his knock on Samantha's door. "Please come in. We've been expecting you. Samantha's in the living room. This situation is absolutely dreadful."

When he entered the living room, Samantha was seated in an overstuffed wingback chair to the left of a marble fireplace. He was pleased to see she looked alert and composed.

"Hello, Alex. Please have a seat. I seem to have quite a mess on my hands. Don't I?"

"Well, I wouldn't say you, but Carl sure is up to his neck in it. I take it you haven't heard from him."

"No, and I honestly don't expect to. Henry's probably right. The son-of-a-bitch is sitting on some island somewhere laughing hysterically at all of us for being such chumps."

Seeing the pain and hurt in her hazel eyes, Alex fervently hoped she was wrong, and Carl was still within reach.

Alex took a seat on the sofa across from her. "If he's still in the country, do you have any idea where he would go? I mean are there friends or relatives he might contact?"

"I know he wouldn't contact any relatives. As for friends, he didn't have any close friends here in town. That is, not any I'm aware of. I guess your best bet is to check all of the sleazy bars from here to the coast. There's bound to be someone who knows the creep."

"Samantha, I realize this is extremely difficult for you, and I wish I didn't have to ask painful questions, but…"

"Alex, don't worry about it. I understand the awkward position you're in, and I appreciate your thoughtfulness. Please feel free to ask me anything you need to."

"Okay, let's start with Friday. At what time did you become concerned over Carl's absence?"

Pauline gave her granddaughter's hand a reassuring squeeze. "You may as well tell him everything, my dear. It's time to stop making excuses for Carl's behavior."

A single tear trickled down Samantha's cheek. "I know, Grandma." She took a deep breath. "I wasn't really concerned about Carl until Saturday morning. You see, Alex, lately my so-called husband has had a tendency not to bother coming home at night. He made such an ass of himself on Thanksgiving at the Butterfield's, Henry ended up throwing him out. He wasn't here when Charles brought me home, and he didn't show up until Friday afternoon. I can tell you we had one hell of a row. Well, the situation went from bad to worse. After telling me what he thought of me, my family, and this town, he went storming out, and that's the last I saw of him."

"Do you have any idea where he goes when he doesn't come home?" Alex asked.

"I imagine he goes to the first bar he can find and talks some tramp into taking him home with her. I've heard he's not welcome at the Cork & Bottle anymore."

"Are you saying there's a chance he could be staying with another woman? Again Samantha, I'm sorry I…"

"Oh, Alex, like Grandma says, what does it matter anymore? Yes, more than likely he's with another woman, and to answer your next question, I haven't a clue who she might be."

When she'd begun to speak, her small hands had been lying loosely in her lap. Now they were clenched into tight little fists, and her tears were flowing freely. Her voice was harsh with anger. "So you see, my husband isn't only a liar and a thief, he's an adulterer as well. Oh, damn-it-to-hell." She wiped at her tears. "It's bad enough he's been cheating on me for years, but I can't believe he'd stoop so low as to steal. I thought once we moved here he'd change and everything would be okay. Now I'm so humiliated I don't know how I'll ever show my face in town again."

"Samantha, I'm not going to sit here and listen to you talk like that," Pauline said. "You are not responsible for his actions."

"Grandma, I'm the one that wanted us to move here, and I'm the one who suggested to Granddad that he hire Carl at the bank. I'm so glad Granddad isn't here to see all of this. It's bad enough Henry has to deal with it."

"Pauline's right, Samantha," Alex said. "No one is going to think any less of you. If you feel up to it, I'd like to ask you some more questions."

Pauline stood. "I'm going to make us some tea. My mother always said it helps in any situation."

"I'm sorry, Alex. I thought I had myself more under control," Samantha said wiping her eyes with a tissue. "Please ask me whatever you'd like."

"Let's go back to Friday night. Did you go out at all after Carl left?"

After hesitating slightly, she replied, "Yes, for a little while. I was furious with Carl, and I got tired of pacing back and forth in this room, so I went for a short walk."

"Do you remember what time this was?"

"I'm not sure, but I think it was pretty late."

"Where did you go?"

"I just walked on Main Street for a few blocks. Alex, what does this have to do with Carl?"

"His car was seen behind the bank around midnight. I was wondering if maybe you saw him leave town."

"I didn't see anyone, certainly not Carl. Besides, I didn't go as far down as the bank."

"Samantha, I'm not only looking into Carl's disappearance. You know Kathleen was murdered Friday night. So if you were out, I need to know if you remember seeing anyone."

"Oh Alex, you must think I'm the most self-centered person you've ever met. Here I'm going on about my problems and didn't once ask you about Kathleen. I understand Abigail was the one who found her. How awful. Is Abigail alright?"

"She's doing fine now, but it was an experience I don't think she'd like to repeat."

"I should say not. Do you have any leads? I couldn't believe GH's description of Kathleen's body in today's paper."

Alex frowned. "Neither could I. I'm quite curious where GH gets his information."

"Are you saying GH's description wasn't true? It's pretty well known around town that there wasn't any love lost between Kathleen and myself, but I wouldn't wish something like that on anyone."

Before Alex could reply, Pauline arrived with a large silver tray placing it on the coffee table.

"Here we are. A nice hot pot of tea. We also have a wonderful pound cake Henrietta made."

As Pauline served the tea and cake, they heard the front door open and close.

It's a pity you didn't know, when you started your game of murder, that I was playing, too.   - House on Haunted Hill (film), 1958

9

The three watched in stunned disbelief as Carl Edwards nonchalantly sauntered into the living room as if he'd just been away for a couple of hours, not a couple of days.

"You god damned son of a bitch," Samantha screamed as she shot from her chair, hurling the contents of her teacup into his face. Before Alex could react, Samantha followed this up with an impressive right jab to Carl's nose.

Pauline jumped to her feet. "Samantha, stop it. Stop it right now."

Carl covered his bloody nose and backed away. "What the hell? You crazy bitch, have you lost your mind?"

Samantha picked up a heavy crystal vase and headed toward Carl. "You no good, lying, cheating bastard. I'm going to kill you."

"Alex, please do something," Pauline cried.

Alex was already moving. "That's enough. Samantha. Stop it. I said stop it." He managed to get himself between the two. "Carl, go clean up your face. Samantha, put the vase down. Then the both of you take a seat."

For a long moment she stood trembling in the middle of the floor, clutching the vase.

"Samantha, please put it down," Alex asked in a gentler tone.

She took a deep breath and finally did as he asked. Still trembling, she slowly turned and walked back to her chair

"What the hell was that all about?" Carl asked around a wad of paper towels. "She's nuts. I think she just broke my nose."

Alex scowled. "Shut up, Carl."

"What the hell?" Carl mumbled.

"Pauline, please take Samantha into another room. After you have her settled, call Henry and tell him what's happened."

Carl removed the towels from his nose. "Why in the hell are you calling Henry?"

"We're calling Henry, you stupid son of a bitch, because your sorry ass is going to jail, and I hope you rot there," Samantha exclaimed, again advancing toward Carl.

Pauline grabbed her arm. "Samantha, come with me now. Alex is perfectly capable of handling this."

Carl turned to Alex. "What's she talking about? Who's going to jail?"

Alex smiled. "Why, Carl, I'd say you are."

"Excuse me?"

The four turned to see Sylvia Schmuckler standing in the living room doorway, looking stunned and embarrassed.

"I'm...I'm...sorry," she stammered. "I knocked, but no one answered. I heard voices, so I let myself in."

"Sylvia, what are you doing here?" Samantha cried.

"We...we...had a three o'clock appointment. Don't you remember?"

Samantha covered her face and ran from the room.

"Miss Schmuckler, as you can see, this is not a good time for us. We would appreciate it if you would please come back on a later date," Pauline said, with obvious irritation.

"Mrs. Silverspoon, I apologize," Sylvia said. "Please tell Samantha to call me at the inn whenever it's convenient for her."

Pauline shook her head after Sylvia left. "What impertinence. Imagine just walking into someone's home like that. Alex, I'm going to check on Samantha, and then I'll call Henry." After giving Carl a look of utter loathing, she hurried out.

Carl stood in the middle of the floor, opened his mouth, then closed it again.

"Carl, you have quite a lot of explaining to do, but I think we'll wait for Henry to get here. In the meantime, you'd better get some ice on that nose."

Carl moved toward the drinks cabinet. "I'll ask for the last time, what's this all about? I come home to find my wife has turned into a crazy woman, and you and Pauline act like I'm some kind of leper."

Alex stared in amazement as Carl calmly made himself a drink. Then putting some ice in a bar towel, he sat down in the wingback chair and applied the cloth to his nose. "Why is Pauline calling Henry?"

"I thought Henry might like to be here in person so he can ask you what you've done with the money you stole from his bank." Alex smiled. *That got your attention you arrogant ass.* He watched with satisfaction as the color drained from Carl's face. "That's right, Carl. We know all about your little bank account in the Caribbean."

Carl downed the contents of his glass in one swallow and contemptuously asked, "Alex, what are you talking about?"

Alex could hardly control his temper. "I'm talking about the money you've been embezzling from the good people of Newcomsville. I'm talking about how you not only screwed over a decent man who trusted you, you've managed to make your wife feel lower than dog shit, and how you've made me want to pound your smug face to pulp."

Before Carl could reply, Henry could be heard coming into the entrance hall.

Alex nodded to himself. Carl looked sicker than before. Good, you little weasel. Let's see what you have to say now.

Henry Butterfield at seventy-five was still a tall imposing figure. Henry Butterfield in a rage looked downright dangerous. Upon entering the living room, Henry crossed to where Carl was seated. In one swift move he had Carl by his shirtfront, lifting him to his feet.

"You, god damned pitiful excuse for a man. By the time I'm through with you, you worthless little worm, you'll wish you'd never heard of Henry Butterfield or this town." Henry's words were like shards of steel cutting through the silent room. "You'd better have every damn dime of that money, or I'll make sure you spend the rest of your miserable life behind bars." He flung Carl back into his chair, turned to Alex, and asked, "Has he told you anything at all?"

"No, he seems to be having a hard time understanding why we're upset. I thought I'd wait until you arrived before asking him any questions. The first thing I'd like to know is why he came back."

"Greed would be my first guess," Henry stated. "Is that it, Carl? Did you decide the amount you'd already stolen wasn't enough? Did you think you'd just help yourself to more of this hick town's money?"

Carl, looking belligerent, glared first at Alex, then at Henry. "I don't know what the hell you're talking about," he said rising to his feet. "If money is missing from your bank, maybe you should ask Barb Winters. Just how do you think she can afford to send her son to that uppity college? Why I…"

That's as far as Carl got before finding himself flat on his back with Henry standing over him.

"Okay, Henry, I think that's enough," Alex said. "Carl, get to your feet. We're going to my office to continue this conversation."

"I'm not going anywhere with you two assholes," Carl mumbled, now holding his bloody mouth. "I'm calling my attorney, and I'm going to sue for assault."

"Carl, your face isn't looking all that great right now," Alex said. "So unless you want two black eyes to go with your broken nose and busted mouth, I suggest you shut up and come with me. You can call your attorney from my office." He turned to Henry. "I'd like you to stay here until you've calmed down and then join us. We're not going to get anywhere like this."

Henry rubbed his knuckles. "You're right. I can't remember the last time I've been angry enough to actually punch someone. I'll see you in a little while when I think I can stand the sight of this piece of shit." After giving Carl a thoroughly disgusted look, Henry left the room.

"Okay, Carl, get some more ice for your lip and let's go," Alex said. "I'll make sure you get anything you need from here later."

Carl held a cloth to his bloody mouth. "Why should I go with you? Are you arresting me?"

Alex sighed with impatience. "We have a slip of paper found taped to the back of your safety deposit box with an account number for a bank in the Caribbean. Barb and Henry spent most of yesterday going over the books, and there seems to be quite a lot of money missing, not to mention your empty safe. So I'd say we have some talking to do."

Carl defiantly stared at Alex for a long moment. Then all the fight seemed to drain from him. Slumping down in the chair, he dropped his bruised face into his hands. Groaning, he said, "Son-of-a-bitch. I thought it was finally over. I thought now everything was going to work out." He wearily got to his feet. "Let me clean up and I'll be ready to leave."

***

"I'm glad you're here, Chief," Bonnie said, as Alex and Carl entered Alex's office. "You wouldn't believe the number of calls we've had. Everyone in town has an idea about who killed Kathleen. We've also had several calls from some of our senior ladies. They're all in a panic thinking there's a crazed murderer on the loose. I told them I was sure they were perfectly safe. I've written down the messages I thought you'd want to see."

"Thanks, Bonnie. Leave them all on your desk, and I'll look at them later. You can leave the voicemail on and go on home. I appreciate you taking care of these calls."

"It wasn't a problem, Chief. Like I told you earlier, I wasn't doing anything this afternoon. And there's a message from Kathleen's brother. He said he wouldn't bother coming until the coroner released the body. So you're to call him when..." Bonnie's words trailed off when she noticed Carl's battered face. "Carl, what on earth happened to you?"

"My continuing bad luck," he replied.

"Thanks again, Bonnie. I'll see you in the morning," Alex said opening his inner office door. "Come on in, Carl, and have a seat. Before we begin, do you want to call your attorney?"

Carl laughed derisively. "What's the point? You've got me by the balls. My only hope is for Henry to ease off once he hears I have the majority of the money left. What I'd like to know is how Henry found out."

"Other than Barb Winter's suspicions, Charles and Agatha happened to see your car behind the bank late Friday night. Henry had already been alerted by Barb that she thought you were up to something. When your car was seen, Henry went in Saturday to investigate."

Carl shook his head. "Doesn't it just figure, caught by those two clowns. So tell me, what happens next?"

"First, I don't appreciate Barb Winters, my son, or daughter in-law, being called clowns." Henry's harsh voice came from the doorway. "And to answer your question, I would imagine you're going to jail."

"Come on in, Henry, and have a seat," Alex said. "Carl was just telling me that he still has most of the money."

"That's right, Henry. It's sitting safe and sound in a Caribbean bank," Carl replied with some of his usual tenacity showing once again. "All I need to do is contact the bank tomorrow and have the money transferred back here. Then everything will be back to normal, and no one else needs to know otherwise."

Henry stared at him with amazement. "So you think it's as simple as that? You give back the town's money, and I forget the whole incident. Do I have that right?"

Carl visibly warmed to this plan. "I don't see why not. As Alex said, I still have most of the money. As for the remainder, I'll have to owe it to you. I should be able to pay it back in no time. Think about it, Henry. I can hardly find a way to repay the bank's money sitting behind bars, can I?"

"Your audacity is astounding," Henry said with incredulity. "I imagine next you'll be telling me I should give you back your job at the bank."

"Contrary to your opinion of me, I'm not that foolhardy." Carl replied. "I have some stocks of my own that have nothing to do with the bank's money. I can sell my shares and pay part of what I owe from those."

Henry studied Carl for a long moment and sighed. "Try as I might, I just can't understand what possessed you to do this. Don't I deserve an explanation?"

Carl's sneer was back in place. "If you want an explanation, thank that controlling wife of mine. It was her fault I quit my broker's job in the city and moved to this hick town. Then when I had some foolproof investment ideas, do you think she'd part with any of Granddad's money? Hell no. Or do you think she'd let me have any of her precious savings? Again, hell no. So I decided the hell with her and the hell with this town."

Henry got to his feet. "Carl, I think it's time you stop blaming your wife not only for your inadequacies but your criminality as well. Alex, I can't listen to this any longer. I'm going home. I have to decide what needs to be done. What do you think we should do with this piece of shit?"

Alex watched Carl's face turn red with fury. Before he could reply, Alex said, "The suggestion that comes to mind is letting him enjoy the hospitality of the town of Newcomsville. We spent a lot of money restoring the town hall and putting in that nice jail cell. I don't think we should waste our taxpayers' money and let it sit unused, although I'm going to have to find someone to stay all night in the outer office. We can't leave Carl locked up alone in case of an emergency. I have my hands full with Kathleen's death. I can't waste an evening watching over him."

Henry smiled. "I know just the person. I'll call Charles. I'm sure he'd be more than happy to help you out."

Alex nodded. "That's an excellent idea. Tell him he can set up a cot in the jail's outer office. I'll call Granny Jo and see if she'll send over something for their dinner, and for breakfast tomorrow."

"Wait just a damn minute," said Carl looking not at all pleased with the arrangements being discussed. "You expect me to spend the rest of today and all night locked up here with Charles? I told you I'd give the money back. Why can't I just go home?"

Both men, staring with dismay, couldn't quite believe what they'd heard. "Considering the reception your wife gave you," Alex finally replied, "jail is probably the safest place for you."

"Alright, so I don't go home. How about if I stay at the inn?"

"You're not welcome at the inn either. You don't seem to understand. You're going to stay right here where we can keep an eye on you. Henry, if you'd like, you can use Bonnie's phone to call Charles."

"Thanks, but I think I'll go home and explain all of this in person. I'll call you when he's on his way."

After Henry had left, Alex relaxed back in his chair, casually propping one booted foot on the corner of his desk. Carl, looking sullen, sat slouched in his seat.

"So tell me, Carl, in total how much did Kathleen take you for?"

Bolting upright, his eyes bulging, Carl stammered, "What...what did you just say?"

"I asked you how much Kathleen Cooper blackmailed you for."

"What...what makes you think I was being blackmailed by Kathleen?"

"Let's see. I know for a fact Kathleen had been blackmailing someone. You work in a bank, and you've been embezzling large amounts of money. Kathleen overheard a conversation between Henry and me which seemed to unnerve her. She also made some sly hints to others as to where her money was coming from. And I just happened to find this interesting little book on her bookcase." Alex reached into his pocket and tossed the small paperback on his desk.

Carl leaned closer to see the title and swore as he read, "Embezzlement — How to Keep Your Business Safe".

"So you see," Alex continued. "Even though Kathleen owned her own business, I can't see her being concerned over someone stealing her money. She was the sole employee. Somehow she discovered what you were up to and took advantage of the situation. She bought this book on embezzlement to help her understand what exactly was going on. Am I right so far?"

Carl's face filled with hatred and he snarled, "That bitch."

Alex smiled. "So I'm right?"

Carl nodded. "Congratulations." He leaned forward in his chair. "You want to know how much she took me for? Well, I'll tell you. Thirty thousand. Do you think that was enough? Hell no. She still wanted more." By this point Carl's face was suffused with anger and his hands were clenched into fists. "The bitch would call me at work or send me nice little notes telling me how much she wanted. One time she actually had the nerve to come to my office at the bank. I told her she wasn't getting another dime. She just laughed and told me she'd have great pleasure telling that spoiled wife of mine just what her handsome husband had been up to."

"Is that why you murdered her?" Alex calmly asked.

Carl leaped to his feet and shouted. "Murder. I'm not the one who murdered her. You know what? You're nuts."

"Sit down, Carl."

"No, I'm not going to sit down," he said still shouting. "You may have me on embezzlement, but I didn't murder anyone, and you're not going to pin that on me."

Alex also rose, placed both hands on his desk, and leaned forward. With thunderous gray eyes, between gritted teeth, he repeated, "Carl, I said, 'sit down'."

Carl, somewhat subdued, promptly did as he was told. "Alright, alright, I'm sitting down. Alex, man, you have to believe me. I didn't kill Kathleen. Not that I didn't think about it, but I'd never have the nerve to actually do it. Besides, do you honestly think I'd come back if I had killed someone?"

Alex sighed and retook his seat. "I'm having a hard time understanding why you came back in the first place. To my way of thinking, if you had the guts to come back after stealing, why not after you committed murder?"

"Don't you see? I came back because I read about Kathleen's death. Remember, I didn't know Henry was on to me. I knew the blackmail would be over, and I thought I was safe. For god's sake, Alex, you have to believe me."

Alex snorted. "Safe to do what, steal more of the town's money?"

"Well, I, ah…"

"Spare me your bullshit, Carl. I know damn well you'd try and get away with anything you could."

Before Carl could reply, the office phone rang.

"Alex, Charles is on his way," Henry said. "Agatha wanted to come, but I persuaded her to just bring their dinner over later."

"That's fine," Alex replied. "Who knows? More good than harm may come out of both of them being here. Henry, I'll be in touch with you later."

"Okay, Carl, let's go. We can continue this conversation tomorrow," Alex said, rising from his chair. "Charles should be here any minute."

"Where are we going?"

"I told you, you're going to be staying with us for a while. Your temporary home is downstairs."

"You can't be serious. You honestly expect me to stay here while Charles plays Festus guarding me in my cell."

Alex smiled. "I'd say more like Eliot Ness. Anyway, Charles isn't here to guard you. He's here in case of an emergency. I can't leave you locked up alone in an empty building. What if there was a fire or you had a heart attack or something?"

At that moment, Charles appeared in the outer office wearing a brown Cheviot suit with matching overcoat, tan spats, and a brown felt hat.

He glowered at Carl. "So you've nabbed the little scoundrel, have you? Don't worry about a thing, Alex. I'll make sure the blackguard doesn't escape."

Alex held back a laugh at Carl's crestfallen expression. "I have total confidence in you, Charles."

After Alex escorted a still-protesting Carl to his jail cell, he made sure Charles was comfortable in the outer room. He called Will Boone at the county Sheriff's office to tell him they had Carl then headed down Main Street to GH's newspaper office. Even though it was late Sunday afternoon, GH could be seen through the plate glass window typing away.

"Well, hello there, Chief," GH said as Alex walked into his office. "I hope this visit means that you have more information for me."

"It seems you're already full of more information than I'd like, GH," Alex replied taking a seat across from the little man. "I'd really like to know how you come by all of it."

"Perseverance, Chief. A good newspaperman never stops digging."

"GH, there was a reason I didn't want the entire town knowing how Kathleen's body was left. I would appreciate it in the future if you would talk to me first before you go printing special editions."

"Freedom of the press, Alex. Freedom of the press."

"Damn it, I'm all for freedom of the press, but I have to be concerned over peoples' reactions. Thanks to your vivid description of Kathleen's body, I now have hysterical old ladies calling my office afraid there's some sicko running around who's going to murder them in their homes. Now, GH, there were only four people who saw Kathleen's body: Abigail, Jack, the coroner Louis Tate, and myself. I can't picture any of them giving you details on the body, so who did?"

"A good newspaperman also never reveals his sources, Chief. You should know that."

Alex narrowed his eyes in irritation.

"Okay, Alex, perhaps I was a little zealous with my special edition, but you have to admit Kathleen's murder is the biggest news story this town has ever had."

"Of course I realize that, but at least talk to me before you print detailed information."

GH nodded. "Fair enough. Now tell me. What's going on at the Edwards' house? I was at the inn earlier when that decorator came storming into the bar. She looked mad enough to chew nails. She ordered a martini and downed it in three swallows. When Ben asked her if there was a problem, she just went off on him. She told Ben, 'I'm not the one that has a problem. It's the Edwards, and they seem to have one hell of a big one.'"

"What happened then?"

"Nothing really. Ben just looked bewildered. You know how people will do when they don't know why what they've just said was wrong. Then he laughed and said, 'I don't think the decorating job is going well.'"

"So, GH, what makes you think I know something about any of this?"

"Because when I left the inn, I drove by the Edwards' house. I saw you and Carl getting into your Bronco. I also saw Henry's car parked out front. Now I have to tell you, my internal news alarm has been going off ever since Saturday when you hurried Henry out of Two Bits for a private chat. I later found out that Henry, Charles, and Barb Winters were all at the bank until the wee hours. Another interesting tid-bit is that Carl left town Friday and hadn't been heard from since. That is until today. So as the old cliché goes, 'I smell a rat.'"

While contemplating how much he should tell GH, Alex was saved by the arrival of Molly Bright.

"Oh, hello, Alex. I hope I'm not interrupting. GH, Sally, and I are going to the inn for dinner, and I'm running a little late."

Alex stood. "Your timing couldn't be better. I kept GH longer than I had planned. I think I'll head home and see what Abigail has cooking."

"Alex, she's not there. I just picked up Sally at the tearoom. Business had finally slowed down so Abigail left Peggy to close up. She went with Henrietta, Carolyn, and Grant to see Pauline's house."

"Why are they all going to look at Pauline's house?" Alex asked. "No, wait, don't tell me. This has to have something to do with Carolyn and Grant. Abigail has been match-making those two since Thanksgiving."

"Yes, and isn't it wonderful," Molly exclaimed. "They just met and are getting along so well, and they make such a great looking couple."

"You'd better not tell me any more. Abigail will be upset if she's not the one to fill me in on all the details."

GH removed his green visor and reached for his signature white trench coat. "Alex, are you going to tell me what was going on at the Edwards?"

"As soon as I have something that's worth printing, I'll call you. Until then, I'd appreciate it if you kept what you saw to yourself."

As Alex, Molly, and GH stepped out onto the snowy sidewalk, they saw Abigail, Carolyn, and Grant hurrying toward them.

"There you are, Alex. We've been trying to get in touch with you, but you're not answering your phone," Abigail said. "We just came from your office and met Agatha going in. She said she was bringing dinner for Carl and Charles. Alex, what's going on? When did Carl come back, and what are Charles and Carl doing at the town hall?"

GH nodded. "That's what I've been asking as well."

Abigail jumped. "Oh, GH, I didn't see you standing there behind Alex."

Alex pulled his phone from his pocket. "Abigail, I'm sorry. My phone needs charged."

"We're on our way to the inn for dinner," Molly said. "Why don't all of you join us?"

"That's a great idea," GH replied. "I made reservations for three, but I'm sure Ben will make room for all of us. Then perhaps Alex will satisfy the public's curiosity and tell us what's going on at the town hall."

"Actually, that's why we were trying to find Alex," Carolyn said. "We were headed to the inn as well."

GH grinned. "That's perfect. Shall we go?"

"Why don't all of you go on ahead," Alex suggested. "I'll meet you in a few minutes. I need to stop by my office."

"Alex, if you'd rather just go home, I can make us dinner," Abigail said.

"No, Hon. That's okay. Go. I'll be there shortly."

"I, for one, plan on riding in the car with Molly," Carolyn stated. "I've been tromping around in this snow long enough. My feet are frozen."

"It may be a little snug," GH said, "but I'm sure we'll all fit."

After retrieving the messages from Bonnie's desk, Alex headed downstairs to check on Carl and Charles. He found Agatha, Charles, and Carl enjoying fried chicken with mashed potatoes and gravy.

"Howdy-do, Alex," Agatha said. "Would you like some of Annie's scrumptious fried chicken?"

"No thanks, but it smells great. I'm on my way to meet Abigail at the inn. I wanted to check on things here first."

"We have the situation well in hand," Charles said. "Carl is just finishing his dinner. Then lowering his voice he continued, "Aggie and I have been subtly questioning him about Kathleen's murder."

Alex arched one brow. "Really. What do you two think he knows about Kathleen's death?"

"Just think about it, Alex dear," Agatha said, in a stage whisper. "What a better motive for murder than to silence the one person who knew about his sticky-fingered activity."

"You think Kathleen may have known something about the embezzlement?"

Charles eagerly nodded. "That's right. To our way of thinking, Carl not only had a motive, but opportunity as well. And as Thomas Linley will tell you, those are two of the three key elements any smart detective looks for in a murderer."

"But what do you think his motive was?"

Agatha smiled. "Blackmail of course."

Charles beamed with self-satisfaction. "This takes us right back to our earlier conversation. If you recall, Aggie and I concluded Kathleen died because she was a nosey Parker, but she had a big mouth as well. It makes sense she was the one to somehow find out what Carl was up to and take advantage of the situation."

"Remember, Alex," Agatha continued. "Chucky and I saw Carl that night. The bank isn't but a hop, skip, and a jump from Kathleen's shop."

"An interesting theory," Alex said. "I'll make sure to keep that in mind. Now I'd better get over to the inn before Abigail comes looking for me. Charles, do you have everything you need?"

"Oh, yes, I'll be just fine. Aggie brought some things from the house and made my accommodations nice and cozy."

"Alex!" hollered Carl from the next room. "Damn it. Let me out of here. I'd rather take my chances with Samantha than stay here with these two lunatics."

Alex smiled. "Don't be too hard on him."

Ben greeted Alex as he walked through the inn's front door. "Everyone is in the dining room. This is turning into quite a party."

"Hi, Ben. I hope we're not causing you any seating problems."

"Not at all. We were busy at lunch, but now you'll practically have the dining room to yourselves."

"I'd like to ask you and Sam a couple of questions later."

"Sure, I'll be in the tap room when you're through eating. We normally close at nine on Sunday, but if business doesn't pick up, I'll probably close early."

Upon entering the gas-lit dining room, Alex was pleased to see Jack and Claire had joined their group.

"Perfect timing," Grant said. "The appetizers just arrived."

"Jack and Claire walked in right after we did," Abigail said. "Ben was nice enough to push these tables together."

"What can I get you to drink, Chief," Meg asked.

Alex took a seat next to Abigail. "I'll have a draft beer, thanks. Meg, when did you start waiting tables in here? I thought you worked the tap room."

"I only work the dining room on Sunday. Would you like an appetizer?"

"No, thanks, it looks like we already have plenty."

"Carolyn and Grant were telling us about their visit to Pauline's house," Claire said. "It looks as if Grant may become our newest resident."

"Alex smiled at Grant. "Really? That's terrific news. I think you'll enjoy Newcomsville."

"It's not a done deal yet, but I did like the house. It's a little large for just me, but Carolyn says it's better to have too much room than not enough."

"I already have some ideas for fixing up the third floor," Carolyn said. "And Abigail and Claire have promised to help."

Alex shook his head. "Good luck, buddy. With those three, you're going to need it."

Abigail frowned. "Alex, really."

"There may still be one major stumbling block, and that's employment," Grant said. "I had quite a bit saved, but my ex got half of it, and I'm going to need an income."

"Here's your beer, Chief," Meg said. "Is everyone ready to order?"

While Meg was taking dinner orders, Alex was studying Grant. An idea had come to him. "Grant, when are you heading back to Pittsburgh?"

"Sometime tomorrow. I'm meeting Samantha about the house in the morning."

"Do me a favor. Stop by my office before you leave town. I'd like to talk to you about something."

Grant looked at him with curiosity, but just nodded. "Sure thing."

"Alex, how's the murder investigation going?" Jack asked. "Or would you rather not talk about it?"

Alex shook his head. "There's really not a lot to tell."

"You must have some suspects in mind," GH said. "I imagine there are a number of people in this town who disliked Kathleen enough to kill her."

"You're right about that. Kathleen certainly wasn't liked by very many. The problem is they're not exactly lining up to confess."

"Speaking of confessing," GH continued, "What's the scoop on Carl Edwards? Why is he at the town hall, and what are Charles and Agatha doing there? And…"

Irritated, Alex interrupted. "I'm not at liberty to go into any of that. So please let it go for now."

"That was quite an informative special edition you put out, GH," Jack said, in a reproachful tone.

Not fazed in the least, GH sipped his beer and smiled.

"Some of the kids were talking about it before Sunday school," Sally said. "Some of the boys were pretending they were the murderer and they were going to strangle the little girls. Miss Henrietta, who taught our class today, put a stop to that real quick. She said it was important to be informed, but we shouldn't make a joke about it or dwell on what happened."

"Henrietta's absolutely right," Molly said. "I think you and your friends could find something nicer to talk about in church than murder."

"I, for one, think we've covered this subject enough for one night," Claire said. "Let's talk about something more pleasant."

Abigail nodded. "I agree. You'll be pleased to hear the tea room sold a goodly number of tour tickets today."

Claire smiled. "From what I've heard, that's true all over town."

"Nothing like a murder to boost Christmas tour ticket sales," Jack said with a wry smile. "Maybe the tour committee can come up with a way to make murder an annual event." Claire rolled her eyes. "For heaven's sake, Jack."

***

"Abigail, I need to talk to Ben and Sam for a few minutes," Alex said as they were preparing to leave. "Do you want to wait, and we'll walk home, or would you like a ride?"

"I don't mind waiting."

After saying goodnight to the others, Alex and Abigail went into the empty taproom. Meg had gone home, and Ben was straightening up.

"Help yourself to an after-dinner drink." Ben said. "Sam is about through in the kitchen. How were your dinners?"

Abigail grinned. "Terrible. It would be nice if Sam learned to cook."

"Complaints, complaints, that's all I get around here," Sam said, removing his apron as he came from the kitchen. "I work my fingers to the bone, and all I get is complaints."

Alex laughed. "You tell her, Sam. Your food was so awful my ravenous little wife not only cleaned her plate, she ordered dessert."

Abigail rolled her eyes. "Alex, you ate most of the dessert."

"Let's sit in front of the fire," Ben said. "Does everyone have something to drink?"

"We're fine," Alex replied. "This shouldn't take long. I imagine you're both ready to call it a night."

Sam nodded. "You can say that again. I'm dead on my feet. Abigail, did you have a large crowd for lunch?"

"Did we ever. We were packed. At one point, I was actually concerned we were going to run out of food."

"I can tell you one thing about today," Ben said. "The Christmas tour ladies should be happy. I think we sold at least twenty tickets."

"Oh, I know," Abigail said. "I didn't get a chance to ask Sally for the final count, but I know we sold quite a few. Alex thinks Kathleen's murder has a lot to do with our sudden popularity."

"People can be ghoulish," Sam said. "Kathleen's shop and apartment were on the tour. Did you find a replacement?"

"Thank god for Stewart. He came through for us with the bookstore. Henrietta and Stewart have been working like crazy to get it decorated."

"Too bad you didn't leave Kathleen's shop on the tour," Ben said. "We could have dressed up a mannequin in the window."

Abigail grinned. "Or hang Christmas lights on the crime scene tape."

"Real funny," Alex said with a frown.

Ben cleared his throat. "Sorry." He turned to Abigail. "Do you think Samantha will have her house ready?

"I certainly hope so."

"I heard Carl left town on Friday and hasn't been heard from since," Ben continued.

Alex nodded. "For a couple days Samantha didn't know Carl's whereabouts, but he's back."

"Too bad for Samantha," Ben said. "She's too nice to be stuck with a jerk like him."

"I agree," Abigail said. "I wish she'd divorce Carl and find someone to treat her better."

Sam frowned. "Alex, you'd better tell us what you wanted to talk about, or Ben and Abigail will spend the rest of the night matchmaking Samantha."

"I think that's Abigail's new hobby," Alex said, giving his wife an exasperated look. "But I'd like to ask you about Friday night. I need to know if just Grant and Sylvia were staying at the inn."

"Yes, except for Ben," Sam replied.

"Ben spent the night here in the inn and not in the carriage house? Why was that?" Alex asked.

"One of us always stays in the small room in the back when we have guests," Sam explained. "Someone has to be here in case we're needed."

"Ben, when we spoke yesterday, I don't recall you telling me you slept here the night before," Alex said with slight irritation.

"Sorry, it was an honest mistake," Ben said. "I'm so used to taking turns when we have guests, I truly didn't think about it."

"Did you go back out after you returned from taking Bob O'Neal home?"

"No. After Sam went out to the carriage house, I closed the doors leading in here and into the dining room. Then I worked in my office for a while and went to bed. Why, what's up?"

"Did you hear either Sylvia or Grant leave the inn?"

"Actually I'm not sure if Grant was here. As for Sylvia, I don't know. I didn't hear anyone leave or come in after I went to my office. But there's really no reason I would unless they were to ring for me."

"Do your guests have keys?"

"They have a key for their guest room but the front door has a key pad so we can change the code. As Ben said, we close off the rest of the inn, so the only place they can go is upstairs. We have a small ice machine, coffee maker, and microwave in an alcove for them."

"Did you go directly to the carriage house when you left the inn?"

"Yes, Alex, I did. Now what's going on?"

Alex studied each man before he said, "I've been told that sometime around one o'clock in the morning someone was seen on the corner near the inn."

"You're saying someone was seen, but whoever saw them isn't sure who it was?" Sam asked.

Alex nodded. "That's right. I was hoping one of you might have seen something."

"Maybe it was Grant walking back from Carolyn's," Ben suggested. "Like I said, I'm not sure if he stayed here that night."

"The only other one it could be is Sylvia," Sam said. "But why would she be out at that time of night."

"Why don't you just ask me?" Sylvia said, standing in the taproom's doorway.

That woman has the most disconcerting habit of showing up uninvited, Alex thought, but he said, "That's exactly what I'd like to do, Miss Schmuckler, if you'd please join us."

After Sylvia was seated and given a small brandy, Alex continued.

"Obviously, Miss Schmuckler, you overheard our conversation, so I needn't go over it all again. I'd like to know if you left the inn Friday night."

"No, Chief Mackenzie. As I said earlier, I had dinner and then went to my room to get organized for my meeting with Samantha."

Alex's gaze went from face to face, then he got to his feet. "Well, we'll be going. It's been a long day." He looked at each of them in turn. "I appreciate you answering my questions. If you remember anything else, don't hesitate to call."

"I'm sorry we couldn't be more help," Ben said. "Are you walking? I'd be happy to give you a ride."

Abigail smiled. "Thanks, but I need to walk off all that food my husband claims I ate."

Alex turned back to the three still sitting by the fire. "By the way, before Kathleen's murder, had any of you recently gone into her shop?"

Ben snorted. "You've got to be kidding. I'd rather be stabbed with hot pokers than set foot in that woman's shop."

"I don't know about the hot pokers," Sam said. "But I certainly wouldn't have had any reason to go in there."

"How about you, Miss Schmuckler?"

"Well, I believe I went into her shop once, when I was first touring the town, to see if she had anything I could use in Samantha's house. She didn't."

The night was cool but clear as Alex and Abigail stepped onto Main Street. The tourists had all left, and the little town lay quiet in its blanket of snow.

Abigail pointed. "Oh, Alex, look. Didn't the garden club ladies do a wonderful job decorating the Christmas tree in the traffic circle?

And doesn't Main Street look all festive with the wreaths on the lamp posts and the shop windows lit with candles? God, I just love this little town. Who could believe murder happened here?"

"I know, Hon. Even though a place can seem idyllic, evil can be hiding just beneath the surface."

***

"Okay, I can't stand the suspense any longer," Abigail said as they headed toward home. "Start at the beginning, and tell me everything."

"It all began this morning after you went downstairs." He told her about his conversation with Henry and Charles, GH's special edition, and his trip to Nan's with the cat.

"I was ready for a cup of coffee, so I went to Flapjacks to find out what Nan was going on about. After about twenty minutes of coaxing, I finally got her to tell me she thought she saw Samantha go past her front door late Friday night."

"No, Alex, not Samantha too."

"I swear, Abigail, I think you and I were the only people in town at home and in bed. Remember Murder on the Orient Express? Maybe the whole town took turns killing her."

Abigail laughed. "You might be right. Considering the way Ben and Sam felt about Kathleen, what made you ask them if they'd been in her shop?"

"The fingerprint boys found a book of Cork & Bottle matches on the floor."

"But, Alex, anyone who had visited the inn could have dropped those matches at any time."

"Yes, I know. I just wanted to see their reactions."

"They reacted exactly the way you would have expected. Didn't they?"

"I suppose."

"What do you mean 'I suppose'?"

"Hon, I'm not sure. I feel one of them wasn't telling me the entire truth, which probably would turn out to be nothing anyway. People clam up about the dumbest things. Now, would you like to hear what happened at Samantha's?"

"Of course."

Alex proceeded to tell his increasingly wide-eyed wife the tale, ending with meeting her outside of the newspaper office.

"My god, what an ordeal for Pauline and Samantha. Carl nonchalantly walking in and Sylvia witnessing the confrontation. I can see why Carl would be your first choice for Kathleen's blackmail victim. But do you really think he's her murderer?"

"I don't know. I kind of believe him when he says he wouldn't have the nerve. But as Charles and Agatha pointed out, he definitely fits the top three elements for a murderer: means, motive, and opportunity. But so do a few others."

"You mean Samantha? I know there wasn't any love lost between her and Kathleen, but I can't see her being *that* violent."

"Besides Samantha, we have Ben, Sam, and Bob O'Neal. Not only did they all hate Kathleen intensely, they all at some time that night were out and about on their own. In addition, there's Tom Scraper. He was working in his display window and saw someone walk by. Now I only have his word that he didn't leave the store. And to be fair, Charles and Agatha were out as well, although two more unlikely murderers I can't imagine."

"What earthly motive could Charles and Agatha possibly have?"

"Remember how angry Charles became at the Butterfield's on Thanksgiving? I agree it's far-fetched, but Charles is crazy about Agatha, and Kathleen was pretty cruel to her."

"Do you think it was wise of you to leave Carl alone with Charles?"

"I think the worst that will happen is that Charles will make Carl's incarceration rather miserable."

"Why did you include Sam when you asked if any of them had left the inn? Wasn't he working there the entire evening?"

"Yes, until they closed up, but Ben stayed at the inn that night. Sam said he went directly to the carriage house, but who's to say. You and I know Ben was a lot more vocal about Kathleen than Sam was, but I think Sam's dislike of her ran just as deep."

"What time did Louis Tate think the murder took place?"

"Between eleven and two, but that was just his initial examination there in her shop. I hope to hear from him sometime tomorrow."

"Unfortunately all of the people you've mentioned were out during those three hours. My first suspect has to be Carl, but I don't understand why he came back. I mean, he had stolen millions, and he was well away from here. If he had killed her, why didn't he just get on a plane and lose himself somewhere?"

"Maybe he came back for Samantha."

Abigail looked incredulous. "You don't think Samantha was in on the embezzlement, do you?"

"No, I don't think she knew anything about that. She was sure mad as hell when Carl walked in. What I'm saying is that Carl is so arrogant he may have thought Samantha was in love with him enough to go with him. I know this sounds crazy, but I truly believe Carl could convince himself."

"Even after he's been cheating on her, not to mention stealing money from her grandfather's bank, he'd believe she'd run away with him?"

"Well, you hear about couples that constantly fight yet seem to be in love. I'm just speculating on why Carl came back. It may be as simple as greed. That's what Henry's first thought was."

"There's the town hall. Do you want to check on Charles?"

Alex chuckled. "No, I think I'll leave Carl to whatever Charles and Agatha have in store for him. When I left to meet you for dinner, Carl was hollering that he would rather take his chances with Samantha."

"That's so funny," Abigail said. "Who knows? They may get a confession out of him by morning. Do you think eventually the entire town will know about Carl embezzling the bank's money?"

"I suppose. I can't imagine being able to keep it quiet. Even if Carl returns the money, the whole ordeal is bound to get out."

"I'm sorry I blurted out in front of GH about seeing Agatha at the town hall. I was so excited to find you. I honestly didn't see him standing there."

"That's okay. GH is a good guy. He can be a little over enthusiastic at times. Here we are, home at last. I plan on typing up the rest of today's events, then going to bed."

"I plan on taking a long hot bubble bath, and then I'm also going to bed."

"Do you think we can time it where we both get into bed at the same time," he murmured, nuzzling her neck as they stood under the porch light.

"I think maybe we could," came her whispered reply.

Nor is there any law more just, than that he who has plotted death shall perish by his own plot. - Ovid, Ars Amatoria

10

At their oak breakfast table Monday morning, over French roast coffee and apple-cinnamon pancakes, Abigail was filling Alex in on the previous day's tour of Pauline's house.

"If you could have seen Grant's and Carolyn's faces. I tell you, when they look at each other, they just glow."

"That's great, Hon. I only hope they're not moving too quickly. Remember, Grant just got divorced.

"At this point, I think they're just enjoying each other. If Grant buys the house, Carolyn will help him decorate, but she's not planning to move in, not right away anyway. The only fly in the ointment I see is Grant finding employment. It would be a shame if everything falls through because of that."

"I may be able to help with a job for Grant."

"Really? How?"

"I have to talk to Henry first, but I happen to know there's recently been an opening at the bank."

"Oh, Alex, that's a wonderful idea. I'm sure Grant would be qualified."

"Now, Abigail, don't get too excited and don't say anything to Carolyn yet. Henry may be thinking of asking Barb Winters."

Abigail nodded. "If Grant can't take Carl's place, Henry might find another position for him."

"I'll call Henry as soon as I get to the office and let you know what he says. What are your plans?"

"Since the tea room is closed today, I'm going to run errands. I have a hair appointment later this afternoon. What's on your schedule?"

"I'll be in my office most of the day. I need to go through the messages Bonnie took. Also, Carl is supposed to transfer back the money from the Caribbean bank."

"I wonder how it went with Charles and Agatha. It was nice of them to help you out."

"I'm sure I'll get an earful from Carl. I've got to get going. I want to be there a little early so Charles can go home."

"Okay, have a good day. I'm making a pot roast for dinner. When you get a chance, call and let me know when you'll be home."

***

"Good morning, Charles, how was your night?" Alex asked, coming into the small office outside the jail room. "I hope Carl didn't give you a lot of trouble."

"No trouble at all," Charles replied, neatly folding the blankets on his cot. "Aggie should be here any time now with fresh clothes for Carl, and our breakfast."

"Alex, damn it. Let me out of here!" Carl yelled from the other room. "If you leave me with Charles any longer, I'm going to sue for harassment."

With raised brows, Alex asked, "Charles, have you been harassing our guest?"

"Not that I know of. I thought our conversation was quite copasetic."

Alex smiled. "I imagine it was. Why don't you come up to my office after you've had your breakfast?"

Back in the lobby, Alex met Agatha heading for the elevator. She was wearing a chocolate brown mink coat with a matching hat and carrying a large picnic basket and a clothes bag.

"Good morning, good morning, Alex dear." she said, as she approached him. "I bring both clothes and sustenance for our two men below."

"I appreciate that Agatha. I can't thank you and Charles enough for helping me out."

"Not at all, not at all. Chucky and I were happy to help. Will you be needing us again tonight?"

"Probably, but I need to speak to Henry first."

"Papaw-in-law is waiting for you in your office. He was kind enough to give me a ride. We have Chucky's car here to go home in."

"Okay, Agatha, thanks. I'll let you know about tonight."

"Good morning, Bonnie," Alex said upon entering his office. "I understand Henry is here."

"Yes, Chief. Would you like me to hold your calls?"

"Buzz me if you think it's important. Also, Grant Cummings will be stopping by. Please let me know when he arrives. Hello, Henry. I ran into Agatha in the lobby on my way up from the jail."

Henry nodded. "Agatha was ready and waiting for me when I woke up. How is Charles getting on with his charge?"

"Everything seems fine, although Carl is screaming that he's going to sue for harassment."

Henry smiled. "Is that right? Are you telling me Carl didn't care for his companions last night?"

Alex also smiled. "He didn't seem to. Henry, before we go on with our discussion about Carl, I have something I'd like to run by you."

"Sure, what's that?"

"I don't know if you'll be interested, but I may know of someone who could fill Carl's position at the bank."

"Really, who would that be?"

"Grant Cummings. He was my college roommate. He's recently divorced and has been visiting here since Thanksgiving. He's been wanting to make a move from Pittsburgh, and he really likes it here. Actually, he's already looked at Pauline's house and is meeting with Samantha this morning."

"Is that right? What are his qualifications?"

"He has an MBA, and has been ZX Corp's chief financial officer for ten years or so. I haven't mentioned any of this to him. I wanted to talk to you first. I didn't know if you were planning on offering the job to Barb Winters."

"Actually I did, but she said that with her busy schedule she was happy staying the bank's VP. Grant sounds like a perfect choice for the job. To tell you the truth, I wasn't looking forward to recruiting and interviewing a bunch of applicants. I'd like to set up a meeting with him as soon as possible."

"That shouldn't be a problem. He's planning on heading back to Pittsburgh today, so I asked him to stop by here before he left town."

"Fine. Now, on to more unpleasant matters, such as what to do about Carl. I discussed the situation with Victoria last night. She feels that if Carl gives the money back and leaves town, perhaps we can all avoid a lot of unpleasantness, as my lovely wife put it, and I'm inclined to agree."

"I personally think the less community uproar the better. If we can deal with this situation quickly, and the citizens realize they have their money back, I don't feel taking Carl to court will accomplish anything. Although, Henry, I have to tell you, Carl isn't just being held on embezzlement charges. I'm going to hold him on suspicion of Kathleen's murder as well."

Henry sighed. "Unfortunately, I'm not surprised. I have to admit I've wondered if he was the one responsible. Does the embezzlement have something to do with the motive?"

"I'm only holding him on suspicion. I don't have any proof he committed the murder. All I know for sure is, yes, Kathleen did find out about the embezzlement and had been blackmailing him."

"Do you know how much she got out of him?"

"Carl says $30,000 over the last few months. He says she was after him for more. In fact, I happened to come across $10,000 hidden in her apartment. I have it here in my safe."

"She truly was a nasty piece of work, wasn't she," Henry said with repugnance. "I guess this explains Carl's erratic behavior lately. Between embezzling money and being blackmailed, no wonder he was turning into a drunk."

"My problem is, if I don't come up with some tangible proof he murdered Kathleen, I can't hold him for very long. At this point, he just thinks he's being held until we get this embezzlement situation dealt with. Henry, I'd like to bring Carl back up here so he can do whatever he has to do to return the bank's funds. Then I'd appreciate it if you'd tell him you aren't sure whether you're going to press charges. That way I can keep him in jail for a little longer."

"I don't have a problem with that. I honestly haven't decided what I want to do with him anyway. Do you really think Carl killed Kathleen? I'd like to believe he's responsible, but somehow I can't see him having the guts to actually do it."

"That's what he's saying. He told me he hated her, but that he would never have had the nerve to pull it off. Like you, I have a hard time seeing it as well, but he has a damn good motive. Although a few others' actions that night are questionable, so I'm definitely not through investigating."

"Well, let's get Carl up here and take care of getting the money returned."

"There's one other minor problem," Alex said. "That's GH. He knows something's been going on at the bank, and he's asking questions. What do you want me to tell him?"

"Hell, Alex, I don't know. The fewer people know about this the better, but sooner or later the entire town is going to hear all about it. Maybe it would be best if GH hears the story from me first."

Alex's phone rang and he reached to answer it. "Excuse me for a minute."

"Chief, Charles and Agatha are here, and Pete Vanderwood is on line one," Bonnie said.

"Send Charles and Agatha in, and put Pete through. Thanks. Hello, Pete. This is unusually quick. I hope this means you have something for me."

"Buddy, you lucked out on this one. We got one hit."

"No kidding. Where was it?"

"It came off of the exterior rear doorknob. The print belongs to a Carl Edwards. We were able to make the match so quickly because he works for a bank and is required to be fingerprinted. I sure hope this will be of some help."

"It's definitely going to make the situation more intriguing," Alex replied. "Thanks for getting back with me so soon."

"No problem. My best to Abigail. Happy holidays."

"Same to your family. Keep in touch."

While Alex was on the phone, Charles and Agatha had joined them.

"We have an interesting development," Alex said. "That was Pete Vanderwood on the phone. He works for the county sheriff's office. He gathered fingerprints for me from Kathleen's shop. You can imagine the number of prints you'd find in a business like that. Well, there was one print lifted from the back door knob which luckily was on file." At this juncture, he paused. "It belongs to Carl."

"Aggie sure had the little sneak pegged," Charles exclaimed. "I myself thought he was the perfect suspect, but too cowardly for the deed."

Alex held up his hand. "Hold on, Charles. I agree this doesn't look good for Carl, but it doesn't prove he's guilty. All it tells me is that at one time he entered Kathleen's back door. I need to talk to him and find out when. Did he say anything last night about going to see Kathleen?"

"No, even though Chucky was as cunning as Hercule Poirot, he couldn't get Carl to come clean," Agatha replied. "In fact, he remained closed up tighter than a clam most of the time."

"Let's get Carl up here. He can take care of the bank's business. Then he and I will have a little conversation about fingerprints and door knobs. Charles and Agatha, I need to interview him in private, but I could use your help again here tonight if you would be willing."

Charles nodded enthusiastically. "We'd be happy to assist you in any way we can. We will return later on this evening. Should we provide the prisoner with dinner?"

"No, that won't be necessary, but thanks for offering. I'll just have something sent over from Flapjacks. Go ahead and have your dinner before you come back."

"Alex, dear, Chucky and I will stop and pick up Carl's dinner on our way back tonight. We'll go over there right now and tell Jo what we'll need."

"That would be great."

Henry sighed. "I may not have to decide whether to press charges. Carl may be going to jail for murder."

***

"It's about damn time you got down here," Carl complained as Alex came into the jail. "I've about had enough of you and this damn place."

"Well, Carl, I've had just about enough of your bullshit," Alex replied curtly. "So I suggest you think twice before you start mouthing off. Now let's go."

"Where are you taking me?"

"We're going to see Henry. He's waiting in my office for you to give him back the bank's money. I assume you can do this over the phone?"

"Of course I can. How do you think I did it in the first place?"

"Considering I've never stolen money from a bank, I'm not exactly sure how it's done."

"Good morning, Henry," Carl said with a smile upon entering Alex's office. "I'll have this matter taken care of in no time."

"You're damn right you will," Henry replied. "And you can wipe that disingenuous smile off your face. I not only want you to call your bank in the Caribbean, I want you to get in touch with whoever handles your stock portfolio. I want to know exactly what your stock holdings are worth."

"Okay, okay, Henry, no problem. Alex, where do you want me to sit?"

"You can sit there next to my desk. Go on and use the phone, computer, whatever."

"Barb Winters is at the bank," Henry said. "She's going to call me when the transfer is completed."

While Henry and Alex waited for Carl to conclude his transactions, Bonnie again buzzed Alex's office phone. "Yes, Bonnie?"

"Mr. Cummings is here."

"Ask him to have a seat. Tell him I'll be with him in a few minutes."

"Grant Cummings is here," Alex told Henry. "When we've finished with Carl, would you like to interview him in here, or your office?"

Henry kept an office in the town hall for handling any necessary community business.

"I'll see him in my office. That way you can take care of other matters."

"I'll go out and fill Grant in on what we discussed and see if he's interested."

***

"Hey, Grant, thanks for stopping by," Alex said. "Henry Butterfield is using my office at the moment. So if you don't mind, we'll talk out here. I have a proposal to run past you."

"No problem. I have to admit you've piqued my curiosity."

"I'm really not trying to be mysterious over this, but I needed to talk to Henry first."

Alex filled Grant in on what Carl had been up to. "Henry is going to need someone to run the bank. I thought of you last night while we were at dinner. Henry would like to interview you after he's through with Carl if you're interested."

"Interested, of course I'm interested," Grant exclaimed. "Alex, buddy, the job at the bank would be perfect. I can't thank you enough. Wait until I tell Carolyn."

"Hold on. Talk to Henry first. Not that I don't think you're a shoe-in, but I wouldn't call Carolyn just yet. Also, for the time being, Henry is trying to keep this situation with Carl quiet."

"No problem. I won't say a word until after my interview. Then if I get the job, I'll just tell Carolyn the position came open. What's going to happen with Carl? Is Henry going to press charges?"

"I'm not sure. Carl claims he'll be able to give the money back. As you can imagine, Henry is rather pissed."

At that moment, Henry walked out of Alex's office looking grim. "The situation has been taken care of."

Alex nodded. "Henry, this is Grant Cummings. Grant, I'd like you to meet Henry Butterfield. Henry's family was one of the earliest to settle in Newcomsville. The Butterfield's, along with the Silverspoons, were instrumental in the town's revival."

Grant shook Henry's hand. "I'm pleased to meet you, Mr. Butterfield. I understand I may be able to help you with a job vacancy."

Henry smiled. "That's what Alex tells me. Let's go into my office, and we'll see about that."

"Grant, I'll catch up with you later," Alex said. As he turned to go into his office, he glanced down at Bonnie's desk. Swearing to himself, he picked up Monday's Newcomsville News. "The Yuletide Strangler Still At Large" was the headline on the front page. "Well, Bonnie, thanks to GH we're probably going to get another flood of phone calls. Tell anyone who asks that it's an on-going investigation, and I'll have a statement for GH as soon as I have something to report. Also, please get our star reporter on the phone for me."

"So, am I free to go?" Carl asked, as soon as Alex reentered his office. "Barb called Henry to let him know the money has been transferred."

Alex resumed his seat behind his desk. "Unfortunately for you, Carl, there's another little matter we need to discuss."

"I hope it isn't about Kathleen. I told you I had nothing to do with her death."

"Then can you explain to me why your fingerprints were found on her shop's back doorknob?" The surprise in Carl's eyes told Alex all he needed to know.

Carl shifted in his seat. "I have no idea what you're talking about."

"Bullshit." Alex folded his arms on his desk and scowled. "I'm not in any mood to play games. They're definitely your prints. So stop denying it."

"For god's sake, Alex, I didn't kill her. You have to believe me."

"I'd like to Carl, but it's not looking good. So you need to explain to me why you went to Kathleen's shop that night."

"Okay, this is what happened. I went to tell her she wasn't getting another dime from me. But, Alex, I never saw her."

"What time did you get there?"

"I'm not sure. It was after I'd left the bank. You see, earlier that day I'd had one hell of a fight with Samantha and decided to get out of this town for good. But instead of leaving right away, I stopped off at a bar. I guess I stayed too long and had a little too much to drink. That's when I came up with the brilliant idea of going to the bank. I cleaned out my safe and went through my desk looking for anything that could lead Henry to my whereabouts. Then I came up with my second brilliant idea. I decided to tell Kathleen her money supply was being cut off."

"What happened when you got to Kathleen's?"

"Not a damn thing. Either she wasn't there, or she didn't hear me at the back door. I knocked and called her name, but she didn't answer. I could see a dim light coming from the front of the shop, so

I tried the door and it was locked. So I left, Alex. I swear that's the truth."

"Could you see anything besides the light when you looked in?"

"No, she has some kind of blind covering the window. All I could see was a faint light."

"Didn't you walk around to the front of the shop?"

Carl shook his head. "No, I didn't go anywhere near the front. I was getting cold and thought the hell with it. I was parked in the back, so I got in my car and left."

If Carl is telling the truth, he could have easily been there at the same time as the murderer, Alex thought. *Because the back door definitely wasn't locked the next morning.*

"How long would you say you were at the back door?" Alex asked.

"It couldn't have been more than a few minutes."

"Are you sure you didn't see anyone?"

"Damn it, Alex. No, I didn't see a soul. It was snowing like hell. I was cold so I left." Slowly the realization of what Alex had been thinking dawned on Carl's face. "My god, Alex, are you saying she was already dead when I got there?"

"Well, Carl, she was either already dead when you got there, or you made sure she was dead before you left."

"Damn it, I didn't kill her. How many times do I have to say it?"

"I guess until I have proof one way or another. For the meantime, I'd like you to remain my guest downstairs."

"Are you arresting me? If so, I'm calling my attorney."

"No, I'm not arresting you, not yet anyway. I'd just like you to stay where I can keep an eye on you. Besides, Henry still hasn't decided whether he's going to charge you with embezzlement." The phone rang. "Just a second, Carl. Yes, Bonnie."

"I'm sorry to bother you again, Chief, but GH is out here."

"What's he doing here? I just wanted you to get him on the phone."

"I know, Chief. I couldn't reach him. The next thing I knew he was walking through the door."

"Give him a cup of coffee, and tell him to sit down and wait."

"Carl, that's all for now. I'll take you back downstairs. I have to warn you GH is in the outer office. He knows something's up, but he doesn't know what. I'm going to have to tell him a little of what's going on. I'm going to say you're being held as a material witness."

"I didn't do it," Carl exclaimed. "Even though I don't really give a shit about this town, I don't want people thinking I'm a murderer."

"Like I said, I'm just going to say you're being held for questioning, nothing else. Carl, it's Monday, and a number of people work here. It's not going to remain a secret you stayed here last night. Isn't it better if I talk to GH instead of him getting misinformation from someone else?"

"Does he know about the embezzlement?"

"Not that I know of. He suspects something's been going on at the bank, but he doesn't know what. Look at it this way, if GH thinks you're the murderer, he may lose interest in what's been happening at the bank. But I don't know how long it will be before GH, and the entire town, find out."

"Oh, that's just great. Everyone will think I'm either a thief or a murderer."

Alex grinned. "Well, Carl, we already know you're one of those."

Carl's mouth formed a thin line. "I may have had a reason to kill her, but I imagine so did a number of others. I'll stay in jail until Henry decides what he's going to do, but I didn't murder her, and I'm not taking the blame for it. So you had better find out who it really was."

"Carl, if you're innocent, you have nothing to worry about. Now let's get you back downstairs."

"Hello, Alex, I hope you don't mind. I dropped by to see if you had anything new to report," GH said his eyes lighting up upon seeing Carl. "Hello there, Carl. I understand you spent last night here in jail. Can you tell me what that's all about? Does it have something to do with the bank?"

"No comment, GH," Carl replied, heading out of Alex's office.

Alex turned to GH. "Wait here. I'll be back in a few minutes."

When Alex returned, GH and Bonnie were in the middle of a rather heated conversation. Bonnie's pleasant face was red with fury and she was saying, "For the last time, GH, I have nothing to say in regards to Carl Edwards or Kathleen Cooper's death. Chief Mackenzie will tell you exactly what he feels you need to know."

"Come on into my office, GH," Alex said. "I think you've annoyed Bonnie enough."

GH took a seat across from Alex's desk. "I'm just trying to find out the truth." He removed a notebook and pen from his shirt pocket. "Are you finally going to give me a statement?"

"I haven't given you a statement up to this point because I had nothing for you to write. Now I want you to listen very carefully to what I'm about to say. I don't want you reading any more into this than what I tell you, is that understood?"

"Understood, Alex. Go on."

"Carl Edwards is being held for questioning in regards to Kathleen's death. Now, GH, he claims he's innocent, and he's just a material witness at this time. He has not, and I emphasize the word 'not', been arrested."

"What are your suspicions? Did Kathleen catch him up to something at the bank?"

"As far as any statement dealing with the bank, you'll have to talk to Henry."

"So all you're going to tell me is that Carl is being held on suspicion for Kathleen's murder and not why? Come on, Alex, you can do better than that."

"I didn't say that he's a suspect. He may have information material to the case, and I have the legal authority to hold him for questioning. I'm sorry, GH. That's all there is."

"You're telling me that you have no suspect?"

Alex shook his head. "I didn't say that. How about if I put it this way. Carl Edwards is being held for questioning, but his activities that night aren't the only ones I'm looking into. It seems there were a number of Newcomsville's citizens, for one reason or another, out that night. So right now, you might say there are too many possible suspects. Is that better?"

"Not much. It would be helpful if you'd tell me exactly why you are holding Carl, and who else is on your list?"

Alex smiled. "You know I can't do that."

GH closed his notebook with a snap. "Okay, the little I've been able to gather on my own, along with my gut instinct, tells me Carl, the bank, and Kathleen are all somehow connected. Kathleen didn't miss much that went on in this town. If she found out that Carl was, oh, let's say, helping himself to money that wasn't his, I think the citizens of this town have a right to know what's been going on in their bank."

Alex shrugged. "I told you all I'm going to. If you want to talk to Henry, you're free to call him. He's here in his office."

"How long are you going to hold Carl?"

"I'm not sure."

"Answer me this, Alex. If Carl killed Kathleen, and left town, why did he come back?"

"Because he claims he's innocent and has nothing to hide. Like I said, I'm just holding him for questioning."

"Can you tell me why Charles stayed downstairs with Carl last night?"

"I'm still investigating Kathleen's murder. I can't leave Carl locked up in an unattended building, so I asked Charles to stay in the outer room next to the jail."

"Is Charles going to be staying with Carl until you release him?"

"Probably, but don't get any ideas about coming over here tonight and interviewing Charles and Carl. They are both off limits."

"Why is Charles off limits?"

"I'm talking about while he's downstairs with Carl. Other than that, it's up to him whether or not he talks to you."

"Okay, well, I guess I need to see Henry. Is he still in his office?"

"As far as I know."

GH stood. "I appreciate you taking the time to talk with me. I'll definitely be in touch."

After GH left, Alex began going through the phone messages Bonnie had taken from the previous day. Once again he was interrupted by the ringing of his office phone.

"Yes, Bonnie."

"Chief, Louis Tate is on line one. And don't forget you're to call Kathleen's brother as soon as the body is released."

"Okay, thanks, put Louis through."

"Hello, Louis. That was quick. Did your examination turn up anything new?"

"No, it was exactly as I expected. Strangulation was definitely the cause of death, and the ribbon is what was used. As far as the time of death, I'm going to stay close to my original estimate, 11:00 PM to 2:00 AM."

"Did it look as if she tried to struggle with her assailant?"

"No, not at all. I believe you're right that she was taken by surprise."

"Did you find anything else I should know about?"

"No. Other than being overweight, she was in pretty good health."

"Well, thanks a lot. I assume you're ready to release the body?"

"Yes. Where would you like her to be taken?"

"I have to get in touch with her brother and see. I believe he's her only living relative. I'll have Bonnie call you once I've spoken to him."

"That will be fine, Alex. Good luck with this one. Do you have any leads?"

"I'm holding one person for questioning, but my evidence against him is pretty circumstantial. That reminds me, Louis. Our local newspaperman, GH Greeley, put out a special edition the morning after the murder. He described the body in detail. I've been wondering how he got that information."

"I can tell you it wasn't from me."

"I truly didn't think it was you. Could there be someone in your office that would give out that kind of information?"

"I would like to think not. Let me check into this and get back to you. There were only a couple of people in my office that would have seen my report."

"I'd really appreciate that. Thanks again."

"Bonnie, would you get me Kathleen's brother's phone number," Alex said, after hanging up with Louis.

"Sure thing, Chief. Mr. Cummings is out here. Would you like me to send him in?"

"Please do. Then I'd like you to call Flapjacks and ask Granny Jo to send over lunch for Carl. Also make sure she knows Agatha will be picking up his dinner later on."

"You look as if you have good news," Alex said as Grant walked in.

"I got the job," he exclaimed. "I've already called Carolyn. I'm going to postpone leaving for Pittsburgh until tomorrow. Carolyn and

I want to go out and celebrate. We were wondering if you and Abigail would like to join us."

"Congratulations. That's really great. When do you start?"

"I'm going to call my office today and give a two-week's notice, so hopefully I can begin before Christmas."

"This definitely calls for a celebration. I think we could all use a night out. Where are you planning on going?"

"Carolyn wants to go to the Wine Cellar for dinner since the inn is closed on Monday."

"Sounds good to me, but I need to talk to Abigail."

Grant smiled. "That won't be necessary. She was at Indulgence when I called Carolyn. She said the timing was perfect since she was having her hair done."

Alex rolled his eyes. "We can't waste a new hairdo, now can we? What time do you want to leave?"

"We'll pick you up at six-thirty? I'll make reservations for seven. Alex, I can't believe how my life has changed in just a few days. If you hadn't invited me for Thanksgiving, none of this would have happened."

"Buddy, I'm truly happy for you, but be careful. I don't want you rushing head-long into something you'll regret."

"I know what you're saying, and I appreciate your concern. This job at the bank is exactly what I need right now. You know I haven't been happy in Pittsburgh for quite a while. I've been thinking long and hard about making a move. And Carolyn and I are getting along great, but we're both smart enough to know we need to take it slow."

Alex chuckled. "If I needed someone to help me through some rough times, Carolyn would certainly be a perfect choice."

A wide smile spread across Grant's face. "Buddy, you don't know the half of it."

***

"Abigail, isn't this terrific news?" Carolyn said, after hanging up from Grant. "I don't know what's going on with Carl the toad, but I'm glad he managed to get himself fired."

Abigail had decided to have a manicure too, and her nails were drying. She sipped vanilla cappuccino at the coffee-wine bar wondering how long it would be before the news got out that Carl was being held in Kathleen's murder. She shook her head. Knowing how gossip spread through the town, she guessed not very long.

"Abigail! Are you listening to me?"

"What? Oh, yes, Carolyn, that really is great news," she said with a smile. "I was just thinking about what Alex said this morning. He's concerned you and Grant are moving a little too quick. I told him you were just enjoying your newfound, ah... how do I say this?"

"The word is lust, out and out lust, and it's wonderful."

Abigail laughed. "Well, that's one way to put it."

"Did I hear someone say something about lust?" Agatha asked, taking a seat next to Abigail.

"Hi, Agatha. I was just telling Abigail how much fun I'm having with my new man."

"Oh, yes, Carolyn, I've been hearing all about the rather attractive gentleman you've been seen around town with," Agatha replied. "How I remember the first time I met my Chucky. Now you talk about lust..." She gave them an exaggerated wink.

"What are you three laughing about?" Claire asked joining them at the bar. "If I had to guess, I'd bet it has something to do with men."

Carolyn grinned. "Men and lust. What a perfect combination."

"We must be talking about Grant," Claire replied, smiling back.

"Yes, and I have wonderful news. Grant is going to be Newcomsville's new bank president. Carl managed to get himself fired, and Henry hired Grant to take his place."

"Getting himself fired isn't all Carl's managed to do," Agatha said, pausing for effect. "He's also being held for questioning about Kathleen's death."

"I knew something was going on last night when we saw you taking food into the town hall," Carolyn said, "but I couldn't get Abigail to tell me what was up."

"I couldn't say anything until Alex gave his okay. Besides, I've only known since yesterday."

Claire's brows drew together in puzzlement. "Why would Carl kill Kathleen? I don't see the connection."

Carolyn turned to Abigail. "Do you know?"

With three pairs of expectant eyes staring at her, Abigail squirmed in her seat. "Yes, but I'm sorry, I can't tell."

Carolyn put her hands on her hips. "Abigail."

"I'm sorry, girls, I really can't. Alex asked me not to go into any details right now."

"How about you, Agatha," Carolyn coaxed. "You must know what's going on. After all, you were the one bringing Carl and Charles their food."

"Now you really have me curious," Claire said. "What does Charles have to do with any of this?"

"I apologize. I shouldn't have opened my big mouth," Agatha said, with downcast eyes. "I can't go into any details either."

"I just saw GH coming out of the town hall," Claire said. "Whatever it is, it will be all over town by tomorrow."

Carolyn nodded. "That's true. So, Agatha, you might as well tell." Agatha brightened. "I can tell you why Chucky is involved. You see Alex needed someone to stay with Carl at the jail during the night. So he asked Chucky to help out. You know Chucky is really rather fond of Alex, so when he asked for help, well, Chucky was delighted. We really don't do much. We're there in case of an emergency. Chucky sleeps in the outer office, and I bring Carl his dinner. Tonight we'll be picking up his food from Flapjacks around six, then taking it to Carl. I'll keep Chucky company for a little while. You know Carl and my Chucky have never hit it off."

"So, you and Charles must know why Alex thinks Carl murdered Kathleen," Carolyn stated. "Come on, Agatha, tell all."

"I'm sorry, dears, I really can't say any more."

Carolyn's eyes opened wide. "I'll bet somehow this all has to do with why Carl was fired. Abigail, is that it?"

Abigail glanced at her watch. "Oh, look at the time. I need to get going."

"I was at the bank this morning, and everything seemed perfectly normal," Claire said. "But I wonder."

"Wonder what?" Carolyn asked.

"If perhaps Kathleen found out Carl had been up to something. We all know Kathleen didn't miss much that went on, and it's obvious Carl had to have done something pretty awful to get himself fired."

Carolyn nodded with excitement. "I think you're right. You know I saw Kathleen come out of Carl's office not long ago. She looked like the cat that ate the canary. In fact, she didn't even seem to see me when I said hello."

Abigail picked up her purse. "I think I'll head home now. Carolyn, what time are you picking us up?"

Carolyn gave Abigail a wry smile. "Claire, we're definitely on the right track. Abigail is getting a little uncomfortable."

"Don't be silly. I have things to do. I can't sit here all day gossiping with you girls."

"Yeah, right, Abigail. I'll see you at six-thirty. I bet I know the whole story by then," Carolyn taunted.

"Cindy, dear, are you ready to shampoo me?" Agatha called to her stylist. "I'll just get a smock and be right there. Ta-ta, ladies," she said to Claire and Carolyn as she headed for the changing room.

Claire laughed. "I don't know that I've ever seen Agatha or Abigail move that fast. I think we were getting a little too close to the truth."

"I believe you're right. And I imagine if GH knows what's up, we'll all hear about it by morning."

Claire smiled. "Isn't that the truth. With GH on the trail, there will be no stone left unturned."

The salon phone rang, and Carolyn excused herself to answer.

"You're awfully busy today," Claire said after Carolyn hung up.

"I can't believe the number of walk-in's we've had." She lowered her voice. "See that blond woman over at the first manicure station, that's Samantha's decorator. She was supposed to meet with Samantha this afternoon, but the appointment was canceled. So she decided to get a massage and manicure."

"With all this going on, I'm surprised Samantha hasn't withdrawn her house from the tour."

"Maybe it's helping her to stay busy. I just hope she finally divorces the bum. Speaking of the tour, how are things going?"

"Actually, everything seems to be right on schedule," Claire replied. "Ticket sales are booming. I just hope nothing else happens before the first tour on Saturday."

***

"Damn it, Charles, I need to talk to Alex," an extremely agitated Carl demanded for the umpteenth time that night. "I don't give a damn where he is. This is important. I need to talk to him now."

166

"Okay, okay, just tell me what it is, and I'll call him," Charles said with irritation. "You know, Carl, it isn't necessary for you to be so quarrelsome."

"You idiot. I'll show you quarrelsome if you don't find Alex. I don't want to tell you anything. I want Alex. It's about Kathleen's death."

"Alright, alright," Charles replied through gritted teeth. "Aggie has been kind enough to bring your dinner. So after you eat, I'll see if I can find Alex."

***

"This really is a nice restaurant," Abigail said as the two couples waited for their cocktails. "This is only the second time we've been here."

"I normally order their carry-out," Carolyn said. "The food is delicious, and I love the Italian atmosphere. The last time I was in here was when I saw Kathleen hiding behind those plants over there." She pointed. "I sure wish I'd seen who she was spying on."

"That was the same night she was killed. Wasn't it?" Alex asked.

"Yes. I was having Grant over for dinner, so I called in a carry-out order."

"Do you remember what time that might have been?"

"Let me see. I would say around one or so. I know I was back at the spa by two. Alex, when are you going to tell us why you're holding Carl? Claire and I are convinced it involves Kathleen and the bank."

Alex took a sip of his drink before he replied. "Abigail told me that speculation over Carl was beginning to run wild. So I called Henry to see how he wanted to handle this. He decided it was foolish to try and keep what happened quiet, and I agreed. You see, for a few months now, Carl has been embezzling money from the bank. It seems that somehow Kathleen found out and was blackmailing him. I plan on asking Carl tomorrow how she discovered what he was up to. Now, Carl says he's innocent in Kathleen's murder, and I can't prove he's not. Henry also told me he's decided not to press charges against Carl. Carl has returned most of the money he stole and can make up the difference from stock holdings."

"He's been stealing our money?" Carolyn exclaimed. "I knew he was a slime ball, but this is incredible. How long has he been doing this?"

"Actually that's the good news. It's only been a few months, and he didn't go on a spending binge. He's been sending it to a bank in the Caribbean. I think that's the reason Henry isn't going to press charges. If I find Carl is innocent of Kathleen's murder, Henry said he'd be happy if Carl just disappears. I can tell you one thing. If Carl is able to leave, he'll leave without a dime."

"If Carl turns out not to be the murderer, do you have any other suspects?" Grant asked.

Alex sighed. "Unfortunately some of our neighbors' alibis that night are questionable. That reminds me, Grant, someone was seen on the sidewalk outside the inn late Friday night. Could that have been you?"

Grant's face turned slightly pink. "Ah, no. I didn't stay at the inn Friday night."

Carolyn smiled. "He's been with me every night since Thanksgiving. Did you ask Ben and Sam?"

"Yes, but they didn't see anyone. It seems there's a mystery person, and to make it more intriguing, I don't even know if it was male or female," Alex said.

"Who saw this person?" Grant asked.

"Charles and Agatha," Alex replied. "They were out in their sleigh, and they claim to have seen someone near the corner as they passed the inn. They say it was snowing pretty hard, and they weren't able to get a good look."

"So there's a chance they didn't see anyone?" Abigail asked.

Alex nodded. "It could have just been a trick of the light."

"Kathleen being a blackmailer doesn't surprise me," Carolyn said. "There are some people who are downright evil, and she was definitely one. I think she and Carl deserved each other."

"I never liked Kathleen," Abigail said, "but blackmail was low even for her."

"I'm probably being totally tacky by saying this, but if all of this hadn't happened, Grant wouldn't be getting his new job and buying Pauline's house in town." Carolyn raised her glass. "So here's a toast to Carl the toad."

Abigail laughed. "Carolyn, you're absolutely incorrigible." She turned to Alex. "That's not your cell ringing, is it?"

"I'm sorry, Hon, but I have to answer it." He pulled the phone from his pocket. "I don't recognize the number. Excuse me a minute." He stepped from the table.

Their meals had just arrived when Alex returned.

"Alex, what is it? What's wrong?" Abigail asked.

"The call was from Charles." Alex had to open and close his mouth, more than once, before he was finally able to say. "Carl's dead."

I love the old way best, the simple way of poison,
Where we too are strong as men. - Euripides

11

"Dead? How can he be dead?" Abigail exclaimed.

"I don't know, Hon. Charles was nearly incoherent. All I could make out was that Charles gave Carl his dinner, and when he went back to remove the dishes, he found him dead. I'm sorry, everyone. I'm going to have to leave. I can call a cab, and Abigail can stay here with you."

"No, that won't be necessary," Grant said. "We'll have the waitress pack up our food, and we'll all leave together. That's if the ladies agree."

Carolyn nodded. "Of course. Charles didn't indicate at all what happened?"

"He did say something about Carl insisting he talk to me, but like I said, Charles wasn't making a lot of sense. I told him to call Jack, and I'd be there as soon as possible."

"Alex, you don't think this could be foul play do you?" Abigail asked.

He shook his head. "I don't have any more information than I've already told you. I don't see how it could be anything else but a natural death. The man's been sitting in jail. How in hell could someone have killed him?"

***

When Alex arrived at the jail, he found Jack, Charles, Agatha, and the coroner, Louis Tate.

"Alex, thank god you're here," Jack said. "I'm afraid I have bad news. After I examined Carl, I called Louis. This is unbelievable. I think Carl may have been drugged."

"Now, Jack, let's not jump the gun," Louis said. "There's a chance Carl just had a heart attack."

Skepticism was scrawled all over Jack's face. "I sincerely hope you're right, but I've been his doctor for a couple of years now, and I've never seen any indication of a heart condition."

Alex narrowed his eyes. "What are you two talking about? How the hell could he have been drugged? As far as I know, no one has been in here except Charles and Agatha."

"I'd say that if it turns out to be foul play, whatever was used was put in his food," Louis replied. "I understand he had chili for dinner. The spiciness could have hidden any unusual taste. I'll be taking the remaining chili with me to analyze. I'm pretty sure I know what to look for. I'll get the results to you as soon as I can. One murder in this town was surprising. Two is astounding."

Alex frowned. "Tell me about it. Louis, I hate to pressure you on this, but I'd really appreciate it if you could examine Carl as soon as possible."

"I'll take care of it first thing in the morning. You'll know as soon as I do."

After Louis left with Carl's body, Alex wearily sat down in a well-worn leather swivel chair behind a rather battered looking desk. Running his hands through his hair, he said, "Have a seat, Jack, and tell me what happened after you got here and why you think Carl was drugged."

Jack sat in a hard-backed chair and leaned forward. "Like I said, I've been Carl's physician for a couple of years, and as far as I know he didn't have heart trouble. But when I first saw him, he appeared to have had a massive heart attack."

"And you don't think this could have been his body finally rebelling over his lifestyle of late?"

Jack shook his head. "I know what you're saying. He smoked and drank to excess, and he didn't watch what he ate. I might be wrong, but I thought it would be best to have Louis take a look. Who knows, after Kathleen maybe I'm getting paranoid."

"No. You did the right thing calling Louis. I just hope you're wrong. But if it turns out to be a drug, do you have any idea what was used?"

Jack hesitated. "I can't say for sure. That will be for Louis to determine. If I were to take a guess, I'd say some form of digitalis."

Alex lifted a questioning brow. "Isn't that used to prevent heart attacks?"

"Yes, but if a person who doesn't have heart trouble is given digitalis, it can have the opposite effect, and it can be deadly."

"So if Carl was murdered, and you're right about this drug, I'll now be looking for a killer with a heart condition?"

"I'd have to say, more than likely, yes. We're talking about a drug which is pretty common. There could easily be twenty to thirty people in Newcomsville alone taking the medication. I'm sorry, but it may not be all that easy to narrow it down to your murderer."

"Thanks a lot, Jack. That's just what I needed to hear. Let's say it is digitalis. How easily could it have been dissolved in Carl's food? I mean, is it a tablet or liquid?"

"Both. A liquid would be the easier to use, but it's more often prescribed in tablet form. You could dissolve it ahead of time, I suppose."

Alex sighed. "Nothing against you professionally, Jack, but I hope you're wrong on this."

He turned his attention to Charles and Agatha who had been quietly sitting side by side against the wall holding each other's hand. Dismayed at the sight of Charles' sickly pallor, Alex asked, "Charles, are you alright? Jack, have you had a chance to look at him?"

"Chucky is just a little overwhelmed at the moment, but he'll be okey-dokey any time now," Agatha replied, giving Charles a reassuring pat on his knee. "Finding Carl like that was a bit of a shock, don't you know."

"I imagine it was," Alex said. "Apparently I should have been on the alert for something like this, but it never crossed my mind Carl would be in danger. Hell, I thought he might be the murderer."

"I don't see how you could have anticipated someone wanting to kill Carl," Jack said. "Besides, most people would assume he'd have been safe in jail. Claire told me Carl was being held for questioning, but I don't understand why."

"It's all about blackmail and greed, Jack. I'll fill you in on the details tomorrow, but in the meantime, if you're suspicions are correct, I obviously missed something important. Now, instead of solving one murder, it looks as if I have two."

"So you think the killings are related?" Jack asked.

Alex nodded. "I have a hard time believing we have two murderers here in town. Yes, Jack, I believe whoever killed Kathleen also killed Carl."

"But what would have been the motive for killing both Kathleen and Carl?" Jack asked.

"If I knew the answer to that, I'd probably have my murderer. And to make matters worse, if digitalis was used, I have to believe the murder was premeditated."

"Why is that?"

"Answer me this. If a person took digitalis, would they carry it around with them? I mean it's not like nitroglycerin is it?"

"I see what you're saying. It's unlikely someone would normally carry digitalis. Do you know where the chili came from?"

"I assume it came from Flapjacks. Agatha, is that right?"

"It certainly did. I picked it up myself."

"Do you remember what time this was?" Alex asked. "I'd say I got there around six, but didn't immediately bring the food over here."

"Let's begin with exactly what happened from the time you walked into Flapjacks," Alex suggested.

"Well, I called Granny Jo as Chucky and I were leaving the house to let her know we were on our way. She told me she'd have Carl's meal ready when I got there, but when I walked in, the place was a mad house. Granny Jo had gotten so busy with the tourists she hadn't had a chance to prepare Carl's dinner. You see, one of her usual helpers had sprained her ankle ice-skating which left Jo in a pickle. So a young waitress I didn't recognize finally went and fixed Carl's food, but in the meantime I became engaged in conversation with Samantha, so I didn't notice when she placed the bowl on the counter. Unfortunately I'm not sure how long it sat there before I picked it up."

"Was the chili closed inside a container?" Alex asked.

"No. I think the poor young girl helping Jo is new and didn't understand what I wanted. She just placed the bowl on the counter. I had to ask to have it repackaged before I left."

"Agatha, when you first went into the diner, did you ask Jo for Carl's meal, or someone else?"

"Jo saw me come in, and I heard her tell that new waitress that I was there to pick up the chili and to get it ready."

"Was Jo's voice loud enough for others to have heard?"

"I suppose if they were nearby."

"So would you say, if poison was used, anyone in the restaurant at the time would have had an opportunity to put it in his food?"

"I'm afraid so, Alex dear."

Alex rubbed his temples. "Great. Can you remember who all you saw at the restaurant?"

"Aggie has a first rate memory," Charles replied, speaking up for the first time since Alex had returned. "I'm sure she'll be extremely helpful."

"Thank you, Chucky dear, but I'm afraid I'm not going to be of much help at all. I really wasn't paying close attention to the restaurant's patrons."

"At this point, anyone you can remember will be helpful," Alex stated.

"Let me see. As I mentioned, I was talking to Samantha, and that decorator person was there as well. I also remember seeing Bob O'Neal and his wonderful brood. There was that nasty Nan Katz and, oh yes, I briefly saw Sam, Ben and that delightful couple, the Scrapers, who I believe are expecting a baby. I'm sorry, Alex dear, I can't think of anyone else."

"That's okay. You've done just fine. Other names may come to you when you're not trying so hard. Did you spend the entire time talking to Samantha, or did you stop to speak to anyone else?"

"I really didn't have a long conversation with Samantha. She was telling me about some of her decorating ideas. Then, oh yes, that's when that clumsy man knocked over his beverage which splashed down the back of my skirt. The odious man had the nerve to say it was my fault for bumping against his table. I had to hurry off to the 'Ladies' hoping I could remove it before it stained."

"How long were you in the ladies' room?"

"That's the good news. When I walked in, Judy and Peg were just coming out, so they were kind enough to lend me some assistance."

"What did you do next?"

"I believe that's when I noticed the bowl of chili sitting on the counter. You know, Alex, you have to walk past that long counter to get to the restrooms. Well, as I was coming out, Jo happened to be walking by. I asked her if that bowl of chili was for Carl. When she saw it just sitting there, she reprimanded that young waitress quite severely."

"Did Granny Jo put the chili in a carry-out container herself?"

"Most definitely. I stood right there by the counter and watched her do it."

"Did you leave right after that?"

"Of course. I knew Chucky would be wondering what was taking me so long, not to mention Carl becoming surly due to hunger."

"Thanks, Agatha, you've been a lot of help." Alex turned to Charles. "Can you tell me what happened after Agatha got here with Carl's dinner?"

"Actually, Alex, in order to be absolutely accurate over this evening's events, I'll need to begin before Aggie's arrival with the chili," Charles replied.

Alex inwardly smiled, hearing Charles sounding more like himself, and seeing the color returning to his face. "Charles, please begin wherever you feel is necessary."

"First I'd like to apologize for my lack of diligence over my charge. You put your confidence in me, and I let you down."

"Charles, did you put the drug in Carl's dinner?"

"Absolutely not."

"I didn't think you had, so I don't want to hear any more about you letting me down. I can't see what you could have done to prevent this."

"That's what I've been trying to tell him," Agatha interjected. "I think it's as plain as punch whoever did this bit of hanky panky had to have put the drug in at the diner."

Alex nodded. "Charles, go on and tell me what happened before Carl ate the chili."

"You see, from the time I arrived, Carl was being his pugnacious self. He rather loudly kept insisting he needed to tell you something. I told him I would try to get in touch with you. I asked him to tell me what he wanted, but he stubbornly refused. He said he couldn't tell anyone but you, so I told him that after he ate his dinner I'd try to find you."

"Did he give you any idea at all what he wanted to tell me?"

"All he would say is that it had to do with Kathleen's death."

"How much time passed between your conversation with Carl and the time he ate?"

"Oh, not long at all. As soon as Aggie arrived, I gave him his food. Alex, I had every intention of calling you after Carl finished. I didn't think a few minutes would matter. I didn't want to interrupt you while you were enjoying your evening."

"Did you hear Carl call out or make any sound of distress?"

Again the crestfallen look came over Charles' face before he replied. "No, I didn't. You see, Aggie and I stepped out of this room for a few minutes."

"Chucky was rather upset at the way Carl had been expressing his need to speak to you, so I suggested we take a little walk while Carl ate. It was when we returned that we found Carl deceased."

"And you didn't see anyone enter or leave this room?"

"No, not a soul," Agatha replied. "We took the elevator to the lobby, and then walked around admiring those lovely paintings that nice young woman that runs the apothecary donated. Then we came back down here."

"And Carl hadn't said anything else?"

"No. He just kept repeating he had to tell you something, and it had to do with Kathleen's death."

"Did you get the impression he had an idea who Kathleen's murderer was?"

Charles frowned. "I'm not sure. You see he was being so incredibly churlish I wasn't really paying close attention. I was planning to contact you as soon as Carl finished his dinner."

"Alex, do you think he might have wanted to confess?" Jack asked.

"I don't think so. From the first I really had a hard time believing Carl was our man, but he was the only one who seemed to have a clear motive. Besides if he wanted to confess, why didn't he just wait until tomorrow morning? Why be in such a hurry? No, Jack, I think somehow Carl had figured out who murdered Kathleen."

"He was eliminated because he was about to reveal the murderer?" Charles exclaimed. "Oh, if only he hadn't been so obstinate in refusing to tell me, perhaps we could have apprehended the perpetrator."

"Wait a minute, slow down," Jack said. "In the first place, how could this person have known Carl suspected them, and how did they know they'd be able to drug his food? Not to mention, how did this person know Carl would be the one to actually eat the drugged food?"

Alex smiled without humor. "I'm afraid that at this time, Jack, those are the million dollar questions. Beginning with who knew Agatha would be bringing Carl his food from the diner. Agatha, do you remember telling anyone today that you would be going to Flapjacks for the food?"

"Take your time, Aggie, and put your thinking cap on," Charles said. "Not only who you were talking to, but anyone else who could have been nearby and overheard. This may be a vital clue."

"I'll give it a try, Chucky dear. Now let me think. I do recall discussing Carl's situation with the girls at Carolyn's spa this afternoon. They were pressing Abigail and me for details, but we didn't reveal any more than the fact that Carl was being held for questioning."

"What girls are you referring to?" Alex asked.

"Besides Abigail and myself, just Claire and Carolyn. We were sitting at the coffee bar. Abigail was waiting for her nails to dry, and I had a hair appointment. We were discussing how wonderful it was for Grant to be taking Carl's place at the bank. Carolyn was wondering why Carl had been fired, and one thing led to another, and I ended up telling them about Carl being questioned, and how Chucky and I were helping you out."

"Did you see anyone else you recognized while you were waiting who could have overheard you?"

She wrinkled her smooth brow in concentration. "Not at the coffee bar. But on my way past the manicurist tables, I'm sure I saw Peggy O'Neal and Meg. You see the spa was rather busy, and the delightful girl who does my hair was running behind, so I was in a hurry and didn't stop to speak to them, but they might have overheard us." Alex nodded in encouragement. "You're doing great. Can you think of anyone else?"

"No, Alex dear, I'm afraid that's it. By the time I was ready to leave, the only person I recognized was Ben, and he was sitting at the bar talking to Carolyn. I just waved as I went by."

"How easy do you think it would have been for the conversation at the coffee bar to have been overheard?"

"As I said, the spa was rather full, and someone could have easily walked behind us. Alex, I'm sorry I can't be of more help."

"Aggie, any information, regardless of its insignificance, may prove vital in solving a murder," Charles stated. "You're absolutely right, Charles. You never know when a little piece of information could turn out to be the critical piece of the puzzle."

"We won't know anything for sure until we hear from Louis whether the chili was drugged," Jack said. "And if digitalis was used, there's something really ugly going on in this town. If I hadn't seen both Kathleen and Carl with my own eyes, I'd have a hard time believing any of this."

"You and me both, Jack," Alex replied.

"On the bright side," Agatha said with a smile, "we all believe your murderer has to be one of the people at the diner, so that should help narrow your suspect list down. Unfortunately, as I said, Jo's place was an absolute mad house."

"Yes, Aggie, but don't forget the digitalis," Charles interjected. "Eliminating possible suspects should be easier once Alex ascertains whether or not any of them are users of this drug. You know, Lord Peter had a similar case, and he was able to successfully apprehend his murderer."

Alex grinned. "Well, I'm not sure I'm anywhere near as clever as Lord Peter, but I'll give it a try. So I'll call Granny Jo and tell her I'm on my way over. I just hope she's not already in bed."

Jack stood. "I'm heading home. Let me know as soon as you hear from Louis. I truly hope I'm wrong about digitalis."

"So do I, Jack. So do I."

"Ah, Alex dear," Agatha said. "I don't want to interfere with your need to speak with Granny Jo, but shouldn't someone tell Samantha about Carl's death?"

"Oh, hell, how could I have forgotten Samantha? Thank you for reminding me. I'll go over there and tell her what happened before I talk to Jo."

"Aggie, and I could be of assistance with Samantha," Charles suggested. "We could explain to Pauline what happened, then drive her over to Samantha's house. It may be easier on Samantha if it's her grandmother who breaks this distressing news to her."

"I'd really appreciate that, Charles. I'm afraid that since Granny Jo had such a busy day, she'll go to bed early, and I'd really like to talk to her tonight."

"You can count on us to expedite this matter for you," Charles said as they rose to their feet. "Again I can't express strongly enough my sorrow and regret that I wasn't able to prevent this unfortunate mishap."

"Charles, believe me. The way it looks; noone could have prevented this. I think our killer would have stopped at nothing to get to Carl. Please tell Samantha how sorry I am, and tell her I'll be in to see her as soon as I can. One more thing, I'd appreciate it if you wouldn't say anything about digitalis, even to Samantha. Tell her we won't know exactly what happened until tomorrow. If it turns out Jack is right, I'd rather any possible suspects aren't forewarned that I may be questioning them on their medications."

"I understand, but shouldn't we fill Papa in on what has occurred?"

"Yes, of course. Henry should definitely know what has happened."

"You can count on us to carry out your instructions to the letter," Charles replied. "Our lips are sealed."

After Agatha and Charles left, Alex took a minute to jot down the information that could be relevant, then reached for the phone. "Granny Jo, this is Alex Mackenzie. I'm sorry to bother you at this time of night, but I need to talk to you. It's rather important. Would you mind if I dropped by?"

"Of course you can come by. I'm just finishing cleaning up. What's wrong?"

"I'll explain when I see you. I'll be there in a few minutes."

When Alex arrived at the diner, Granny Jo was pouring him a steaming cup of coffee and had sliced him a thick piece of pumpkin pie. "Alex, sit yourself down. I have a little more straightening up to do, so I hope you don't mind if I work while we talk."

"I'm sorry for interrupting you, Jo. I understand you were pretty busy tonight."

"Lord o' mercy, busy ain't the word for it. I usually have a decent crowd on Mondays because the inn's closed, but I can't ever remember a Monday such as this. To top it off, that dang fool Roberta has to go off ice-skating, acting as if she's still a young girl, and winds up spraining her ankle. That's not bad enough, Roberta sends in her teenage niece to help out. Now I know Roberta meant well, and I do appreciate her trying to help, but Sissy knew nothing about waiting tables. So in a nutshell that's why Carl's dinner wasn't ready when Agatha got here. I hope he wasn't too hungry by the time he ate it."

"Actually that's why I'm here," Alex began. "I need to talk to you about the chili. Carl's dinner may have been tampered with."

Jo stopped refilling the napkin dispensers and stared at Alex. "Tampered with? What in the world are you talking about? I had a bowl of that chili myself, and it was just fine."

"Sorry, I'm not explaining this very well. Let me tell you what happened, and then we can see if we can figure this out." He began with Agatha's arrival and ended with their suspicions. "So you see if the chili was tampered with, it had to have been while it sat here on the counter."

Jo turned slightly pale and swayed on her feet. "I think I need to sit down."

Alex quickly rose and helped her to a booth. "I'm sorry, Jo. I didn't want to upset you, but I didn't know any other way to tell you. Are you alright? Do you want me to call Jack?"

"No, no, just give me a minute. I'll be fine."

"Would you like a glass of water?"

"To tell you the truth, Alex, I think something a little stronger than water is required. There's a little bourbon in the cupboard above the sink in the kitchen. If you'd get me a small glass, that would be just fine."

Alex returned with two glasses. "I hope you don't mind, I poured myself a little as well."

Jo gave him a slight smile. "Perhaps you should have just brought the bottle." After taking a sip, some color returned to her face. She took a deep breath. "Alex, I don't understand any of this. First, this afternoon I hear Carl's being held for questioning in Kathleen's death. Now you tell me he's dead, and it could have been my chili that killed him."

"Like I said, we're not sure what happened, but it's not your fault the chili was used. Somehow someone knew Agatha was going to bring Carl his dinner. They used the opportunity to do their dirty work. I just thought if I talked to you tonight, you might remember seeing someone around Carl's chili. On the other hand, I may have upset you for no reason."

"No, you did the right thing calling tonight. I'm seventy-five years old, and if you want me to remember something, asking me sooner is definitely better than later. Now, what do you need to know?"

"Let's start with everyone you can remember, either already here, or who came in while Agatha was here."

"Land sakes, Alex, this place was packed. I don't know if I'll be of any help to you at all," she said, her soft round grandmotherly face crumpling in despair.

"That's okay. You're going to do fine. Please just relax and take your time."

She narrowed her eyes in concentration. "Let me see. I spent most of the time in the kitchen, but I did come out a time or two to help serve. I remember seeing Ben, Sam, and the Scrapers. Isn't that wonderful news that Judy is expecting? I just think they're the sweetest couple."

"Yes, they're really great. You say Ben and Sam were with them?"

"Oh, yes, and I was so pleased to see both of them. They don't usually come in for dinner. They're normally just here for breakfast. I suppose it was because their place is closed on Monday. I imagine

Sam gets a little tired of his own cooking. I have to say that as much as I love this place, I also enjoy a break now and then."

"Were you the one who served them their dinner?"

"No, I just saw them sitting with the Scrapers. It was Sissy who waited on them."

"Did you happen to see if any of them left the table?"

"My goodness no. I was so busy. I…wait a minute. I do remember Sam poking his head around the kitchen door. He told me my chili and corn bread were the best he'd ever had. How about that?"

Alex grinned. "I agree your chili is great. Jo, you're doing fine. Can you remember anything else that the Scrapers or Ben and Sam may have said or done?"

The delight on her face vanished and concern clouded her brown eyes before she said. "Alex, I don't want to get anyone in trouble. I can't believe any of those good folks could have had anything to do with murdering anyone."

"I understand, and I wouldn't be asking you these questions if I didn't think it was important. You see, if I know where people were and what they were doing, then I can talk to them and ask them what they remember. Then maybe by listening to everyone I'll be able to put all the pieces together like a puzzle. You never can tell. What may seem insignificant could be important."

"My word, Alex, this is too awful to believe, and here you are having to sort it all out. You're a good man. I don't know what this town would do without you."

"Thanks. Hopefully I can live up to everyone's expectations. Now, if you're not getting too tired, I'd like to go on."

"Oh, I'm okay. Now, let me see. Nan came in just before I got really busy and took her usual seat at the counter. I tell you, Alex, I think that woman is getting even more hateful since Kathleen's death, if that's possible. I know they were good friends, and she really misses Kathleen, but Nan can't be taking her grief out on folks."

"Really? What has she been doing?"

"For starters, she's been talking even nastier about Samantha than she and Kathleen used to. I came out of the kitchen to help serve the O'Neal's their food, and I saw Nan right in Samantha's face. I couldn't hear what she was saying, but Samantha was red as a beet. I tell you what, if Nan Katz doesn't watch her mouth, she'll be the next one to get murdered."

"You couldn't hear anything that was being said?"

"No, but I wish I had."

"Who was waiting on Samantha's table?"

"It should have been Sissy, but I didn't notice if they'd been brought any food."

"Was Samantha sitting alone?"

"When I saw Nan standing by her, it was just the two of them, but she came in with her decorator."

"Did Sylvia leave without Samantha?"

"No. While Nan was at their table, she must have been in the restroom because while I was ringing up this nice couple from Michigan, I saw her and Samantha leave. You know, I'm not sure they even had dinner."

"You say Nan was sitting at the counter. Were all of the stools full?"

"Well, yes, but there're only eight seats."

"At which end of the counter was Nan sitting?"

"She always sits on the first stool near the front door next to the cash register. I think that's so she doesn't miss anyone who comes in."

"So she was sitting at the opposite end of where the chili was left on the counter?"

"Yes, that's right. As I said, Sissy put the chili down on the counter by the door leading into the kitchen. As you can see, there's a section where there aren't any stools. I use it for carryout orders. Alex, it's beyond me how I missed that bowl sitting there, but I didn't come out of the kitchen that often. Besides, hard telling when Sissy actually got around to filling Carl's bowl. She was in and out of the kitchen all night."

"Okay, Jo, you said you helped serve Bob and Peggy O'Neal. Did they have all the kids with them?"

"No. Just Meg and Sally. I don't know where the boys were."

"Did any of them say anything you think might help?"

She hesitated before shaking her head. "Not really."

"What is it, Jo? You look as if you want to say something."

"It's just, well, none of them were acting quite right. The girls were real quiet, and Peg seemed awful fidgety. And every time I looked at Bob, he had an awful frown on his face."

"Did any of them leave the table?"

"I didn't see her leave their table, but I saw Peg, along with Judy, come out of the ladies' restroom behind Agatha."

"Is that when Agatha asked you about Carl's dinner?"

"That's right, and I still can't get over Sissy not understanding when I told her to get a 'to go' bowl ready for Agatha. How confusing is that?"

Perhaps she didn't hear you clearly. So you don't have any idea how long the bowl sat on the counter?"

"No, Alex, I'm sorry I don't. All I know is I told Sissy to get the chili ready when Agatha came in, and it was still sitting there when Agatha asked me about it later. You're going to have to ask Sissy, that's if she even remembers being here. Don't get me wrong, I'm sure she did her best, but I just don't understand teenagers today. They can't seem to pay attention to anything for more than a minute unless it's one of those computer games or a cell phone."

"Just a couple more questions and I'll let you go to bed," Alex continued. "Did you at any time see anyone around Carl's bowl of chili?"

"No, I'm sorry, I didn't. Anyone could have walked past that counter on their way to the restroom and put something in that bowl." Her eyes filled with tears. "I just can't believe someone used my good food for such an evil deed. This will be one more reason for my daughter to bring up selling out and going to a retirement home."

"Granny Jo, no one in this town is going to think you had anything to do with this. I don't know of one person that's ever had a meal here who has had anything but praise for your down-home cooking."

She dabbed her eyes with a tissue. "Thank you, Alex. I still don't want to think it was one of the nice people of Newcomsville who would do something so terrible."

"I understand, but you never know what lengths people will go to if they're angry enough. Jo, there's something that has been bothering me. If the bowl sat there all that time and was probably cold, then why didn't someone just get Agatha a new bowl?"

"I told her I'd get a fresh bowl when I realized what had happened, but she said not to. She'd heat it up in the microwave at the jail, so I just packed it up for her."

Alex stood. "If I can get Sissy's phone number from you, I'll be on my way."

"Sure, I have it right behind the counter."

"Before I leave, is there anyone else you can recall seeing?"

"Well, there was Stewart and Henrietta. I think they came in after Agatha left, although I'm not sure. I'll tell you one thing I am sure of," she smiled for the first time since Alex had walked in, "As awful as these murders are, it's not stopping the tourists from coming into town. Tell Abigail I sold several more Christmas tour tickets today."

"I'll do that. Thank you for your help. If you remember anything else, please call. It doesn't matter what time it is."

***

At home, Alex found Abigail, Carolyn, and Grant sitting around a blazing fire and drinking hot chocolate.

Grant sighed with relief when he saw Alex. "Buddy, am I glad to see you. These two women are making me crazy with all of their speculations. Carolyn wouldn't budge until you got back and filled us in."

Carolyn rolled her eyes. "Grant's as curious as we are. So, Alex, do tell all."

"Before you begin, are you hungry?" Abigail asked. "I've kept your dinner warm in the oven."

"In a bit, Hon. I had a large piece of pie at Granny Jo's. What I would like is a beer. How about anyone else?"

Grant nodded. "Sure, sounds good."

Carolyn waved impatiently. "We're fine. Just tell us what happened."

Abigail frowned. "What were you doing at Granny Jo's?"

He took a seat on the sofa next to Abigail. "I don't want to disappoint you ladies, but there's really not a lot I can tell you. All I can say for sure is that Carl is dead, and there's a chance he was drugged."

"Drugged?" The girls cried in unison.

"How could he have been drugged?" Abigail asked.

"We think it might have been in the chili Agatha brought Carl from Flapjacks," Alex replied.

"Granny Jo's chili," Abigail exclaimed. "You're not saying you think Granny Jo or Agatha murdered Carl are you?"

Before Abigail could continue, Alex held up his hand. "Here's what I know."

He explained that Carl wanted to tell him something important about Kathleen's death, about Agatha arriving at the diner to pick up Carl's dinner and finding it a mad house, ending with Sissy leaving the bowl of chili sitting on the counter. "So, you see, if the chili was drugged, how easily it could have been done."

Abigail narrowed her brows. "But how could the murderer know Agatha would be taking Carl his food?"

"That's easier to explain than you'd think. A number of people, one way or another, could have found out."

"Also, how did this person know Agatha would be getting the food from Flapjacks?" Carolyn interjected.

Alex sipped his beer. "According to Agatha, you three were a probable source."

"What are you talking about?"

"Think back to the conversation you were having with Agatha and Claire at the coffee bar in Indulgence," Alex said.

"Let's see." Carolyn tapped her lip with the tip of her finger. "We were talking about Grant getting the job at the bank. Then Claire sat down next to Agatha and…"

"Oh, no, Carolyn," Abigail interrupted. "That's when Claire mentioned seeing GH coming out of the town hall, and Agatha told about Carl being held for questioning."

Carolyn nodded. "You're right. Claire and I started pressing you and Agatha for more information about Carl."

Abigail turned troubled eyes to Alex. "I'm sorry, but it's true. The four of us were discussing Agatha and Charles helping you and that Agatha would be taking Carl his dinner."

Alex gave her a reassuring smile. "Don't get upset, Hon. You four weren't the only ones in town discussing Carl. Between GH and the guys at Two Bits, it wasn't a big secret. Besides, who would have known discussing Carl's dinner arrangements could possibly lead to his murder," he sighed. "Actually, I spoke to GH this morning. I knew as soon as the town hall workers arrived, they'd know Carl was in the jail, so I wanted to talk to GH first, although I only told him I was holding Carl as a material witness. I thought it would be best to let Henry explain the embezzlement charge. What I need to know from you ladies is if you remember seeing anyone who might have overheard your conversation at the coffee bar."

"Anyone in the spa could have heard us," Abigail replied. "Carolyn was extremely busy today."

Carolyn nodded. "Abigail's right. We were so engrossed in our conversation, I don't know who might have walked past."

"The easiest way of finding out who was at the spa is to look at Carolyn's reservation book," Grant suggested.

"That's perfect," Carolyn exclaimed. "That will give us everyone's name and appointment time. Abigail, wouldn't you say it was around one o'clock when we were talking?"

Abigail shook her head. "Closer to two. My hair appointment was at twelve-thirty. But you're right, Grant. That's a great idea."

"The only problem I see is the walk-ins," Carolyn said. "Hopefully I kept today's list, but I'll have the receipts."

"You know, I recall seeing Peggy and Meg, but that's probably because their nail appointment was right after mine," Abigail said.

"Carolyn, are you the one who checks the customers out?" Alex asked.

Carolyn shook her head. "Heavens no. I have a very competent girl who takes care of that. I'm in charge of the wine and coffee."

Abigail chuckled. "There's a lot more interesting gossip around the coffee bar."

"She's exactly right," Carolyn agreed. "It's always important for one to remain informed on current events."

Grant snorted. "And with that great witticism, I think we'll take our leave."

Carolyn got to her feet. "Yes, let's go. I'm anxious to look at today's reservations. Alex, I'll call you in the morning and let you know which of our neighbors could have had big ears today."

As Grant and Carolyn were leaving, the phone began to ring.

"I'll get it. Hello, this is Alex Mackenzie."

"Alex, Henry here. What in god's name has happened now? Charles just arrived home and tells me Carl's dead, and you think he was murdered."

"That's what I'm trying to find out. I have to wait for Louis Tate to call with autopsy results before I'll know for sure. Did Charles mention how Samantha was doing?"

"Agatha said she collapsed, and Pauline called for Jack. How in the hell could something like this have happened? Charles is telling me drugs may have been put in the chili at Flapjacks. Is that true?"

"If it turns out to be drugs, that's the most likely place for it to have come from."

"Just a minute, Alex. Charles is saying something. He wants me to tell you he and Agatha intercepted GH outside the town hall. Evidently he heard about the coroner's van being parked out front. They were successful in persuading him to wait until he heard from you, but they did inform him of Carl's death."

Alex sighed. "That's great. I suspect we'll greet the morning with another special edition. I'll call him tonight and give him some details, otherwise hard telling what he'll write."

"I asked GH to give me twenty-four hours before printing the embezzlement story. Please call me in the morning to let me know what Louis says."

Alex had no sooner hung up the phone than it rang again. "Hello, Alex Mackenzie."

"Hello, Alex. GH here. I'm glad I caught you in. What can you tell me about Carl Edward's death?"

"I was just about to phone you. I understand you've been talking to Charles."

"That's right. He and Agatha told me Carl was dead, but I couldn't get any more out of them. So what's the scoop? How did he die? Was it foul play? Do you think his and Kathleen's deaths are related? Or was he so full of remorse over killing Kathleen that he took his own life?"

"Hold on, GH," Alex replied with exasperation. "The first thing I want to make clear is that Carl did not take his own life. All I know at this time is that it was a sudden death, and I have to wait for the coroner's report. I'd appreciate it if you didn't print anything about this until I know what's happened. Would you do that for me? I promise I'll call you as soon as I know something."

"Well..."

"Come on, GH, you don't want to print a half-assed story do you? Wouldn't you rather wait until you have all of the facts?"

"Henry asked me to wait twenty four hours before printing the embezzlement story which will be tomorrow morning. How about this? I'll just say Carl was found dead and you're investigating. Alex, you know as well as I do, you can't keep Carl's death quiet."

"Alright, but just print what I've told you. It's not necessary for you to dramatize it." "Sure thing. I assume Louis Tate already has Carl's body?"

"Yes. He's going to do the autopsy first thing in the morning, then let me know the results." A sudden suspicion came over Alex. "GH, do you by any chance know someone who works in the coroner's office? Is that how you knew so much about Kathleen's death?"

"As I told you before, Alex, a good reporter never reveals his sources. I'll be in touch." With that the line went dead.

"Damn it to hell," Alex said slamming down the phone.

"What's happened now?" Abigail asked, coming back into the room.

"It's GH. I have a feeling he's going to know how Carl died before I do. I'll have to call Louis in the morning and let him know he may have an indiscreet employee. Hon, did you say my dinner is in the oven? I think I finally could eat something."

"Sure. Sit down at the table and I'll get it for you." She shook her head. "I still can't believe Carl was drugged."

"I know, but it's too much of a coincidence for Carl to have a heart attack just when the town finds out he's being held for questioning in Kathleen's death. I think the murderer felt Carl was a threat to him, or her, and took an easy opportunity to get rid of him."

"But if Carl knew who the murderer was, why didn't he say something earlier?"

"We'll never know exactly what happened. You have to remember that Carl wasn't a stupid man. Yes, he was an incredible ass, but he had a sharp brain, not to mention good self-preservation instincts. I suspect sitting alone in jail with nothing else to do but think, he realized he knew something he hadn't thought of before."

Abigail placed Alex's warmed food in front of him. "So if he had an idea who the murderer is, wouldn't that mean it must be someone close to him? I mean wouldn't it have to be someone he knew rather well for him to think of this person?"

"Not necessarily. Think about Carl's lifestyle. He spent most of his time sitting in one bar or another. Most people, after consuming a large quantity of alcohol, have a tendency to talk too much. Carl could have been in a bar telling someone who-knows-what, or someone could have overheard him. Don't get me wrong. I feel the murderer definitely knew Carl. I'm just not ruling out those who may have only been casual acquaintances."

Abigail sat down at the table with a cup of tea. "I just can't believe someone nonchalantly sat eating their dinner at Flapjacks knowing that at any time Carl would be dying. Granny Jo must be beside herself at the idea of it being her chili that was used. How was she when you left?"

"Tired, but she's a tough old bird. You're right that she was pretty upset at the thought of someone using her food for such an 'evil deed' as she put it. I guess the first thing I should do in the morning is call Sissy. With any luck she'll remember seeing something, but I'm not counting on it."

"I don't understand how that chili could sit there for all that time and no one wonder why it was there, and why didn't Jo just give Agatha a fresh bowl? Don't you think the murderer was taking quite a chance that someone else would eat the chili by mistake?"

Alex nodded. "Those questions bothered me too. The diner was unusually busy, and with Roberta not there, Jo became flustered. I think Roberta must be Jo's right hand worker. Jo not only had to deal with customers, but also with Sissy not knowing what she was doing. I did ask Jo about a fresh bowl, and she said Agatha insisted she'd just heat it up at the jail. I think Agatha was in a hurry and thought it would be quicker. Maybe it didn't take as long as it seems from the time Agatha walked in until Jo finally packed up Carl's food. As for someone else eating Carl's chili, that would be unlikely. Jo wouldn't serve a customer food that had been sitting out. She would just throw it away."

"Did Jo say if the stools at the counter were also full?"

"Yes, but the only person Jo remembers sitting there was Nan, and she was at the far end from the carry-out counter where the bowl was."

"Nan," Abigail exclaimed. "Alex, Nan Katz doesn't miss a trick, and it wouldn't matter at what end of the counter she was sitting. Have you talked to her?"

Alex glanced at the clock over the stove. "Do you have any idea how late it is? Tomorrow I plan on talking with everyone who was in the diner, but first I'd like to type up my notes while my thoughts are clear. Then I'm going to bed. Why don't you go on ahead? I won't be too long."

"My goodness, it's almost one. You must be exhausted. Can't this wait until morning?"

"No, Hon. I'd rather work on it now. I'll try not to wake you when I come to bed."

She wound her arms around his neck. "I'm beginning to get really scared. There's a cold-hearted killer in this town. What if they decide you're getting too close to the truth and come after you next?"

He held her tight and kissed the top of her head. "I'm going to be just fine. This person may be a cold-hearted killer, but they're going to make a mistake, and I plan on being right there when they do."

History is a needle, for putting men asleep,
anointed with the poison of all they want to keep.
-Leonard Cohen

12

Abigail awoke early Tuesday morning to find Alex's side of the bed was still made. She put on her slippers and robe and went out into the great room. She found him sound asleep in his leather desk chair in front of his computer with Thomasina curled up in his lap.

"Alex, wake up," she said, gently shaking his shoulder. "It's morning."

"What?" he mumbled slowly opening his eyes. "Abigail, what time is it?"

"It's 6:30, and you've slept in this chair all night. What time did you quit working?"

"I'm not sure. I thought I'd just close my eyes for a minute and, well, here I am. Damn, my back," he said as he started to rise, pain doubling him over. Hon, you're going to have to help me get out of this chair."

"For god's sake. Sit back down. Let me call Jack. Look at you. You can't even stand up straight."

He waved her away. "I'll be alright in a minute. I just need a hot shower."

"Let me help you into the bathroom. Thank goodness we have a walk-in shower. Yell if you need any help."

Abigail had the coffee made and was taking bagels from the toaster when Alex shuffled in.

"Well, at least you're standing upright. Does your back still hurt?"

"Only when I try to sit, stand, or walk," he replied gruffly as he lowered himself into a chair. "I'll stop by Jack's on my way to the office and see if he can give me something."

"Why go into the office? Can't you just work from here?"

"I need to go through some information I have on the computer at work. Then I'd like to talk to as many people as possible that were in Granny Jo's last night. I want to question them while their memories are still fresh."

She placed breakfast on the table. "So, did you figure out who our murderer is?"

"Unfortunately no, but I can't help thinking that somehow Carl is the key to both murders."

"Really?"

"Let me run this theory by you. We know Kathleen was blackmailing Carl over his embezzlement. How she found out about this, we may now never know. What if Carl just happened to have a close friend he confided in about the embezzlement and blackmail? Seeing what could be an opportunity to join Carl in getting some easy money, this person became Carl's accomplice. What if while sitting in jail, Carl came to the conclusion that this person must have decided on their own to get rid of Kathleen, and this is what he wanted to tell me last night. Remember Carl said he went to her shop the night of the murder, and she didn't answer his knock so he left. He confessed rather easily to the embezzlement charge, but was emphatic that he didn't kill her, and now I feel it's clear he didn't.

"So after hearing about Kathleen's death, he comes back to town thinking he can continue stealing from the bank since she is no longer a threat to him. I didn't have any substantial proof he was Kathleen's murderer, but no one else knew that. So why did someone think Carl needed to be kept quiet, unless they were afraid Carl would spill his guts to save his own hide? I think both Kathleen and Carl became threats to our murderer. Now all I have to do is figure out the connection. I can't help but think the answer is right in front of me, and I'm just not seeing it."

"Do you honestly think Carl would tell someone he'd been embezzling and was being blackmailed?"

"What if he confided this to someone he thought he could really trust? From the time Carl came strolling back into his house, events have moved quickly. I don't see how he could have had an opportunity to communicate with this person. Then this person heard Carl was being held for questioning and feared he wouldn't hold up under pressure. Carl has been sitting in jail with nothing to do but think. It's hard to say whether he knew his life was in danger, but my guess is Carl may have believed the person he told about the blackmail could be capable of murder."

"That's an interesting thought. If you're right, we're back where we started. Anyone in town could have been Carl's accomplice, although I can't think of anyone that close to him."

"Ah, yes, but there may be another twist. Last night I didn't tell you that the drug may have been digitalis. So you see, if Louis finds Carl was drugged, hopefully I'll be able to narrow down our suspect list from all those who were in Flapjacks last night."

Abigail gaped incredulously. "Good grief, Alex. You're telling me you're looking for someone who was not only in Indulgence yesterday afternoon, they were also in Granny Jo's last night, and this person takes digitalis heart medication and was close to Carl?"

"If Louis tells me Jack's suspicions were right, I think that would be the obvious answer. Remember, it wasn't just those who were in Indulgence who knew about Charles and Agatha helping me out with Carl. By the afternoon, it was pretty common knowledge Carl was back and in jail."

Abigail sighed. "I suppose it couldn't just be a crazy coincidence that practically the same group of people who were in one part of town or another the night Kathleen was killed just so happened to be in Flapjacks the night Carl was drugged."

Alex shook his head. "I believe coincidences do happen, but not this time." No sooner had he said this than the phone began to ring.

"I'll get it." Abigail reached for the phone. "Hello, Mackenzie's'."

"Good morning. This is Louis Tate. I'd like to speak to Chief Mackenzie, please."

"He's right here. Just a moment."

"Hello, Louis. Thanks for calling me so soon. What did you find out?"

"Good morning, Alex. Well, you can tell Jack he had it right. Carl was given a large dose of digoxin in his chili, which I'd say worked very quickly."

"Digoxin? What is that? I thought Jack said it could be digitalis?"

"Digoxin is a type of digitalis. It comes in a liquid form. Mixed in food or a beverage, it works more quickly than digitalis. Your murderer wanted to make sure Carl would die. When I say a large dose, I mean extremely large. A quarter of what was used would have done the job."

"So there isn't any doubt the murder was premeditated."

"Your murderer knew exactly what they were doing."

Alex released a long breath. "I was afraid of that. Okay, Louis. Thanks for getting on this so soon. I'm sure someone in the Silverspoon family will be calling you with funeral arrangements."

"That's fine. You know this had me so curious I couldn't sleep. I was up before dawn to run the tests on Carl. Alex, considering the amount of the drug that was used, I'm afraid this person won't hesitate to kill anyone they feel is a threat. You take care of yourself, and I hope the next time I see you we're in court trying this murderer."

"You've definitely got a date. I'll see you in court. By the way, Louis, please make sure no one else in your office sees this report. The editor of our newspaper, GH Greeley, may have a friend in your office who is giving him information they shouldn't. I don't want to get anyone in trouble. I just thought you should know."

"Is that right? I'll be damned. Thanks for telling me. I'll lock the report in my desk, and then I'll look into the matter. Keep in touch."

"When Alex hung up, Abigail said, "I don't have to ask. I can tell by the look on your face Jack was right. What are you going to do now?"

"I'm going to start by seeing Jack. I need to know if any of those on my list take digoxin. Besides, I'm hoping Jack can give me something for my back," he said with a grimace as he rose. "Then I'd better see Roberta's niece. Hon, I'd like you to wait until you hear from me before you tell anyone it was digoxin that killed Carl. Even though his death will be all over town, I don't want the specifics known yet."

"I won't say anything, but I don't think Jack can disclose personal medical information like that."

"You're probably right. I'm not familiar with the law when it comes to revealing prescriptions, but since this is a murder investigation, I'm hoping Jack can help."

She frowned. "If you find out one of our friends takes digoxin, I don't want to know. I just can't imagine anyone we're close to being this evil, not to mention being in on the embezzlement."

"I understand, Hon, but think about it. How well do we really know our neighbors? We consider a number of them our friends, but sometimes people aren't what they seem. They can have a darker side which isn't shown until they're pushed beyond their limits."

"But if your theory is wrong, what other motive would someone have to kill both Kathleen and Carl? I mean we both know Kathleen wasn't liked by a number of people, and Carl wasn't exactly popular either, but what reason would one person have to want both of them dead?"

"There's self-preservation, but hate is a strong emotion, along with revenge, and let's not forget love."

"Love? Are you crazy?" Abigail exclaimed. "Samantha couldn't kill Carl."

Alex shrugged. "He's treated her terribly for years now. Maybe she finally had enough. You know there's a thin line between love and hate. Remember she was seen out the night Kathleen was killed, and she was also in Flapjacks last night."

"But why would she kill Kathleen? I can't imagine Samantha thought she and Carl were having an affair."

"Maybe she found out about the embezzlement and went over to try to talk Kathleen into stopping the blackmail."

"But if she wanted to protect Carl, why turn around and kill him? Alex, that doesn't make any sense."

"Maybe all Carl has done finally became too much for Samantha to bear. I'm not saying there's any proof of this. I'm just considering all possibilities." He hesitated. "Or I could be looking at this all wrong. What if the only connection between the two deaths is as simple as Kathleen's killer seeing Carl at the back door and thinking he saw them. I feel the murderer was still in Kathleen's shop when Carl came by. He said the back door was locked when he tried it, but when I got there it wasn't locked."

Abigail nodded vigorously. "That has to be the answer. The murderer thought Carl saw them and panicked. This person heard about Agatha taking the food to Carl and took the opportunity to kill him."

"It may be that simple, but my gut instinct tells me it's more complicated." Alex reached for his coat. "If I have time, I might come back for lunch."

"Great, today we've got beef stew and homemade biscuits," she replied as she also rose. "Are you sure you don't want me to drive you to Jack's?"

"No thanks, I'll be fine. You have a good day." He held her close and gave her a long reassuring kiss.

***

"Good morning, Alex," Claire said opening her oak-paneled front door. "Jack had a feeling he'd be seeing you. Come on in. He's just finishing breakfast."

"Thanks, Claire. I'm sorry to be bothering you so early."

"No problem. We're early risers. Jack told me a little of what happened last night. Since you're here, I expect Jack's suspicions were right."

"Unfortunately, he was right on," Alex replied. "I kept hoping Carl's heart just decided to give out, but it looks as if our murderer has struck again."

When Alex entered the kitchen, Jack was seated at a round maple table with matching cane-bottom chairs. Cream and brown tiles covered the floor. The cabinets were a glossy cream and the walls a pale green.

"I knew it would be you when I heard the doorbell," Jack said motioning Alex to the chair across from him. "Have a seat. Coffee?"

"I'll leave you two alone," Claire said. "I'll be in the front room if you need anything."

"Thanks, Claire, and, yes, coffee would be great."

"Louis must have been as eager as we are to find out what killed Carl," Jack said pouring Alex a cup of coffee.

"So was it digitalis and was it put in the chili?"

197

Alex gingerly lowered himself into the chair. "You were right except it was digoxin instead of digitalis. Given in a large dose it can act quickly, and according to Louis quite a large dose was used. So now, Jack, we come to the part when I ask you which of our residents, who happened to be in Flapjacks last night, takes digoxin."

"Before we go into all of that, would you like to tell me what's wrong with your back?"

"I fell asleep in my desk chair. Actually I'm much better than I was. You should have seen me when Abigail woke me up this morning."

"I can imagine. I'll give you some anti-inflammatories and a mild muscle relaxer. If that doesn't help, come back and see me in a couple of days."

"Thanks, I'd appreciate that. Before we get into this digoxin thing, I'd like to bring you up to date."

"Let me make sure I have all of this straight," Jack said after Alex finished. "For a few months now, Kathleen has been blackmailing Carl after she found out he'd been embezzling from the bank, but now that Carl has been murdered, you don't think he could have been Kathleen's killer."

"That's right. From the beginning I had a hard time seeing Carl as the murderer. Even after he told me about the blackmail and how much he hated Kathleen, it just didn't feel right. I can easily picture Carl as a liar and a thief, but not as a cold-blooded killer."

"I'm still absorbing the fact Carl was embezzling. What's Henry going to do about this?"

"The good news is that Carl still had the majority of the money sitting in a Caribbean bank and transferred it back yesterday."

"So you're still thinking the same person who killed Kathleen also killed Carl?"

"Yes, and in some obscure way Carl's the key to both deaths."

"Do you have any idea what the connection is?"

Alex hesitated. "Perhaps, but I'd like to find out the answers to a few more questions before I say more. The other possibility is that whoever killed Kathleen thought Carl saw them in Kathleen's shop that night."

"That certainly would be the simplest explanation."

"You're right. It would be. But as I told Abigail, I have a gut feeling Carl's murder is more involved than that."

"I'd like to muddy the waters a little more with a theory I have," Jack said.

Alex smiled. "Sure, go ahead. What's a little more mud at this point?"

"This might be far-fetched, and you've probably thought of this, but what if the two deaths aren't connected. What if someone thought it was the perfect opportunity to get rid of Carl? What if someone hated Carl so much that they killed him betting you'd think exactly what you are thinking, that the same person committed both murders?"

"I have to admit that scenario hadn't crossed my mind. Damn it, Jack, could I be so focused on the same person doing both killings that I've missed the obvious?"

"I don't know. You've had a lot more experience with this type of situation than I have. It's just that lately Carl has managed to piss off a lot of people, and maybe one of them decided to get rid of him."

"And some of them happened to be in Flapjacks that night. Jack, you've given me something to think about. Even so, whether there's one murderer or two, right now I need to follow up on the digoxin lead."

Jack nodded. "I agree. The digoxin is probably your best bet."

"Now on to stickier matters. Can you reveal the names of your patients who take digoxin?"

"No."

"That's it, just no? I know about patient-doctor confidentiality, but can't there be an exception if there's a murder involved?"

"No!"

"For god's sake, Jack, can't you say anything besides 'no'? You may have the information which could lead me to a killer."

Jack exhaled a long breath before he replied. "I've been thinking about nothing else since I got home last night. I'm sorry, but not only legally, morally my hands are tied. Wait a minute," Jack said cutting off Alex's next retort. "Like I said, I've been thinking this over for most of the night, and I have an idea which may be of some help."

"Okay, I'm listening."

"First, I can tell you I only have a few patients who are taking digitalis, and I honestly don't think any of them is your murderer. Also, remember, I'm not the physician for everyone in Newcomsville."

Alex nodded. "Good point. Go on."

"Who knows for certain digoxin was used?"

"Not many. Only you, me, Abigail, and Louis are aware of the test results. There are a few more that only know you suspect he was drugged. I'm not sure exactly what Samantha and Pauline were told, but why does it matter?"

"When I went to Samantha's last night, after Pauline called, I didn't tell them any more than Charles had, that Carl had been found dead, and we wouldn't know any more until Louis called with his report. So I was thinking, if people hear that some kind of drug was given to Carl, but not exactly what type, you may be able to find out who knows of a friend, or may have indirectly heard of someone, who takes digoxin. I know this may be unorthodox, but I can't think of another way for you to get the information. I think speculation on Carl's death will be the number one topic of conversation all day."

Alex nodded again. "The problem is who would think of digoxin as being something that could kill? It will be opioids such as oxycontin, percodan, percocet and vicodin that come to people's minds."

Jack rubbed his chin. "You're right. Digoxin is known as a heart medication. I would imagine not many people know it can cause death if given to someone who doesn't have heart trouble."

Alex thoughtfully sipped his coffee. "Why don't we just tell the truth — that Carl was given an overdose of Digoxin — and see what comes of it. We may get more information that way."

"Good point. Someone might know somebody who takes the drug and come forward." Jack smiled. "From what I hear from Claire, there's more town information shared at Carolyn's spa than you'd find on the evening news."

Alex laughed. "I believe that. In fact, Carolyn and Grant were at the house when I arrived home last night. They both knew Carl might have been drugged. I think I'll recruit Abigail and Carolyn to see what they can learn about our neighbors."

"Maybe you should tell the girls to use the word digitalis," Jack suggested. "It's a more familiar term than digoxin."

With a grunt of pain, Alex got to his feet. "I'll let you know how our little plan works."

Jack also stood. "Give me a minute and I'll write you that prescription. Alex, I'm really sorry I can't be more help."

"I appreciate you trying, and I understand your position. Now I think I'll call Abigail and see if I can get the tongues wagging."

As he entered the living room, Claire asked, "Alex, how's Granny Jo? She must be so upset that the murderer put drugs in her chili."

"She was pretty angry last night, but she's a tough old girl. She'll be just fine. In fact, she told me she was so busy yesterday she was able to sell quite a number of tour tickets."

Claire laughed. "Is that right? Well, good for her. Who knows, after all of this gets out, Flapjacks may end up being top in ticket sales."

Before Alex could reach the door, his cell phone rang. "It's Abigail. She must have known I wanted to talk to her."

"Female intuition," Claire said. "Tell Abigail I'll see her later. I'm having lunch with Victoria. She wants a Christmas tour update before our committee meeting. Now I'd better get Jack moving. His first patient will be here, and he'll still be in his pajamas."

***

"Hi, Hon."

"Alex, I'm glad I caught you. Carolyn called, and she'd like you to stop by her place as soon as you can. Where are you now?"

"I'm at Jack's. Did Carolyn say why?"

"It has to do with her reservation book."

"Is she at Indulgence now?"

"Yes, but she said for you to go around back to her private entrance. Grant will meet you upstairs in the loft. Carolyn will join you as soon as she can."

"Okay, I'll head over there now. Abigail, I need you to try and do some investigating for me."

"Sure, what do you want me to do?"

"I'd like you to discretely find out who in town is on heart medication."

201

"So Jack wasn't able to tell you anything?"

"He helped as much as he could. I really want you to be discreet with this. The town is going to be talking about nothing but Carl's death and speculating on what might have killed him. I'd like you to mention digitalis as a possibility. Do you think you can do that?"

"Do you honestly think the murderer is going to admit they take digitalis?"

"I'm hoping someone else will mention names. I know this sounds pretty iffy, but what do I have to lose? Just sound as casual as possible when you mention digitalis."

"This may be easier than you think," she said with reassurance. "Is it alright if I say the drug was put into the chili?"

"That's fine. I suppose half of the town already knows. I'm also going to recruit Carolyn for this fishing expedition."

"That's a great idea. Indulgence is the perfect place for town gossip."

Alex smiled to himself. "That's what I understand. Okay, I'm heading there now. See you later. Good luck."

"Here you go," Claire said, handing Alex the prescription. "Jack said to let him know if this doesn't help."

"Thanks, I'll do that." As Alex stepped out onto the Monroe's front porch, he barely missed tripping over the Newcomsville News lying on the doormat.

"Newcomsville Embezzler Latest Murder Victim?" was the bold headline.

"Damn it to hell, GH" Alex said through clenched teeth as he picked up the paper and began to read the front page.

Newcomsville Embezzler Latest Murder Victim?
By GH Greeley

Carl Edwards, president of the Newcomsville Bank & Trust was found dead in his jail cell at the town hall last night. Did Mr. Edwards die of natural causes or was it foul play?

Mr. Edwards was being held as a material witness in the Kathleen Cooper murder.

This reporter recently discovered that Mr. Edward's fingerprint was found on Kathleen Cooper's back doorknob the day after her body was found in her shop window.

And that's not all. Our illustrious bank President had been caught embezzling the life savings of Newcomsville's own citizens. Was Kathleen killed because she found out about Carl's dirty little secret? If so, who killed Carl?

According to bank owner Henry Butterfield, Mr. Edwards still had the majority of our money residing in a Caribbean bank and graciously returned it. Mr. Butterfield decided not to press charges since the money has been returned on condition Mr. Edwards leave our village permanently.

Well, Mr. Edwards has left alright, but not in the way Mr. Butterfield or Chief Mackenzie might have preferred.

All Chief Mackenzie would say last night is that the death definitely wasn't suicide, and he was waiting for the coroner's report.

So does a healthy forty-something man just keel over dead, or did someone help him along? Was Mr. Edwards just in the wrong place at the wrong time? Could the murderer have seen Mr. Edwards at Kathleen's back door? Could the murderer have thought Mr. Edwards saw them? Did Mr. Edwards see the murderer?

This reporter has a hard time believing that someone being held for questioning on a murder charge coincidently dies of natural causes. Was Mr. Edwards, in fear of his own life, about to point his finger at Kathleen Cooper's murderer?

If so, how did the murderer get past the watchful eyes of Charles and Agatha Butterfield who Chief Mackenzie had deputized to keep an eye on Carl? We hope to soon have the answers to these questions.

Police Chief Mackenzie promises to give a full report as soon as Coroner Louis Tate completes the autopsy.

Until then, there is still a murderer at large in our idyllic little town. Stay alert.

"GH certainly has a colorful way with words, doesn't he?"

Alex looked up to see Pauline Silverspoon standing next to him. Frowning, he refolded the paper and laid it back on the mat. "Oh, GH has a way with words alright. Has Henry seen this?"

Pauline nodded. "Victoria called me this morning to see how Samantha was doing. She said Charles was outraged with GH for implying he and Agatha were lax in their duties, but Henry didn't think it was any worse than expected."

"I guess Henry's right. I just wish GH wouldn't write about murderers running loose around town. How's Samantha doing? I planned on stopping by later to talk with her."

"Actually, she's doing much better this morning. The shock has finally worn off. Henrietta and I have her staying with us. I thought it would be for the best to get her out of that house. I wanted to see if Jack would write a prescription for a mild sedative in case she has trouble sleeping."

"Samantha certainly has had a lot to deal with lately. I hope she'll make it through okay."

"She's stronger than one would think. She's beginning the funeral arrangements today. Not only that, she's insisting on still having her house on the Christmas tour. I understand that 'Sylvia-person' called Samantha to ask if under the circumstances she'd like to cancel the decorating. According to Samantha, it was she who had to convince Sylvia to stay in town and finish the job. They're meeting later this afternoon. Though I find myself agreeing with Sylvia. Samantha has enough to deal with without worrying about a house tour. I told her I was sure Claire would understand if she dropped out. On the other hand, perhaps decorating her house is the distraction she needs right now."

Alex's brows rose. "So Miss Schmuckler isn't as enamored with our little town as she thought she was."

"I can't say I blame her for wanting to go home. I don't know how long I'd stay in a town where there were two murders in less than a week."

Alex sighed. "I know. Hopefully I'll have all of this cleared up soon."

"I'm not blaming you. I know you're doing your best," Pauline said giving him a reassuring smile. "Have you heard from Louis Tate yet?"

"He called me early this morning. In fact, that's why I'm here. I wanted to discuss the outcome of the autopsy with Jack. All I can tell you is that the drug that killed Carl was definitely put in the chili Agatha brought from Flapjacks."

She grimaced. "That's dreadful, but honestly I can't say I'm surprised. Considering his lifestyle of late, some kind of tragedy was bound to happen, but I didn't expect this. There wasn't any love lost between Carl and me. As hard as I tried, I couldn't like him. Ethan kept telling me there was good in him, and he just needed a chance to show it. Now I don't say this very often, but I'm glad Ethan isn't here. He didn't at all like to be proven wrong," she said with a wistful smile. "I would like to think for Samantha's sake that at one time there was good in Carl. I can't help but think the so-called Silverspoon money was always in the back of his mind, although I would never say that to Samantha. For god knows what reason, she loved the man."

Alex smiled. "One never knows where our emotions will lead us. Well, I'm off." He cautiously eased himself down the steps. "I'll probably see you later."

"Oh, by the way, Alex, I understand the young man buying my house is a friend of yours. Samantha was meeting with him this morning to finalize the sale."

"His name is Grant Cummings, and he's a really nice guy. I think he'll be a great addition to the community."

"I also understand he'll be our new bank president."

"Yeah. He can't believe how perfectly everything has worked out for him here. And I'm sure we won't have to worry about Grant running off with the town's money. You'll have to call Abigail. She'd love to fill you in on the details."

"I will. You take care of yourself."

When Alex arrived at Indulgence, he slowly climbed the exterior back stairs to Carolyn's loft apartment.

"Come on in," Grant said opening the door to Alex's knock. "I'll call down and let Carolyn know you're here. She's been biting at the bit to talk to you since last night. She's hoping the names she found in her appointment book will help. Have a seat and help yourself to coffee, and there are some sweet rolls."

While sipping his coffee in the contemporary kitchen/dining room, Alex appreciated the stylish simplicity of the open loft with its tall bay windows overlooking Main Street. The cozy living room, with its soft buttery leather circular sofa, matching armchairs, and smoked glass coffee table set on a colorful Oriental rug, faced a raised brick fireplace. Down a hall to his right, Alex knew there was a snug little den with floor-to-ceiling bookcases and an entertainment center that made him green with envy every time he saw it. The master bedroom and adjoining luxury bath completed the loft's striking transformation.

"Carolyn will be right up," Grant said. "Alex, I can't thank you enough for asking me to come for Thanksgiving. I now have Carolyn, a great new job, a fantastic house, and I feel my life may finally be heading in the right direction."

"That's all well and good thanking him for bringing you to town," Carolyn said coming up behind the two men. "As for your imminent pleasure and impending happiness, well, handsome, I think that's where I take over." Smiling, she reached up and kissed Grant's blushing cheek.

Alex chuckled. "I'm sure he's in capable hands. Now, before Grant's face gets any redder, maybe you should tell me about your appointment book."

"I have it right here," she said eagerly opening her book to the correct page. "And wait until you see who was at Indulgence yesterday." She handed him the reservation book. "Here's the sheet listing all of our walk-in clients as well."

Alex scanned the lists. "Could I have a sheet of paper? I'd like to jot down some of these names."

"Sure. Here you go." She handed him a notepad. "I was surprised at some of the people on this list who I don't recall seeing. Usually if they're a regular, they stop by the coffee bar and at least say hello."

"Really, who didn't stop?"

"Let me see. There's Peggy and Meg, but Abigail said she remembered seeing them. Also Henrietta. Now that one really surprises me. She always stops on her way out and has a cup of tea. As for Nan Katz, well, it depends on her mood that day whether she deigns to speak to me."

"What interests me the most is the number of names who also happened to be at Flapjacks last night." He hesitated. "I don't see

Ben's name on the list. I'm sure Agatha told me she saw him sitting at the coffee bar."

Carolyn frowned. "Ben? I don't recall. Oh, wait a minute." Her face cleared. "Yes, he did stop by. We close at six on Mondays, and it was a little before that when he came in and had a glass of wine."

"Do you recall what you talked about?" Alex asked.

"I told him about Grant's new job at the bank. I was telling everyone I could," she said smiling at Grant. "And I'm pretty sure we talked about Carl being in jail and speculating why."

Alex, watching her closely, saw the muscles in her face grow taught and what looked like fear cloud her eyes. "Carolyn, what is it? Did you remember something having to do with Ben?" When she hesitated, he gently coaxed. "I know how close you and Ben are, but this is important. I need to know any information you have."

"But it may mean nothing, and I'll have dragged Ben into this for no reason."

"I sympathize, but any little thing could be important. You have to trust me to judge its significance."

Carolyn silently turned to Grant and he nodded. "You can trust Alex to keep an open mind."

She let out a long breath. "Damn, I hate this, but here goes. I was telling Ben about Grant's new job, and I told him we were driving into the city to celebrate. He asked where we were planning on eating. Since the inn was closed, he and Sam were also going out so maybe they could join us. I told him I thought that would be fine with you and Abigail. He said he'd let me know. Then just before Grant picked me up, he called and said Sam had been working on decorating the inn all day and was too tired."

Alex sighed. "And they ended up at Flapjacks. By any chance did you two talk about Agatha's plan to bring Carl his dinner that night?" Alex shook his head. "You don't need to say any more. The answer is written all over your face."

"Now what?" Grant asked.

"I need to find out why they changed their dinner plans."

"It could be just as Ben said," Carolyn added. "I know they've both been working like crazy to finish decorating. You know what perfectionists they both are. It's possible Sam really was just tired. Besides, Alex, why would either one of them want Carl dead?"

Thinking they may have been seen by Carl in Kathleen's shop the night she was murdered would be a damn good motive, Alex thought. Aloud he said, "Yes, it could be as innocent as Sam being worn out, but I'll still have to question them."

Tears filled Carolyn's eyes. "Ben's going to know I was the one who told you, and he'll probably never speak to me again."

"Oh, baby, that's not true," Grant said folding her into his arms. "Ben will understand. He knows Alex has a job to do, and questioning all of us is part of that job. Now stop crying. You can't have your customers downstairs see you with a blotchy face, can you?"

"Carolyn, I'm sorry. I didn't mean to upset you."

She gave Alex a slight smile. "It's alright. As Grant said, you have a job to do."

"If you don't mind, I have more questions in regards to this reservation list."

"Sure, just give me a minute to fix my face."

"Buddy, I don't envy you your job in the least," Grant said when the bathroom door closed behind Carolyn.

Alex snorted. "Tell me about it. When I left the county sheriff's office, I have to admit I sure as hell didn't anticipate anything like this. To be honest with you, I felt I had fallen into a pretty cushy job. Now I have to go around antagonizing my neighbors. But I am determined to find out who committed these murders and put them in jail for the rest of their life."

Grant smiled. "I hear you."

"Okay, I have myself back together," Carolyn said rejoining them. "So ask me anything. I promise no more hysterics."

Alex turned the reservation list so she could see it. "Are the letters next to the customer's name some kind of abbreviations?"

Carolyn nodded. "First is the name of the person who provides the service, the code is what type of service the client wants. Such as PC for pedicure, MC for manicure, and SCC would be style cut and color. See what I mean."

"Okay, what does FBM stand for?"

"Full body massage."

"So if someone was coming in to have more than one service, the code for each one would be listed?"

"Yes, what are you thinking? You have a funny look on your face."

"I'm not sure. There's something I should be remembering," Alex said studying the list of names and service codes. He sighed. "Hopefully I'll remember what I'm trying to remember. Carolyn, I really appreciate all of your help. Now I'd like to talk to you about doing a little undercover assignment for me if you're interested."

"Of course I'm interested. What do you want me to do?"

Alex explained about the digitalis/digoxin in the chili and the plan to have her and Abigail keep the Newcomsville gossips humming with speculation. "I know this is a long shot, but somebody may remember someone taking digitalis and put two and two together."

"If I had to guess, I'd assume the fact the drug was put in the chili at Granny Jo's is going to become common knowledge." Carolyn said.

"As I told Abigail, I'm sure that fact has already made its way all over town."

"So you do want me to mention digitalis?"

"Yes, but just casually mention it as a possibility. You could say you've heard that if digitalis is given to someone who doesn't need the drug, it can be deadly, or something like that."

"And if I come up with anything, what should I do?"

"You call me. Under no circumstances are you or my lovely wife to go investigating on your own. I'm serious. This person has murdered two people, and I'm sure if they feel trapped, they'll kill again."

Grant turned Carolyn to face him. "I want you to listen to Alex. It's one thing to try and discretely gather information. It's quite another to go snooping around on your own. I don't want to be worried about what you're getting up to while I'm gone."

"I promise I'll be careful and let Alex know if I learn anything. But wouldn't it be exciting if I'm the one who discovers who the murderer is?"

Grant narrowed his eyes. "Carolyn."

She kissed his cheek. "I'll do as Alex says. Now I'd better get downstairs and get this in motion."

"Do you have my cell number?" Alex asked, getting off the barstool. "Damn."

"Alex, what's wrong?" Carolyn hurried around the counter to help.

"It's my back. I fell asleep in my desk chair last night, and this is how I woke up. Jack gave me a prescription, but I haven't had it filled yet."

"Come downstairs with me," Carolyn said. "I'll see if my masseuse, Burt, has an opening. A good massage is exactly what you need."

"Thanks, but I have too much to do to waste time getting a massage."

"Don't be silly. I'll find out if he has an opening. It will only take an hour, and won't it be worth it if you can move without pain?"

"Buddy, you might as well give in," Grant said. "She's not going to give up."

"Okay, thanks," Carolyn said as she hung up the phone. "Alex, Burt is booked until 4:30, but he can take you then. So I told them to write you in."

Alex sighed with resignation. "I'll see how I'm doing later on and let you know." He turned to Grant. "You have a safe trip to Pittsburgh. Abigail and I are really looking forward to having you here permanently. I'm sure Henry is in a hurry for you to come back as well. Who's going to be running the bank during your absence?"

"Barb Winters is willing to take charge temporarily. If everything goes according to plan, I'll be back in two weeks."

"Sounds good, and with any luck, you'll be coming back to a murder-free town."

When Alex turned the Bronco onto Main Street, he noticed Charles was parked outside the Apothecary Shop. Its window display of unique glass bottles combines a modern pharmacy with old time charm. Alex decided to stop and get his prescription filled. He pulled in behind the classic Packard.

"Good morning," Charles said as Alex walked up to the car. "Have you seen today's GH special edition?" Not waiting for Alex to reply, an agitated Charles continued, "I find myself extremely vexed at the insinuation that if I'd been on my toes, the murderer wouldn't have been able to slip Carl's drugged chili past me." Barely stopping for a breath, he went on, "Now, Alex, I feel GH has been quite unjust. How would he expect me to know someone had deliberately injected something into Carl's food?"

"Charles, I wouldn't be too concerned with what GH writes," Alex replied. "Once the town learns how the chili was tampered with, no one is going to fault you."

"I sincerely hope you're correct. Actually, after reading the article, father expressed the same opinion. May I inquire if you've received the coroner's report?"

"Yes, Louis called me this morning. The drug was definitely put in the chili."

"After reviewing all of last night's events, Aggie and I came to the conclusion that Jack's surmise of the situation had to be correct. May I assume Jack's hypothesis on the type of drug used was also correct?"

Alex nodded.

"I have to tell you, Aggie has been cogitating over her time in Granny Jo's last evening. Unfortunately, she hasn't remembered any additional information, but she's not giving up. Please don't become disheartened. With your untiring vigilance it won't be long until you have a satisfactory conclusion to this case, just as in Agatha Christie's 'Appointment With Death'. Although in that particular case, it was the leaves of the foxglove which were used. Just remember to fully employ your little gray cells."

Before an amused Alex could think of a reply, Agatha came out of the Apothecary Shop carrying a small prescription bag.

"Howdy-doo, Alex," she said in greeting as she approached the passenger side of their car. "Would you join us for brunch? Chucky and I are on our way to Flapjacks. I'd like to reassure Granny Jo that no one is going to blame her for Carl's death."

"Thanks, Agatha, but I'll have to pass. I need to get to my office. But I'm glad you're going to see Jo. She was pretty upset when I left her last night."

"The poor old dear," Agatha said getting into the car. "We'll do our best to cheer her up."

"You know, Aggie, perhaps returning to the scene of the crime is all you need to make a hidden memory come back," Charles said.

"Alex, we'll keep you informed of any new developments." With a hearty wave, Charles gunned the Packard and sped off.

A few minutes later, Alex left the Apothecary Shop prescription in hand. Glancing at his watch, seeing it was still too early for the lunch crowd, he decided to walk the short distance to the inn and ask Sam and Ben about their change of plans the night before.

Alex found Ben stringing fresh garland and hanging antique brass lanterns around the inn's front porch. Wreaths adorned with pine cones, holly berries, and elaborately tied green and red plaid bows hung in all of the windows with the soft light of Christmas candles glowing behind them.

"Hey, Ben, the inn looks great," Alex called, approaching the porch steps. "You've put my decorating to shame. I'm going to be in trouble when Abigail sees this. She'll want me to do more to the outside of our house next year."

Ben smiled. "Hey, no problem. Sam and I will help you out. We charge by the hour."

Alex smiled back. "I appreciate that, but the town of Newcomsville doesn't pay me enough to hire you two. I hate to interrupt your work, but I need to talk to you and Sam. Can you take a short break?"

"Sure, what's up?"

"Can we go in and talk. I need to sit down."

"No problem, but why are you walking like you have a stick up your…"

Alex rolled his eyes, then explained. "Jack gave me some pills which I'm about to take. Hopefully they'll work."

"Well, come on in. Are you hungry? Sam's making roast beef hot shots for lunch."

Alex nodded. "Sure, that sounds great. A cup of coffee also sounds good. I suppose you two have heard about Carl's death?"

"How could we not have," Sam replied. "Thanks to GH, it's all over town."

"What the hell happened?" Ben asked. "We heard a crazy story about someone poisoning the chili Carl got from Flapjacks."

"Who told you that?" Alex asked.

"This morning when I went to the post office, Molly said she went to Flapjacks for breakfast, and Granny Jo told her something was put in the chili. Molly said Jo is really worked up over this. Molly asked for French toast, and Jo gave her pancakes," Ben said.

Alex sighed. "Unfortunately it's true. During the crush at Granny Jo's, someone managed to slip something into the bowl Agatha was to take to Carl."

Sam frowned. "How would they have known Agatha was taking Carl the chili?"

"From what I've learned, there were a number of people who by one means or another had become aware of this."

"Are you thinking the same person who murdered Kathleen also killed Carl?" Ben asked. "Could one of GH's theories be right?"

"I definitely think the same person murdered both people. As for GH's theories, well, I'd rather not speculate on those."

Ben cocked his head and smiled. "I'll bet GH is right. Kathleen was blackmailing Carl for embezzling. And that's why you were holding Carl. Come on, Alex, tell me I'm right."

Alex finished his coffee and with mild irritation pushed the cup aside. "Yes, Kathleen had been blackmailing Carl, and, yes, Carl was being held for questioning in Kathleen's death, but considering that he's now dead, it's unlikely he was her murderer. Now if I've cleared that up to your satisfaction, I'd like to get on with why I wanted to talk to both of you."

"Sure thing. We're all ears," Ben replied.

"I understand you were both at Flapjacks having dinner last night."

"That's true," Sam said. "When we walked in, we saw Tom and Judy who had just gotten a table, and they asked us to join them."

"The bowl of chili was sitting on the counter where there aren't any bar stools, near the short hall to the restrooms and kitchen," Alex explained. "Did either of you see the bowl, or see anyone around it?"

"I went to the restroom and poked my head into the kitchen to speak to Jo," Sam stated. "But I didn't pay any attention to a bowl of chili."

"How about you, Ben?" Alex asked.

Ben shook his head. "I didn't leave the table. Tom, Judy, and I were too busy watching that hag Nan Katz going off on Samantha. I couldn't hear what she was saying, but Nan was right in Samantha's face. Carl was a real ass, but it's too bad someone didn't give Nan the chili instead."

Sam gave Ben a reproachful look. "I don't think this is the time to be joking about killing people."

With a 'whatever' shrug, Ben lit a cigarette and waited for Alex to continue.

"I agree," Alex said. "Ben, was Samantha alone at the table when Nan approached her?"

"Yes, she was. Earlier I saw her sitting with Sylvia, and at one point I saw Agatha talking to them both."

"Did you see Agatha come in? And did you hear Jo ask the waitress to get Carl's chili ready?"

Ben grinned. "I saw her come in. She's kind of hard to miss. But after that I didn't pay a lot of attention until I saw Nan with Samantha."

"Did Tom or Judy leave the table at any time?"

"Oh, come on, Alex," Sam said. "You can't seriously suspect Tom or Judy."

Alex's mouth tightened into a thin line. "I don't know who messed with the chili, but somebody in Flapjacks sure as hell did and I need to know as much about people's movements as I possibly can. So, did Tom or Judy leave the table?"

Ben angrily stubbed out his cigarette. "Judy did. I suppose she went to the ladies' room and, no, I didn't see her put anything in Carl's chili."

Alex ignored Ben's sarcasm and asked, "Carolyn said you two were going to join us for dinner in the city last night to celebrate Grant's new job. What happened?"

Sam gave Ben a sideways look before saying, "It was a personal matter between Ben and me. It had nothing to do with not wanting to celebrate with you guys."

"That's right," Ben spoke up. "We think Grant getting the bank president's job is terrific. Although if the poor guy doesn't watch it, Carolyn will have him walking down the aisle before he knows what hit him."

Alex chuckled. "That's what I'm afraid of. I hope they have enough sense to take it slow, although I haven't seen Grant this happy in years."

Ben grinned back. "Oh, I think Carolyn is keeping him real happy. I just hope he has the stamina to keep up."

Sam rolled his eyes. "Okay, guys, I need to finish my lunch preparations. Alex, is there anything else you'd like to ask?"

"No, that will do for now. Thanks for lunch." Alex rose from the barstool. "If you remember anything, please let me know."

"I'll walk you out," Ben said. "Hey, you seem to be moving better. Maybe the pills are working."

"I hope so. It's kind of hard to conduct an investigation when you can hardly walk."

Ben stopped at the foot of the staircase in the entry hall. "About last night, Alex. Well, you know, Sam likes to keep our personal life private. So he didn't want to tell you about, ah...well, the little disagreement we had. You see, I came back home all hyped to join you for dinner, but Sam had been decorating in here all day and was tired. One thing led to another, and we just ended up going to Flapjacks. It was as simple as that."

Alex nodded. "Thanks again for lunch."

"Hey, Alex, wait a minute," Ben called. "You didn't tell us what was put in the chili."

"I didn't, did I." As Alex headed back to his Bronco, he saw Nan Katz marching down the sidewalk towards him brandishing a newspaper.

"Well, there you are, Chief Mackenzie." She stopped in front of him waving the paper in his face. "I see there's been another one. I demand to know what you're doing about these murders. First, poor Kathleen. Now that drunkard Carl Edwards has been killed right under your nose. Is anyone safe in this town? You know I had dinner at Jo's last night. I could have been the one who ate the toxic chili. And where do I find you? Instead of being out doing the job the residents of Newcomsville pay you to do — which, in case you've forgotten, happens to be looking for this insane person who's going around town killing people — I find you coming out of that heathen bar, and it's not even noon. It wouldn't surprise me in the least if it turns out one of those sickos is the murderer. We all know how they felt about poor Kathleen."

Gritting his teeth in an effort to keep his anger under control, Alex unceremoniously grabbed the paper out of Nan's hand causing her diatribe to stop mid-sentence. His temper somewhat in check, he said, "Nan, I assure you I'm doing the job I was hired to do. So unless you witnessed something useful last night which will help me do that job, I suggest you keep your opinions to yourself, and let me get on with it." With effort, Alex waited to see if by chance she did have something to tell him. He watched as her pinched face turned brick red with anger, and she snapped her thin mouth shut.

"Well, I've never," she spat before turning away.

I'll bet you haven't, Alex thought watching her stomp off. *And that's probably half your problem.*

"Having a pleasant morning are you?"

Alex looked up to see Judy Scraper smiling at him from the doorway of Yesteryears Antiques. "I have a feeling I'm not going to get her vote next election."

She laughed. "I think you're right, but you'll certainly get mine. I didn't mean to eavesdrop. I heard shouting and came out to see what was going on. Alex, she deserved everything you said."

"I suppose, but it wasn't very professional of me. I just hope she's not so pissed that she won't pass on useful information."

"Are you kidding? If Nan Katz knew anything she thought would be important, she'd crawl on her hands and knees to be the first one to tell you."

"Abigail says she doesn't miss a trick."

"And she's exactly right. By the way, speaking of Abigail..." Judy gave him a wide smile. "Have you bought her Christmas present yet?"

"No. Why?"

"Well, then, follow me. I just happen to know of something she'd love to have."

A half-hour later, Alex, left Yesteryears carrying a beautifully wrapped Baccarat vase under his arm.

Murder may pass unpunish'd for a time,
but tardy justice will o'ertake the crime.
                    - John Dryden, The Cock and the Fox

13

In the Tearoom kitchen lunch preparation was underway. Abigail had recounted the night's events to Beatrice and Peg.

"I just knew Carl Edwards would come to a bad end," Beatrice said. "And poor Josephine. Imagine someone putting drugs in her chili. She must be torn all to pieces. As soon as I can, I'm going to call and see how she's doing."

"My god, Bob and I were there last night with the kids," Peg said. "The murderer could have been sitting right next to us. It was awful when Kathleen was killed, but somehow that's different from having dinner with a murderer."

"I know," Beatrice said. "But Alex is going to find out who's been doing these terrible things, and then everything can get back to normal." She shook her head. "That's if you call this town normal."

"Isn't that the truth," Abigail said. "I'd better go unlock the front door. It's almost eleven." She pushed through the swinging kitchen door and walked down the central hall thinking about how to bring up different drugs with her customers. She had hoped to be able to talk more about it with Peg and Beatrice, but that would have to wait. Lost in thought, she opened the front door and jumped in surprise.

"Goodness, Claire, you startled me. Are you early, or am I late?"

"Sorry," Claire said stepping into the entry hall. "You don't have the time wrong. I was hoping to talk to you before my lunch with Victoria. Do you have a minute?"

"Sure. Everything is under control. Let's talk in the tearoom. Beatrice, Peg and I were just discussing Carl. Unfortunately Peg, Bob, and the girls had dinner in Flapjacks last night.

"I would imagine quite a few people are a bit unnerved by the thought of having eaten where someone was drugging the food."

"It gives me shivers just thinking about it. Can I get you a cup of coffee or something?" Abigail asked as they sat down on a wicker settee.

"No thanks, I'm fine. I just wanted to talk to you about Carl's death. I couldn't get any more information out of Jack except that a drug was put in Carl's chili, and I was wondering what you knew."

Considering how much she should tell her friend, Abigail hesitated. "Well..."

Claire smiled. "Come on, Abigail, you know that anything you tell me will go no further."

Deciding Claire could be helpful ferreting out who might take digitalis, Abigail told her the entire story. "So Alex wants us to discretely see if we can get any information on who may be taking the drug."

"Hmm, let's see," Claire said. "I know of two people who take digitalis, but I can't imagine either one of them as a murderer."

"Really, who's that?"

"Pauline Silverspoon and Victoria Butterfield."

"What?" Abigail exclaimed.

"Yes, it's true. Both of them take it."

"But Claire, neither one was in Flapjacks last night."

"No, but both Agatha and Henrietta were."

"Claire! You don't really believe either of them had anything to do with this. Do you?"

"It's far-fetched, but they both really disliked Carl."

"But what about Kathleen?" Abigail asked. "What motive would Agatha or Henrietta have for killing her?"

"As for Kathleen, her constant ridiculing of Samantha was a definite sore spot for Henrietta. And what if Agatha just took this opportunity to get rid of Carl? Maybe Alex is wrong, and the murders aren't connected."

"*Claire.*"

"Oh, I know, Abigail. It really is too outlandish. And I do like both Agatha and Henrietta, but it's pretty obvious someone in Flapjacks had to have done the deed, and they both were there."

"Oh, my god," Abigail exclaimed. "They were both there!"

"Who was where?"

"Agatha and Henrietta were both in Indulgence yesterday."

"And the importance of this is...?"

"The murderer had to have known Agatha's plan to pick up Carl's dinner from Flapjacks. Remember we were all sitting at the coffee bar talking about it."

"Are you sure Henrietta was there? I didn't see her."

"She was waiting to get her hair done when I left."

Abigail shook her head. "I don't see how we can even consider Agatha as a suspect. She'd be pretty stupid to drug Carl when she was the one Alex asked to pick up the chili. Besides, if anyone had taken some of Victoria's or Pauline's digitalis, wouldn't they have noticed?"

"Not necessarily. Maybe it wouldn't take much to kill someone who didn't need the drug."

"I can't picture either of them being a killer. But, Claire, you have an interesting point. It doesn't have to be the killer who uses the drug. They could have stolen it from someone they know."

Claire nodded. "And doesn't that open another can of worms?"

"It certainly does." Abigail frowned. "I'll mention it to Alex and see what he thinks. Even so, we still need to find out who's taking the drug, and who has access to it." Before Abigail could continue, Peg interrupted.

"Hi, Claire. Sorry to interrupt but the dining room is starting to fill up."

"Thanks, Peg. I'll be right there."

"I'll keep my eyes and ears open dend see if I can get anything useful out of Victoria during lunch, but I'm not sure how to go about asking if she happens to be missing any digitalis." Claire smiled and got to her feet. "We also have our last tour meeting this afternoon.

Who knows what may come out of that. Are you sure you don't mind having the meeting here?"

"No, that's fine. We'll meet upstairs, and if we get together around three o'clock, that should work for me."

"Hopefully it will be a quick meeting." Claire grimaced. "That's if Nan isn't on some kind of rampage. I still can't figure out how that woman managed to get on this committee."

Abigail laughed. "Doesn't she make sure she's on every committee? I don't think anyone has the nerve to tell her no. Have a good lunch, and I'll see you later."

Claire had no sooner sat down at a linen-covered table in the dining room than Victoria walked in.

"Good afternoon," Victoria said taking a seat across from Claire.

"Good afternoon. Or is it?" Claire frowned, seeing the agitation on the older woman's face. "Are you alright?"

Victoria gave a dismissive wave. "Oh, yes. It's this loathsome business with Carl Edwards. I don't mean to sound callous, but I won't be hypocritical either. I just hope Alex can sort this out before the tour. All we need is to have another dead body turning up in the middle of the dessert."

Claire smiled. "Other than dead bodies, all of the tour preparations seem to be going along just fine. At last count we've sold four hundred and eighty tickets, and, from what I understand, over the last few days it's been Granny Jo who has sold the most."

"That poor woman. I can't imagine how distressing all of this must be. Agatha and Charles were in Flapjacks this morning and said Josephine was overwrought."

"I can imagine," Claire said. "The murderer had to be pretty desperate to take a chance like that. I mean, anyone in there could have seen them put the drug in the chili. Talk about brazen."

"Oh, well, it's obvious this person has to be quite insane," Victoria said. "I find it extremely unsettling to think someone that deranged is living amongst us."

"They say poison is a woman's weapon. I wonder if that's true?"

"I have no idea," Victoria said with disdain. "I wouldn't have a clue how to go about obtaining drugs to kill someone."

"Hello, ladies," Peg said with a smile. "Are you ready to order lunch?"

"Good afternoon, Peg," Victoria replied, the disdain still clear on her face. "I'm sorry, we've been discussing this latest nasty business and haven't had an opportunity to look at the menu."

"It is horrible, isn't it? Bob, the kids, and I were in Flapjacks last night. It makes me ill to think we were sitting having a nice dinner while someone was tampering with Carl's food."

Victoria frowned. "I must say the information I received was rather vague. I understand the diner was busy, but how a bowl of chili could sit unattended without Josephine's notice is beyond me."

"Roberta's niece was helping Jo out because Roberta sprained her ankle skating," Claire replied. "Sissy had no experience waiting tables. I guess Jo told Sissy to get the chili ready, and what happened with the chili after that seems to be the mystery."

Peg narrowed her brows. "I've been thinking about that. I'm sure I saw that bowl sitting there, but at the time I didn't think anything about it. I was in the 'ladies' with Agatha and Judy helping remove a stain from Agatha's skirt. When we came out, Agatha stopped at the counter and asked Jo about the chili. Now I realize that had to have been the deadly bowl of chili."

"Did you happen to see anyone else coming in or out of either of the bathrooms?" Claire asked.

"Just Bob coming out of the men's room," Peg said with a laugh. "I swear that man can't eat anything without spilling some of it on his shirt. Now, ladies, I hope all of this talk about drugged food hasn't ruined your appetite."

"Well, I must say, it will probably be quite some time before I feel compelled to eat chili," Victoria said with a grimace. "So please don't tell me that's the special."

Peg smiled. "You're safe. We have beef stew and biscuits, or if you'd like something lighter, we have ham and cheese quiche with a salad."

"I'll have the quiche and salad," Victoria replied.

"Make that two," Claire said. "And a glass of white wine as well."

"How about you, Victoria?" Peg asked.

"Yes, I believe I will. Considering how this day began, wine is definitely called for." "I saw Pauline," Claire said after Peg left. "She said Samantha is holding up fairly well. I thought perhaps she'd rather not do the tour, but Pauline said she was determined to go on."

Virginia nodded. "I had the same thought. It seems hiring that decorator is turning out to be a godsend."

Claire smiled. "Isn't that the truth."

"Here's your wine, ladies," Abigail said. "Peg will bring your lunch shortly."

"Thank you," Victoria said. "You seem to have a large lunch crowd this afternoon."

"I think the news about Carl's murder must have already made its way to the city," Abigail said. "That's all everyone is talking about, but I'm not complaining. I'm selling more tour tickets. Although I'd like to believe it's our quaint little town bringing them in, not ghoulish curiosity."

Victoria frowned. "I can't believe I'm actually going to say this, but if ticket sales continue at such a rapid pace, I'm concerned we'll be unable to handle this many people, although god knows this town needs the income. Claire, what do you think?"

"We have experienced volunteers," Claire said reassuringly. "The guides could split the tours into smaller groups. Don't worry. I'm sure the tour will go off without a hitch. I'll bring it up at the meeting."

"Yes, it would be prudent to be prepared for an excessive number."

"Well, ladies, here's Peg with your lunch," Abigail said. "Please enjoy it. And don't worry about the tour, Victoria. I'm sure Claire's right, and everything will be fine."

Victoria sighed. "I sincerely hope you are right."

***

When Alex returned to his office, he found an eager GH waiting for him, determination filling is round face.

"Hello, Chief. I told him I didn't know when you'd be back, but he insisted on waiting," Bonnie said glaring at GH.

"That's alright, Bonnie. I had a feeling I'd be seeing him today," Alex said as he opened his office door. "Come on in, GH, but I'm warning you, I can't tell you much."

"Now, Chief, I find that kind of hard to believe," GH said taking a seat across from Alex. "The citizens of Newcomsville have the right to know how Carl died and why."

"I can tell you that last night at Flapjacks someone put enough drugs into Carl's dinner to kill him. Why this person did it remains unknown."

"Okay, how about telling me something I don't know. Like what type of drug was used?"

"Further tests are being conducted to determine that."

"Oh, baloney, Alex. You know and aren't telling me. What difference could it make?"

"GH, that's all I have to say about the drug. Let it go."

Looking disgruntled but determined, GH persevered. "Okay, I know Charles and Agatha were with Carl last night before he died. Did Carl say anything to Charles?"

"Like what?"

"Like maybe he thought he knew who Kathleen's murderer might be, and he wanted to spill his guts."

"Why would you think that?"

"Alright. I'll tell you how I see this. Carl is embezzling money from the bank. Somehow Kathleen finds out and blackmails him. For some reason, Carl goes to Kathleen's shop the night she's killed. Then Carl leaves town. Kathleen is murdered. Carl comes back. You put Carl in jail. Now he's dead. So either Carl saw who did the deed, or he had a pretty good idea who it was."

Alex smiled. "That's an interesting summary."

"Am I wrong?"

"No, I wouldn't say you're wrong. I think either of your possibilities could be the right one. But, GH, if you're asking me to choose one, I can't. I don't know if Carl saw who killed Kathleen, or if he just thought he knew who it was. What I would bet the farm on is that the same person who killed Kathleen also killed Carl."

GH leaned forward. "Do you have any suspicion who this person might be?"

"No comment."

"Come on, Alex,"

"GH, I've told you all I can."

"Okay, answer me this. If Carl thought he knew who the murderer was, why didn't he tell you as soon as you brought him in?"

Alex laughed. "How would I know? Maybe he didn't realize what he knew until he had time to think it through. Listen, GH, Carl came back to town knowing Kathleen was dead and thinking the coast was clear for him to continue embezzling. Maybe sitting in jail, he put two and two together. We'll never know. Hopefully when I catch the murderer, they'll fill in the blanks."

"You sound pretty confident you'll catch this person."

Alex nodded. "I am."

"Is that all you're going to tell me?"

"Yes."

GH rose from his seat. "Okay, Alex, thanks for nothing. I'm going to Flapjacks to see what I can learn from Jo. It's amazing nobody saw anyone put drugs in the chili. From what I understand, there were people everywhere. You would think somebody would have seen who did it." GH cocked his head. "Do you think someone did see something and is afraid to come forward?"

"It's possible. If that's the case, wanting the killer caught might override their reluctance."

After GH left, Alex, sighing, sat back in his desk chair and began reviewing all that had occurred since Kathleen's death. Glancing out his window, he idly watched as a male and female cardinal gracefully landed together on a bare branch. The female cardinal, seeming extremely annoyed, walked back and forth on the branch, fluttering her wings and chirping loudly at her partner.

Alex grinned. "Well, buddy, you sure managed to piss her off." After one more indignant flap of her wings, she flew off to alight on a higher branch as the male bird looked mournfully up at his sweetheart. Two emotionally-charged faces swam before his eyes. Alex sat up straight in his chair, thoughts racing, as the pieces fell into place.

"Damn it, that has to be dehe answer. Now how in the hell am I going to prove it?" Rising from his chair, Alex began pacing the length of his office. Finally, opening his safe, he removed the matches, brooch, and glue gun and placed them on his desk.

"Knock, knock."

Alex looked up to see Samantha standing in his office doorway. "Hi, Samantha, come on in."

"Hello, Alex. I just saw Bonnie in the hallway, and she said it would be okay for me to drop by. I've been in Henry's office discussing Carl's funeral arrangements. Grandma told me she saw you at Doc Jack's this morning, and you said you wanted to see me. So here I am." The unending stress and strain she'd been dealing with for the past few days showed harshly on Samantha's pretty face.

She looks as if she's about to drop, Alex thought as she took a seat. "I appreciate you coming in, Samantha. I don't know what to say," Alex began. "'I'm sorry' sounds pretty lame. I can't help but feel somewhat responsible for Carl's death, but believe me, I honestly had no idea Carl would be in danger."

"I know that," she replied giving him a wan smile. "Thinking back over the past few months, deep down inside, I've kind of had, oh, say, a premonition something like this was going to happen. I'm not saying I thought Carl would be murdered. I guessed it would be more on the order of him driving himself drunk into a tree or something. Do you have any leads at all?"

"Unfortunately I can't say I have anything definite."

"I understand it was poison. Do you know what it was?"

"Yes, but it wasn't poison exactly. It was digitalis."

She frowned. "Digitalis. My grandmother takes that. Isn't that a heart medication?"

"Yes, but if you don't need the drug, it can be deadly."

"Oh, my god, who would do such a thing?"

"That's what I'm trying to find out." He folded his arms on the desk and leaned forward. "I do have some questions I'd like to ask in regards to you being in Flapjacks last night."

"Sure. What would you like to know?"

"Were you there when Agatha came in?"

"Yes. Sylvia and I had just sat down."

"Did you hear her ask Granny Jo to get Carl's chili ready?"

"No. The restaurant was packed. I just saw her come in, and I think she waved at Jo."

"Were you and Sylvia alone at the table all night?"

"No. Agatha came over and talked to me for a few minutes."

"Did you talk to anyone else?"

She frowned. "Well, if you could call it talking. That horrible Nan Katz came up to me and started yelling about Kathleen. I'm telling you, Alex, I don't think that woman is right in the head."

"What was she saying?"

"Oh, I don't know. She wasn't making a lot of sense. She went on about how I hated Kathleen, and Kathleen hadn't ever done anything to me, and how hard Kathleen had to struggle, and how I was handed everything. Then she had the nerve to tell me she wouldn't be surprised if I was the one who killed Kathleen."

"What did you say to that?"

"What do you think I said? I told her she was crazy and to get out of my face."

"What did Nan do?"

"She wouldn't shut up. I finally pushed past her and left. Sylvia and I ended up going to my house and ordering a pizza."

"Was Sylvia with you the entire time Nan was yelling at you?"

Samantha hesitated. "No, I believe she was smart enough to walk away when Nan started in on how I can't do anything on my own. God knows she might have gone off on Sylvia as well. When I finally turned to leave, Sylvia was waiting for me by the door."

"Did you know Agatha would be taking Carl his dinner?"

"I knew Agatha and Charles were helping you out. I didn't know the specific arrangements."

"Samantha, please think hard. I need to know if you saw anyone around the bowl of chili."

"Alex, I wish I could tell you 'yes', but I didn't see anything. Carl and I may have had our problems, but I didn't want him dead. Run out of town penniless and in disgrace, yes, but murdered, no. I know people are talking about how callous it is for me to go on decorating my house for the tour on the day after my husband is killed, but if I don't keep busy, I'm afraid I'll go crazy."

"I wouldn't pay any attention to anyone who has the gall to criticize you. Those who care about you understand."

Samantha sighed. "I hope so." Her eyes fell onto the brooch. "How pretty. Is it Abigail's?"

"No, I found it on the floor in Kathleen's shop the day she died."

"Really." She leaned closer for a better look. "It seems familiar to me. May I pick it up?"

"Sure. I thought it might have been Kathleen's, but Nan said she wouldn't have worn something like this."

Frowning, Samantha closely studied the brooch. "Alex, I'm sure I've seen this somewhere."

"Take your time. This could be important."

"It looks like one Aunt Henrietta has, or maybe Agatha. I can't be sure."

"Perhaps when you're not trying so hard, the memory will come back. If you do remember, please call me. It doesn't matter what time it is."

"Okay, I'll let you know. Now I'd better get going. Sylvia is coming over to finish decorating. I don't know what I would have done without her. We're down to two days until the pre-tour showing. I understand you and Abigail are hosting this year's residents' party."

"That was Abigail's idea, not mine." He smiled. "She loves any excuse for a party."

"Hats off to her. Having that many people over is a lot of work. If I don't talk to you before, I'll see you on Friday." Rising to her feet, she took one final look at the brooch. After Samantha left, Alex put the matches and glue gun back in the safe. He put the brooch in a plastic bag, then into his coat pocket. I'll have Abigail look at it.. If she sold it in her shop, maybe she or Sally can remember who bought it.

Before Alex could sit back down, Bonnie called to him. "Chief, a call just came in I think you need to look into."

At his open door, Alex paused with raised brows at the stifled laughter filling Bonnie's face. "Okay, I take it there's something amusing going on?"

Bonnie finally controlled her mirth and said, "Judy called from Yesteryears. There seems to be a problem at the traffic circle involving a delivery truck, Charles and Agatha, a horse, and the Christmas tree. She was laughing so hard I couldn't understand any more than that."

"Christ." Alex grabbed his jacket and headed for the door.

There are glances of hatred that stab,
and raise no cry of murder.   - George Eliot

14

When Alex arrived at the traffic circle, he took in the scene before him with amusement and exasperation. A beer delivery truck sat at an angle blocking Main Street. A large man, presumably the driver, was gesticulating angrily at Charles and Agatha who sat in their open horse-drawn carriage in the middle of the circle with the top of the garden club's perfectly decorated twelve-foot Christmas tree lying across their laps.

Alex sighed and stepped into the melee. He worked his way through the noisy crowd who were all trying to tell him what had happened. He finally reached Charles, Agatha, the truck driver, and an extremely agitated horse.

"Okay, alright. Just everyone calm down." Alex shouted. "I can't understand anything with all of you talking at once, and you're scaring the horse." Finally quieting the crowd, Alex turned to Charles. "Calm this horse down, then tell me what happened."

"I'll tell you what happened!" the furious truck driver said glaring at Charles and Agatha. "I had just pulled out onto Main after making a delivery when these lunatics came out of nowhere and cut right in front of me. I honked and hit the brakes, but by that time the carriage had already jumped the curb and hit the tree."

"Alex, if I may be allowed to expound upon what actually transpired..." Charles interjected, as he extricated himself from the tree's upper branches. Before he could continue, Nan Katz came thundering through the crowd.

"What is going on here? What has happened to our Christmas tree?" She came to a halt by the carriage. "Look at our beautiful tree. You imbeciles, you've ruined it." She glared at Alex. "Do you know how much hard work the garden club ladies put into decorating this tree? And now look at it. Chief Mackenzie, I'd like to know what you're going to do about this."

"Nan, I'll take care of it," Alex replied. "Just step back and let me sort this out."

"I hope you don't expect the garden club to pay for the damage. That is if anything can be salvaged. Look at all that has been broken! Chief Mackenzie, just who's going to replace this?"

"Nan, I said I'd take care of it. Now please stand over there and be quiet."

"Chief Mackenzie, I don't appreciate your tone. The town council is going to hear how rudely I've been treated."

"That's fine, Nan. You do whatever makes you happy. Now get the hell out of my face."

"You haven't heard the last of this," she snarled. "This town is out of control, and you're totally useless." She turned and roughly pushed her way through the crowd.

Running his hands through his hair, chiding himself for losing his temper, Alex took a deep breath and surveyed the now silent crowd.

"Okay, everyone, the show's over. If you saw what happened, and you have something to tell, please stay. Everyone else, I'd appreciate it if you'd go about your business. I want to have this cleared up as soon as possible."

He turned to Charles who had escaped the tree and was comforting Professor Plum, the Chestnut who had been pulling the carriage. "Charles, please tell me your side of this."

"Alex, I'd like to apologize for putting you in the position of having such a disagreeable exchange with that odious woman."

"Don't worry about it. Just tell me what happened."

"Aggie and I thought it would be prudent for us to take the carriage out for a trial run before Saturday. You know we drive around during the tour adding a bit of atmosphere."

"Yes, Charles. Go on."

"Well, you see, we were having trouble with the carriage bogging down in the snow. We'd had just such an occurrence before approaching the traffic circle. I was encouraging the Professor to pull harder, when suddenly the carriage shot forward. It was about then that we encountered the truck."

"I believe it was the blowing horn that spooked Professor Plum," chimed in Agatha, smiling through a tangle of Christmas lights. "Before Chucky could stop him, we were heading directly toward the Christmas tree."

"But, Alex, the collision with the tree wasn't Professor Plum's fault," Charles said vehemently. "He veered at the last minute. Unfortunately the carriage isn't as agile as he."

"I assume Professor Plum is the horse?" Alex asked.

Charles nodded. "That's correct."

"His lady friend is Miss Scarlet," Agatha explained. "She wasn't feeling up to par today, so she's waiting back at the stable for his return. Won't she be disappointed when she learns what excitement she's missed."

"Can I leave now?" the disgruntled truck driver asked, giving Charles and Agatha a 'you're both nuts' look. "I'm running late, and I have other stops to make, and other than the tree, there doesn't seem to be any damage."

"Sure," Alex replied. "No one's hurt. No reason for you to stay. Sorry for your inconvenience."

He gave Charles and Agatha one more shake of his head, then walked toward his truck.

"He's a rather excitable fellow, isn't he?" Charles observed as the delivery truck pulled away.

Alex rubbed his temples. "I need to see if we can stand this tree back up and assess the damage. Can a couple of you men help me?" Alex asked of the few remaining spectators.

Managing to get the tree upright, and securing it back in its stand, with his back vehemently protesting the exertion, Alex stepped back to inspect the damage.

When the idea arose of placing a Christmas tree in the traffic circle, a weatherproof outlet was installed. Kneeling down and feeling around under the tree for the electrical cord to plug the lights back in, Alex froze as his eyes fell upon a small prescription bottle hanging from a branch. Using two fingers of his gloved hand, Alex gingerly removed the red ribbon which held the bottle to the tree. An insurmountable rage shot through him as he read the Merry Christmas label stuck to the outside.

"So, now you're taunting me," he murmured through gritted teeth, knowing for a certainty the bottle in his hand once held digoxin. *You're getting cocky and that's when I'm going to nail your ass,* he thought, gingerly rising, his back protesting with every move. Discreetly placing the bottle in his pocket, he turned back to the little group.

"Alex dear, is there a problem?" Agatha asked. Finally disengaged from the tree, she was able to alight from the carriage. "I must say, your face is a rather alarming shade of purple."

Alex tried to regain his composure. "It's nothing. Now let's see how many strands of lights are out."

"Alex, I take full responsibility for our little misadventure," Charles said. "Aggie and I will assume all expenses and will be expedient in setting everything to rights."

"That would be great," Alex replied. "We don't want to upset the garden club ladies any more than they probably already are. I'm sure by now Nan has given them a full account."

Agatha smiled. "Considering Mamaw-in-Law is president of the garden club, I'm sure she'll express to the other ladies her confidence in our ability to have the tree back as it was in no time."

Most likely Mamaw-in-Law is going to have a fit when she hears about this, Alex thought. Aloud he said, "Well then, I'll leave this in your capable hands."

***

"Well, we're all here except Nan," Claire said as the tour committee took seats around Abigail's dining room table. "I can't imagine what's keeping her. She's always on time."

"Maybe we'll be lucky, and she won't show," Molly whispered.

Abigail laughed. "I think our luck just ran out." The three women turned as they heard footsteps on the stairs. A red-faced Nan soon came into view.

"Oh, oh," Abigail murmured. "She doesn't look happy."

"Well, hello, Nan," spoke up Molly. "We were getting worried about you. It isn't like you to be late."

Nan tossed her coat across the back of her chair and abruptly sat down. "I'll tell you exactly why I'm late. I've just come from the traffic circle where those two village idiots, Charles and Agatha, have managed to knock over the Christmas tree."

"What?" the other three said as one.

"That's right. Our beautiful tree is lying in shambles. And Abigail, let me tell you, your husband was extremely rude to me when I asked who was going to repair the damage. In my opinion, it shouldn't be the garden club's responsibility."

"Perhaps you should give us more details," spoke up Claire, seeing the angry flush burning Abigail's cheeks.

"I stopped in at Yesteryears to do some shopping," Nan began. "Although I think Judy Scraper must think this is New York considering her prices. Anyway, while I was looking around I heard horns honking and people screaming. Judy and I went to the front door, and I couldn't believe what I saw. I was outraged, but Judy for some reason thought the sight was humorous."

Claire sighed. "Nan, please get to the point. We have a lot to get through this afternoon."

"The point is, Charles Butterfield managed to drive his horse-drawn carriage into the town's Christmas tree which now lays in ruin. When I asked our illustrious police chief what he intends to do to repair the tree, he told me to get the hell out of his face."

Abigail visibly strained to keep her voice calm when she said, "Nan, I can't imagine Alex talking to you like that unless he'd been provoked."

Nan narrowed her eyes. "I didn't provoke anyone. I'll tell you, Abigail Mackenzie, why I think your husband lashed out at me. I told Kathleen when he was hired as police chief that I didn't think he was qualified. The entire town can now see how right I was. It's obvious how over his head this job really is. There have been two murders in less than a week practically right under his nose, and our police chief still doesn't have a clue who the murderer is. Why I wouldn't be surprised if it doesn't turn out to be Charles and Agatha. Of all people to put in charge of a prisoner, that idiot and his wife would be the last people anyone with any sense…"

Abigail rose to her feet. "Nan, I suggest you stop right there. I'm not going to listen to this. Unless you can refrain from trashing my husband, or anyone else for that matter, you can just leave."

Nan's nostrils flared. "Well, I never."

Before she could continue, Claire spoke up. "Perhaps, Nan, it would be for the best if you went home. Obviously you're upset, and arguing among ourselves isn't going to accomplish anything."

Nan rose. "I'll do that happily. As a member of the Garden Club, it's more important for me to inform Victoria of this disaster than to sit here being insulted."

***

Claire shook her head. "I must say our tour meetings have been anything but dull."

"Poor Victoria," Molly said after Nan had left. "Do you think we should call and warn her?"

Claire smiled. "I'm sure Victoria can handle Nan."

"I'm sorry I lost my temper," Abigail said. "I just couldn't listen to her any longer. Alex is a damn good police chief, and Charles and Agatha couldn't have done anything to prevent Carl's death."

"Abigail, if you hadn't shut Nan up, I would have," Claire said. "Now, ladies, shall we try and get through these last minute arrangements."

"You know, Nan was in Flapjacks the night the chili was tampered with," Abigail said. "What if Alex is wrong, and the same person didn't kill both Kathleen and Carl? What if Nan killed Carl in revenge for Kathleen's death?"

Molly nodded. "That's right. You may be on to something. Nan's an avid gardener and is probably knowledgeable about certain poisons."

"It wasn't a garden poison that killed Carl," Abigail said, thoughtfully tapping her pen on the tabletop. "But Nan is older. She could very well be taking digitalis."

Molly, perplexed, looked from Abigail to Claire. "I hadn't heard exactly what killed Carl. I was in the Apothecary a couple of weeks ago, and Nan was picking up a prescription. I heard her say something about her heart."

"No kidding," Abigail exclaimed. "I'll have to tell Alex. This is awful to say, but if the killer is one of our neighbors, I'd rather it be Nan."

"Abigail, I know Nan isn't one of your favorite people, but why would she have killed Carl?" Claire asked. "Where's her motive? She would have had to suspect Carl, and she wouldn't have had any idea why Alex was holding him."

"She was in Indulgence on Monday, and at Flapjacks Monday night," Abigail replied.

"Yes, but even if she overheard Agatha talking about Carl's food, like the rest of us she still didn't know why he was being held. Nan didn't know about the embezzlement or the blackmail."

Abigail sighed. "You're right. Okay, then Nan is pretty much out of the picture. Although it would have been nice to pin it on her."

"Abigail," Molly cried.

Abigail grinned. "That was an awful thing to say, but at this point, I really don't care."

"Ladies, trying to pin a murder on Nan is certainly more fun than working on tour business," Claire said, "but we really need to get this done."

"Okay, boss, we'll be good," Abigail said.

Claire flipped through her notes. "Let's see. The tour guides are all lined up. Ben and Sam have the desserts under control. The houses and businesses look fabulous. Abigail, do we have a current total on ticket sales?"

"No, but we may exceed five hundred. I hope that's not going to cause problems."

Claire nodded. "Victoria voiced the same concern. My thought on this is since we've already sold more tickets than usual, we cut off sales as of tonight. What do you think?"

"I agree," Molly said. "If there're too many people on the tour, it will take longer, and people will get restless."

Claire turned to Abigail." What about you?"

"Sure, I think cutting off sales is a good idea. The last thing we want are groups of cold, unhappy people."

"Great. Okay, next is parking," Claire said. "If this snow continues, where are we going to put all of these cars?"

"Abigail, we have a problem," Peggy called from the bottom of the stairs. "You need to come down."

Claire threw up her hands. "Now what?"

"I'm sorry. You two continue. I'll be right back."

"What's wrong, Peg?" Abigail asked as she reached the bottom of the stairs.

"Alex can't get out of the Bronco."

"What?"

"It's his back. He's in a lot of pain."

"What happened?" Abigail asked as she hurried through the back door behind Peggy.

"I don't know. Beatrice saw him out the kitchen window."

"Alex," Abigail cried when she saw Alex laying half in and half out of the car. "What have you done?"

"You're going to have to help me," he said through gritted teeth. "I can't make it into the house on my own."

"Do you want me to call an ambulance?"

"No. Just help me walk."

"Alex, I'm afraid I'm not strong enough. Let me call for help."

"No!"

"Abigail, I'm going to call Bob," Peg said. Not waiting for a reply, she hurried back inside.

"Where do you want him?" Bob asked a half-hour later as he and a cursing Alex finally reached the top of the stairs.

Abigail pointed down the hall. "Put him in the bedroom. Jack's on his way. He said to lay him down flat."

"I'm here," Jack called coming up the stairs. "Hang on, Bob, and I'll help you."

***

"Alex, I still can't believe you did something so idiotic as helping pick that tree up," Abigail said for what Alex was sure was the tenth time since Jack and Bob had left.

"As I've said, I did it without thinking. Will you please let it go? And please stop fussing. My pillows are fine. Aren't Claire and Molly waiting for you?"

"No, they decided to finish up at Claire's."

"Then aren't you needed downstairs to help close up?"

"Peggy and Beatrice can handle it," she replied stepping back from the bed. "And getting annoyed with me isn't going to help. It wasn't me who told you to lift a twelve-foot decorated Christmas tree. Also it wasn't me who said you needed to lie still for at least two days." She placed her hands on her hips. "Now if you're hungry, I can get you something before Beatrice puts everything away. Jack said you should have food with the medication."

"Sure, whatever," he muttered irritably, thinking that getting him food would at least keep her busy for a while.

"I'll be right back. Don't move," she smiled, lightly kissing his forehead.

Alex scowled to her retreating back. "Yeah, yeah, yeah." *I may be on the brink of solving two murders, and I can't move,* he thought with disgust. *Okay, you may not be able to walk, but you can still use your brain. The first matter of business is to get the prescription bottle checked for prints. Then call Bonnie and tell her what's happened.*

"Here you go," Abigail said coming into the room a few minutes later carrying a tray. Can you pull yourself up against the pillows?"

"Abigail, in my coat pocket there's a prescription bottle. I need you to get a handkerchief and a zip-lock, and carefully bag it. Then I'd like you to call Pete Vanderwood. Tell him what's happened to my back, and ask him if he'd come and pick it up. Then I need you to…"

"Alex, slow down," Abigail said with exasperation as she set the tray across his lap. "I'll take care of anything you need, but now you should eat."

"Abigail, listen to me. This is important. I found a prescription bottle hanging from the Christmas tree, and I want Pete to check it for prints."

"You found what?"

"A prescription bottle, and I'd bet the farm it once held digoxin."

"Wait a minute, are you telling me the murderer purposely hung their empty digoxin bottle on our Christmas tree hoping someone would find it? That's crazy."

"Someone killed two people, one by strangulation with a Christmas ribbon leaving them looking like a grotesque window display, the other by putting poison in a bowl of chili in a public restaurant. I don't think we're dealing with a rational person here."

"Okay, I'll give you that. After I 'bag' the bottle, what do you want me to do next?"

"Call Pete and tell him what happened to my back, and see if he can come and pick the bottle up. I'd like to have this done as soon as possible."

"Wouldn't it be quicker if I just took the bottle to Pete at the county sheriff's office myself?"

"Sure, if you have time."

"I can go first thing tomorrow morning. I could be there and back before we open for lunch."

"That would be great, Hon. Hand me the phone. I'll call Pete and explain all of this. Also please bring me my laptop and that blue file containing my notes. Even though I'm confined to bed, I can still get some work done."

"Do you know who the murderer is?"

"I think so, but I need proof, and that little bottle might give me that."

"Alex, you can't keep me in suspense. Who is it!"

"Hon, I can't jump the gun on this. I could be wrong. Please be patient."

"Alex!"

"Abigail, please."

She sighed. "Alright. But promise that as soon as you're sure, you'll tell me."

"That's a promise."

***

Before nine o'clock Wednesday morning, Abigail left Alex propped up on pillows with his phone close at hand.

"I'll be back as soon as I can," she said from the bedroom doorway. "Beatrice should be here within the hour. Call downstairs if you need anything."

"Sure thing. Pete knows you're on your way. He should be waiting for you."

A short time later, Alex pushed his laptop, along with the notes he'd been reviewing, to the side of the bed, and sighed with frustration. *Damn, I know I'm right, and I can't do a thing about it*

237

stuck here in this bed. Just when he began thinking about trying to get out of the bed, his phone rang.

"Hello, Alex Mackenzie."

"Alex, Pete."

"Hey, Pete, don't tell me you have a match already?"

"No, that's why I'm calling. I thought Abigail would have been here by now. Has she left yet?"

Alex glanced at the clock, surprised to see how much time had passed. "Pete, she left over two hours ago. Actually she should have been back home by now."

"Buddy, I haven't seen her. She wouldn't give the package to another officer, would she?"

"No. She knows to take it right to you. Damn it to hell, Pete, something's wrong."

"Hold on, buddy. Let's not panic yet. Maybe she just decided to stop on her way and do some shopping."

"You don't understand. Abigail is as obsessive as they come. If she says she's going to do something, she does just that. She would never deviate from her plan. Besides, the tearoom opens at 11:00 for lunch. She'd never be late for that unless something was wrong."

"Could she be in the tearoom, and you not know it?"

"I doubt it. Let me check downstairs, and I'll call you back. Pete, if she's not there, I'd like you to send out a patrol car looking for her."

"Sure thing, buddy. I'll do it myself. Call me back."

"Abigail's Tearoom," answered Peggy cheerfully. "Can I help you?"

"Peg, it's Alex. Is Abigail down there?"

"Hi, Alex. No. She left Beatrice a note telling her she had an errand this morning, but she's not back yet. How are you doing? Do you need something?"

"No, Peg, thanks. I was just wondering if she got back. If she comes in, please tell her to come up."

"Okay. Are you sure you don't need anything? I can bring some lunch up. We're not busy yet."

"Thanks, Peg, but I'm fine."

Alex quickly called Pete back. "Pete, she's not here."

"Okay, Alex. What is she driving, and what route would she have taken?"

"She's driving a new red Beamer, and she should have taken the main highway from here into the city, then 224 right to you."

"I'll let you know as soon as we find her. Hang in there, buddy, I'm sure she's fine."

"That's easy for you to say," Alex mumbled as he hung up the phone. *I have a murderer on the loose who's killed two people, my wife is missing, and I can't hardly walk. Yeah, I'll hang in there alright.*

Alex, trying to control his nervous energy, fantasized over his victorious capture and subsequent arrest of the would-be murderer. *If you have her and harm her in any way, god help you when I get my hands on you*, he thought, his fists clenched, knowing that if he laid there a minute longer, he'd drive himself mad. Tentatively easing his legs over the side of the bed, trying to rise, he grimaced as the pain shot up his back.

"That's probably not a good idea," Jack said from the bedroom doorway.

"Christ, Jack."

"Sorry, I didn't mean to startle you. The door at the top of the stairs was open, so I just came on in. And it looks like I got here in the nick of time. May I ask what you think you're doing?"

"Abigail is missing. She left this morning to do an errand for me and never got there." Alex filled Jack in on the prescription bottle and his desire to have it checked for prints. "So you see why I'm trying to get out of this damn bed."

"Yes, I see, but I also see it's not working. If you don't stay still, it's going to get worse. You said Pete was looking for Abigail. So my medical advice is to lay back down, and let him do his job. In fact, if it would make you feel better, I'll go look for her as well. Chances are there's a simple explanation."

"You're probably right, Jack, but I've got a murderer out there, and this isn't normal behavior for Abigail."

Jack frowned. "Talk about normal behavior. I can't believe someone actually hung that prescription bottle on the Christmas tree."

"Yeah, and if Charles and Agatha hadn't knocked it over, that bottle wouldn't have been found until the tree was removed."

Jack shook his head. "Whoever the murderer is seems to enjoy taunting you."

"Yes, Jack, and what if that person was standing there and saw me find the bottle and is beginning to panic. What if through some twisted thought process, they're thinking they can get to me through Abigail?"

"Abigail wouldn't let some stranger get in the car with her."

"No, but what if it wasn't a stranger, or what if they forced their way into her car. Jack, you know what this murderer has already done."

"Alright, you've managed to alarm me as well, but I still think our best course at this time is to wait to hear from Pete."

"She left over three hours ago. I can't just sit here and..." Before he could finish, his phone began to ring. With his heart in his throat, Alex managed a shaky, "Alex Mackenzie here."

"Alex, it's me."

"Abigail, Hon, thank god, where are you? Are you alright?" The relief he felt upon hearing her voice was short-lived.

"Yes, I'm okay. I'm at the hospital. Pete is…"

"Hospital? What hospital? What's happened?"

"Alex, I'm fine. Please just listen to me."

Alex took a deep breath and tried to calm his racing heart. "Sorry, go ahead."

"I had a blow out. The car hit some ice, and I ended up in the ditch. The airbag deployed hitting me pretty hard. Pete, along with some state police, found me and brought me here. They insist I should see a doctor. My chest hurts and I'm a little bruised, but I'm alright."

Relief washed over Alex. "Okay, Hon, but Pete is right. You should let a doctor check you over. Jack's here. I'll ask him to pick you up. What hospital are you in?"

"City Hospital. Oh, Alex, you should see my beautiful new car."

"That's okay. Relax. Jack's on his way. The car's insured. I'll find out where it was towed. Everything will be fine."

"I don't care about the insurance. My beautiful car is wrecked."

"Abigail, I really think you need to go lay down," he replied with as much patience as he could muster. He'd been in a living hell all morning, picturing the love of his life in the hands of a murderer, and all she could talk about was her damn car. "Please just go see the doctor, and put Pete on. I'll see you shortly."

"Hey, Alex, I told you we'd find her."

"Pete, I can't thank you enough. Our friend Jack Monroe is on his way to pick Abigail up."

"No problem. I'll wait until he gets here."

"I can't believe no one passing by saw her car in that ditch."

"You know along sections of 224 the snow banks can get pretty high. Well, somehow she managed to go into the ditch between two of these, although I don't think she sat there for very long. And before you ask, I have the package and it's intact. I'll let you know if we get a match."

"I definitely owe you one, Pete. Thanks again."

Pete laughed. "You can buy me a beer at the Cork & Bottle."

"Will do."

Alex sighed with relief as he hung up the phone and lay back on the pillows. Hearing footsteps coming up the stairs, he turned toward the door and saw Peggy carrying a lunch tray.

"Jack told us what happened to Abigail. So I thought you'd probably feel like eating something now," she said setting the tray across his lap. "Also, Beatrice wanted me to tell you that when Jack gets back with Abigail, she's going to put the both of you to bed, and you're both supposed to stay put until Jack says you can get up."

"Thanks, Peg. Suddenly I find I'm ravenous, and this really smells great." Smiling, he sniffed the vegetable soup's heady aroma. "Tell Beatrice that after the morning I've just had, I'll be more than happy to do just that."

"You must have been worried out of your mind," Peg said. "You know, Alex, with everything that's happened lately, I'm beginning to think there's a permanent black cloud hanging over Newcomsville."

"I don't blame you. But with any luck, that black cloud will soon be blown away."

Later that night, tucked into bed, with Thomasina curled up at their feet, Alex gently brushed the hair away from his sleeping wife's face and again sent up a thankful prayer for her safe return. "I'm going to make your picture perfect little town safe again," he whispered, placing a light kiss on her cheek. "I promise, love."

15

Friday, December Third
5:05 PM, Alex's office

"I'm leaving, Chief," Bonnie called from the outer office. "Is there anything else you need?"

"No, Bonnie, thanks. Will I see you on the pre-tour?"

"You sure will. I'm running home to put on heavier boots before going to the inn."

"Okay, I'll see you shortly."

"Chief, are you sure you're up to the walking? You know the tour goes from one end of town to the other."

"Between Jack insisting I do nothing for two days and a lot of TLC from Beatrice, my back is feeling pretty good, but I appreciate your concern."

Bonnie smiled. "I'll get it, Chief," she called, as her phone began to ring. "Yes, Mr. Vanderwood, he's right here."

"Chief, it's Pete Vanderwood on line one, and make sure to keep track of the time. You don't want to keep Abigail waiting."

"Thanks, Bonnie, I will. Hello, Pete, tell me you have good news."

"That depends on what you consider good news," Pete replied.

"A known print off that bottle would be at the top of my list, but I can't imagine I'm that lucky."

"First, Alex, I apologize for taking so long to get back with you. My wife's sister broke her leg skiing, and her husband is out of the country. We had to pick up her children. Needless to say, my house is in an uproar."

"I can imagine. So, Pete, don't keep me in suspense. Tell me what you have."

"We got a match. It wasn't a known print, but it's a match to one we lifted when we swept Miss Cooper's shop, and it definitely was digoxin in the bottle."

A chill ran up Alex's spine. "Pete, what are you telling me?"

"I'm telling you that whoever owned that prescription bottle was at one time in Miss Cooper's shop. We were able to lift the print from the underside of the cap."

"No shit," Alex murmured. "Pete, that's great. Thanks for letting me know."

"Sure thing. I hope this will help."

"Buddy, thanks to you I think I may be close to catching a murderer."

"Go get him. Let me know how this turns out."

Glancing at the clock Alex cursed. He grabbed his jacket and hurried out of the office. Waiting for the elevator, he reached into his pocket for his gloves. Instead he felt a plastic bag.

***

5:20 PM, Abigail's tea room

"Abigail, are you sure you're feeling up to having people over for a party?" Sally asked from behind the counter.

Abigail nodded. "I'm feeling much better."

"Is it okay if I leave? I have everything closed up. I'm meeting Mom at the post office on my way to the inn. I don't want to miss the beginning of the tour."

"Sure, Sally, go ahead. Beatrice and I have everything ready for the party. I don't understand where Alex could be. He promised he'd be home by five o'clock. Oh, good, here he is now."

"Sorry, Hon," Alex said hurrying through the front door. "Pete Vanderwood just called me with great news. Give me a minute to change into warmer clothes, and I'll be ready to go. Take a look at this and tell me if you've seen it before." He handed her the small plastic bag he drew from his jacket pocket.

"What is it?" Sally asked, as she put on her coat.

"It's a brooch, and I believe it's one of ours." Puzzled, Abigail laid the bag on the counter. "Look, Sally, what do you think?"

"Sure. I recognize it. Why is it in that plastic bag?"

"I have no idea. We'll have to ask him."

"Ask who what?" Alex questioned from the doorway.

"This brooch. It's one of ours. We were wondering why it's in this bag?"

"So it did come from here. Sally, do you remember selling it?"

"Yeah, I thought about buying it myself for my mom for Christmas, but I couldn't afford it."

"This is important. Who did you sell it to?" Alex asked.

"Let me think. It couldn't have been that long ago. Wait a minute, I have it." Sally smiled in triumph. "She was a really nice lady who said she was new in town and would only be staying for a few days. She went crazy over the brooch."

Alex's pulse quickened. "Do you remember her name, or anything else about her?"

With her eyes scrunched up behind her glasses, Sally thought as hard as she could. Eyes popping wide, she cried, "I have it."

"Hurry up, Abigail. Get a coat," Alex demanded. "We have to get to the inn."

"Alex, for god's sake, will you please tell me what's happened."

"I don't have time to explain. Come on. Let's go."

"Don't leave without me," Sally called, close on Abigail's heels.

"Alex, it's snowing like hell. Are we taking the car?" Abigail asked, as she tried to button her coat and run down the front steps.

"No, it will be faster on foot," Alex yelled over his shoulder as he headed down Main Street.

***

5:45 PM, Indulgence

"Carolyn, I'm finally heading out," Burt said as he put on his parka. "Here are today's massage medical history forms. Oh, by the way, there's a couple in there from the other day."

"Thanks. Are you going on the pre-house tour?" Carolyn asked.

"I sure am. I'm one of the guides this year so I need to learn the route and pick up my top hat and cape before tomorrow night, and I hope I'm not going to be too late. The group is probably already gathering at the inn."

"Really, what time is it?"

"Almost six."

"Oh, my goodness, I didn't realize how late it was," Carolyn said as she began to glance through the papers Burt had handed her. "I understand we'll be doing the tour route in reverse since we'll all end up at the Mackenzie's later for the party. Oh my god, oh my god," Carolyn exclaimed as she stared down at the paper in her hand.

Burt hurried over to the coffee bar. "What is it?"

"Oh my god, what do I do?" she looked around uncertainly. "Shit, shit, shit. How could I have been so stupid? Where did I lay down the phone?"

"It's right here. Carolyn, what the hell's going on?"

"I don't have time to explain," she said franticly dialing Alex's number. "Come on, come on, answer the phone." She tapped her foot impatiently. "Damn, I have to go find Alex." She headed for the front door.

"Carolyn, slow down. You need a coat. It's snowing like crazy."

"My coat's in the break room." She dashed to where her coat hung and was back at the door in seconds.

"I'm coming with you." Burt hurried after her, slamming the door behind him.

A blast of cold snow hit Carolyn in the face. Turning into the wind, she ran toward the inn as fast as her two-inch heels would allow.

"You're going to break your damn neck," Burt shouted as he ran up next to her. "For god's sake, Carolyn, where are you going?"

"To the inn," she shouted back.

"Fine. I'll carry you." And with that Burt swung Carolyn over his shoulder and took off.

***

5:55 PM, The Cork & Bottle Inn

"Hey, Ben, where are you?" Sam called from the entry hall. "People are starting to gather out front."

"I'm up here," Ben said from the top of the stairs. "I was turning the candles on in the front windows and one was out. I think it's the extension cord. I'll replace it and be down in a minute."

"Okay, I'll have everyone assemble out front before letting them in." Sam stepped back onto the porch to the sound of jingling sleigh bells. Chuckling, he watched as the Butterfields' big red bobsleigh turned the corner, driven by none other than Mr. and Mrs. Santa Claus. Sam grinned as he approached them. "You look great. When did you get the costumes?"

"Aggie found them in a shop in the city. Aren't they terrific?"

Agatha grinned. "We thought they would add a bit of merriment to the festivities. Do you think everyone will like them?"

"I imagine you'll be a big hit."

Charles beamed. "We were supposed to ride around town in the carriage for a bit of atmosphere during the tour, but with all this snow we thought the sleigh would be just the ticket. Then Aggie came up with the costumes."

Upstairs, Ben wedged his hand behind a tall antique cherry dresser, trying to unplug the old extension cord. Swearing, on his hands and knees, he jammed his arm in as far as it would go. His hand brushed against a piece of paper wedged between the dresser and the wall.

Pulling the paper out, his eyes narrowed when he read, "Personal Prescription Information" for digoxin.

"Holy hell," Ben exclaimed as he raced down the stairs, grabbing a coat as he ran. Bursting from the inn's front door, he franticly searched the noisy crowd for Alex. Spotting Sam in the crowd around the sleigh, he worked his way toward him. Finally reaching the sleigh, not yet registering that Mr. and Mrs. Claus were present, he grabbed Sam's arm and yelled, "Where's Alex?"

"I don't know. I haven't seen him. This is quite a group isn't it?"

"Sam, you have to help me find Alex. I think I know who the murderer is."

"What did you say?" Sam asked with astonishment.

"Help me find Alex!"

As Ben and Sam reached the edge of the crowd, Sam pointed. "Look." They watched in astonishment as Burt hurried toward them carrying Carolyn over his shoulder. Before either man could speak, their attention was drawn to the middle of the snow-covered street where Alex, Abigail, Sally, Molly, and a puffing GH, were all running full tilt toward them.

"Burt, put me down," Carolyn shouted, as they came to a halt in front of Ben and Sam.

Out of breath and puffing, Burt set her on her feet. "She would have broken her damn neck if I hadn't carried her. I don't know what's going on, but she had to get here in a hurry."

"Where's Alex?" Carolyn asked. "I need to talk to him."

Sam pointed. "Here he comes."

"Alex, thank god you're here," Carolyn cried. "I just found out who takes digoxin. It was listed on the medical form from a massage last Monday."

"That's not all," Ben said excitedly. "Just now upstairs I found a paper with the digoxin prescription refill."

Alex tried to catch his breath, while waving the group to silence. "Okay, everyone. First I need to find Samantha. Has anyone seen her?"

"She's not here," Sam said. "Is Samantha in danger?"

"Alex found a brooch in Kathleen's shop the day her body was discovered," Abigail gasped. "Sally just identified it as one she sold." Abigail turned to Alex. "If Samantha isn't here, she must be waiting at home for everyone to arrive. We have to get over there."

"You'll never get anywhere in a car with all this snow," Ben said.

"Wait a minute," Sam said. "Stay here. I'll be right back."

Jack Monroe walked up. "Alex, is there a problem? Can I be of any help?"

"Jack, I have to find Samantha. She may be in danger."

"What do you need me to do?"

Just then the sound of sleigh bells could be heard emerging from the crowd.

"Alex," Charles called, stopping the sleigh at the edge of the group. "Sam has explained the situation and your dilemma over the most expedient way of reaching Samantha. I suggest that without delay you accompany us in the sleigh, and we'll make haste to apprehend the villain."

Alex paused briefly to take in the sight of Mr. and Mrs. Claus and the horse drawn sleigh with Sam already in back and thought, what the hell. He jumped in next to Sam.

"Wait for me," Abigail called.

"You're not leaving me," Carolyn cried.

"I'm not missing this," Ben yelled.

"I'm going along," Burt said.

"Christ," Alex exclaimed.

Jack smiled. "I guess I'd better come to."

"Hey, what about me?" GH shouted.

A slack-jawed crowd stood in front of the inn watching as Santa stood up in his red sleigh, cracked his whip and called, "Hyah!"

***

5:56 PM, Samantha's house

"These are the last ones," Samantha said as she lit the candles on the mantle in the parlor. "Everything looks beautiful." She stepped back to take in the room. "You've done a wonderful job with the entire house. I couldn't have done this without you."

Sylvia smiled. "I'm glad I could help. These last few days have been dreadful for you, but you're holding up famously."

Samantha gave her a wan smile. "As the old saying goes, 'the tour must go on.'"

Sylvia put her arm around Samantha. "You know what? I think we both deserve a glass of wine. I brought a nice bottle of Merlot. Let me get it from the car. We should have time to have a glass before everyone arrives."

"That sounds wonderful."

As Sylvia stepped away, slipping on her black cashmere coat, the reflection from a flickering candle caused her snowflake pin to sparkle. Samantha stared at the lapel pin with dawning recognition. Shock and confusion filled her face. "It was yours," she whispered.

"What? Samantha, what's wrong?"

"It was yours," Samantha repeated. "The brooch, it was yours. You bought it in Abigail's shop."

Sylvia frowned. "What are you talking about? What brooch?"

"The brooch Alex found in Kathleen's shop. I saw it in his office, and I knew I'd seen it before, but I couldn't remember where until I saw that pin on your coat. Sylvia, you really liked that brooch. If you lost it in Kathleen's shop, why didn't you go back looking for it?"

"I don't understand why you're getting so worked up over a brooch. It was a day or so before I realized it was gone, so I had no idea where I'd lost it. It wasn't that important."

Samantha shook her head. "You liked that brooch too much, and it was too expensive for you to just ignore its loss." Samantha watched as Sylvia's pretty smiling face turned ugly and menacing. Before she could stop herself, Samantha cried. "My god, Sylvia, it was you. You killed Kathleen. And Carl. It had to be you. My god, why?"

"You really are a stupid little rich bitch, aren't you," Sylvia snarled. "Can't you figure it out?"

"Wait a minute. Wait just a god damned minute. You were his latest whore." Her laugh was without humor. "You're right, Sylvia. How could I have been so stupid. I knew he was messing around, but with you? Just how long had you been screwing my husband?"

Sylvia gave Samantha a contemptuous smile. "Oh, it began the first time I decorated your house in the city. Carl and I had a perfectly pleasant affair going on until you made him quit his job and move to this piss-ass town. Then, what a surprise, last summer I ran into Carl at a bar. We picked up right where we left off. He told me all about the neat bit of embezzlement he had going on. Then when he told me about you needing a decorator to help you with this tour, well, we thought what a laugh it would be for Carl's lover to come to his incompetent wife's rescue."

Every word Sylvia uttered was a shard of glass piercing Samantha's heart. Her rage simmered as Sylvia went smugly on. "Then that greedy nosey bitch Kathleen had to ruin everything. After

I finished making this house of yours presentable for the tour, Carl and I were going to take off. I had a perfect little place picked out in the Caymans. But that bitch kept asking for more money. Then she saw us together in the Wine Cellar and everything started to fall apart. I told Carl I'd handle Kathleen, but the idiot panicked. He got drunk, cleared out his office, and took off not knowing I'd checked into the inn. Then what does the asshole do?"

Sylvia's voice was becoming shrill, and her hands were shaking. "The moron came back. If he had just let me know where he was, I could have met up with him, and we could have been out of the country. I couldn't believe my eyes when I walked into this house and there he stood. I saw the terror in his face and knew he realized I was the one who had killed that bitch and that he was going to crack. I had to save myself. Luckily I overheard that ludicrous Agatha talking about taking Carl his dinner, and how her equally ridiculous husband would be staying with Carl. God, this town is full of clowns." Sylvia laughed sardonically. "It was so easy for me to put the digitalis in the chili while Nan Katz was accusing you of killing Kathleen. How rich is that?"

Incredulity in every word, Samantha quietly asked, "What if some innocent person had eaten that chili and died?"

Sylvia shrugged. "I would have tried something else. You see, Samantha, Carl was a lot of fun, and I would have enjoyed helping him spend all that lovely money, but I sure as hell wasn't about to sacrifice my life for him."

My god, she's mad. Samantha took a few steps back, fear beginning to displace her anger.

Sylvia glanced at her watch. "Now I have to do something about you, and I don't have much time. That gang of village idiots will be here soon. Maybe after I kill you, I'll make you look all festive like I did that cow Kathleen. I don't know what I enjoyed more, winding that red ribbon around her fat neck or smearing that hot glue all over the bitch's big mouth. But don't worry, Samantha, I won't let you down. I'll have you looking so good they'll want to use you as part of your own Christmas display because, you know…" Her insane laughter filled the room. "I'm your decorator, aren't I?!"

Samantha watched Sylvia's grotesque laughing face. Her heart pumping with fear and rage, not wanting to take her eyes off of

Sylvia, she desperately tried to think of something she could use as a weapon.

Seeming to have read her thoughts, the laughter left Sylvia's face replaced by a knowing smile. "Don't think you can hurt me, you stupid bitch. I've already gotten away with two murders. Killing you is going to be just as easy." She lunged.

***

"I believe this is where we're going to have to park," Henry said to Victoria, as he tried to peer through the snow blowing across the Mercedes' windshield. "I don't think there's anything closer. Wait and I'll come and help you out. We're going to have to walk, but it's only a block or so from here to the inn."

"If this snow doesn't stop in time for the tour tomorrow, we'll have a mess on our hands. Where are all of those people supposed to park?" Victoria said with agitation as Henry helped her from the car. "Also, I don't see how Charles will be able to take the carriage out in weather like this."

"Don't worry my dear. Everything will work out just fine. It always does. We should cross here," Henry said. "The snow doesn't look as high on the other side. Victoria, be careful. This snow is deep."

"Looook ouut, Mamaw!"

Startled, Victoria and Henry looked up at a sight which would haunt Victoria for years to come. Careening toward them at breakneck speed was the big red sleigh drawn by Professor Plum and Miss Scarlet, their hooves pounding down the snowy street with Santa Claus precariously balanced in the front seat grasping the reins. Beside Santa was Mrs. Claus, and behind them, all jumbled together every which way and seemingly hanging on for dear life, were Carolyn, Ben, Sam, Abigail and Alex, Jack Monroe, and, if Victoria wasn't mistaken, Burt the masseuse, with GH Greeley running after them, stubby legs pumping, coattails flying, yelling, "Wait...for...me!"

"My god, Henry, what in the world?"

"Victoria, watch your step."

"Really, Henry, this is too much," Victoria exclaimed as Henry helped her up out of a mound of snow.

Henry chuckled. "I know, I know." He brushed snow from the back of his wife's fur coat. "But look at the bright side, my dear."

Victoria narrowed her eyes. "Oh, yes, Henry, and just what might that be?"

"At least whatever is happening, isn't happening tomorrow during the tour."

***

Samantha, pivoting to avoid Sylvia's lunging grasp, caught her heel on the edge of the rug. Trying to keep her balance, her hand grabbed onto a large potted poinsettia. Swinging the plant with all her might, she managed to clip Sylvia on the shoulder, staggering her back. The momentum of the swing, and her snagged heel, caused Samantha to fall forward. Both women crashed together onto the living room carpet.

Sylvia, reacting quickly, rolled away reaching for the green ribbon tied around the poinsettia pot.

Samantha, seeing her intent, got to her knees and gave Sylvia a quick jab to the nose.

"You bitch." Sylvia screamed, wiping at the gushing blood. "I'm going to kill you."

Before Samantha could get to her feet, Sylvia grabbed a handful of her hair pulling her back down to the floor where her head connected with the upended porcelain poinsettia pot. Dazed, her vision blurred, Samantha watched in horror as a bloody-faced Sylvia loomed over her winding the green ribbon around her hands.

"Now I've got you. Don't worry. I'll make this nice and quick." Grinning insanely, blood running down into her mouth, Sylvia put the ribbon over Samantha's head. "I promise you'll hardly feel a thing."

Drawing on all the strength she had left, Samantha clawed at the hands which were gleefully tightening the ribbon around her throat. *Oh god, she's going to really kill me,* Samantha thought, as the pressure on her neck increased. *Someone, please, please, help me. I don't want to die.*

Faintly, as her vision began to dim, she heard the distant sound of tinkling bells. *I didn't know that when you're dying you hear bells,* was her last conscious thought. A cacophony of wood splintering, glass breaking, shouts, screams, and the easing of the pressure around her neck were the next sensations Samantha was aware of as she began to regain consciousness. Upon opening her eyes, Samantha blinked, not quite believing who was grinning down at her. Feebly she croaked, "Santa?"

"Right-o," Santa said beaming back.

Outside of the killings, we have one of the lowest crime rates in the country.   - Marion Barry, Washington DC Mayor.

Epilogue

Newcomsville Murderess Captured! by GH Greeley, Editor

The successful, if chaotic, capture of Sylvia Schmuckler, the alleged deranged murderess, occurred last night at the home of Samantha Edwards.

This reporter was right on the scene when, following a harrowing dash across town, Chief Mackenzie, Mr. & Mrs. Claus, along with their assorted helpers, arrived in the big red sleigh just in the "Nick" of time to save Samantha from the clutches of the demon decorator.

From what this reporter was able to ascertain from Chief Mackenzie, this web of intrigue includes adultery, blackmail, embezzlement, and murder.

Kathleen Cooper had been blackmailing Carl Edwards after discovering he was embezzling money from the Newcomsville Bank & Trust. Miss Schmuckler and Carl Edwards had an on-going relationship and were partners in the embezzling scheme. According to Chief Mackenzie, Sylvia said she killed Miss Cooper because Kathleen was a threat to their plan to retire to the Cayman Islands with their ill-gotten gains.

Miss Schmuckler also stated that after Carl's incarceration she feared he would crack under pressure and confess, prompting her non-traditional use of digitalis in a bowl of Granny Jo's chili.

Now, as our idyllic little town breathes easy again, we can enthusiastically welcome Grant Cummings as our new bank president.

And we eagerly await the arrival of tonight's happy horde of Christmas tour patrons. The winner of this year's Christmas decorating contest will be announced in tomorrow's issue.

Good luck to all entries.

"Well, Alex, I'd say it turned out to be a satisfactory conclusion to a rather baffling case," Charles said. "I told you all it would take was using your little gray cells, and you would be able to wrap this up."

Charles, Agatha, Alex, Abigail, Ben, Sam, Carolyn, Jack and Claire were gathered together in the taproom of the Cork & Bottle Saturday afternoon. Alex had driven a cursing Sylvia to the county Sheriff's office that morning. Now, over cups of hot cider, the group was discussing the previous night's rather unorthodox rescue of Samantha and Sylvia's capture.

Alex smiled. "I'm not sure my little gray cells were working all that well. If I wouldn't have canceled my massage appointment on Tuesday, I would have seen the medical information form. When I was looking at Carolyn's list of walk-in clients, something kept niggling at me. It wasn't until I saw the form that I recalled having a massage once before and having to list medications. Not to mention carrying Sylvia's brooch around in my pocket to show to Abigail, then, between her accident and being obsessed with the prescription bottle I found on the tree, forgetting to show it to her."

"Alex, you're being too hard on yourself," Abigail said.

"Perhaps, but identifying the brooch as belonging to Sylvia placed her in Kathleen's shop the day she died. The massage form would have given me what I needed for the digitalis connection."

"Putting that poison in a bowl of chili in a busy restaurant was a truly vile act," Claire said. "Imagine not caring if it was eaten by the person it was intended for or an innocent bystander."

"When did you figure out Sylvia was in this with Carl?" Carolyn asked.

"Actually you gave me my first clue. You saw Kathleen in the Wine Cellar hiding behind some plants as if she was spying on someone. Then when you tried to see who she was looking at, all you saw was Sylvia. I got to thinking about that. Kathleen wouldn't have worried about Sylvia seeing her unless Sylvia was with someone Kathleen wanted to make sure didn't see her. Since she already had Carl on the hook for embezzlement, seeing him with Sylvia had to be the icing on the cake, so to speak."

"I still can't believe she was careless enough to fill out the massage form," Ben said.

Agatha nodded. "I agree. I find it amazing, as cunning as the little viper was, for her to turn around and slip up by filling out the form."

"You're not thinking the chain of events through, Aggie," Charles interjected. "When Sylvia had her massage, she probably hadn't determined how she was going to snuff out Carl. Isn't that right, Alex?"

"I believe you're right, Charles. According to Carolyn's list for walk-in clients on Monday, Sylvia was down for a massage and manicure. She had the massage first, so it was while she was having her nails done that she overheard the girls talking about Carl and that Agatha would be taking him dinner. So once again, Carolyn, you held a vital clue."

Carolyn smiled. "Thanks, but it was Grant who suggested we look at my appointment book."

Jack shook his head. "I find the entire chain of events unbelievable. Who could have imagined all three elements would come together at the same time."

"No kidding," Ben said. "Sally identifying the brooch, Carolyn finding the massage form, and me having to change an extension cord and finding Sylvia's prescription."

Abigail smiled. "I don't think I'll ever forget the look on Victoria's face when she saw all of us go past in the sleigh."

Charles nodded. "I must say, until I apprised her of the circumstances which made it vital to use the most rapid form of transportation to rescue Samantha, Mamaw was rather distraught."

"That's true. Mamaw-in-Law was a teensy upset," Agatha said. "But when she heard what a hero Chucky was, well, she overlooked the few minor mishaps which occurred during the rescue."

Claire laughed. "Mishaps? I guess that's as good a word as any to describe half of the town running after the sleigh when they were supposed to be enjoying the house tour."

"I know last night didn't go according to plan," Ben said. "But I must say that was one hell of a sleigh ride."

"Has anyone heard how Samantha is?" Sam asked.

"She's home and feeling pretty good," Jack answered. "She had a minor concussion from that flower pot, and her neck is sore, but she'll be fine."

"Alex, in the beginning did you suspect Sylvia was Kathleen's murderer?" Claire asked.

"No. That one had me pretty baffled. In fact, Charles and Agatha saw Sylvia the night of the murder. They told me they saw someone outside of the inn, but they couldn't identify the person. Also there were the Cork & Bottle matches that were found on the floor in Kathleen's shop. I knew Sylvia smoked, but so do others who could have been in her shop. For one reason or another, half our neighbors were out and about the night she was killed, and each of them had a motive to want her dead."

"Were you ever able to ascertain how Kathleen knew about Carl's sticky-fingered activity," Charles asked.

"That turns out to be quite a story. According to Sylvia, it was a matter of Kathleen being in the right place at the right time. As for Carl, it was continuous bad luck. There was a small discrepancy on Kathleen's bank statement. She went to the bank to ask about it, but wasn't satisfied with the service she was getting. Kathleen being Kathleen, she insisted on speaking to someone with more authority. As fate will have it, she was directed to Carl. So without knocking, she just walked into his office. Carl was in the process of transferring stolen funds by phone. When he saw Kathleen, he slammed down the phone and shoved some papers under a stack of folders. Seeing the guilt written all over his face, and considering Kathleen's inquisitive nature, alarm bells must have gone off in her head. Before Carl was able to deal with Kathleen, Carl was called out of his office to resolve some dispute. He could hardly drag Kathleen along, so he had to leave her sitting there.”

Ben chuckled. “Oh, Alex, this is too rich. What did the little snoop do then?”

“When Carl returned, he found Kathleen sitting in his chair smiling, waving a copy she’d made of the transaction he‘d shoved under the folders. She was even quick-thinking enough to push redial on his phone, and who answered but a Cayman Island bank. Now, with the evidence in hand, it was easy for her to begin her blackmail.”

Claire frowned. “It’s hard to believe Carl was so careless doing his illegal money transfers.”

“The man was a moron,” Carolyn said. “What do you expect?”

“I think arrogant is more like it,” Alex replied. “With Carl it was always someone else’s fault.”

“All’s well that ends well,” Carolyn said smiling. “Look how it all fell into place. We exceeded all of our past tour ticket sales. Yesteryears Antiques is going to win the decorating contest. Samantha can finally have a life. The town is free of Kathleen’s vicious tongue. Newcomsville has a gorgeous new bank president. And we were able to get all of our money back before Sylvia slipped Carl the poisoned chili.”

“Carolyn.” Abigail cried.

“What? What did I say?”

Ben laughed. “Nothing but the truth, love. Nothing but the truth.”

Outside of the inn, as the snow clouds parted, the sun shone brightly down upon the little town of Newcomsville as it once again lay peacefully under its pretty mantle of snow.

About the Author

Debby Grahl lives on Hilton Head Island, South Carolina, with her husband, David, and their cat, Tigger. Besides writing, she enjoys biking, walking on the beach and a glass of wine at sunset. Her favorite places to visit are New Orleans, New York City, the Cotswolds of England, Captiva Island in Florida, and her home state of Michigan. She is a history buff who also enjoys reading murder mysteries, time travel, and, of course, romance. Visually impaired since childhood by Retinitis Pigmentosa (RP), she uses screen-reading software to research and write her books.

Her first published romance, <u>The Silver Crescent</u>, was released by The Writer's Coffee Shop in January, 2014. The Paranormal Romance Guild awarded it 5 stars and First Place in the 2014 PRG Reviewers Choice awards in General Romance. Her second book, <u>Rue Toulouse</u>, a contemporary romance set in New Orleans, came out January, 2015. It was a Finalist for the First Coast National Excellence in Romance Fiction Award. Decorated to Death was self-published in 2017. Debby belongs to Romance Writers of America, Lowcountry Romance Writers, Florida Romance Writers, First Coast Romance Writers, and the Hilton Head Island Writers' Network.